THE
EMPEROR'S
RIDDLES

Satyarth Nayak

AMARYLLIS

AMARYLLIS

Copyright © Satyarth Nayak 2014

This edition first published in 2014
Third impression 2015

AMARYLLIS

An imprint of Manjul Publishing House Pvt. Ltd.
• 7/32 Ground Floor, Ansari Road, Daryaganj, New Delhi 110 002
Email: amaryllis@amaryllis.co.in   Website: www.amaryllis.co.in

Registered Office:
10, Nishat Colony, Bhopal 462 003 - India

Distribution Centres:
Ahmedabad, Bengaluru, Bhopal, Kolkata, Chennai,
Hyderabad, Mumbai, New Delhi, Pune

Sword image on cover courtesy:
The Los Angeles County Museum of Art

ISBN: 978-93-81506-45-5

Printed and Bound in India by
Thomson Press (India) Ltd.

For my mother...
For believing a lot more than I did,
that I could write a book

Yo Dhammam passanti so mam passanti
(He who sees Dhamma sees me)

VAKKALI SUTTA

CONTENTS

BOOK ONE

Buddham Sharanam Gacchami

'*He* has come.'

The messenger ran as fast as his legs could carry him, but the walls were running faster than him. The doors were folding themselves. The steps were flying high and sinking low.

He had come.

They had called him Teacher. He had told them about him.

'He will come.'

They had asked who will come.

'He will come, one hundred years after I am gone. He will rule the four directions of one of the four continents of the world. He will love me and my word. He will build shrines for me and they will number eighty thousand and four. His name will conquer hills and cross the seas to spread far. He will love us all like no one before. There will be blood. There will be death. And there will be life.'

One hundred years had lived and died.

The messenger was running through the garden now. His bare feet trampled the rose bushes, crushing the new blooms. The flowers scattered and fell to the ground, slayed in their prime.

'They are dead. All of them,' the gardener mourned.

His companion bent over and dug the earth some more, mixing the torn petals and leaves with the soil.

'They will live. The dead will bear new life.'

The messenger meanwhile hobbled into the royal chamber. A thorn resolutely stuck in his foot, drawing blood. The king was looking out of his bedroom window. Waving at someone in the sky.

'What is it?'

'A son, sire. The queen has given birth to a boy.'

'Boy?'

'Another son, sire.'

'How's she?'

'Alive. She is resting.'

The king was quiet. He took out a box engraved with an image of Vishnu astride his Garuda. The silver chakkra held aloft on the god's finger glowed like a giant flying disc. From it the king scooped out a fistful of navaratnas and flung them at the messenger.

The man bowed and limped out, leaving behind a faint trail of blood in his wake.

He looked at the red letters that stained the page.

OM PATNAIK

Falaknuma literally meant 'resembling the sky' and the restaurant laboured hard to justify the epithet. It had climbed eight storeys of the Clarks Avadh, an imposing structure towering over all the surrounding buildings, fountains and gardens in its vicinity, to perch on the rooftop. Falaknuma opened its doors to all who entered this vintage hotel and Patnaik loved to haunt the place whenever he was in town.

Tonight he and his friends had returned to the restaurant again, and sat looking through its all-glass windows at the glittering nightscape of Lucknow. The traditional Avadhi *hors d'oeuvres* on their table were as distracting as the ustad from the Agra Gharana whose vocals clasped a wistful bandish in its arms. Patnaik had turned to marvel at a throbbing alaap when a fan had come clamouring for an autograph.

As she walked away gratified, his friend pointed at the book he had signed. 'That was *Open Your Eyes and See*. Your debut novel.'

The writer grinned. It was his first baby and what a birthday it had seen. They had taken it in their hands and sung lullabies of love. They had clothed it in sheets of gold and cut bright red ribbons around it. The bestseller had remained on top of the charts for months and the chapter on Swine Flu had even needled the WHO. Over the years, the thirty-six-year-old writer had gained a cult following for his work on the esoteric. He had written many more books and even his harshest critics had applauded their scholarly content. But the candles for the first-born were still melting into the cake.

He asked for the menu. 'Shall we order the main course?'

'Sure. Although I already know what you will be having,' his friend winked. 'Navratan pulao.'

'With some Navratan korma,' the woman seated from across him simpered.

Patnaik grinned, 'Everytime!'

They were laughing again. The author's bizarre fixation with the number nine, had in recent years, become quite an urban legend. Not only his friends, even his readers were constantly curious about his extraordinary association with the number. By now, Patnaik knew all possible explanations had become exceedingly obsolete and he had resigned himself to the phenomenon that nine was determined to be a persistent presence in his life.

The friend leaned forward. 'So what is it with you and nine? Let's hear it once and for all.'

'Cover the basics first,' the woman added, 'You were born on the ninth day of September, which is the ninth month of the year. Your name has exactly nine letters. The titles of your books, your phone number and your car number all add up to nine. And when your mobile rings, you are treated to Beethoven's Ninth Symphony. Anything else?'

They were giggling. But Patnaik knew that the number had touched him in many different ways. At times it had come as a blessing, as though it were a sprinkle of holy water. Sometimes it seared him, like a pair of hot iron tongs. He was nine when his parents had separated. Nineteen when he cried over his first heartbreak. He was twenty-nine when he had finished his debut novel, which had gone on to become the ninth bestselling book of the year.

'You want the latest? My page on Facebook touched ninety thousand "Likes" last night.'

'Your Hidden Truths page where you and your heretic fans bicker about assassinations, UFOs and secret documents?' the woman chuckled. 'What's the current topic?'

'Pluto,' Patnaik answered, devouring a galouti kebab. 'We are talking about how the planet was suddenly demoted to a piece of junk floating in the Milky Way.'

The man thumped his glass on the table. 'I knew it.'

'Knew what?'

He looked at the woman. 'Pluto. It was the ninth planet in our solar system!'

She turned towards Patnaik as the waiter piled steaming murg korma on their plates. He was smiling.

'Yes. The number nine has a way of sneaking into my life at all times. It's the devil in disguise. Did you know that many ancient leagues and prehistoric cabals are believed to worship the number?'

'That's creepy. What the hell is so extraordinary about nine?'

'Quite a bit. The fact that it's the highest single digit in our decimal system makes it one of the most revered numbers in all civilisations. The position of the numeral is also special. As the last number standing between single digits and double digits, nine symbolises an end and a new beginning. A mathematician will also tell you that it is the first composite Lucky Number and multiples of nine always add up to nine. This does not happen with any other number. Try it.'

The numbers were in their mind. 18-27-36-45-54 ... each adding up to nine.

'All these factors have singled out the number as a symbol of perfection across religions. So Hindus venerate nine heavenly planets called Navagrahas and nine celestial gemstones in Navaratnas. The Navaratri festival invokes nine forms of Shakti or the Mother Goddess while our traditional aesthetics celebrate nine emotions or Navarasa. Hindusim also divides the temporal cycle of creation, preservation and destruction into nine parts. Hindus have 108 names of gods while Islam has ninety-nine names for Allah and nine spheres of the universe.'

'Sounds like Dante's *Inferno*.'

'It does. Christian mythology also pays homage to nine. Besides nine spheres of heaven and nine circles of hell, you have the nine-fold hierarchy of angels. Abraham was ninety-nine when God spoke to him while Christ was thirty-six when he was crucified. He died nine hours later and appeared nine times after Resurrection. Saint Paul lists nine spiritual gifts of God while a Pope's death is mourned for nine days. Even Buddhism talks about nine levels of the sky and their Stupas house ninety-nine Tathagatas.'

'Don't forget the nine Muses of Greece.'

'Sure. Greek thinkers like Pythagoras have celebrated nine for being the highest single number. Even ancient Egypt mentions Ennead or a group of nine gods judging men after death. Go through pagan cultures and you will find them replete with nine. Norse mythology narrates the tales of Odin who ruled nine worlds and hung from the World Tree for nine days. Druids and Celtics mention nine virtues while the Aztecs say the soul goes through nine stages. The Sabines in Italy have nine gods and the Freemasons regard nine as the number of human immortality. Been to the Bahai Lotus Temple in Delhi?'

'Of course.'

'The temple is a tribute to the number nine. It has twenty-seven petals in groups of three to form nine faces. There are nine doors and nine ponds surrounding the temple. The word Bahai itself has a numerical value of the magic number.'

'Now you will tell me that Akbar had nine wise men.'

'So did Vikramaditya. And don't forget your English expressions. Whether it's nine lives, cloud nine or the whole nine yards, the digit is everywhere, taking us closer to excellence.'

Patnaik paused, spooning the last morsel of the Shahi Tukda.

'Sweet tooth still intact?'

'Always intact,' he chuckled. 'And here's the clincher. Man is born after nine months. Nine nurtures life. Our universe may simply be an arithmetic number. Life is perhaps a mathematical equation and we are all numbers existing inside a bracket.'

'I thought you were numerophobic. I have seen how numbers can frighten you to death,' the man spoke.

'They still do. But never the nine.'

'But why only the esoteric?' the woman shrugged. 'You are such a well-read man. There's a lot you can write on. What fascinates you so much about these conspiracies?'

'It's hard to explain.'

'It's not. When a man is a bachelor at thirty-six, he'll have nothing better to write.'

The writer's green eyes smouldered like nuggets of coal. 'It's the unknown. The unidentified. Secrets that are beyond reach. Don't you want to unravel them? Grab the knowledge that has been denied to us? What else is life about?'

'Knowledge is a blessing, Patnaik. But knowledge can also demolish.'

'Perhaps. But it pushes you into the real world. A world without illusions. Nothing can be more important.'

'Sometimes I feel you are still that child who never understood why his parents separated. You wanted answers then. You still want answers today.'

'Interesting.'

'You found no faith in them and now you look for other things to believe in. Your questions keep changing. You undertake new journeys but you seek the same truth.'

'And why do I do that?'

'You think the truth loves you. Does it talk to you? What do these conspiracy theories tell you?'

The writer smiled. 'I don't know what they say. But it's crucial that they are given a voice. A chance to speak. It's always tempting to kick them out and choose easier options. We all seek that peace. But there are some who seek the truth. They choose roads less travelled. You may or may not make such a journey but it is vital that you are given that choice.'

Getting up, his friend twirled his fingers and hissed. 'Guess what? I just realised that we have been talking about all this on the ninth floor.'

As they walked out of Falaknuma in peals of laughter, Patnaik glanced behind. His admirer was showing the autographed copy to her friend. He looked at the title again.

Open Your Eyes and See.

*H*e was walking down the stone steps.

It was dark but Ram Mathur knew his way about. This was not his first time, nor would it be his last. There was no escaping this place. Not that he was seeking one. It was beautiful here.

The world can be good.

Mathur lit a clay lamp and watched as it floated alone over the water. Alone like him today. There was no one to talk to or listen to except the river next to him. His hand unconsciously went to the large locket hanging from his neck. The place was deserted, its inhabitants asleep. Sleeping across the river by the burning pyres. He wanted to touch their foreheads. The next day was on its way but for now they were at peace. He knew that the morning sun would bring men to these shores again. They will come and drown in this water.

Like they drowned every day.

It was raining again. He stared at the flames choking in the distance, their wet reflections lighting up the river with a thousand points of light. He liked to see fire and water hold hands. It pulled him out of his house every once in a while. It was said that this place marked the spot where time had struck its first gong. This was where a devata had perspired and his sweat had swollen into this stream. It had seduced the gods to make a refuge inside it. It was now calling out to him.

Mathur entered it, wrapping the waters of the river around him like a shroud. As the rain continued to pound on his head, the omnipresent liquid seemed to fill up his being. He lowered his palms deeper, gathered some water in them and then lifted his hands and drank all of it. The river was now inside him. It knew now. It knew what his mind was running after. It heard the voices trying to break him. It saw what he had done tonight. It touched what his soul was seeking.

Someone who could take what he had to give.

The river knew something else. He was not alone.

Suddenly, the water broke. A silhouette appeared. It grasped Mathur's dripping hair and pushed him under the water letting him writhe and wriggle about as the river flowed into his nose and stabbed his lungs. Then the man hauled him out. Mathur's fingers were pushing him away but he clung to his chest.

'The Nine.'

Mathur laughed. He was laughing like a little boy getting wet in a shower. The thunder was laughing with him. He stretched out his arms and embraced the man. The two drenched bodies clung to each other. A spark of lightning bared its teeth and in its light he saw the man pull out something.

A syringe.

The needle rose and tore into Mathur's right eye. The man's clammy fingers were jabbing the syringe deeper into the socket. Mathur seemed to just stand and watch his thumb move viciously in and out, jabbing at him as though he were a slab of ice. The needle penetrated deeper and deeper, squirting all the fluid it had inside its belly, which had begun to scrape the insides of his eye like a piece of glass. The man yanked out the empty syringe coated with the innards of Mathur's head. He wiped it on the old man's face and tossed him away.

The rain was drenching his eye now. The night was darker and his brain boiling.

Mathur groped his way to the shore. He flayed his arms blindly, reaching out to the stony steps of the ghat, but the pounding rain and rising waters pushed him back and he slipped. His nails viciously scratched the mossy green stones of the river-bed and then with effort, he hauled his body up. His assaulter was gone. By now his skull was on fire. He pushed a finger inside his socket.

His eye was draining out of his head.

Just then his left eye caught the glint of a bronze trishul stuck to the steps. Holding on to its shaft, he heaved himself higher up, but the trishul gave away. The downpour was whipping his bare back now as the wet cloth clung to his skin. The next moment he felt a spongy object slide down his right cheek. He instinctively held out his palm.

A blue eyeball stared at him.

Where is the fucking flashlight?

All around him were what seemed like the intestines of a galactic pit. There were no walls. No floor. No knobs or bars. Only darkness. His hands clawed at the slimy emptiness. Trying to touch the void. Feel the nothingness. He was in the presence of absence. Was that a man standing, breathing heavily in the vacuum? The sound was driving him insane. He ran. But each time he looked back, the motherfucker was there. Tied to him like gravity. Pasted to the dark like a cut-out. He was getting closer with each step. Before long, he felt the man stand right in front of him, touching his lips with his blood-coated fingers. They dug into his neck and tugged at his throat.

Suri yanked on the light switch.

Bloody nightmares!

As he sat up on the bed, his eyes fell on the bedside photograph of himself. A silent witness to the reeking drama that was the life of police officer Parag Suri. He knew the colour of blood. The smell of death. As one of the most feared officers in the department, his reputation preceded him to every posting. There were rumours that he had once urinated on a MLA who had offered to pay him off. But the nightmares that sank their teeth into him at night did not seem to fear him. They had found him one Friday evening twenty-seven years ago. And they had never left his side since. Nobody knew that this fearless thirty-six-year-old officer often woke up squirming at night, afraid of his own dreams.

He looked up. 'Yes. My fucking dreams.'

Suri picked up the glass of water from the night stand and drained it. He began pouring himself another glass when the phone rang. The voice on the other end sounded as if it too had woken up from a terrible dream. The words kept bouncing off his brain. Then one word strangled him.

Murder.

The officer was awake now. As the man's rapid speech began to make more sense, Suri's fingers curled tighter around the receiver, harder with each new detail. Was he still inside his filthy nightmare? Then he saw his face in the mirror. It was no dream.

It has happened again.

'Send the car,' he heard himself say.

Suri shivered as he splashed cold water on his face. The words were still ringing in his ears. Murders were a part of his life but this was something else. Something that should not have happened. Something that was going to screw his life.

But I had warned her.

He heard the siren wailing outside his house. Eighteen minutes later, he was standing on the bank. The beacon on his vehicle was staining the river with red. Sprinting over the wet stones he reached the spot where some of his men were crouching near the water. He knew what had happened. But he had never seen such faces.

Two of the men came forward. 'There.'

They were shining their torches. The light seemed to set something on fire. A blue sapphire flashing in the dark, begging to be picked up. Then he saw what it was. What the voice on the phone had meant. A single blue eye, like that of a ragged doll stared up at them, unblinking. The corpse. The white hair. The bloody socket. The eye ball in his hand. He looked up and instantly his throat muscles cramped into a coil.

What was that?

There was something else. Something on the face.

What the hell?

He realised he had his hand on his mouth; something seemed to be crawling over his skin. He looked. He wanted to flick it away. There was nothing. He turned towards the body again. The torchlight shone brightly on the bloodied face. The stench of rotting flesh was mingling with the smell of incense burning nearby. People sleeping on the steps faraway were beginning to peek out of their covers now.

'Put up a tent around it. Get more men here. Keep everyone away.'

His men ran like the dead. Gaping at him in shame. Asking him to hold their hands and cover their eyes. He did nothing. His nightmares were going to get more vulgar.

He looked up. 'Yes. Those fucking nightmares.'

Suri took out his cellphone and dialed a number. A voice asked him to 'please check the number you have dialed'. He pressed the buttons a second time. The voice spoke again. He furiously punched the numbers once more. This time it rang.

*N*o one was answering his call. He disconnected and took out a bottle.

Nothing like alcohol after work.

Six glasses later he sat breathing softly. Killing always made him thirsty. It also made him feel like God. How they always begged and pleaded with him. And how he hated those pleadings. One day he would sit and write down the many ways in which men could beg for mercy. He had heard them all. Pathetic worms writhing to carry on with their existence. Wishing to live a few days more. The world said life and death was in God's hands. Was he not God then? Did he not hold the power to take or give lives as he pleased? Live or die? He had no dice. Only one rule.

Die.

Death for those who disobeyed him. Defied him. Told him that he did not deserve the prize. It was they who had no merit. No respect. They did not know how to use it. How to honour it. It was so simple. It only had to be given its slot. He stood up.

Everything must be catalogued.

He will show them what to do. What it was worth. An enigma that cannot remain an enigma any longer.

The Nine.

Tonight he had failed again. One more had challenged him. This man had not pleaded. He had laughed at his ignorance. But this failure was going to push them towards the revelation. He took out the syringe. Laying it carefully on the table, he picked up a stick-on paper and red marker. He liked red markers. They reminded him of blood. He took out the cap and inhaled the tip for a while. Then he wrote.

MATHUR

He pasted the paper around the syringe and opened a drawer. Eight used syringes were resting in peace. They all had labels on them. Names of the eyes they had gouged out. The man dropped the syringe into the drawer.

The police called him Scorpion. He did not like the name. His cellphone rang.

'I was calling you.'

'I know.'

'Is it done?'

'Yes. But it's complicated now.'

'What are you saying?'

'He has spoken. But you can't hear him.'

'Are you doing something?'

'I have taken care of it. We will go that way.'

'It might spill out of hand.'

'Everything will work out. You cannot change it. It's a matter of hours now.'

'Then the Nine?'

'Yes. The Nine.'

'He knew. They all knew.'

'We will know now. '

'And then?'

'There will be light.'

6

$\mathcal{T}$hey watched the stars appearing as they arrived. He had never come here before. The whistling wind seemed to agree with the belief that it was a sacred spot. Yudhisthir had once performed penance on these hills. He had spoken a lie in the battle of Kurukshetra to create a just land. A land that upheld the highest principles of sociology.

'Will I see you again?' the king asked.

'No one returns from this path. It takes you home. You will know when your time comes. Make the journey.'

'Is this necessary?'

'It's a pledge I made with myself. I will respect it.'

'You can carry it out living here. With your family. Amidst your children.'

'Those are two lives. I cannot live both. I will end up lying to both. The life here was good. I have lived it. I have given it to you. We must rise and fall.'

'But we love you.'

'That's why I must go.'

'Do you love me, Father?'

'Do you love me, Son?'

The wind blew away the answer.

'Have you decided? Who shall come after you?'

'You know my answer, Father. You have always known it.'

'You will not change?'

'I know your choice. It's not mine. I am free to choose.'

'What do you have against him? He is also your son.'

'The seat will go to the eldest.'

'You are forgetting the prophecy.'

'I remember it every day. You believed in it. You made the daughter of a priest my wife because she will give birth to a great emperor. She has the lowest rank among all my queens. Her son will never wear my crown.'

'You cannot fight the future.'

'You don't believe in the Teacher. How can you have faith in his prophecy?'

'I have faith in your son. I have seen him. He is the only one.'

'What about his anger?'

'You have created the wrath that is consuming him. You are responsible for his demons, yet he continues to be noble. Undo the harm you have done so far or it will consume everything.'

'My eldest will not let it happen.'

'You have blind love for your eldest. His ways have already created a revolt. That does not happen to rulers.'

'My mind is made, Father.'

'I must leave then. Ascetics have nothing to say to rulers.'

He took out his sword and advanced towards the king. Raising the blade in the air, he brought it down on his son's neck. The wind howled as the blood began trickling down his back.

The old man spoke. 'I have severed my link with you now.'

The king touched the wound. The tip of the sword had made a small nick.

'I gave you my blood. You have given it back.'

He walked towards the cliff. Standing at the edge he bowed before his sword and hurled it into the void.

7

What is he trying to say?

It had been a morning well spent. He had returned to his favourite childhood haunt, the world famous Bada Imambara, which he used to visit often as a boy with his mother. Today, the writer had strolled all alone through its central chamber, which contained the tomb of Nawab Asaf-ud-Daula, a room made remarkable by its gilted mirrors. With an ambition to surpass the glory of Mughal edifices, the Nawab had turned Lucknow, or Avadh as it was then called, into an architectural Eden. Patnaik had once again wondered at one of the largest arched constructions on the planet, marveling at how the fifty-feet high ceiling stood without the support of any beams, making the hall a gigantic hollow shell.

Having had his fill of the mausoleum, Patnaik had walked over to the Bhulbhulaya again. The three-dimensional labyrinth had an astonishing four-hundred-and-eighty-nine doorways, enough to confound anyone who dared to enter. The Imambara had its own share of homespun conspiracies. Legend had it that the building had secret underground passages to Faizabad, Allahabad and Delhi. Some even said that great treasures lay hidden in its tunnels and that many had gone missing while exploring them.

Patnaik had then returned to the comfort of his hotel's lawns and sat waiting for the Imam. The old man had promised to tell him a magnificent secret from the pages of eighteenth-century Avadh for his next book. With time to kill, he had opened his laptop and logged on to his Facebook account. He had found many more voices whispering about the ninth planet. Some believed Pluto had been stripped off its status since it symbolised negative energies of the human consciousness like rebellion, schizophrenia and death. Others had theories that the planet was a myth and had never existed in space. There were suggestions that the next topic of discussion should be the story about Taj Mahal originally being an ancient Shiva temple called Tejo Mahalaya. Then a chat window had popped up.

Patnaik had smiled. It had been a while since he had spoken with him. Then he frowned.

Need u Patnaik. Matter of life and death.

His first instinct had told him that his friend was playing the fool. But something didn't add up.

What happened?

You must come. You cannot refuse.

You know I will never refuse. Are you alright?

I can't speak now.

The writer had felt the long grass blades of the unmowed greens poking his skin.

What's going on? You are scaring me.

There's no time. It's already too late.

Too late? For what?

Patnaik had stared as the person keyed in a single word.

Come.

Where are you?

I am waiting.

He rubbed his eyes. The afternoon breeze from the Gomti

was making him feel sleepy. After the arrival of the steam engine in India, the Awadhi royalty had added a Venetian flavour to the river. They had fashioned steam boats and spent hours lazing over the waters in magnificnent gondolas. Patnaik took out a stick of chocolate wafer and bit off the top.

What does Mathur want?

He had called him right away, but his mobile was switched off. Whatever it was, he knew he had to heed to his friend's call. The Imam would just have to wait.

'Where to?'

The cab driver outside the hotel was peeking through the window. Patnaik slid inside and slammed the door.

'Varanasi.'

8

The land had become a river of lightning. Water like milk was spilling from the heavenly hills. The white elixir spread over earth and turned grey. Sixty thousand urns of ash were bathing in the reservoir of Ganga.

That had been another yuga. Men had lived and men had died, but the river still went on in Varanasi. It was the oldest inhabited place in the world. Shiva had stood here with Parvati at the beginning of time, when the universal clock had just begun ticking. Each passing hour had smeared a new layer of endlessness over this eternal space. The journey from Lucknow to Varanasi took just four hours. Patnaik looked out of the cab's window to get a sense of the city's sanctity. He only found chaos.

Police and media vans were lined along the ghat with a horde of officials scampering in and out. Priests were shouting into cell phones behind barricades at the entrance. Somewhere a siren was blaring. Reporters with pens and cameras were trying to break through the lines. A voice from a loudspeaker was yelling at them to behave. The writer frowned.

What the hell is going on?

Getting out of the cab, he walked towards the policeman guarding the ghat entrance.

'Excuse me.'

'No entry. No entry today.'

'What's happened here?'

'The ghat has been sealed.'

'Sealed?'

'This is a crime scene. Stay away.'

Patnaik's eyes sprinted down to the Ganga behind the man.

'Crime scene? Is Mathur alright?'

The officer stiffened. 'You know Ram Mathur?'

'Yes. I am a friend.'

'What's your name?'

'Om Patnaik. He called me here. Where is he?'

The man hollered at another guard to take his place and walked off at a brisk pace towards the river. Minutes later he returned with a giant of a man, who, judging by his yawns, had not slept all night. 'Mr Patnaik? Parag Suri, Investigating Officer.'

'What's going on here?'

'So you knew Ram Mathur?'

'Quite well.'

'I have bad news for you. The man was murdered. Last night.'

Suri was speaking. But for Patnaik, time seemed to have stopped.

Mathur dead?

He heard an echo. One word had changed.

Mathur murdered.

They were telling him to follow them. They were descending the wet stones. They were taking him to where Mathur lay as a corpse.

But who would kill Mathur?

He had met Ram Mathur a couple of years ago regarding an ambitious volume on the Buddhist esoteric. The fifty-four-year-old historian, dubbed as the 'recluse of Sarnath', was one of the most respected minds in world academia. Patnaik had never forgotten how the man had touched him on his forehead, just as his father used to. He still remembered his wonderful tales of mythology and folklore. Especially the miracles of Buddha from *Divyavadana*. The Teacher had taken birth without giving his mother Mahamaya any pain. And right after emerging from her womb, he had walked seven steps towards the north.

They were walking along the Ganga now.

At Sravasti, the Teacher had searched for a mango tree but they had all been cut down. He had then planted a mango seed and it had instantly ripened into a tree.

As Patnaik walked on in a haze, he realised men with mics were surrounding him for quotes. They wanted him to speak. They were saying he knew why Mathur was dead.

The Teacher had also risen into the air. He had issued flames from his shoulders and water from his feet. Then he had divided himself into multiple Buddhas. One personal Buddha for each man standing there.

The multitude swarming today had not come for the Ganga. They were here for the corpse. They were waiting to see it appear from that makeshift yellow tent on the steps. They were pointing at the guards. Pointing at the men coming out of its folds with cotton swabs and plastic cachets. Pointing at the camera flashes lighting up the canvas inside.

Three weeks after his Enlightenment, the Teacher had created a Golden Bridge in the air and four weeks later he had created a jewelled chamber.

Patnaik had been a guest at Mathur's house several times, staying there for prolonged periods of time. He had asked the old man why miracles were performed. Were they not violations of cosmic laws? Did they not mock the routine of the universe? Mathur had disagreed. Miracles simply explored new dimensions of the world that we had never seen before. They showed us unknown realities that existed within our environment. Told man about scientific interactions that were possible. Perhaps God was vain after all.

'Just card tricks of Nature,' Mathur had winked.

Suri was watching his face. 'I see the news has shocked you. I had known him for a while. They say he was a good man.'

'He was extraordinary. Are you sure he was murdered?'

'The body leaves little doubt about that. A local priest discovered it at around four in the morning and informed us.'

The writer seized the officer's arm. 'No. It's not possible. Not possible. The chat…' His voice convulsed. 'He was killed last night?'

'Yes.'

'But we had a chat on Facebook in the morning. He asked me to come here. You are wrong. There's a mistake.'

'We are sorry, Mr Patnaik. I don't think it was Mathur you chatted with.'

'What?'

'You had the conversation with someone else.'

'Someone else?'

'Someone who knows that you knew Mathur. Someone who told us that she has called you here.'

'Who is this?'

Suri pointed. 'Mathur's daughter. She has flown in from Ahmedabad.'

Patnaik's eyes followed his finger.

'She isn't allowing us to remove the body until you see it.' He scanned the writer's face again. 'Why exactly has she invited you?'

'I have no idea.'

'Neither do we, Mr Patnaik. Understand clearly that we have not called you. We are not even pleased about involving an outsider in the case. This is a police matter but she insists. We have no clue what's on her mind. You had better speak with her and find out what she wants.'

He was looking at a young woman. Black hair. Black eyes. Gazing at a blue image of Shiva on the banks. Her body was taut like a pulled string. Her fingers were clenched tight, making her ring bulge out. Her face was static. She stood looking lifelessly at the sculpture. Patnaik wondered if that gaze had turned the god into stone.

He walked up to her.

'Does it do any good to drink poison? Is anything in this universe worth dying for?' She murmered, almost to herself. Patnaik paused and followed her glance. Shiva was standing with a cup of poison that had surfaced during Samudra Manthan. According to the Puranas, the gods and demons had churned the Ocean of Milk in search of nectar; the churning had yielded fourteen ratnas including Lakshmi. In the end nectar had floated up but it was followed by poison from the ocean's womb. The venom was so fatal that it had threatened to dissolve the entire universe. Finally on Vishnu's advice, Shiva had consumed the poison and become the Neelkantha.

'Shiva took the poison so that life could be saved,' Patnaik spoke up. 'It's not easy to see your creation crumble into dust. Every man has his own universe. It may be his life, his family, his work or simply an idea. A faith or a belief that puts meaning into him. When that is threatened its creator will willingly ingest any poison. Your own life seems like a small price to pay.'

She looked at him. Her eyes were red from crying. Patnaik could almost feel her grief like a heavy shroud over her. But there was something else too. Was it anger? Yes. Beneath her suffering lay a chilling fury. And a decision to act.

'I am Sia. Thank you for coming, Om.'

'It was you?'

'Yes. I beeped you from my father's FB account.'

'But the password…'

'It was never a secret. He had told me long back that his password was my name. I had logged into his account today to hunt for any information that could explain his murder. I found you were online and pinged.'

Patnaik was trying to remember their words. What had she written?

It's already too late.

'Why this deception?'

'Ask him. He wanted you here.'

'Mathur?'

'Yes. I haven't called you, Om. It is his command. He used to speak a lot about you and your writing. When I saw you on FB, I gave you his message. I knew you would heed his call. I typed those words but he has summoned you here.'

'I don't understand, Sia.'

'You haven't seen the body yet.' She grabbed his hand and dragged him towards the tent. 'Come. He is waiting for you.'

Her fingers clutched Patnaik's fist in a cruel grip. The man cringed.

Waiting for me?

Sia's voice squeezed his heart with an icy fist.

'See what happens to people who drink poison for others.'

9

$\mathcal{S}$tepping inside the dripping tent, he felt an anonymous terror biting into his limbs.

What did Sia mean?

As both of them advanced, the circle of men surrounding the corpse parted. Their official masks were on. Professional. Detached. Indifferent. But Patnaik could see the paint flaking – somehow, despite their efforts, those facades seemed to be crumbling. These men had seen something that had cracked their shells to reveal the flesh inside. Patnaik looked down.

And immediately recoiled.

Mathur.

He knew he was dead. Murdered. He knew he would be seeing his corpse. But he was not prepared for this. Certainly not this. Mathur was lying on the floor loosely wrapped in his loin cloth. His right hand was clutching a thin bronze trishul. But Patnaik was looking at his face.

His eye. They have gouged out his eye.

The right eye was gone and in its place was a gaping, accusing hole, swarming with flies. The fluids had dried and huge blobs of tissue and fibre clung to his face and neck. Some had dripped over the silver locket he was wearing. The left eye was staring at him. A single blue eye watching him silently like Cyclops. But there was something else. The writer gaped at his mouth.

He is smiling.

Smiling softly. They had slaughtered him and pulled out his eye, but he was still smiling. There was no pain. No rage. He had found peace. This was not the face of a man brutally murdered. This was a face that had seen God.

What have they done to him?

Patnaik turned to Suri. 'His face…?'

'Yes. It's fucking extraordinary.'

'Are you sure he was killed?'

'I know what you are thinking, but no one pulls out his own eye. The bastards injected a corrosive poison through the socket. It drained the eye and snapped the brain but this look on his face is something else. I have seen corpses. Faces twisted with fear. Tongues hanging out in pain. But this calm is terrifying. It looks as if he felt no pain.'

Patnaik glanced at Sia. Her horror was ringing out loud now.

See what happens to people who drink poison for others.

She was standing alone at a distance, tugging at her hair. Staring at her father grinning at his death. Suri pointed at the historian's left cheek.

'Look.'

Patnaik gaped.

A letter.

Someone had carved on his face.

Patnaik slumped to the floor. Mathur's cheek bore a single mark. A large Om. The letter clung to his skin like a red leech that had sucked his blood all night. Something sharp had been used to slash his face to make this bizarre graffiti. The wound had clotted and swollen up. Spots of congealed blood on his neck and arms were glistening like sores.

Suri indicated the bronze trishul in the historian's grip. 'Someone used this to gash his cheek. We have scraped flesh from its tips.'

'Why is he holding it? The handle also looks bent.'

'We are looking into that. What's confusing us right now is that mark. Why did the killer scrawl on his face?'

'Yes. Why?'

'There's also report of some animal matter on the corpse.'

'Animal matter?'

'Yes. It's apparently on the trishul and his fingers.'

The medical team walked inside to cart the body away. As they lay Mathur on the stretcher, Patnaik gently touched his feet. He saw Sia's bare fingers caressing her father's forehead. After a minute she withdrew her hand in a tight fist. They heard the crowd outside roar wildly as the stretcher emerged like a deity from his sanctum. They were not folding hands. They were pointing fingers. Suri walked out barking at them.

They were alone now. Alone with nine photographs of the corpse lying on the floor. Sia picked one. 'I have two questions for you, Om. Why did my father slash himself?'

The writer spun towards her. 'Your father? You mean Mathur...'

He never finished. Sia had taken out an orange sheet. 'And what is the meaning of this?'

'What is it?'

'A piece of paper. My father emailed it to me three minutes after he died.'

10

He was watching darkness and light play before him again.

The dark never blinded him. It held his hand and welcomed him in its fold. Stepping inside, he saw light from a bracket of eighteen lamps on the side wall. They always shimmered there like tiny suns of incandescent gold. A pot with a few lotuses stood in a corner along with a ritual vase of water. The censer hanging from the ceiling sanctified him again. Wisps of smoke were curling from the joss sticks and running into the twilight.

The Samanera closed the door behind him. One of the many novices here, he was training to become a monk. Traditionally, all Samaneras were below the age of twenty. They were expected to follow ten percepts of ethical conduct before being considered for Upasampada or the Ordination. The practice had originated with Buddha's son Rahula who became the first Samanera. The story went that when the Teacher returned to Kapilavastu, his wife Yashodhara took Rahula to his grove.

'Look at this wandering Bhikkhu, my son. His golden complexion shines like the face of Brahma. He is your father. He left you when you were born. He is back now. Go and ask him for your inheritance.'

When the prince came close to Buddha, he was instantly filled with affection for his father. 'Your shadow gives me great comfort, O Monk,' he bowed. 'I have come to ask for my inheritance.'

Buddha touched Rahula's head. 'Material wealth will divert you from the true path. I will give you the most sacred treasures that I have earned at the foot of the Bodhi. You will inherit my bliss.'

The father tonsured his son. He asked him to cast away his princely attire and gave him the orange robes of a Samanera. Buddha's first discourse to Rahula was on the importance of nine virtues. These teachings later became known as the Rahulovada Sutta.

Walking on tiptoes, the Samanera approached the centre of the room. Every time he stood in this space, he trembled with veneration. This womb nurtured a divine consciousness that always invited him to a higher plane of energy. The lamps in this cell glowed like an awakened mind. They told him they had all the answers he sought.

The Bhikkhu was sitting in the centre. His eyes were closed and he was holding a turquoise prayer wheel.

The Samanera bowed three times before the meditating figure. He pressed both his palms together and touched them to his forehead.

'It has happened, Bhante.'

The Bhikkhu opened his eyes.

'Ram Mathur is dead. He was killed last night.'

'Yes.'

'They have found a drawing on his face.'

'I know.'

The Bhikkhu closed his eyes again. After a while he folded his hands.

'Grieve not, Tathagata. We are powerless before death. It binds us and drags us away. You cannot cut through that rope. But it is not the conclusion of life. To die is to find a portal. The being is reborn. The soul is a bundle of habits, memories, sensations and desires. The Tibetan Buddhists say that the spirit goes through forty-nine doors. In the end it will all come back.'

The Samanera got up. While nearing the door, he heard the Bhikkhu's voice.

'Tathagata. You turn twenty in two years?'

'Yes, Bhante.'

'I heard you get restless these days.'

'I have nothing new to read. I have asked them for a book on Taoism.'

'Have you seen what I had given you?'

'Yes, Bhante.'

'The moment has come. Are you ready for the Sights?'

He did not reply.

'You have understood them more than anyone else. You have seen their soul. They have seen yours. All actions are not pleasant, Tathagata. They offend the eyes. Pinch the spirit. Create doubt. But they are all children of a grand design. You must hold on to your faith. We need it right now.'

'I have heard you, Bhante. But I only want to serve.'

'You say you want to make humanity more humane.'

'I do.'

'We also want the same. We have seen your work for the unfortunate. Why do you love them? Why are you drawn towards their suffering? Their punishment?'

'I don't know, Bhante.'

'You cannot battle your destiny, Tathagata. You already are what you will be. Some lives are for others. Like trees. Like rivers. Suns and moons. That's the only way to serve. Taoism will tell you the same. It teaches you to flow with the universe. Realise the natural order within. Follow yourself, Tathagata. The elements inside you. Will you walk?'

He was quiet.

'We have run out of time. It's not about us anymore. You still hold your right to choose but my hands are empty. I never knew these walls could be so vacant. Stand under the tree today and you will find only wood. We have to bring life to live here once more. Go for the Sights. See what is being done and what you can do.'

'You have too much faith in me, Bhante.'

'I have nothing else now. Our gates have opened again. They will need you more than ever before.'

'I know.'

'Don't heed my words for yourself. Heed them for those that are about to come.'

An hour later, the Samanera left. The Bhikkhu looked at the tree in the distance. They said that the legendary chant *Buddham Sharanam Gacchami* had been created in its shade.

The Bhikkhu picked up his mobile phone. He knew Buddha was watching.

'What are you saying?'

'I am asking you why my father scarred his face?'

'You think Mathur did that?'

'I know it was him. I will tell Suri when he comes.'

Patnaik stared at her. 'You are insane, Sia. Why will Mathur carve on his own skin? It was obviously made by his killers.'

'No, Om. They surely poisoned him. But they did not draw on him.'

'Why are you so sure? It's not an alphabet that you can recognise. It's a doodle.'

'That's why I am so certain. Letters and words would have confused me. My father's handwriting was not very distinctive. I am glad he chose to draw. He made it easy for me.'

The writer looked at the photo. 'Easy for you?'

'Do you see the mark?'

He nodded. The Om was glinting through the pixels like a hieroglyph etched on papyrus.

'This is exactly how he used to draw the syllable. He could never make a proper one and always puffed up the upper half. This Om was most certainly drawn by his hand. That's why he was holding the trishul. He used it to write on his face.'

Patnaik stared at the mark.

Mathur did this to himself?

'The symbol is no mystery to me. What I don't understand is this piece of paper.'

The writer took the orange sheet from her hand. 'What is this? You say your father emailed it to you after he died?'

'Yes. I was working late on a report last night when I got an email from him. This came as an attachment. Suri has told me the exact time of his death and this came precisely three minutes later.'

'You are telling me that a dead man sent you an email?'

'Yes, Om.'

Patnaik looked at the paper. Printed in the centre were two rows of lines and circles. The upper row comprised a huge circle with two semi-circles on both sides. The semi-circles were perfect mirror images of each other. The lower level had a row of seven vertical lines. The first line was the shortest while the second was the longest and the remaining five were of equal length. Directly below the print was an ink autograph.

'This is Mathur's signature.'

'I know.'

Patnaik was looking at the printed images on the paper. And suddenly something stirred within him. What was it? Something had nudged his brain. He gritted his teeth. The moment had lapsed. Something had flickered within and died.

'I really don't understand, Sia. How could Mathur mail you after he was killed?'

'More than how, I want to know why,' Sia lashed out. 'Why did he send me this? What's going on here? Is this some sort of a message?'

'If your father mailed it to you then that might be the most possible explanation. This is a strange message. He might be trying to communicate something in secret.'

He looked at Mathur's photos again.

This looks like a puzzle. Is that why he smiles?

He handed the sheet back to her. 'It is obviously for your eyes only. And that probably means that he is telling you something that cannot be shared with others. Maybe that's why he was killed. But Mathur…' He paused.

Did this man know secrets that could take his life?

She seemed to have read his mind. 'Exactly, Om. You knew him. Was he really a man with secrets?'

'I know, Sia. It all looks impossible but look at this picture. The eye. This mark on his face. This is no longer Mathur.' He held her hand. 'Think hard, Sia, you may know something that can explain all this.'

'I have no idea, Om. I hardly lived with him. I was very young when my mother died. My uncle in Delhi became a parent figure. That city has always been my home and now my job with ISRO keeps me in Ahmedabad. I know nothing about my father's business.'

'But he used to tell me that you visited often.'

'Yes. I always came down to Sarnath during holidays. That place had become his only world. We loved being with each other. He always tried to make up for lost time. We would go for long walks and I would hold his hand. He knew such beautiful stories. He was a strangely fascinating man.'

'He was. Anything else?'

'I always found him keeping to his books and papers. He was very particular about them. Sometimes he disappeared for days saying he was visiting old friends. Sometimes he would go to Varanasi to sit by the Ganga. We respected each other's work. He used to say that we both served society. He looked at the past and I looked at the future.' Sia paused. 'There is one thing.'

'What?'

'He once said that he wanted to give me his mind. I remember it only because he had an extremely bizarre expression on his face. It almost scared me. I think he was talking about his knowledge of history and mythology.'

But Patnaik's brain was already entering another dimension.

Mathur wanted to give his mind to Sia. And now he has sent her an email.

Patnaik felt a wire tighten inside his spine. What had happened here? Someone had killed Mathur, yet he had reached out from the beyond to hand them a last letter.

'Hold on. I don't understand this. If Mathur left a message for you, what am I doing here? This is obviously a family secret. A private covenant. Why have you shared this with me?'

Sia smiled. 'I have told you that you are here because he wanted it. I haven't dragged you into this, Om. Your presence here was my father's wish. I simply carried it out.'

'What do you mean?'

'You still don't get it.' She stopped. Footsteps were approaching the tent.

'We will talk later. This is not the place. And not a word to anyone.'

Suri stormed in looking totally worn out.

'Damn these reporters. Such a sticky lot. They all want bloody breaking news. The body is on its way now. How does it feel being part of a real murder, Mr Patnaik?'

He kept quiet. The officer turned to Sia. 'You should rest now. The flight from Ahmedabad must have been tiring. I have made arrangements at a guest house nearby…'

'We'll go home, Suri.'

'You want to go to Sarnath?'

'Yes.'

'Both of you?'

'Yes.'

'Alright, Sia. I am really sorry about this. You know I tried to warn your father. But he did not listen.'

Patnaik stopped dead in his tracks. 'What's that? You had warned Mathur?'

'Yes. I had met them both. They had just come back from a trip.'

'Tibet.' Sia smiled weakly. 'Our last trip together.'

Suri lowered his voice. 'I clearly told him that his life was in danger.'

'What danger?'

'There have been several murders like this in the past few months.'

'More murders?'

'Yes. Initially they seemed random but soon a very definite pattern emerged.'

'What kind of pattern?'

'That is confidential. We had managed to hush the murders or get them reported in the media as natural deaths to avoid panic. Mathur seemed into fit in the pattern perfectly. I warned him right away but he shrugged me off.'

The writer was thinking furiously now.

Similar deaths in the past months. And Mathur fit into that pattern.

He looked at the photographs again. The old man had turned into a stigmata that held a question inside the wound. Was the answer hiding among those geometrical lines and circles on the orange sheet? The figures were sneering at him. And the river outside was asking him a question.

Do you want to hear what he told me last night?

'What do you want?'

'You know what I want. Why pretend?'

'Watch where you are sitting.'

'I am not blind like you, sire.'

He was sitting on the throne. There was no one in the court. Only the king standing before him.

'Are you playing a game?'

'There are no rules here.'

'Is it true?'

'What, sire?'

'You have brought an end to the revolt?'

'Yes.'

'What did you do?'

'It ended on its own. When I arrived with the army, they all came together and put down their arms. They should have been calmed months ago.'

'Are you saying my eldest is not worthy?'

'He was ruling them. He failed.'

'I hear you have started commanding too many regiments of the army.'

'Are you afraid?'

'I know what else you have done.'

'Tell me.'

'You have my father's sword. He had thrown it away when he left us. You found it.'

'I have it. It's mine.'

'Will you give it back?'

'Will you fight for it?'

'You are insolent. I hear that you have no heart. You are arrogant and have no mercy. Some say you have read all the four Vedas.'

'I am what I make myself.'

'Have you been plotting against me? Or your elder brother? Do you want this throne?'

'You cannot place me here. I will place myself.'

'I can stop you.'

'You cannot stop me. You can only kill me.'

'You have a wall around your mind. I want to reach it. Hold it. Smash it into pieces.'

'You have tried. They have failed.'

'I exile you from the kingdom.'

'What have I done?'

'Go away.'

'Do you love me, Father?'

'I wish you were never born.'

'Yes, sire.'

The king wrenched the jewels off his body. His ears were bleeding now. Then he pulled his garments away. The prince walked out naked. Outside the palace, Krishna stood on a wall teaching Arjuna that the greatest wars are those that vanquish the mind.

13

$\mathcal{H}$e picked up another one.

The stink of charred tobacco had transformed his living room into a gas chamber. They were dying. They wanted to breathe. But the men knew better than to make a noise. Their boss was pissed. He had failed and the cigarette smoke was a perfect cover to hide his face.

Suri flung the photos through the fumes. 'It's that motherfucker again.'

They already knew that.

'How could we let this happen? What the hell were we doing?'

He stubbed his cigarette furiously. He knew the killer. This was not the first time he had struck. He had already dug his fangs eight times before. Eight deaths. And Mathur was number nine.

Nine murders.

The horror show had been running for the past three months. Bodies had been littered across eight different places, before Mathur joined the list. A glass jar in one of their offices now held nine eyeballs in formaldehyde, staring at each other. The Intelligence had informed him that it was a single man. One killer walking around with poison.

They had named him Scorpion.

No one knew his motive but the pattern was flawless. The same corrosive poison had been the instrument of doom and every corpse had turned up with the right eye hanging from its socket. They had been warned about the historian but they had failed. Because he had not listened. Because they did not know one thing.

Who was this bloody Scorpion?

He looked at his men. 'This mark of Om. Is Sia sure about it?'

'Yes, sir. She is positive that her father slashed his face himself.'

'We may have an edge then,' another officer spoke. 'In all the murders elsewhere, the victims did not leave any last words. But Mathur has scribbled a letter on his cheek. It surely means something.'

Fantastic was the word. What was the historian up to? Who scars his own face like that? Suri's eyes fell on the newspapers. They had not been able to con the media this time. The press had picked up every gory detail and dished it out for breakfast. Headlines and TV slugs were trying to outwit each other in a dazzling contest of wordplay.

Murder In Holy Land screamed one headline; *Blood Stains The Ganga* said another. *Dead Man's Evil Eye* and *Historian Brands His Own Face.*

He looked up. 'Some fucking wordplay.'

Suri had been dodging their calls so far. But he knew he could not avoid them forever. Murder in Varanasi was a colossal media event, especially a sensational murder such as this. They were already calling him a failure. Memos were raining from his bosses to hold a damned press conference. Give a statement. But he had nothing to give. So the exile continued.

'What about Om Patnaik?' He heard an officer speak. 'Sia Mathur wanted him here.'

Suri closed his eyes. He was right. The arrival of the writer was a strange event. Why was he here? Why had Sia claimed that his presence was vital? She had said that the man was a family friend. He had seen them both whispering in the tent. What were they hiding?

He looked at his team. 'Any news from forensics?'

'Nothing.'

Suri took a deep breath.

What I need is a bloody miracle.

The intercom buzzed. The voice on the other end sounded excited.

'Yadav here, sir. The Forensic Department just called. They have completed their lab tests.'

He waited.

'They say they have a breakthrough.'

Suri's fingers clenched the phone's neck.

'Breakthrough?'

'Yes, sir. One of their officers will be arriving shortly.'

Suri placed the receiver back on the cradle and lit another cigarette.

Had the bloody miracle happened?

The deer nodded.

The sky was blushing pink before the morning sun. He got up and sniffed. He was hungry. Last night a woman had fed him rice but now he wanted tender green grass. Not too much. Just enough to fill his belly.

The grass in the park had soaked up all the dew. He was nibbling at the juiciest blades. Suddenly he froze. Someone was standing there. Watching him.

A man.

The deer turned to run. Then he stopped and looked at the man.

The man was smiling.

The deer walked up to him and rubbed his head against his legs. Five ascetics came walking along that road. One of them laughed.

'Look. Here stands our luxury-loving brother. He used to partake six grains of rice a day. I have seen him falling unconscious from starvation. He told me that when he touched his belly he could feel his spine. Look how nourished he is now. He has changed. He is no longer worthy of our respect. Do not speak to him. Do not greet him or invite him to join us.'

The man was caressing the deer. 'What wrong have I done?'

'You have forsaken your vows.'

'You have turned away from asceticism.'
'You have given yourself to enjoyment.'
'You have strayed from the path of wisdom.'
'You will never understand truth.'
The man spoke. 'I heard a girl sing. She said:

Fair goes the dancing when the sitar is tuned
Tune the sitar neither low nor high
The string overstretched breaks
The string over slack is dumb
Tune the sitar neither low nor high.'

He smiled. 'I have not renounced my vows. I understand them now. Austerities and luxuries obscure the mind alike. Deprivation is as much a hindrance as indulgence. One can no longer understand truth in either state. I have given up both extremes. I have discovered another path.'

They looked at him with awe. 'What have you discovered, O wise one?'

'The Middle Path.'

The deer saw the five ascetics fall at the man's feet.

Sarnath had seen this miracle centuries ago when Buddha preached his first discourse to the five men. They had become his first disciples and formed the Sangha or the Order of Monks. Following that, the Triratna or Three Jewels – Buddha, Dhamma and Sangha – had come into existence. Buddha was the enlightened mind. Dhamma was the body of teachings. And Sangha, the awakened beings. It was here that the Dhammachakra Sutta or the Wheel of Dhamma had rolled into motion.

Patnaik felt an intense thrill every time he stepped into this landscape. Sarnath had the fragrance of thousands of years. The Buddha had walked here and touched the five elements. The wind resonated with the Teacher's Four Noble Truths. They said we suffered because we craved for things that were not permanent. Not everlasting. Renouncing that attachment would end all the pain.

But was it so easy?

Sitting in Mathur's house, the writer felt a sudden pang of loneliness. The montage embedded in his brain was playing once more. That smile. The eye. The lines and circles on the paper. He wanted to pull open their mouths and make them talk. Walking into the living room, he stopped before a picture of the historian. He was smiling at him again. Next to it was another picture of Sia and Mathur holding each other and laughing. The words on the frame told him why.

YOUNG SCIENTIST OF THE YEAR – SIA MATHUR

She was sitting on the terrace. The red of the sky had touched her eyes. Or perhaps she had been weeping again.

'Looking for answers?'

Sia shook her head. 'I sometimes wish the answers would come looking for me. It would make life so much easier.'

'Easier yes. But it will stop our evolution. Our growth lies in our search. The journey we make. The pain. The doubts. The failures. And then the ecstasy. When the answer is revealed. When it sits on our hands and warms our soul.'

'Beautiful words! No wonder your readers love you.'

'It's true. The answer may dodge you for a while. It will tie a cloth over your eyes and hide in some corner. It will giggle as you stumble around with your hands stretched. But the epiphany comes and you drag the answer out of the hole by its hair.'

He looked at the book in her hands. 'What are you reading?'

'Hansel and Gretel. It was Father's favourite. Hansel was so clever to drop a trail of pebbles behind him in the forest. When the moon came up, they twinkled like stars and guided them home.'

Patnaik was silent. Mathur had also emailed a few stones.

I only have to follow them and reach home.

'I didn't know the award-winning scientist loved to read about gingerbread houses and witches.'

'It's this house, Om. I can always be myself here.'

'Your father used to tell me about your work at ISRO. I remember how excited he would get. When did the award happen?'

'Last year at our Research Facility in Ahmedabad. They thought my work on solar planetary physics was good enough. I am now training for human spaceflight programmes for 2016.'

'Sounds thrilling.'

'Totally. Our solar system is quite a billiards table. There are so many colours to play with. So many secrets waiting to be hit upon.'

'Your father was very proud of you, Sia.'

'I know.' She was looking at the sun sinking before her.

'Have you eaten? You look hungry.'

She nodded. The writer picked up the orange sheet lying on the table. 'You still don't recall anything that might help us?'

'Nothing. He never told me anything. And he never listened to anyone.' Her voice sounded bitter.

'You mean Suri's warnings?'

'Yes. He laughed at him. You didn't know him, Om. He could be very stubborn when he wanted. Almost as if he was another person. I kept begging him for days but he did not care. If only he had listened.'

'You still don't want to tell Suri anything?'

'He will never understand it,' she wiped her eyes. 'Besides, my father did not intend it that way. It's a sacred trust. I will never share it with another person. Never.'

Patnaik looked at the paper again. He recalled that moment inside the tent when something had floated before his eyes, light as a feather. It had stroked his face and vanished.

'It makes no sense.'

Sia got up. 'Let's take a walk.'

'A walk? Now?'

'There is still light. It will do us good.'

'But shouldn't we sit and rack our brains? Your father has handed us a rather impossible problem.'

'I know. That is why we need this walk. There is a place here in Sarnath. It's holy ground. People go there looking for answers. It may speak to us.'

$\mathcal{T}$he mound was silent.

Erected around 500 AD, the Dhamek Stupa was one of the oldest Buddhist shrines in the world. Standing at a height of 144 feet, the cylinder was easily the most colossal structure in Sarnath. Geometrical swastika patterns, floral designs and human figures sat on those red bricks while a ring of lotuses ran around the centre like a ribbon. The stupa marked the hallowed Mrigdava or the Deer Park where Buddha had preached his first sermon to the five. The deer park also represented one of his past lives mentioned in the Jataka. Born as a deer, the Buddha had saved the life of a doe from the King of Benares. Even the modern name Sarnath was a contraction of the name Saranganath or Lord of the Deer.

Walking around the stupa, Patnaik understood what Sia meant. He could sense an energy in his fingers as he caressed the ancient stones. He was walking on consecrated ground.

The Teacher had answered the questions of the five here. He may have answers for us.

Sia was looking at a woman. An old woman who returned her stare. There was something unknown in her eyes. Was she coming towards her? She was wrong. The woman walked past them. Sia turned towards the massive mound.

'People love the Sanchi Stupa but I have always been drawn towards the Dhamek. It has raw power.' She craned her neck. 'I wanted to see it one last time.'

'What do you mean?'

'I will not be coming to Sarnath again.'

'Your father loved this place.'

'I know. I cannot face Sarnath without him. It is no longer the same place. But I'll miss it. There is something in the air here. It heals.'

He heard voices of her past simmering in those words. She was right. This place healed. Could it heal her?

'I'll miss the temple too.'

'Temple?'

'Yes. The Sarnath Temple. We used to go there together. My father was devoutly attached to that shrine. He would go there daily to offer flowers to the Buddha.'

Patnaik was sucking on a chocolate nugget, turning it round and round in his mouth.

'He deeply revered the Buddha. Having lived here for so long, he was greatly influenced by Buddhism.'

'I know, Sia. Mathur had told me once that he thought of himself as the Teacher's sixth disciple of Sarnath.'

The writer sat down on the grass. He was looking at a cluster of Buddhist monks circumambulating the Dhamek Stupa. They were walking in the traditional clockwise direction symbolising the apparent movement of the sun around the earth. The rotation announced that the Buddha was the centre and essence of their lives. Each of the monks were holding a bell and a dorje. These were symbols of the masculine and feminine like the Tibetan Yab-Yum or the Chinese Yin-Yang. The men were constantly revolving the dorje around the bell, creating a vibrating resonance. This mystical union of Wisdom and Compassion was believed to lead to an enlightened mind. They were chanting.

Buddham Sharanam Gacchami
Dhammam Sharanam Gacchami
Sangham Sharanam Gacchami

He was by the river again. Inside the tent. Looking at Mathur. Those images on the paper.

The lines... the circle.

The monks were encircling the stupa. They were singing. The dorjes were revolving. The bells were humming.

Mathur was attached to the Sarnath Temple. Buddha had first preached at Dhamek in Sarnath. In this deer park he had set the Dhammachakra in motion. The Wheel. The historian said he was the sixth disciple. Six because there had been five disciples in the beginning. The five devotees of Sarnath. The five original sons of the Sangha.

Patnaik got up. His green eyes were sparkling as he felt the pieces fall rapidly into place.

Five disciples... lines and circles... Buddhist monks... Deer park... The stupa...

The air was resonating now with the music of the bells. He got up. The sound was everywhere. Outside the Dhamek. Inside his mind. Patnaik was chanting too. He was not alone anymore. He had unconsciously become a part of a divine chorus.

I go for refuge in Buddha
I go for refuge in Dhamma
I go for refuge in Sangha

He seized Sia's hands wildly. 'I think I have cracked it.'
'Cracked what?'

'The lines and circles on the paper. I know what they mean.'

She glared at him, 'Are you being funny?'

'No, Sia. I see it now. There is a part that I still don't understand. But I have got the rest. Don't you hear the elements?'

He turned towards the stupa. The monks had gone but the air was still pregnant with the chiming of the bells.

'We have to go to the temple.'

'What temple?'

'You were right, Sia. Sometimes your answers come looking for you. The Dhamek has spoken. Sarnath Temple. That's where the answer lies.'

16

$\mathcal{S}$he watched his face change.

He seemed to have burst forth from the giant rocks that dotted the landscape. He was moving towards her now and yet somehow appeared to be quite still, as though his body were being transported without his own physical effort. His feet seemed to grind the mud into finer particles and his eyes were burning holes in her body.

'I see you again, princess.'

He was smiling like a child.

'You have to stop calling me that. I am no princess. I catch fish.'

'You are my princess. And you will be my queen.'

'So you are going to be king?'

'Your king. Their king. All four directions will be under my rule.'

'The king has never told me his name.'

'I have no name. No family. I only have you.'

'What else do you have?'

'I have myself.'

'What's he like, the king?'

'He has many qualities. He knows what the Vedas have to say. He can lead any army to victory. He can defeat the gods when he picks up his sword. He has no mercy when he hunts.'

'You are cruel. You are too proud.'

'No, princess. I am just a liar.'

'You lied?'

'Yes. I am nothing. I have nothing but my loneliness.'

'You were lonely before you met me. Are you lonely still?'

'Man is all alone until he gets what he wants.'

'What do you want?'

He grasped her hand. 'Come.'

And just like that, moments later, the ground beneath her feet turned to water. They were standing in the shallow part of the river. They said Hanuman had flown over it carrying the Sanjivani herb that had healed Lakshman and purified the fatal infection of his flesh. The river water flowed like blood in the dry veins of the region. It nurtured the children of the land and gave life to the living.

'See, princess.'

'It's our river.'

The prince handed her his bow and arrow. 'Shoot me.'

She loaded the arrow. He pointed at his reflection in the water. The bowstring twanged and the arrow splintered the image into a thousand ripples.

'I want to see my face in this river.'

*S*he was watching him.

His face was like a magnet, pulling her towards him as though she had no will of her own. She only had her faith. She did not ask him any questions; she was following him for answers.

The prophet had promised her the ultimate truth.

The three triangles of the shrine had turned orange with the setting sun. Patnaik had always loved the utter simplicity of the Sarnath Temple. Walking towards it today, he felt an energy coursing through his veins. The temple was radiant, like the face of a pregnant woman. The writer knew it was not the sun. It was the secret within its womb that had given colour to its cheeks.

The secret which I will reveal.

They were standing inside the sanctum now. The last few devotees had left as they entered. The tall walls surrounding them were dressed in murals and frescoes. A Japanese artist, Kosetsu Nosu, had splashed the colours of Buddha's life all over these divine dimensions. In them the Teacher lived and died like a circular loop inside a square.

Patnaik pointed ahead. 'There.'

The altar at Sarnath Temple was a place for hibernation. Once the Vassa or the monsoon retreat of Buddha, the shrine had risen from the ashes of Mulagandhakuti Vihara where the Teacher spent his rainy days. The tradition had lingered on and monks continued to stay dormant within the temple grounds during the three months of rain every year.

Patnaik stopped walking. 'Look.'

Sia's eyes grew large.

It's him!

That mouth smiling softly.

The smile.

She froze with fear. *But he's dead.*

She paused.

His eye.

This was not her father but a golden image. The most famous image in the iconography of Buddhism.

As Patnaik spoke, his voice was laced with fervour. 'This is the answer. Sarnath's Preaching Buddha.'

The Preaching Buddha was hailed as the supreme masterpiece of the Sarnath school of art. Carved by Gupta artists in fifth century BC, it was an abstract union of simplicity and sublimity. Picturing the Teacher's first discourse to his five disciples at the deer park, the makers had trapped both physical charm and mental bliss. The gigantic floral halo stood witness to that moment of transformation when Siddharth became Gautam. The golden image here was an exact replica of the original sculpture preserved at the Sarnath Museum.

They were sitting before the Teacher. It was fascinating to be there and to gaze at the answer. It was also terrifying yet strangely comforting.

'I saw his face, Om. He was here. It was like he never died.'

'I know. This is why Mathur dared to become the Buddha. The disciple became the master because he wanted us to come here. It was his greatest offering to the Teacher. He was the medium and the message, Sia. That's why he smiled.'

'Smiled just like him.'

'Yes. Buddha's smile reflects his transcendental nature. His spiritual delight. Mathur was probably experiencing a similar emotion. He was in terrible pain, Sia. And yet he smiled and slashed his face. He smiled because he was giving you his essence. He bled with joy because he knew that one day you would stand here before the Buddha and realise his final word. He was beyond human, Sia. Only a higher power must have made it possible.'

Sia was watching silently.

He smiled to show us the way. Was he smiling right now?

Patnaik retrieved the orange sheet from his pocket. 'When I first saw this paper, something had touched my mind. It all came back at the Dhamek.'

'What?'

'The circle. It spoke to me at Dhamek today. The story. The deer park. The five disciples. Your mention of the Sarnath Temple. Those monks around the stupa. It all added up to what your father was trying to tell us in his final message.'

'I am still blind, Om.'

Patnaik indicated the Buddha's hands. 'Look at his fingers. This posture of raising the hands to the chest depicts the Dhamma Chakra Pravartana or the Turning of the Wheel of Dhamma. In this mudra the tips of the thumb and the index finger of both hands form circles. The circle depicts the Wheel.'

'The Wheel of Dhamma.'

'Yes. Recall the Dhamek Stupa. Circle. The monks circumambulating the stupa. Circles. The dorjes revolving around the bells. Circles again.'

Sia nodded. 'I see what you saw. But what about the rest?'

'Now you know the circle stands for the Wheel of Dhamma. You can see it there in the centre.'

'Yes. And the semi-circles?'

'They are on either side of the circle. Take a look.'

Sia stared. She could see figures on both sides of the wheel. Suddenly she gasped. They were not only similar but symmetrical. Perfect mirror images of each other.

'They look like animals.'

'Not just any animal. They are the animals of Sarnath. The animals associated with the Dhammachakra.'

'Animals of Sarnath. You mean…'

'Deer. One deer on either side of the Wheel. Deer of the Sarnath park where the first sermon was heard.'

'But why semi-circles?'

'I know. It makes no sense. But now I see they are not just semi-circles. They are letters.'

'Letters?'

'English letters.'

Sia gave a cry. 'D. The letter D.'

'Precisely. Two Ds facing each other. D for deer.'

She laughed. *That was easy!* 'And those seven lines?'

'Look at either side of the deer. What do you see?'

'Human figures.'

'Correct. Count them.'

They were seven.

'Exactly. Seven lines for the seven figures on the panel.'

'What are these figures?'

'The five lines of equal length are the five disciples of Buddha. The Five Fathers. The original Arahants.'

'And the first two lines?'

'They are the first two figures on the panel. The first line is the shortest since the first figure is a child. The second figure is a woman. So that is longer. The identity of these two figures is not clear. They could be Buddha's wife Yashodhara and son Rahula. They could also be the donors of this sculpture.'

Sia turned towards him. 'You have done it. I see why my father brought you to me. So that you could bring me to him.'

'Have I?'

'What do you mean?'

Patnaik took out the photograph of the historian's mutilated face.

'What about this mark? The symbol of Om? I have no idea what this means.'

She took the photo from his hands. 'Let me decipher that for you.'

The writer's body turned rigid. 'You?'

'Yes.'

'You mean…'

Sia laughed. 'I know. I have always known.'

18

*H*e scoured her face like a mad man.

She knows. What does she know?

'I recognised the mark the moment I saw it.' She held his hand. 'That syllable is nothing but you.'

'Me? What are you saying?'

'I am saying that you have got so used to being called by your surname that you have forgotten your first name, Om.'

The writer stood in stunned silence. It took him another second to process the information.

'You mean this mark? It's my name?'

'Yes. Remember his FB password. My name. This was your name. He always did that. I told you that my father had summoned you. This mark was his command. He wanted you here. You were probably the last person he thought about before the poison ate him.'

Patnaik felt a lump forming in his throat.

Mathur wrote my name on his face. He called out to me that night.

He looked at the Buddha. 'What does he want now?'

'There is a reason why we are sitting before the Teacher, Om. He has something for us here. We need to get near the image.'

Patnaik touched the wooden railing that kept men away from

the Buddha. She glanced around. 'Don't worry. There's no one here.'

'That's not what I was thinking, Sia.' He looked at her.

She nodded. 'You have your scruples but I don't have a choice. We will have to do this. We are not desecrating his altar. He will understand.'

They got up and crossed over the railing. The hundred-feet Buddha was sitting atop a high marble plinth. There were offererings of candles and incense, and metal vases stuffed with lotuses, roses and sunflowers, before the imposing statue. They examined every inch of the platform.

Nothing.

'Are we making a mistake?'

She shook her head. She was thinking.

What did he do here?

She was watching her father standing before the Teacher with flowers.

She jolted. *Flowers*

'The vases.'

'What?'

'Look in the vases.'

Patnaik saw what she had realised. They picked up a vase each. Pulling the flowers out, they reached into the vases. Could they be hiding anything?

'It's here.'

He watched Sia pull out a small bundle of red silk from the bottom of her vase. Twenty trembling fingers rolled the cloth away.

'What is this?'

'I don't know. He must have hidden it last night.'

She lifted her inheritance.

A head.

A small bronze head was resting inside the silk. The metallic curves burned in the temple light.

'What a strange face.'

'Not strange, Sia. Look again.'

She saw it now. The mouth was curved into a smile.

Like Buddha. Like Mathur.

His green eyes were gleaming as she moved it about in her hand. What could this mean? Why had the historian concealed it here? Entrusted it to the Buddha?

'No ideas, Om?'

'None. Never seen anything like this. What I can tell you is it's no antique. This has been quite recently manufactured.'

Sia pointed at the figure's forehead. 'It has a mark.'

'Yes. Looks like a question mark but the lower dot is missing.' He nodded. 'Quite symbolic. We are nothing but big question marks right now looking for answers.'

'What now?'

Patnaik took it from her hands and wrapped it back in the silk. 'Let's get out of here.'

Walking towards the door, they glanced at the fresco adorning the walls. The Mahaparinirvana. His disciples had gathered around him as he lay dying under the full moon.

'Who will guide us when you are gone?' Ananda asked.

'My teachings will be your teacher now. Do you have any final doubts?'

They did not speak. He spoke for the last time.

'Nothing in the world is permanent. Work towards your own salvation.'

The voice fell silent.

'What's that sound?'

Sia looked at the entrance. Someone was there.

The woman.

The woman she had seen at Dhamek. She recognised those eyes. They were gazing at her again. Walking out of the temple, Sia turned, to look at her once more.

19

*T*he Goddess watched as the man stumbled into the shrine and fell at her feet. His sword slipped from his hand and clanged to the floor. He looked back in fear at the doorway and saw the prince follow him in, with a sword which dripped blood, his blood.

'Leave me alone. You have got what you wanted. You are the Emperor now.'

'Not yet. You are still alive. The last one.'

'I'll flee from this land. Banish me. Exile me. Do what we did to you. You will never see me again.'

'I know I'll never see you again.'

'How many more will you kill? The palace is bathed in blood. You have slaughtered all ninety-nine of our step brothers.

'This is nothing compared to your sin.'

'Stop it.'

'You have killed too.'

'No.'

'I have killed men. You killed a woman.'

'I did not.'

'An old woman. My mother.'

'Stop.'

'You killed my mother.'

'It was a mistake. We wanted to kill your wife. You married a heretic.'

'She is no heretic.'

'You went against Father. Against our laws. Father is dead. We wanted to kill her too.'

'Not my wife. You wanted to kill what was inside her. In her womb. My unborn. Heir to my throne.'

'Yes. But your seed lives. You live. You are immortal. You have lost nothing.'

'You don't know what I have lost. You will never know.'

'I'll be your servant.'

'Then serve me now.'

The man saw his face reflected in the shining edge of the sword as it came down swiftly. It was no longer a weapon of steel, it seemed to have transformed into fiery gold. As the blade descended, ripping the air into pieces, the Goddess laughed. The man's blood coloured the walls red.

She wanted nothing more than to dip the ten metals she was holding in the blood and lick them one by one.

20

This was the Maha Shamshan. The Great Cremation Ground of the world.

Unlike other places in India, cremation sites in Varanasi were right in the heart of the city. For the inhabitants of this holy city, cremation was a release, not pollution. It did not contaminate the flesh, rather it liberated the soul by melting the threads of clay that tied men to earth. This had always been Varanasi's consecrated task and its ghats embodied conflicting dualities – land and water; life and death; gods and men; sound and silence.

Sia was standing at the Manikarnika Ghat. Vishnu had carved it with his chakra and filled it with his perspiration. Shiva had seen the water glow like a million suns and made a home within it. Today, as she watched the sun scorch the river, she could imagine it boiling like a gigantic cauldron. Her hands clasped the earthen urn that held the remains of her father. It was warm like her father's palm; for one last time, they were holding each other's hand.

The post mortem had confirmed that a corrosive toxin had been injected into Mathur. Sia could not recall the name. She wanted to burn his books and papers with him. Her father would have loved that. In the morning, before coming to the ghat, she had sat by his shrouded body while Patnaik had wept silently. Her father, who had faced life head on, had his face covered in death. Just like that woman she had seen at the Sarnath Temple the other day. She was here again. Looking at Sia with that piercing gaze.

Who was she? Was she following her?

At the ghat, some of the priests had objected to her, a woman, performing her father's last rites. They said cremation was not an act of emotion and that a woman's tears held the soul back from its final journey. Patnaik had stepped forward to do the deed, but then he saw her eyes. They held no tears. The heat of the cremation ground had blistered her naked feet as she performed the seven obligatory circumambulations of the funeral pyre, carrying a cracked earthen pot of holy water. A steady stream of water fell through the hole in the pot like the draining of her father's eye. In the end she had smashed the pot on the earth, hoping it would wake him up.

The four elements were there now. The water of the Ganga. The fire of the pyre. The earth of the ghats. The air of Varanasi. They were embracing the souls. Telling her to let go; to submit her father to them now.

She uncovered the urn. Was her father breathing in those embers? Sia upturned the vessel into the river. The ashes crowded around her for a while and then floated away. While climbing back the steps, she stopped.

The woman was here too.

That old woman. The one she had seen at Dhamek. At Sarnath Temple. At the mourning today. That same woman. She was calling her name.

As she walked towards her, she was, for the first time, able to get a better look at her face. An ageing face covered with hair that was more white than grey and large rimmed glasses that could not hide the question in her eyes. What was it that Sia had been trying to catch all these days? Trying to see every time she had seen her? She saw it now. It was a silent sobbing sorrow. 'Who are you?'

'You don't know me, Sia. I would like to know you.'

'I don't understand.'

'I want to help you.'

Sia walked past her. 'I don't think I need anybody's help.'

'What about that metal head at Sarnath?'

Sia stumbled.

'I saw you holding that bizarre toy. Do you have any inkling what it could be?'

'No.'

'Neither have I. Never seen anything like that. But I would love for both of us to know.'

Sia did not speak.

'Will you come, Sia?'

'I don't know.'

The woman was gone. Sia's head was reeling. She looked at a board on the steps. It bore the word Avimukta, another name for Varanasi meaning 'Never Abandoned.' They said the dead never abandoned the living.

Her father was still there.

21

*H*e was waiting.

Tension was writ large on his face. He was finally going to meet the expert from forensics today. They had been claiming a breakthrough, but he was not celebrating yet. Suri had been in the police force long enough to see many such pieces of evidence get flushed down shit holes.

He looked up. 'Yes. Fucking shit holes.'

The people involved in the case had acquired semi stardom, thanks to the press. Images of Sia holding the urn, being splashed about in newspapers and news channels, seemed to be winning hands down. Patnaik, dubbed as the mystery man, was a distant second. Suri himself was close to being a near celebrity. His pictures were printed with giant question marks stamped on his face. The media, like a hungry dog, was sucking this piece of news dry. Their cameras were now pointing at him.

This had better be bloody good.

The noise outside his room told him that the man had arrived. The door opened to admit the expert, who walked in carrying a blue folder.

'Hello, Mr Suri. Jain from the Forensic Department.'

The men shook hands.

'Very hot today. How about some orange juice?'

Suri jerked his thumb at one of the men who rushed out. Jain was opening his folder and going through the contents.

'So, Mr Suri. How have you been?'

Suri grunted in reply. He saw what the bastard was doing. He was having fun. Gloating over the power he had over him, just then. Jain was only too aware of the media mud-slinging currently in progress. He knew what he held inside his folder was nothing less than ambrosia for Suri.

After two glasses of juice, the man relented.

'Mr Suri, we have good news.'

The officer nodded. *Finally.*

'Our team has finished examining the scene of the murder. We have also closely examined the body of Ram Mathur and the material evidence.'

'What material evidence?'

'There are three. Firstly, his garments. They are clean. Then you have the trishul. It only has Mathur's fingerprints. The tips of the trishul have blood and flesh and the DNA report is a perfect match.'

'So we can confirm that Mathur alone handled the trishul.'

'Yes. But this third object gave us something else.'

He opened his folder and placed it on the table. Suri knew what he was looking at.

'Mathur's locket.'

'Yes. It's silver. We have found a print on it.'

'A fingerprint?'

The man smiled. 'Not exactly.'

He took out a single sheet of paper. The image on the print-out was definitely not a finger.

'An ear?'

'Yes, Mr Suri.'

The kidney-shaped figure looked like the artwork of a child. The officer picked it up slowly. Very slowly.

They have found an ear print.

Suri knew that ear prints were fast becoming the latest forensic favourite. While he still swore by fingerprints, experts were now claiming that the human ear was the new sensation. The shape and size of each individual's ear was unique, making it the masterkey to unlocking a criminal's face.

'Is this good?'

'We believe it is, Mr Suri. The impression is quite clear. We normally don't get such fine ear prints. It indicates a physical scuffle before the killer stabbed Mathur's eye.'

'But this could be Sia Mathur's print.'

'That was a possibility. Our team has already taken Sia's prints. They do not match.'

Suri looked at the sheet.

A second print.

'You think this is the Scorpion?'

'We do. You must come to our forensic base and get this checked. If you find a file match, you will have your man.'

Suri held up the locket. The words engraved on it were not familiar.

'Om Mani Padme Hum.' Jain read them out. 'A six syllable Buddhist chant. It invokes the jewel in the lotus.'

'Anything else?'

'The trishul. We have detected animal matter.'

'I heard that at the ghat. What exactly have you found?'

'Animal bone.'

'Animal bone?'

'Yes. Very minute scrapings. Looks like cattle bone.'

Suri frowned. *Cattle bone?*

'I am glad that the old man was gripping the trishul. The animal matter was clinging to the handle and his palm. It was pouring heavily that night and the traces could have easily washed off.'

'But it makes no sense. Bone shavings?'

'We know. Odd thing at an odd place.'

Suri picked up the sheet again.

Could this be the Scorpion?

He wanted it to be. It could take him to the killer's hole. He would then grasp him by the ear and drag him out. He might have that bloody press conference after all. He might even be able to peel off that Friday from his soul.

That Friday twenty-seven years ago...

'How about some more juice, Mr Jain?'

Leaving him to enjoy the drink, Suri got up and opened the window.

22

$\mathscr{I}$t had begun to rain again. Vigorously.

He was looking at the painting. Shiva was dancing, bruising the universe with his trishul. A servant with salve-smeared fingers was massaging the Emperor's body. Massaging the sore points to release the pain. The flaps of the tent had been drawn to keep the rain and stench away.

'Ghastly weather.'

'Yes, my lord.'

'When will they stop screaming?'

'No one knows, sire.'

'Those women have been going on and on for days.'

'And nights. No one here has slept.'

'It will end. They cannot go on forever.'

'Yes, sire. Nothing is forever.'

'Are there many dead?'

'Many are still dying.'

'Now?'

'Yes, my lord. The rains have brought with them disease and infection.'

'How many?'

'Some say almost one lakh have perished. Like any other war.'

'I have never heard of so many dead in a war.'

'It is like any other war, sire. It's all the same whether it's one hundred or one lakh. All the same.'

'What are you saying?'

'You have won. Your father will be proud.'

'He will wander like a spirit. He never had the power to crush this land. Even my grandfather failed. I am the only one.'

'The land is nothing. You have won much more. Come and see.'

The man opened the flap and rain water gushed in like pus from a gaping wound. The Emperor stepped out and instantly recoiled. He had stepped on a dead woman's naked breast. Milk flowed out and mingled with her blood. The women surrounding the dead stopped wailing. The fire in their eyes was burning the rain.

The downpour continued to soak the corpses littered on the field, bloating them beyond recognition. Men and mud had become one dripping mass. Wading through the pile, his chariot began mowing down the bodies. The Emperor got down and tried walking on foot, but his feet sank into men, women and children. The drenched cadavers were decomposing with layers of maggots wriggling on them. Flies and crows continued to devour the dead, the sight of human innards, rotting flesh and blood making the dance of death even more hideous. His feet were now smeared with the skin and slime of thousands of people. Mortal remains of those who had ceased to be living men and women and were now a mere casualty of war.

The sky over the river had turned grey. As the rain soaked him to the skin, he began to shiver, icy winds biting into his naked skin. The smell of the rotting flesh suddenly rose to engulf his senses. He could no longer hold his food and wine. It came out in a rushing trajectory to smear the bloody mud with poorly ingested meals.

As he looked up, the swollen river had turned red.

23

$\mathcal{T}$he morning sun yawned.

But the city of Kapilavastu was already wearing new clothes. Queen Mahamaya had given birth to its heir and the prince had been christened Siddhartha. Expectancy fulfilled. King Suddhodana's palace had turned into a rainbow. Pots of gold were going out to every household and dance and music were keeping the gods awake. The prince was dressed in satin and rubies and placed on a bed of lotuses. Eight wise Brahmins had come to bless the baby. They were soothsayers who knew what would happen tomorrow. The King folded his hands.

'What is my son's future, Learned Ones?'

Seven of them looked at the king. 'He will be a Chakravarti ruler.'

The eighth one looked at the baby. 'He will become the Buddha.'

A hush fell over the city.

Twenty-nine years later, the prince saw four sights. He saw old age when deep furrows marked the loose flesh. He saw sickness which ruined the body and sapped the mind. He saw death when life fled the flesh and energy borrowed from the universe returned to it. He saw a Bhikkhu who had chosen the begging bowl as his trade. That night he rode away into the dark in search of light.

Sia was watching the departing prince. He looked troubled but peaceful. Everyone was sleeping. He alone was awake.

'The Four Sights and the Great Departure.' Patnaik joined her. 'A very rare oil.'

Besides the painting, the only other element in the room were rows of glass shelves stacked with VHS tapes and DVDs. Sia looked at their titles. *Did You Know?*; *Lost Secrets*; *What Really Happened*; *The Other Side*. Multiple programmes. One maker.

'Jasodhara. Some TV woman.'

'That's what she told me.' Sia nodded. 'Producer and documentary film-maker. Retired a few years ago.'

'Why have we come here, Sia?'

'Because she has called us. She says she can try to help us.'

'But you don't even know this woman.'

'I don't know you either, Om. I want to see if this woman can do what she says. She is not forcing us. She gave me a choice to come or not come and I have chosen.'

'You have chosen to share your inheritance with a total stranger? You who said you will never share it with anyone else.'

Sia threw her hands up in the air in exasperation. 'Do you know what to do with the bronze head?'

He shook his head.

'Neither do I. I know what I had said, but my father has handed us something we can't comprehend. This woman saw us holding the metal at Sarnath Temple. I am curious. She may have a few ideas. I have spoken with her on the phone before coming here.'

'She might be dangerous. You are going against Mathur's plan.'

'I know that. I understand everything you are saying but I had to take this risk. Besides, I am not doing this blindly. I have researched about this woman online and she seems to know her stuff. Look at all these tapes and DVDs. She has obviously spent her life exploring every weird item on this planet. She has approached me and I want to give her a chance. But I will be cautious.'

Patnaik picked up a tape. 'Everything here is far too clean.'

'I don't like dust, child.'

The pair swung towards the booming voice. The woman standing at the doorway was smiling. When Sia introduced the writer, she giggled. 'You think this sixty-three-year-old hag is going to rob your enigma, Patnaik?'

The man did not smile. Sia hastily pointed at the oil. 'That's a beautiful painting.'

'The beginning of Buddha.' Jasodhara walked up to it. 'I love these stories. The old man, the sick man, the dead man, the ascetic. They need not be four different men. They could all be one single person. One who is old, sick and dying.'

Sia looked at her. The old woman was staring distantly into the painting.

'It is said that these four visions were conjured up by deities. Even when the prince was leaving, the powers above made the hooves of his horse silent. It's like the gods were conspiring with the man. They sometimes do that, you know. Lay out a road for us and place us at square one. You cannot fight the itinerary. You can only keep rolling the dice.'

Patnaik pointed at the racks. 'I was reading your show titles. They sound intriguing.'

'Something that kept me busy. The programmes were quite a smash, but much before your time. Mystery has always fascinated me. Give me anything bizarre and I am sold. Then six years ago I waved goodbye and settled here in Sarnath.' She pushed back a tape jutting out of the shelf. 'I hope a part of me lives on in them.'

'Did you know my father?'

'No, Sia. I had never met Ram Mathur. I was only an admirer of his books and papers. Your father's works were a mine of history and mythology. They proved to be excellent research material for my shows. News about his brutal murder came as a blow to me. I had seen reports that said you were in Varanasi but I had no idea you were back in Sarnath. Seeing you at Dhamek was frankly quite extraordinary.'

'Yes. That's where I saw you first.'

'I wanted to talk to you. I really did. Then you both marched off to the temple.'

'Were you stalking us?' Patnaik frowned.

The old woman nodded. 'I confess I was. I should have approached you right away but I kept backing off. And then I saw you both jump the temple railing and begin looking into the vases. That's when I was intrigued. Very intrigued. I hid there and watched you discover the bronze head.'

'I see.'

'My actions may seem suspicious to you but I had been restless since Mathur's murder. Then I saw you both find the hidden metal at the temple. That, and the news about the mark on his face, convinced me that something phenomenal was on. Speaking with you at the ghat was not easy, Sia. I was thrilled when you called today and even more fascinated to hear about that email. I wonder what really happened with him that night.'

Sia tapped on a DVD. 'This looks interesting. *Nepal's Royal Massacre.*'

'One of my most controversial episodes. After this a lot of

people showed up at my doorstep shouting that I was putting up crap on air. I never bothered. We all need an outlet.'

Sinking into a chair, Sia took out a photograph of the bronze head. 'This is what he left us.'

Patnaik looked at her questioningly. He saw Jasodhara smile and knew that she too had understood. Sia had not brought the real thing, mere pictures of it. The woman brought the photo close to her face.

'Let's see. You say he emailed you a puzzle after he was killed?'

'Yes. And that brought us to this figure. Can you identify it or give us any clues?'

Jasodhara was pouring over the prints of the metal figure with curiosity. 'Very interesting. Nothing vintage about it though. Quite modern and freshly crafted.'

'Om told me that. But what is this thing?'

'It looks oddly familiar.'

They looked at each other. 'Give us anything you know, Jasodhara.'

'My memory's gone blunt now. I can't seem to place it.'

'What about that mark on the forehead?'

'Looks like a question mark but it's surely something else. Could be some unknown script. I am sorry.'

Sia was fingering her hair but Patnaik could sense her beginning to get angry. The print was perched on Jasodhara's palm like a sleeping baby. A baby that had not yet learnt to speak.

'If only this metal could talk,' she seemed to echo his thought.

The writer turned towards Jasodhara. 'We should leave. Sorry for wasting your time.'

The woman did not reply. She was gazing at the red silk Sia had placed on the table. It was the cloth wrapped around the bronze head at the temple. She picked it up as if it were a live wire that could cook her. Her face seemed static and ecstatic at the same time. Minutes later she spoke again. 'You want the head to talk? We can make it talk.' She looked up. 'Literally.'

They stared at her and then the photograph.

'This bronze head will talk?'

'Yes. It will tell us what it wants.'

'What are you saying, Jasodhara?'

'I recognise this object now.'

'What is it? How can it talk?'

'It can because it's infused with technology.'

'Technology?'

'The technology of automation.'

The duo stood up.

Automation.

'Wait a minute. Are you telling us…?'

The woman nodded. 'Yes. This bronze head is a robot.'

24

A robot? Mathur has left us a robot?

'It is a robotic head. And not just an ordinary robot.'

'What do you mean?'

'This robot hides an enigma inside it. Just the way they used to do thousands of years ago in India.'

Sia gasped. 'Thousands of years ago? Are you saying the ancient world played with robots?'

Patnaik stood up in a frenzy. 'She is right, Sia. Homer and Aristotle have spoken about robots. Ancient Chinese texts like *Liezi* mention automatic human models. Our Sanskrit texts talk about the use of Yantra Purusha or the mechanical man to serve society. The medieval Arabian inventor Al Jazari even created working humanoid automata in the twelfth century.'

Jasodhara laughed. 'Looks like your writer friend likes me after all.' She went inside and returned with a book. 'This is an English translation of the *Samarangana Sutradhara* written by the twelfth century Indian ruler Bhoja. Read this extract, it actually describes robots in use in medieval India.'

Male and female figures are designed for automatic service.
Each part is made and fitted separately with holes and pins.

The material is mainly wood, but a leather cover is given to complete the impression of a human. The movements are managed by a system of poles, pins and strings attached to rods controlling each limb.

'Not very sophisticated, but such primary models were abundantly used by our ancestors. Besides being tools of entertainment, they performed one extremely critical function.'

'What?'

'They concealed enigmas.'

'Enigmas?'

'Secrets. They were used to hide and pass secrets.'

The trio gazed at the photo.

What enigma was this one hiding inside it?

'Have you heard of Pope Sylvester II?'

'No.'

'Sylvester II is one of the most mysterious figures in European history. Born as Gerbert d'Aurillac, he was the first French man to become pope in 999 AD. The man had a deep fascination for the sciences of the Arab world, which have led to rumours that he was a sorcerer and Satan worshipper. It is believed that after studying magic in Morocco, he sailed to India and acquired various supernatural arts and objects. One of them was a bronze robotic head like this one.'

'A talking head.'

'Precisely. A primitive robot that was programmed to answer YES or NO when it was asked a question. The Pope has explained in one of his writings that it was based on a perfectly simple operation corresponding to a two-figure calculation.'

'This probably means it was a binary robot that responded to stimuli and then processed the data,' Sia said.

Jasodhara keyed into her laptop. 'The toy was destroyed when Sylvester died, but a reference is believed to exist in an old cybernetics journal *Computers and Automation*. This passage frequently appears on the Net. Take a look.'

> This speaking head must have been fashioned under a certain conjunction of stars occurring at the exact moment when all the planets were starting on their courses... Naturally it was widely asserted that Gerbert was only able to produce such a machine head because he was in league with the Devil.

'The Devil.' Sia nodded.

'Obviously. The technology was a zillion years ahead of its time. In fact, many even claimed that the robot was actually a female demon called Meridiana who granted the Pope's wishes.'

'I see that. But how is my father related to all this? What's a historian doing with robots?'

'Not just a historian any longer,' Jasodhara smiled. 'There was a lot more to Mathur than he let on. The robot proves that he was aware of some of the deepest mysteries buried in our past. That could even be the reason why he was killed.'

'What mysteries are you talking about?'

'Here. See this.'

Jasodhara was holding out the red silk cloth. Patnaik spread it on his palm. 'What the...'

'What is it, Om?'

'Words.'

'Words?'

'There's a couplet printed on the damn rag.'

They looked. Two lines in English.

A vision of the second of beloved's tall books
The unknown is never an answer if one looks

'How did we miss it?'

'Kids always grab the toy and forget the packaging,' Jasodhara laughed. 'These lines made it clear to me that we are dealing with a robot. You asked me how will this bronze head speak? This is the manual to bring this machine to life.'

'What is this couplet?'

'I told you that our forefathers used robots to conceal and transport enigmas. All such robots were sealed with a password. To unlock a robot, you needed the pin.'

'And this couplet holds the password?'

'Yes. It will give us the key to unlock this robot. If you go through our past esoteric writings, you will come across hundreds of couplets and verses like these believed to hide passwords that can make such robots speak.'

'But this one's in English.'

'I know. During the British Raj many couplets suddenly started appearing in English. This only meant that our ancient secrets had started creating a space in the Western world. Doors were opening to absorb and assimilate outsiders fascinated with our native genius. This couplet appeared in an anonymous text in 1881 and created quite a sensation. The writer claimed that these two lines contained the password to something extraordinary. He called it a password to the greatest enigma in ancient India.'

'Greatest enigma?' Sia stared at the robot. 'What was it?'

'I don't know. The only way to find out was to crack this couplet, but it eluded experts for years. Finally an African historian was able to extract the password. He revealed that the password was actually a question.'

'Question?'

'Yes. The couplet says "never an answer". What is never an answer?'

'A question.'

'It makes perfect sense. Look at Sylvester's robot. It spoke when it was asked a question. Mathur has also placed a robot in your lap. Speak the password and it will give up its secret.'

Patnaik was still staring at the couplet.

Jasodhara smiled. 'It was easy once the African showed us that the couplet was using the name of an ancient Indian Emperor.'

'Emperor? Which one?'

'Ashoka.'

'Ashoka? You mean Ashoka the Great?'

'Yes. Do you want to try it?'

Sia shook her head. 'Just tell us the answer.'

'Ashoka is the beloved in the couplet. One of the man's many names was Devanampriya.'

'Devanampriya,' the writer cried. 'It literally means Beloved of the Gods.'

'Right. The tall books refer to his nineteen Pillar Edicts. Remember all his edicts carried messages of love and piety. The password we are looking for is inscribed on the second pillar edict. I have the complete translated text here. Can you spot it?'

The trio poured over the inscription of the edict which had appeared on her laptop screen.

'Which one is the password?'

'You have to look for a question.'

A question. They had forgotten. They searched again. There it was. Only one question.

'What is Dhamma?'

'Yes. The password is one of the seminal queries of man. This explains the second line. So many have tried to look for this answer. So many have failed. Not everyone becomes the Buddha.'

She held up the photograph. 'We could have tested the password if you had brought the real goods.'

Sia glanced at her and then unzipped her purse. 'Very well.' They watched as she took out the robot and placed it on the table.

'I was just being careful.'

Jasodhara's eyes sparkled like the bronze figurehead. She extended her hand. 'May I?'

Picking up the robot she touched the cold metal to her cheeks. They saw the sixty-three-year-old transform into a child who had found a hidden stash of candies. Suddenly, everything in her room seemed to turn to dust, compared to this one figure and the ancient secrets it promised to reveal. She nodded at Sia.

'That's wise. You have seen your father's corpse and now you have been forced into a dark passage. Don't trust anyone, child.'

She handed it back. 'Speak the password, Sia. Let's pull the enigma out of its head.'

'I want you to do it.'

'But your father…'

'Do it, Jasodhara.'

The woman giggled like an excited girl. The next moment she looked at the robot's face and whispered.

'What is Dhamma?'

Her eyes dilated wide.

She did not want to believe this, but here it was, sitting right before her. Her eyes darted over the words nine times. Each time they were recounting the same fantastic tale of hatred and love. An enigma that had stayed in hiding for two thousand years. Scrolling down with the mouse, she watched the words jumping up and down. Then she got up and walked to the window, breathing deeply.

Alia Irani was a freelancer. She had no bosses to please, no colleagues to bitch about and no deadlines to adhere to. She worked at her own pace and on her own stories. Like the one that had cost a governor his seat; then the one that had shut down one of the largest hospitals in the country; and the one she was on right now. It was turning out to be a lot more eccentric than she had imagined; the pleasure of unearthing something so exciting practically giving her an orgasm.

Looking out of the window, she gazed at the full moon. She always called it the white balloon. It was a childhood friend that filled up with air every fifteen days. Her eyes traced the outline of the rabbit again. This was her favourite Jataka tale; the creature's selfless act had made it an example for all. Alia sighed. Those were good days. Virtue was no longer rewarded in the world today.

She gazed at the wooden board on the wall. Nine newspaper cuttings pasted there were flapping in the mountain breeze. Stories of nine men. Nine dead men. They were no longer random pieces of paper. They were like the pieces of a jigsaw which seemed to fit in with one another, revealing a harrowing picture.

Someone knocked. She closed the window and opened the door.

It was the Lama. The maroon and yellow robe suddenly brought colour into the room. His broad forehead carried all the lines and cracks he had collected over the years even as his tonsured head seemed to shine with the power of penance. However, he looked weary, as if an invisible weight were crushing him.

'So it is true?'

He was silent.

'Is it true?'

The Lama looked through her into the distance. 'What is Truth? It is how we see and perceive reality on this earth. How we use our senses. Any action in this world is only a relative truth. Relative because everything around us is in constant flux. We must apply it to reach the absolute truth. That truth is free. That alone can liberate us.'

Alia pointed to the world outside her window. 'For me what happened there is the truth. I don't know if it's relative or absolute. But it's hideous and must come out. A crime like this one is precisely what I have been battling all my life. I cannot allow this to go unaccounted for.'

'It's only the workings of a confused mind.'

'It's a sick mind. He must be stopped.' She sat down on the floor. 'Are they cremating him tomorrow?'

'Yes. It has been seven days. They are doing it at dawn. It's only a matter of hours now.'

'I will be there.'

'Everyone is welcome. He will like it.'

'He did not deserve this.'

'We do not mourn our dead. His time had come. He served well in this life. He will serve well wherever he goes now.'

'Have they reached any plausible conclusions in their investigation?'

'They are doing their work. We have been asked to follow orders. One goes through everything in life.'

'We need evidence.'

'What evidence?'

'I must see the body.'

'Body? You cannot see the body. He has been placed.'

'I will strip him down to his balls if I need to.'

'Leave him alone. You want to defile him. Desecrate his bed.'

'And you will help me.'

The Lama folded his hands in pain. 'He is ready for his journey. We respect the dead. We don't break into their sleep. It's against everything that we believe in.'

'I must photograph his face.'

The man trembled violently. 'No. No face. Not the face.'

'Only the face.' 'Don't do this.'

'Why not?'

'There's nothing to see. He's gone. Let him rest.'

'He will not rest unless we do it. He wants to tell us what happened. Will you help him?'

'This is wicked. A sin.'

'What happened to him was a sin. You called him your friend.'

'Yes.'

'Will you betray him now?'

The Lama got up and opened the door. Then he stopped,

as he heard the sound of her voice again, reading something on her laptop. Telling him a story. It sounded familiar. Dangerously familiar. For the next few minutes there was no sound in the room except her voice.

He heard her speak again. 'Is this true?'

The Lama was looking older now. His fingers were fumbling with his robes. 'Don't do this.'

'Is this a relative truth or an absolute one?'

'It's a truth that kills. It loves to draw blood. Stop playing with it.'

'The game is on. Will you help me win?'

'At what cost? It may only do more harm than it already has.'

'It will not. I will see to that.'

'You are making a mistake.'

'I have learnt a lot from my mistakes. I don't mind making one more. You fear I'll fail?'

'I fear that you will succeed. There will be no mercy then.'

'I am not seeking mercy. Only answers.' She pointed at the newspaper clippings on the wall. 'They must know.'

The Lama looked at them. Then he spoke. She heard it all again, but there was more. A lot more than what her research had told her. She could see everything clearly now. The method. The madness. The design in the disorder. It was an enigma worth dying for. An enigma worth killing for.

An enigma so powerful that even gods would kill for it.

When he left, she opened the window again. The red and gold of the monastery were sleeping. The night was about to end. Then she would go there and wake him up.

Standing at six thousand feet above sea, Alia Irani folded her hands in a silent prayer.

$\mathcal{T}$he golden head nodded.

Many had asked him this question yesterday. Many would ask him this question tomorrow. They thought it was a complex calculus. He knew it was a simple alphabet.

'What is Dhamma?'

The man before him was snarling. His skin was the colour of night and his eyes were like burning coals. On his neck he wore a terrible ornament – a grotesque necklace of human fingers. Withered bones strung together on a thread made for a crude and cruel trophy. The sickening necklace hung around his neck and looked as if several fingers were reaching out to strangle his throat at once.

'Why do you kill, Angulimala?'

The man showed his dagger in the Teacher's face. 'I have been cast out. Stop walking.'

'I have stopped. When will you stop?'

'Me?'

'You have killed nine hundred and ninety-nine people. When will you stop, Ahimsaka?'

The dagger fell from his hand. 'How do you know that name?'

'Your father named you Ahimsaka. One who is not violent. Come to the Sangha. Follow Dhamma.'

'What is this Dhamma? I have asked you twice. Tell me now or I will kill you. I want new fingers for my loop.'

'Take my fingers. But lend me your ear.'

They were listening. The robot was no Buddha, but it had wisdom to offer. It started glowing. More and more radiant. More and more euphoric. The face transformed into a rapturous orb of fire as if the sun had stumbled into the room. The aura was holding their bodies and raising them up. Jasodhara was clasping the sun in her palms but it did not burn. There was no heat. Only a light that healed. Words sprang from the face.

Four lines.

The trio stood enchanted. Stunned by the fireworks, they forgot to hear the words. The wonder of the robot had transported them to an alternate universe. When the sound stopped, the light also dimmed and died.

'Did you see that? Did you see how it blazed? It did not blind me or burn me. It just touched me like a friend.' Jasodhara's face was shining.

Sia nodded. 'Like a beautiful solar flare. But it should have heated the metal.'

'It must be the magic of the enigma it carries,' Patnaik said reverently. 'These ancient men were playing with technologies far ahead of their time, much ahead than we can imagine.'

What they had witnessed had wrapped itself around their minds completely. The robot was no longer an ancient relic of the past, but a dazzling avatar of ancient scientific advancement that had burnt to cinders all fragments of doubt that any of them were still clinging on to. In that single moment they had died and were reborn.

'Ask the question again. We missed what it said.'

They crowded around to watch the miracle unfold for a second time. The password breathed life into the figure again and they heard a clear voice render a mystical stanza.

Open your eyes and see them for these are words of Vishnu
Leave me by these copper leaves of the twisted trees fifteen
Did two hands create the science or were the fingers thirty
You can be a new ruler if you repeat with your brain keen

Patanik wrote it down just as the robot turned lifeless.

'What is this, Jasodhara?'

'What?'

'I thought you said the robot will reveal its enigma. The greatest enigma of ancient India.'

'Yes.'

'This looks like a riddle.'

'Riddle?' she grabbed the pad. 'You are right. It is a riddle.'

Sia frowned. 'Now what?'

The woman was silent.

Now what?

A minute later she shrugged. 'If we have a riddle, the only thing we can do is solve it.'

'But you said...'

'I know what I said. Looks like it's not going to be that easy.'

Sia stared in alarm but Patnaik tossed the robot up in delight. 'Awesome. The fun is not over yet.' He smiled at her. 'Relax, Sia. We are doing good. This may tell us all we want to know.'

Jasodhara read the first line.

Open your eyes and see them for these are words of Vishnu.

She looked at Patnaik. 'Words of Vishnu? Vishnu said a great many things.'

'It says you "see" the words. See the words. You hear words when someone speaks them. But you "see" words when someone…'

'Writes them.' Jasodhara filled in the blank.

'This may be referring to something that has words written on it.'

'Yes. Written words. Maybe an inscription or a text. Or a book that contains the words of Vishnu.'

'Is it talking about the *Vishnu Purana*?' Sia spoke.

Patnaik slapped her on the back. 'Wonderful, Sia. The *Vishnu Purana* is regarded as the most important of the eighteen Mahapuranas of Hinduism. It's even called Puranaratna and is full of stories about cosmic wars and creation myths.'

Jasodhara shook her head. '*Vishnu Purana* is a dialogue between Rishi Parashar and his protégé Maitreya. It contains tales and legends about Vishnu. Not exactly his words.'

'Do you have anything better?' Sia asked.

'What about the *Bhagvad Gita*? The book contains the words of the Lord. He spoke about Atma, Dharma and Yoga.'

'She is right, Om. The Lord tells us to do our Karma. Nothing else matters. Not even your own loved ones.'

'But when the Lord delivered the Gita to Arjuna, he was not Vishnu. He was Krishna. This line clearly says Vishnu.' The writer glanced at the notepad. 'Let's skip this line for the moment. What about this one?'

Leave me by these copper leaves of the twisted trees fifteen.

Both the women shook their heads.

Did two hands create the science or were the fingers thirty.

Jasodhara stirred. 'Now this line is loaded. It's talking about science. If this is indeed a book, then it again points to the Gita. Among other things the book has also been celebrated as a highly advanced scientific text. While modern science includes only physical reality in its domain, the Gita strives to push its boundaries and calls for an enquiry of metaphysical reality. Arjuna's conflict is also a metaphor for the eternal psychological crisis inside man.'

'And what about these hands and fingers?' Sia asked.

'This I am not sure.'

'I think this line is talking about the creator,' Patnaik said. 'The hands that did "create the science".'

'And the fingers?'

Jasodhara counted. 'Thirty fingers would mean six hands. A god with six hands?'

Sia grinned. 'You are making it too hard. I think six hands here indicate three men. That's more practical.'

'She's right,' Patnaik nodded. 'The line is asking whether the creator was one man or three men. There seems to be some confusion regarding his identity.' He looked at the line again.

Did two hands create the science or were the fingers thirty?

Jasodhara grunted. 'Gita again. It had two architects. Vyasa and Ganesha.'

'Too many holes there. The first line should have said Krishna. I have never heard anything about fifteen trees in the book. We are looking for three men here. Finally the last line promises to make someone a "ruler" if you "repeat". The Gita is a spiritual text. It tackles doubts and delusions. It does not make men kings.'

Jasodhara stared at the last line again.

You can be a new ruler if you repeat with your brain keen.

'Repeat with your brain. Repeat. Repeat. Of course!'

She was staring at the line. Patnaik took the notepad from her hands. 'What do you see, Jasodhara?'

'That's the clue.'

'What clue?'

'This word confirms what we are looking for.' She pointed at the words. 'Don't you see? The riddle is definitely talking about a book. There's no doubt now.'

'I don't understand.'

She stood up in a frenzy. 'How was knowledge in ancient India passed on, Patnaik?'

'Word of mouth. Through Smriti.'

'Exactly. Smriti. Memory. Books were memorised by one generation and repeated to the next.' She tapped her forehead. 'The "brain keen".'

Patnaik looked at the last line in awe.

You can be a new ruler if you repeat with your brain keen.

Jasodhara was reading the riddle again. Her face glowed with joy.

'The second line. The second line. It's so obvious now. This is brilliant stuff.' She pointed. 'These "copper leaves". Again a book.'

'How?'

'Leaves. Manuscripts. Our ancient texts were written on leaves.'

Patnaik was animated. 'You are right. But which book? A book that makes a "new ruler"?'

'Yes. A "new ruler". But Vishnu? Words of Vishnu that make you a new ruler. Vishnu.' She sat down. 'New ruler by Vishnu. Vishnu. Yes. Vishnu. Not god. Ruler. And trees?'

She grabbed her laptop and drummed at the keys furiously. Her glasses seemed to glow with the colours on the screen. Moments later she stood up and smiled.

'I have the book. You were right. It's not the Gita.'

The writer was holding the robot. He carefully placed it on the table as if it were made of glass.

'Are you sure, Jasodhara?'

She nodded.

'A book by Vishnu?'

'Yes. But not Lord Vishnu.'

'A book with fifteen trees? A book that can make someone a new ruler?'

'Yes. All of that.'

The old woman turned the laptop towards them. One word leapt out of it.

ARTHASHASTRA.

'*Arthashastra*?' Patnaik whispered. He looked at her. '*Arthashastra*. Yes. *Arthashastra*.'

Sia charged at them. 'Why are you both so certain? As far as I know, *Arthashastra* was written by Chanakya.'

'You are right. But Chanakya had many names. One of them was Kautilya.'

She was waiting.

'And another was Vishnugupta.'

She gasped. 'The "words of Vishnu". But what about the rest? The second line?'

'*Arthashastra* was written on palm leaves like most ancient Indian texts. Brown palm leaves look like shiny copper. And it is divided into fifteen books or fifteen adhikarnas.'

Patnaik laughed. 'The "twisted trees fifteen"! What an adjective. Twisted because they teach you to use unscrupulous tactics against your enemy. In fact, the name Kautilya itself comes from the word Kotil which means cunning.'

'What about the third line?'

'Ah! The dispute over authorship.' Jasodhara rubbed her hands. 'The book mentions its author as Kautilya and Vishnugupta. Both the names are traditionally identified with the patronym Chanakya but scholars still debate about the author's identity. While some say Chanakya, Kautilya and Vishnugupta are three different men, others argue that they are three names of the same person. That's the confusion. We are still not sure whether "two hands" created this science or the "fingers thirty".'

'And it can make the reader a ruler. I guess that explains itself now,' Sia grinned.

'It certainly does. The book is one of the greatest treatises on state craft. It says it can condition a man into the perfect king with a perfect mind. But "new ruler" also hides another clue. Can you guess?'

'What?'

'It refers to Chandragupta Maurya who was discovered by Chanakya. He was his dream monarch. Chanakya was the original king maker and Chandragupta was the new psyche of the nation.'

'Great.' Sia clapped. 'But I am still waiting for that fabulous prize you promised. Why is the robot pointing towards the *Arthashastra*?'

'It's obvious. It wants us to make a journey.'

'What journey?'

'A journey to where the *Arthashastra* is kept.'

Patnaik stepped forward. 'What are you saying, Jasodhara?'

'I am merely obeying the second line of the riddle.'

Sia and Patnaik looked at the words.

Leave me by these copper leaves of the twisted trees fifteen.

'That's the robot speaking to us. It's job is done and we now need to return it. Do that and you will get your prize.'

'But I was thinking of keeping it,' Patnaik objected, like a petulant child.

'The bronze head is not a souvenir, Patnaik. It has to go back from where it came. That's where we will find the enigma.'

'Are you sure?'

'I am not sure about anything anymore. Let's just flow with the tide.' Jasodhara sat down and gazed at the robot. A moment later she spoke. 'Can I tell you something, Sia?'

'What?'

'I was craving for one more excitement. One last thrill before I kick the bucket. Thank you for knocking on my door.'

She smiled. 'Thank yourself. Our dreams have a way of coming true on their own. I am running after mine now. It may bring me the release I seek.'

The old woman got up and held her hand. 'You have helped me. Will you let me help you?'

'I don't understand.'

The next moment, Jasodhara sat her down before a camera and switched it on. 'Speak, Sia. Discharge your emotions.'

Patnaik stood up horrified. 'What are you doing?'

'I see what's inside her, Patnaik. She needs to break the bottle.'

'This is not one of your damn shows. Get up, Sia.'

Sia did not move. She was staring at the lens as if the piece of glass had hyptnotised her.

'Trust me, Patnaik. I know what I am doing. She must flush it out.' Jasodhara turned towards her. 'Scream, Sia. Throw your pain at me.'

'My father.'

'Go on.'

'Father.'

'Yes. Give me what you saw.'

'He was lying on the ground. No eye. A cavity there. The other eye was glaring at me. His face was ripped and blood trickled down his hands. The Om was bleeding. Trishul sticking out of his hand. He was smiling. Patnaik was copying. Suri was wiping. Forensic men inside and press reporters outside. I see him in my sleep these days. Letters tattooed on his forehead. And the eye dripping…'

'Enough,' Patnaik blocked the lens. 'Stop it, please.'

Sia stood up. She was quiet. Then she looked at him. 'I feel empty, Om. Empty inside.'

'I know. You have rinsed your system.' The woman cupped her cheeks.

Patnaik picked up the robot. 'Can we move on? Do we need to reach the place where the *Arthashastra* is now?'

'Yes.'

'And where do we find the text?'

Jasodhara smiled. 'It is kept where it was accidentally discovered by a scholar in 1909. The Oriental Research Institute (ORI) in Mysore.'

The building was red and green and blue.

Standing in the vast, windy courtyard of the monastery, Alia felt like a small, insignificant speck of dust. Six golden banners swayed in the wind, glowing like the yellow button on her jacket.

Rumtek Monastery looked ethereal in the morning light. The hills behind were a perfect tapestry for the vibrant colours of the shrine. She watched the sun bring out the colour of the roof, as though bathing it in a fresh shower of gold. A pillar in the centre of the courtyard rose like a tree from the heart of a pyramid. Inscribed in Tibetan, it told the story of the birth of the largest Buddhist sanctuary in Sikkim.

While her eyes read the tale on the pillar, her heart was elsewhere, listening to another story from long ago.

She could clearly hear her mother's voice now. She had walked into a monastery and placed her nine-day-old daughter before the Buddha. He was the first god Alia had seen. Later, there had been many more, but Buddha had become her first love. Strolling towards the entrance, she saw monks preparing for the funeral. The Lama was there. As she walked nearer, she saw his face.

He has decided.

'Are you ready?' he asked her.

'Yes.'

'Afraid?'

'I am never afraid.'

'What have you brought?'

'My camera.'

He handed her a bunch of chrysanthemums. 'You will need these.'

Entering the monastery, Alia saw images of the Four Guardians of the universe. They had given their word to Buddha that they would guard all his shrines on earth. The colossal prayer hall was a splash of colours with Kagyu paintings, murals and frescoes. The monks sat in rows offering flour and butter Tormas to the Teacher.

'This way.'

The ten-feet statue of the Buddha dominated the hall, towering over the thousand small Buddhas of clay and gold. While he was the central attraction of the shrine, people also came to see Lhabab Chodten. The Golden Stupa contained some of the most sacred relics of the Gyalwa Karmapa, considered third to the Dalai Lama in the spiritual hierarchy of Tibetan Buddhism.

'In here.'

He opened a door.

'Stop.'

A police guard had materialised as if from nowhere, and was standing next to the entrance. The man eyed them from head to toe. He shut the door.

'Not allowed inside.'

The Lama stepped forward. 'It's alright. She is with me.'

'Who is she?'

'A friend. I know her.'

'You have permission?'

The Lama pointed at Alia's hand. 'She has come to pay her respects. Do we need permission to honour our dead?'

The guard looked at the white flowers.

'Go.'

They thanked him but the man barred their way again.

'Open your purse.'

Alia stepped back. The guard spoke again. 'Your purse.'

'There's nothing here.'

'Show me.'

He grabbed it. A moment later he fished out the camera. 'Not allowed.'

The Lama's face drained of all colour. Alia tugged at the camera strap. 'I know. I have not come here to click pictures. This is a funeral. Give it back.'

'No. I keep it.' He gave her purse back. 'You come back and take it.'

'But you cannot...'

'Go.'

Walking into the chamber, the Lama tried to pull the door shut.

'Don't shut,' the guard barked. 'Not allowed.'

'We want to pray in our temple. Give us a moment of peace.'

He slammed the door in the face of the police guard. Alia saw a black hole covering them. Two candles were burning like the sun and the moon. Between them the white coffin spread like the milky way. A picture of the monk stood next to it, wreathed in garlands and flowers.

'I am sorry.' She heard the Lama.

'What for?'

His face was darker than the room. 'Your camera. What will you do?'

Alia laughed. 'A good journalist always anticipates. And I am good.'

'What do you mean?'

'That camera's a dummy.'

'Dummy?'

'A little lolipop for the guard.' She took out a large mobile. 'This is the real deal.'

The Lama stared. The next moment he sprinted to the head of the coffin. She could almost hear his heart beat, so palpable was his fear. 'We must hurry. There's no time.' He handed a candle to Alia and lifted the coffin lid.

Instantly a bitter-sweet smell filled the room. Alia was looking at a layer of golden silk. The cloth glistened under the light of the candle like a bed of fire. The Lama lifted the layer revealing the monk's body. He was dressed in simple white robes. His face was covered with cloth.

Alia looked at the Lama. His fingers approached the face and then hesitated.

'Do it.'

He finally loosened the cloth covering the face and pulled it away. The face of the monk.

Alia bent over and brought the candle closer to the face. The Lama turned his eyes away. She kept looking.

I was right.

The face was talking. Telling her everything she wanted to hear. His words were echoing in that silence.

'I can hear them,' the Lama burst.

Her hand trembled and a blob of wax dripped over the monk's face. Noises from outside were beginning to break the silence of the darkness within.

'Fast. Do it now.'

Alia's mobile flashed in the dark. A blinding light. Then again. And again. And again.

'They know we are here.'

The sounds were growing like thunder. Her flashes rained like lightning.

'They are coming.'

His voice was shaking. Her fingers were trembling.

'They are here.'

The mobile slipped and fell to the floor with a bang. As she picked it up, the door swung open. Daylight crashed inside and blinded their eyes.

They saw shadows. A group of monks. A man stood in front of them. He was looking at the open coffin. The Lama fell on his knees.

The Head Monk.

Nobody spoke. The man entered the room and walked up to the coffin. He quickly, but reverently, rearranged the cloth over the dead monk's face, covered it with the gold silk and closed the lid shut. After placing the candle back in the stand where it belonged, he turned to Alia and extended his hand towards her.

Without a word, she placed her cellphone in his hand. His fingers jumped dexterously, deleting all the images she had clicked. One by one.

All of them.

Her picture gallery was empty.

'Leave.'

Alia walked out of the shrine with her mobile and camera. Reaching the monastery's walkway, she performed the Kora or the circular walk. The wind had started howling now. Prayer flags in various hues fluttered violently in the wind, and her hair whipped her face, stinging her skin. She walked along an endless row of giant prayer wheels stretching as far ahead of her as she could see. She touched them one by one as they turned in the wind. Behind her were all the wheels she had set in motion. Before her was what remained to be done.

Back in the courtyard she saw the community gathering just as the bells started ringing. The monks stood with folded hands, each holding a single stick of incense. The Gnan Sop had started. The monk's final release.

Alia walked out. She knew that the body would be consigned to fire. She knew that more ceremonies would follow to give the dead man merit and virtue to carry into his next birth.

She knew something else. She knew this was not a natural death. The police were covering up the crime and lying to the media. She had seen what the Lama had seen. A truth which the coffin could keep hidden no longer. The absolute truth.

The monk had no right eye. Just a rotting hole.

Alia touched the yellow button on her jacket. Taking it out gently, she placed it inside a small case.

28

*T*he man was walking faster now.

The palace was much bigger than the city that served it. Nine halls had swallowed him one by one and turned his legs into lead. He finally found it. The sanctum sanctorum. His fingers tugged at the silk curtains and pulled them back.

Nanda lay on a bed of pearls. The gems clung to the king's body like pox. His fingers were busy pulling out the succulent flesh and fat off a stuffed peacock. With every tug, the roasted bird's body shivered and dropped more feathers on the floor. Blue, green and gold plumes of the lord.

He saw the Brahmin standing before him. The man's face was covered with sweat and grime and his dirty feet had stained the silver carpet he stood on. The naked girls fled in terror and Nanda sat up in rage.

'Who is this ugly animal?'

The man folded his hands. 'I am a scholar from Takshashila. Protect us, lord. The armies are advancing. They have defiled the waters of the Indus and decimated the cities in the north. They are approaching Magadha. Prepare an assault. Lead your men.'

'Go away, fool. No one can dare touch me. What do I care about Magadha?'

'You will live if Magadha lives. If Magadha falls, you will be buried under it. You must wake up.'

Nanda hurled a bone at the Brahmin's face. 'Guards! Catch this dog by the hair and throw him out.' History watched as they dragged the man and flung him into the streets of Pataliputra. He stood up and tied his hair into a knot.

'I, Chanakya, vow to uproot the Nanda Dynasty. I will demolish this rotting empire and put a wise ruler on the throne of Magadha. Then and then alone will I untie my hair.'

Sia shuddered. 'What a terrible man.'

'Not terrible, Sia,' Patnaik smiled. 'Sensible.'

Jasodhara nodded. 'Chanakya had seen how the country was crumbling under the Nandas. Installing Chandragupta on the throne was the most practical thing he did. With one move, he ensured security from external threat for the next hundred years.'

The trio was speeding through the busy streets of Mysore. Up ahead was the the university campus where the Oriental Research Institute was located.

'Do you know where the *Arthashastra* is kept within the Institute, Jasodhara?'

'Yes. I was there when they celebrated the centenary of its discovery. The manuscript is not on display. It lies locked in a steel almirah in the Central Library.'

'How did it end up here?'

'That's a fascinating story. The book had disappeared around the twelfth century. Many even began dismissing it as a fable. Centuries later in 1909, the librarian of this institute was examining ancient manuscripts donated by a priest when one page looked familiar. Upon close inspection he realised he was looking at the lost *Arthashastra*. The man was Rudrapatnam Shamashastry.'

'What a discovery.'

'That was a watershed event in Indological studies. It led to a lot of changes in the way Indian history is viewed today. The text completely disproved the theory that ancient Indians had learnt statecraft from the Greeks. It is now the crown jewel of the ORI.'

'What are we going to tell them?'

'I have no idea. It's impossible to access the manuscript on your own and there's no way we can tell them about our quest. But we must get to the book and return the robot.'

'And then? Shall we find the enigma?'

'Let's get to the text, Sia. Our treasure will find us.'

A large sign on the front of a building announced that they had reached. Getting out of the vehicle they gazed at the structure. Despite being more than a century old, the red and white colours of the institute still looked fresh and beautiful. The building was a mélange of Gothic, Romanesque and Indian architecture. They could see Hindu statues posing under Corinthian columns and a silver lion holding a lamp.

As they walked in, the vast central hall spread out before them. Well lit, it revealed rows upon rows of metal racks. The library was known to house as many as thirty-five thousand palm and paper manuscripts. Lines of towering bookcases standing in parallel ranks contained the bulk of these bundles. The rest, the rarest of rare, were kept safe under lock and key. Among them was the original copy of the *Arthashastra*.

'What's that smell?' Sia wrinkled her nose.

'Citronyl oil.' Jasodhara said. 'They brush it on the manuscripts for preservation.'

There were several people in the hall, all crowded around a

tall, young man. His face, familiar to them, had adorned the covers of many magazine, besides frequenting various television shows. Patnaik drew their attention to him. 'The royal prince. Must be inspecting their ancestral manuscripts.'

'I know.' Sia sighed. 'He's such a dish.'

Patnaik walked up to the librarian nearby. 'Hello, sir. I am Om Patnaik. I am a writer and have come here in search of a particular text.'

'All our manuscripts have been indexed for easy reference. Once you have identified the text, you will need permission from the Director of the Institute. In case he agrees, you can see the manuscript.'

'I see. What if I wanted to see a manuscript locked in one of the almirahs?'

The librarian raised an eyebrow. 'They are the most exceptional ones. You are talking about national treasures. Access is restricted. Do you have any particular text in mind?'

Patnaik passed his tongue over his lips. 'The *Arthashastra*.'

The man's face changed. His eyes seemed to say, *Why can't you people leave the* Arthashastra *alone?*

'Please wait here.'

They knew he was heading straight for the Director's room. The trio waited in anxious silence. Their request had suddenly made them quite conspicuous. There were several people around who were beginning to look at them with curiosity. Word had spread that three people had come looking for the *Arthashastra*.

The librarian returned. 'What is this regarding?'

'I told you I am a writer. I am writing a book on Chanakya.'

The man shook his head. 'You cannot have it. It's a privilege which only a few get. Not everyone who walks in here can see it. You will need to file a written application requesting for permission.'

'It sounds like a long process. I was wondering if I could just get a glance…'

'Didn't you hear me?' His voice suddenly rose. 'You cannot. It's impossible. There is no way you can get anywhere near the book. Leave.'

The librarian moved towards the prince. Sia's face turned livid. 'Why was he being so rude?'

'Must be fed up of people pestering him about the text.'

Jasodhara looked up and saw Shamashastry's portrait smiling at them. He always smiled at visitors who walked into these walls clamouring for the *Arthashastra*. They were all curious to see the wonder he had rescued. It was not the text but the story that brought them here in hordes. Sia yanked Patnaik's hand.

'We will get to that book. I don't care how but we are definitely seeing it. I am not going back like this.' She looked around. 'What's the time?'

It was 1.35 p.m. Sia pointed at a sign.

LUNCH BREAK: 1.30 p.m. – 2.30 p.m.

And right before their eyes, the hall began to empty out. People were leaving for lunch.

'This is our chance,' she whispered.

'What do you mean?'

'There's no one around. We know where the book is. Just go and do it, Om.'

'Do what? This is not the way. We'll think of something.'

'This is the only way. I'll keep guard here. Slip the bronze head in.'

'But the almirah must be locked. Are you carrying a magic key?'

'Yes.' Sia thrust something into his hand.

He stared at the object in surprise. It was a hairpin. She made a face. 'Don't get too pious with me, Om. I am quite sure you know how to use it.'

'No, Sia. Don't do this,' Jashodhara pleaded.

'You are a bloody thief!' Patnaik whispered. 'This is wrong. I want to get there but not like this. Never like this.'

'Your ethics again. We have no time for your conscience. We must get what we want, Om. That's the only thing that matters now. Will you just give up now, when we're almost there?'

'I know, Sia…'

'Will you?'

He looked into her eyes.

'Give me the pin.'

Jasodhara touched him nervously. 'Careful, child.'

The next moment he had disappeared into the archives section. The tall iron racks shielded him on both sides. His heart beat like a terrified rabbit's, but his legs somehow seemed to carry him on. He looked at his watch.

1.44 p.m.

Something within him was telling him to stop.

There is no going back now.

He pulled out an éclair from his pocket and popped it into his mouth. Sucking on it, he pierced the heart of the hall, going deeper and deeper into its depths. As he walked he looked around in awe. Shelves upon shelves of wisdom, stacked up right here. Knowledge was all around him, like a pool of water. He stopped and looked. He wanted a sip. There was so much that man knew and so much he did not. If only he had the time.

Time?

1.53 p.m.

Three steps more and he was standing in front of the almirah. Pushing the pin into the metal keyhole, he twisted it gently.

The hall was still quiet. As he continued twisting, the metals rattled setting his heart pacing even faster. His fingers were now slick with sweat. He was losing his grip on the pin. Just when he was beginning to give up hope, he felt a click. The lock had given way. Patnaik stiffened. He waited for a few heart beats to make sure he was still alone.

Then he pulled the steel almirah open, to find bundles of manuscripts nestled inside long wooden boxes. Each of them had labels with names and figures on them. He sighed in relief; without the labels it would have taken him forever to find his copy. Reading the labels one by one, he paused as he came to the sixth box on the second shelf. The label left no room for doubt.

ARTHASHASTRA – KAUTILYA

As he picked it up and looked at it, Patnaik seemed to forget all his fears. Here he was, holding a piece of ancient India. A fragment of history which lay in his hands like a newborn. Did Chanakya know that the writer would come here one day? Was he standing there to fulfill a prophecy? The box opened to reveal a sheaf of copper-coloured leaves. Touching them he at last understood the rapture of Shamashastry. He had never thought about the *Arthashastra* before, but today it had become a part of his life. He stood for a while feeling secure in the shade of these leaves. Then he gently placed the manuscript back in its resting place and placed the robot next to it.

Now for the greatest enigma of ancient India.

But what was it? Where was it? There had been nothing else in the box. Patnaik's fingers rummaged timidly through the other bundles. Was it hiding somewhere behind these relics? He was hoping the enigma would see him. Call out his name. He only heard the sound of his heart thumping.

What am I looking for?

Before he could answer his question, his reverie was broken by the sound of voices. People were returning.

2:25 pm.

He was late! The writer swung the metal doors in and pushed the pin in again. The hall was echoing with the sound of several voices now. In another quick minute he had fastened the lock and swiftly retreated from the archives. Emerging out of the racks, he rushed towards Sia. Jasodhara was nowhere to be seen.

'I have returned the robot.'

'And the enigma?'

'There was nothing near the *Arthashastra*. Only other boxes.'

'The enigma must be in one of those. Did you check them?'

'Are you insane, Sia? There are hundreds of them crammed inside. There's no way I could have checked all of them.' He looked around. 'Where's Jasodhara?'

'Went to check some books. What do we do now?'

The man opened his mouth to speak but a voice silenced him.

'Excuse me.'

They turned. It was the prince.

They stood gaping. What did he want? Had he seen Patnaik sneaking out of the archives? Had he seen him handling the *Arthashastra*? Had they acted in haste? Was he going to call the Director?

The young man was smiling. 'I found this on the floor. I think you dropped it.'

Patnaik was about to shake his head when he saw the object in his hand.

What?

His blood curdled in his veins.

It was the robot.

He stared at it in wonder, unable to tear his eyes away.

But I just locked it inside the almirah. Where did he find it?

Sia was also staring at the bronze head. Then she looked at Patnaik.

She thinks I dropped it.

The prince was watching them. He stretched his hand. 'Take it.'

Patnaik took the robot from the man. He had failed. This was a failure's trophy. He glanced at it in misery.

What's this?

It couldn't be. He was seeing things. He looked at the head closely again. No. There was no mistake.

This was a different robot.

The truth hit him hard.

Not our robot. Not our robot.

He gawked at the young man. The prince was looking at him with curious eyes. Then he turned and disappeared into the Director's room.

Patnaik turned towards Sia. She was still growling. The man thrust the figure into her face.

'See this. It's not....'

He froze. Jasodhara was walking towards them looking like her own ghost. She was holding an open book. He could make out numbers printed on the page. The woman placed the book in Sia's hands.

'Look.'

Sia and Patnaik recoiled.

'My God! The mark.'

'This is the same question mark! Similar to the one on our robot's forehead.'

'Yes. I found what it stands for. See.'

Their eyes followed her finger across the page.

'Nine?'

'Yes. Nine.' Jasodhara's voice was shaking. 'It says this mark is the original number nine. You are looking at the very first nine ever written by man. The number nine as we know today has evolved from this glyph. This is the original.'

Patnaik was gaping at the number.

Nine again.

Nine always.

Sia frowned at the duo. 'Why is the robot carrying this figure?'

'Not anymore,' Panaik shook his head.

He held up the metal head. The mark was gone. In its place was a new symbol that resembled the earlier symbol. However, the lower stem of this one was tilted towards the left.

She snatched the head. 'What's this?'

'It's a new robot.'

'What do you mean a new robot?'

'It's a different robot. A different robot with a different mark.' Jasodhara mumbled. She scanned the page again. They knew what she was searching for. It was there. Staring back at them.

'The new mark.'

'This is the next nine. This is how the number looked in its second stage of development. We are looking at the evolution of the number nine.'

The number was growing right before their eyes. They watched it rising from infancy to adulthood and finally sinking into old age. The digits followed each other in a single file. Their shapes were different. But the soul was the same. They all represented the number nine.

Suddenly Patnaik let out a squeal. 'But this robot. That man gave it to us. That man. The prince.'

'Prince?' Jasodhara gaped.

They nodded. The woman's eyes had widened into two round saucers. She was not looking at them. She was not looking at anything anymore. Her lips moved.

'You had better remember this series. All these nines. You are going to meet them one by one.'

'What the hell is going on, Jasodhara? These robots. That prince. These nines. What is the enigma?' Sia was fuming.

But Jasodhara seemed far away, as though she could no longer see or hear them. Patnaik and Sia seemed to have disappeared. The Institute had withered away. All the manuscripts had evaporated. The only living, throbbing object was this number. Her world seemed to have contracted into a sequence printed on paper.

A sequence of nines.

The woman took the new robot in her hands. 'I told you the enigma will find us. It has. I know now. Yes. I know. But I can't tell you.' Her fingers trembled.

'I can't tell you anything.'

*T*hey were squinting at the horizon. The war down south had become a bedtime story. They knew about the land that had refused to bow before their army. The shore that commanded the sea. The serpents who stole their riches and men who hid their enemies. Then the Emperor had brandished his sword and darkened their sky. They were no more. Their wombs had dried. They had burned their seeds and turned their river into blood.

Their heroes were coming back now. The Emperor was coming back. They were standing for the drum roll.

But all they heard was silence.

The army entered the doors of the city. One rank followed another. Swords and arrows. Horses and elephants. Drums and trumpets.

Silence.

Then they saw a man walking with a tray. It held the royal crown. Behind him came another man carrying the Emperor's helmet and armour. And then a third bearing his blade and shield. The fourth man was holding a plate piled with his jewels. The last one carried his royal garments, folded in a neat pile.

'Look. The Emperor's not carrying his sword.' A child pointed at the rising sun.

He did not look into their faces. He was looking at the ground below him. He was wearing a bright orange robe and his tonsured head was shining.

Had they lost the war?

The man stopped before the small temple. Inside the sanctum was the image of an infant Hanuman gobbling up the sun. The young god was trying to ingest all the light in the world. The Emperor folded his hands. The silence was broken by the sounds of his chanting.

'Are you afraid, Jasodhara?'

'I am not. Perhaps I am. I don't know.'

They kept quiet. They wanted her to speak.

'I know you want an answer. I am holding it right now. It came and stood before me in the library. All those nines were screaming an epiphany. They have helped unravel the enigma for me, and I am still trying to deal with it. But you, Sia. You are a scientist. Will you be able to do that?'

'Why not, Jasodhara?'

'Because it's staggering. It will force you to distill every drop of faith you have in your body. You must pry open your flesh and soak it in. It will sound intense. Impossible. But see that robot on the table. You have touched it. You can touch it again. It all fits in perfectly and it's all science. The enigma. Mathur. The nines. The robots.'

'Tell us then. Tell us what these damn things stand for!' Sia held up the new robot.

'And what is this nine?' asked Patnaik.

'That's just the catch. I can't.'

The writer grasped Jasodhara's hand. 'You can. You just need to calm down and speak to us so that…'

'You don't understand, Patnaik,' she sprung from her chair. 'I can't talk about it because it's against the rules.'

'Rules?'

'The rules of this test.'

Her voice quivered with emotion. Sia and Patnaik looked at each other.

Test?

'What test?'

'A journey where you must discover the end on your own. I should not have asked you to share it with me and you should not have agreed. It was the intrigue. It was too much for all of us. I have already made you start on the wrong foot. We have brought each other to the edge of a fantastic revelation but in the process we have broken the rules. I wanted a final crescendo but I almost jeopardised your mission.'

They continued to stare blankly at her.

'The silver lining is there has been no serious damage. We are still good. We only need to be extremely careful.'

Sia giggled. 'All this sounds very melodramatic, Jasodhara. I really wish my father's life had been as sensational as his death is turning out to be. The only excitement he ever had was getting his papers published and meeting old friends. The man was just another history professor.'

'Wrong, Sia. Ram Mathur was much more than that. He was a component of the greatest enigma of ancient India. An enigma so powerful that even the gods would kill for it.'

Patnaik banged his fists on the table. 'I knew it. The moment I saw that nine, I knew it had to be something eccentric. A supernormal worm hole leading to some occult. So what is this enigma?'

'A constellation. An ancient constellation long presumed to be either a fantasy or a reality that no longer exists. But these nines are a blinding flash. They tell me that the constellation is not only alive but functioning even today.'

'Sounds like an exotic cabal.'

'I cannot reveal anything more. You will make your own discoveries as you walk on this path. Understand that you both are on a quest. Since I have become a part of it, I can help you along the way. But when it comes to information about this trial, I will have to be careful. I can give you the facts that you need to deal with the test but leaking any other knowledge will render this journey invalid.'

Patnaik turned towards Sia. 'I just remembered what you had told me in Varanasi. You said your father had spoken of giving you his mind.'

'Makes it all the more official,' Jasodhara nodded. 'That and the robot he left leave no doubt that he was a vital organ of the constellation. You told me how baffled you were when you got his mail after he was dead. But it may have been much simpler. I see how the system might have worked.'

'What system?' Sia asked. 'You must speak.'

'You will access that on your own. That's not too difficult. The hard part is the test your father wants you to take. Are you ready for the challenge?'

'What is the challenge?'

Jasodhara bent over their faces. 'You have to reach the cradle of this constellation. The place of its origin.'

'You mean the place where it was born?'

'Exactly. The place of its creation is their most revered spot. The test prescribed by the constellation, since it began, is a pilgrimage to its very source.'

'But why?' Sia choked. 'What does my father want?'

'I believe he wants to reveal the secret wealth of the constellation to you.'

The woman saw the consternation on their faces. But she knew that deep within, their hearts had leapt.

'Secret wealth?'

'Yes. Its prized possession. The most guarded mystery of the cluster.'

'So he is trying to tempt me?'

'No, Sia. I think a father simply wants to share his life's secret with his daughter. You may take the test or decline. It's your choice.'

She was quiet. She knew her father had already chosen.

'Do you know what this wealth is, Jasodhara?'

'Yes. Many voices in esoteric writings have silently whispered about it. But again I cannot disclose anything. Only its name.'

'It has a name?'

'Yes. It's called the Nine.'

'Nine?' Patnaik glanced at the robot. 'Nine.'

'Precisely, Patnaik. That's the link. Remember I had told you that the robot will lead us to the greatest enigma of ancient India. I know I am right now. If you reach the constellation, you will find nothing less than that.'

Sia felt a chill seeping into her bones. Only a few days ago she was looking at her father's corpse from the stands. But Mathur had picked her up and placed her inside the circle. He wanted her to go through the door now.

'How do we proceed?'

Jasodhara smiled, 'The sciences will guide you.'

'What sciences?'

'There is one fact you must know about the constellation to perform this task. It pays homage to nine deities. Not gods or goddesses. It kneels before nine sciences. Nine powerful sciences that were practiced in ancient India and continue to fascinate men even today.'

'Nine again?'

'Of course. You will find the number at every milestone along the way. The constellation celebrates the spirit of curiosity within man. His primal urge to know. To seek answers, to stand before the Tree of Knowledge. It's only natural that their temple honours scientific research and enquiry.'

'Are these sciences also a big secret?'

'No. I'll tell you what they are because you need to know that to locate the cradle. Write them down.' Jasodhara handed Sia a notepad. Patnaik leaned back.

This is exciting.

'The first science of the nine is Psychological Warfare. It deals with the technique of using mind games to achieve desired results.'

'You mean indoctrination?'

'Yes. Indoctrination through various means such as the media and propoganda. It relies on transmitting messages to influence people. Many have called it the most dangerous science, one that instructs how to programme and control a person's behaviour. His thoughts and opinions. Pain and pleasure. Dreams and nightmares.'

'Interesting,' the writer remarked. 'Today most of the violence in the world is a product of psychic brain washing. Propaganda has become a modern-day demon and its claws are only getting sharper by the day.'

'True. The second science is Physiology. It studies the physical and biochemical functions of various forms of life. Do you know the most fatal knowledge hidden inside this science?'

'What?'

'The deepest secrets of life and death.'

'Impossible. Are you serious?'

'Dead serious. But hold on. There are far greater wonders ahead. The next one is Biotechnology. It deals with the use of living organisms and bioprocesses to heal diseases, destroy pathogens and rejuvenate nature.'

Sia shook her head in awe. 'Psychology, physiology and biotechnology. And this is thousands of years ago?'

The old woman smiled. 'That's ancient wisdom for you. You scientists must really give our forefathers a little more respect. It all began with them. Science number four is one of the oldest scientific and philosophical traditions of the world. Alchemy.'

'Now that doesn't surprise me. Alchemy was always one of the spooky sciences.'

'Ancient Indian alchemy was far spookier than all other civilisations. It's not just about the philosopher's stone, known to transmute base metals into gold. Our forefathers were masters of Rasayana, the mysterious art of distilling therapeutic rasa or nectar from nature. It might just be that coveted recipe – the elixir of life.'

Patnaik laughed. 'What's next?'

'Communication.'

'You mean communication through letters, pigeons or spies?'

'Something far more high end than that. This science is not so much of this world, but of the other worlds.'

'Other worlds?'

'Yes. Communication here talks about extra-terrestrial communication.'

Sia's mouth fell open. 'ETs?'

'Exactly. Our ancestors have long dabbled in interactions with life in outer space.'

'This is too far-fetched, Jasodhara. I grant you biotechnology and physiology, but inter-galactic communication in ancient times? Not possible.'

'Tell that to the mass of ancient literature that talks about strange creatures visiting our world from outer space and interacting with man. Tell that to the paintings and sculptures of the past that depict aliens inside flying objects. Your beliefs are your choice, Sia. But the heritage of our ancestors cannot be ignored.'

'She is right,' Patnaik nodded. 'A lot of our ancient art and literature mentions such communication. There are strong theories about ancient astronauts and aliens in the writings of many modern twentieth century writers like Daniken, Icke, Sitchin and Temple. What's the sixth one, Jasodhara?'

'Gravitation.'

'You mean gravity? Did we discover it before that apple fell on Newton?' Sia laughed.

'Nope. Newton can rest in peace. Gravitation here is about defying and manipulating gravity. It teaches us how to construct flying machines.'

'Flying machines?'

'Ancient aeroplanes called Vimanas in our classical texts.'

'Like Ravana's famous Pushpak Vimana that he used to kidnap Sita?' Sia asked. 'Plain myths. Are you telling me now that our ancestors flew around in planes too?'

'They may not be as mythical as you imagine, child. Today, there's enough material to make us believe that almost all ancient civilisations of the world had access to some form of air travel. Books by David Childress and Eklal Kueshana have been shouting for years that our ancestors scaled the skies in various contraptions. And Indians were not far behind. I had even done a special episode on this topic.'

'I am sure ISRO would love to see that tape. Science number seven?'

'The seventh science is Cosmology, dedicated to our universe. Ancient India practised it long before Copernicus and Galileo were born. Some even claim that the science conceals secrets about travelling through the fabric of space and time.'

'You are talking about time travel? This is getting truly bizarre.'

'Maybe. Maybe not. Who are we to question our fathers? Science number eight is Light. Ancient Indians had identified light as a powerful source of energy. This science is concerned with ways to control and exploit the power of light. It could well be the forerunner to LASER.'

'Enough.' Sia threw up her hands. 'ETs, planes, time travel booths and now laser. What were these ancients? Gods or demons? Cyborgs or androids? Give me the last one.'

'The final science is Sociology. The ninth of the nine.'

'Socio? That's a bit of an anti-climax.' She made a face.

'No, Sia. The ninth science is one of the most essential branches of learning in ancient India. It explains the evolution of societies and how to predict their downfall. Sociology may be the least glamorous of the nine, but it forms the base on which this entire edifice rests.'

She looked at the pad.

PSYCHOLOGICAL WARFARE

PHYSIOLOGY

MICROBIOLOGY

ALCHEMY

COMMUNICATION

GRAVITATION

COSMOLOGY

LIGHT

SOCIOLOGY

The nine deities of the constellation.

'This is the order.' Jasodhara tapped the page. 'According to the legend, the nine sciences are slotted in this exact order.'

'It almost looks like we are evolving backwards.'

'I see your point, Sia. Don't forget this was an age that played with robots. Most ancient texts of the world discuss highly futuristic knowledge. Recitation of Vedas is said to generate electricity. The Bible talks about blood circulation and Copernican laws. The Quran supports the Theory of Relativity and the Big Bang. Bahai books warn us about nuclear disasters. And there's nothing more Newtonian than the Hindu theory of Karma.'

'Every action has an equal and opposite reaction.'

'Exactly. We are all standing on the shoulders of the past. Why do you think the constellation has chosen robots as its messengers? They are symbols of an era light years ahead of our times.'

Sia nodded. 'I have heard these stories before. The paradox is that ancient civilisations, including ours, were astonishingly high-end.'

'Our ancestors may well be the original geeks of the world,' Patnaik grinned. 'Look at our Hindu scriptures. They are full of stories depicting weapons with astounding powers. Many experts believe these are actual terrors reflecting the highly advanced technology of the times. Vishnu's chakra or Shiva's trishul could simply be extremely sophisticated forms of weaponry developed back then.'

'Don't forget our epics,' Jasodhara said. 'Do you know what several passages of the *Ramayana* and *Mahabharata* are believed to narrate, Sia?'

'What?'

'Nuclear wars!'

'No way.'

'Yes. The epics picture our forefathers as a technologically supreme race wielding horrors like the Brahmastra and Gandeev. The *Ramayana* mentions weapons that "could destroy the earth in an instant". The *Mahabharata* describes flying spears that could "ruin whole forts" and fireballs that could "destroy a whole city and burn fifty thousand men to ashes". It talks about an "iron bolt" that reduced Krishna's entire clan to ashes. Sounds familiar?'

Jasodhara switched on her laptop and pointed at a paragraph. 'This passage from the *Mahabaharata* is quoted a lot on the Net. Read for yourself.'

> *'The earth shook, scorched by the terrible violent heat of this weapon. Elephants burst into flame and ran to and fro in a frenzy over a vast area. Other animals crumpled to the ground and died. The waters boiled, and the creatures residing therein also died. From all points of the compass the arrows of the flame rained continuously.'*

'This is what happened at Hiroshima and Nagasaki,' Sia exclaimed.

'Precisely. Nothing short of a prehistoric atomic holocaust.'

'But these are epics. All this could be pure imagination.'

'Of course. But what's bizarre is that these prehistoric descriptions are exact images of modern atomic devastation. Every detail of doom matches perfectly. How do you explain that? How did our ancestors give such accurate accounts of nuclear savagery? Is it simply a coincidence?'

Patnaik took over the narration. 'If the epics do not satisfy you, what about relics of a past civilisation?'

'What civilisation?'

'The ruins of Indus Valley. Our very own necropolis. Many believe that the finds in the citadels are a living testimony of nuclear horrors that turned cities into graveyards.'

'What finds, Om?' asked Sia.

'One of the most astonishing discoveries were the glazed glass stones littered on the streets of Mohenjo Daro. Closer inspections have revealed that they were actually shards of clay.'

'Clay had become glass?'

'Precisely. Only an overpowering heat could have induced this extraordinary chemical change. The cities show that huge masses of rocks had crystallised, fused or melted. Even the river is believed to have dried up or changed its course. There are no volcanoes in the Indus valley. What generated such extreme heat that brought about these changes?'

'A nuclear blast.'

'Then you have stories of human skeletons found in these ruins. We have all heard reports that many were seen curled on the ground in foetal positions or holding each others hands as if a sudden cataclysm had caught them unawares. This again hints at a nuclear attack. Rumours persist that many remains found at the excavation site are radioactive in nature. Today, the Indus Valley remains trapped inside an hourglass, Sia. But sift the sands and you will find many such stories.'

'Fine. Point taken. Now how do we start on this quest?'

'Your quest comprises a series of tests,' Jasodhara said. 'Each test will be a riddle spoken by a robot. You must solve each riddle to reach the next level. Every robot is called a Yantra.'

'How many tests are we looking at?'

Jasodhara smiled. 'I thought the number was obvious.'

'Nine? Nine tests?'

'Yes. Nine tests, which means nine robots will give you nine riddles to solve. Each riddle hides the name of an icon.'

'What icon?'

'An icon denoting one of the nine sciences of the constellation. You will have to solve the riddles to find these nine icons, one by one. The riddles will come in the same order as that of the sciences.'

'You mean the first icon stands for Psychological War. The second symbolises Physiology and so on.'

'Exactly. That'll be your clue while cracking the riddles. Each icon is called a prateek. The constellation's cradle will be revealed only after you have found all the nine icons. I told you it's a pilgrimage, Sia. You pay homage to the nine revered sciences before getting to the source.'

'How do we progress in this trail?'

'Once you solve the first riddle, you must go to the first prateek. There you return the yantra and get a second one. That will take you to the second prateek and so on. Complete nine rounds and you finally hit the jackpot.'

They were listening. The route had been laid out before them.

'Sia can have the cradle,' Patnaik spoke up, 'I want something else. Will this trail tell me who killed Mathur?'

'I don't know that, Patnaik. But if this is what he wants, you must do it. It might answer your questions too.'

'Yes.' Sia looked at the robot. 'I will walk. I know I will reach the end.'

Patnaik held her hand. 'We will get there together.'

'So now this yantra will give us the first riddle?'

The old woman laughed. 'You still don't understand, Sia.'

'What?'

Jasodhara looked at Patnaik. His Adam's apple was bobbing up and down as he tried hard to gulp down an unknown fear. He had understood. He wanted to say it a loud, but his tongue seemed to have got caught in his throat. 'Of course.'

'Of course what, Om?'

'Don't you see? The *Arthashastra*.'

'What?'

'That was the first prateek. The icon for Psychological War. This is level two now. Our journey has already begun.'

Sia's eyes grew large as realisation filled them up. Jasodhara tapped on the yantra in her hands.

'Exactly. You forget that you are holding the second robot. The riddle of the first yantra has brought us to Mysore, to the first icon. We were ignorant then, but now we know. This is not the end, Sia. This is the beginning. One prateek done. Eight more to go.'

Patnaik pointed at the mark of nine. 'That's the reason why the number is evolving on these robots. They are an indicator. Each new nine will identify a new yantra for us as we proceed. The number will grow as we make progress in our quest.'

'Yes. It will walk with you as your past and your future on this journey. Every time you get a nine, you will strive to get the next one. Once you complete the sequence, you will stand before the cradle.'

Sia was absorbing every word. It was all coming together. 'Tell me something. How is *Arthashastra* an icon for Psychological war?'

'It's the perfect prateek. Psychological warfare is all about ways to play with the mind. Take over a brain and you take over the man. *Arthashastra* talks about that and more.'

'Yes,' Patnaik nodded. 'Remember that the book had emerged from an age of fear and distrust, when India had split into small independent states. Chanakya wrote a cold text that mirrored those cold times. It became an unapologetic sponsor of Kutyudha or psychological war and Dandaniti or brutal measures.'

Jasodhara was Googling the text now. 'Open the book and you will find that its twisted psyche justifies almost every immoral act for greater good. Using children as spies, violating peace treaties, killing one's own family and even your own heir are all celebrated. And then there is Silent War. It teaches you how to silently invoke fear in the minds of your enemies and then grind them to dust.'

Sia was looking at extracts from the book which were now lighting up the laptop's screen. With every line, her heart beat faster.

'Straight trees get cut down but crooked ones are left standing.'

'A snake may not be venomous but it must pretend to be so.'

'He who is attached to his family will only experience sorrow.'

'Princes like crabs are father eaters.'

'Chanakya actually endorses killing your family for the greater good,' she gaped.

'The book's heart is full of dark conspiracies like *Sam Dam Dand Bhed*. Don't forget that our diplomatic enclave in Delhi has been named Chanakyapuri. But the greatest influence of *Arthashastra* is that the Indian Intelligence has been modelled on this book.'

'You mean RAW?'

'Yes. It follows many tactics and strategies outlined in the text. And not only Chanakya. Alexander, Changez Khan, Hitler and Churchill were all aware of how to play with the psyche of men. Today our brains are getting even more wired and rewired with new messages every day. With modern technology and media power, our minds are exposed and defenseless like never before.'

'Not just these men, Jasodhara. Even the librarian knew it,' Patnaik grinned.

'What librarian?'

'The man at ORI. I have been wondering why he suddenly turned so rude.'

'Who cares?' Sia scoffed. 'His rudeness only strengthened our resolve to get to the book.'

'Exactly. Don't you see?'

'See what?'

'It was a mind game.'

Jasodhara walked towards him slowly. 'You mean…?'

'This was about Psychological War. I think he deliberately psyched us into rising to the challenge and completing the first round. He was conditioning our brains. He must be working for the constellation. They have broken us in.'

The old woman stared at him but Sia seemed skeptical.

'And the prince? He handed us the second yantra. Was he also one of them?'

'Perhaps,' Jasodhara nodded. 'The constellation has been alive for thousands of years. The Indian royalty must surely be aware of it. It makes perfect sense that the present royal families continue to honour their pact.' She picked up the yantra. 'These are very deep waters. Let's not think too much now. We cannot penetrate its aura yet.'

They stood gazing at the yantra. Then she handed it to Patnaik. 'You have won the prize today. You ask.'

The writer asked the question. The robot smeared gold on their faces.

In nine arched petals of a lotus exists a sanctuary of the sky
He raises one leg for us to watch within the upper air's flow
In the cosmic whirl of rage was born the fatal stab of death
Lose me there in empty bliss that a dual veil opens to show

Jasodhara sighed. 'What lyrics. Just a riddle, but see the lines.'

'You are right,' Patnaik grinned. 'I am a writer. I know what you feel.'

Sia clapped at the drooling pair. 'Beautiful but what do they mean?'

The writer laughed. 'Always the scientist. Any answers, Jasodhara?'

'The second science is Physiology. That's a vast subject. We have to narrow down the prateek.'

'You said the most dangerous secret in that science was the secret of life and death.'

'Yes. This ancient science is believed to hold the key to immortal life. Many even claim that its mysteries can revive those who have passed on. But I think this riddle is pointing at something even more dangerous.'

'What can be more dangerous than everlasting life?' Sia asked.

The woman's words came ominously. 'The touch of death.'

'Touch of death?'

'Yes. Among other things, physiology in ancient India describes techniques of killing a man by simply touching the vital points on his body. Read the third line.'

They looked at the riddle.

In the cosmic whirl of rage was born the fatal stab of death.

'The "stab of death" is related to what our texts call Marmakala or Varmakala. The word Marma denotes crucial pressure points in the human body. Hinduism says our body contains 108 Marma points out of which sixty-four are highly vulnerable. When struck, it can maim and even kill a man. Much of this principle lies hidden in the science but parts of it have become components of martial arts like the Kalarippayattu. In fact, even Judo is believed to have leaked from this science.'

'Sounds scary. Is it painless?' Sia asked.

'Probably. The riddle may be pointing to a place where Marmakala is taught.'

'The first line talks about a "sanctuary", Patnaik pointed. 'That sounds more like a shrine. It also mentions "a lotus". Could be a Hindu or a Buddhist prateek. The flower is sacred in both cultures. In fact, the riddle may be about Lord Indra.'

'Why Indra?'

'The oldest mention of Marmakala appears in a story in Rig Veda dedicated to Indra. A serpent demon called Vritra had captured all the waters of the earth. Indra killed him by hurling his Vajra at the demon's navel which is one of the vital points. It's the first ever recorded use of this science.'

'You are right,' Jasodhara spoke. 'But do the other lines agree with you?'

'The first line mentions "nine arched petals of a lotus". The story says that after killing Vritra, Indra hid inside a lotus out of remorse. Then again "sanctuary of the sky" could refer to his heavenly palace. Indra is known as the god of the sky. I am not sure about the rest.'

Realisation seemed to dawn on Sia suddenly and she cried out in excitement, 'If it's Indra, then the prateek could be the Meenakshi Temple in Madurai.'

'Meenakshi Temple?' Patnaik wondered aloud.

'I remember reading about it online. Indra was once roaming the earth when he came across a Shiva ling besides a lake. He worshipped the lord and built a temple there. It later became the Meenakshi Temple and the shrine is called Indra Vimana. What do you think, Jasodhara?'

'The same thought. What about the second line? What is this "cosmic whirl of rage"? And what is the "duel veil" in the last line?'

Patnaik was looking at the second line.

'Someone who "raises one leg" for us. No idea. This "the upper air's flow" is strange.' He paused. 'It rings a bell. I have heard about it. But where? Where?' He started pacing up and down the room.

Sia giggled. 'Do you always dance about like this when you are pissed?'

'I have it on the tip of my tongue,' the writer scowled.

Suddenly Jasodhara's voice crashed through. 'Wait a minute! What did you say?'

'I said I just can't recall.'

'I was asking, Sia.'

'Me? I said he was dancing in anger.'

The woman was silent.

'What is it, Jasodhara?'

'I think Sia has shown us the way.'

'What are you saying?'

Her words were strangely sonorous. 'You have the wrong god. The riddle is not about Indra. It is pointing at Shiva.'

'Shiva?'

'Indra was not born with the knowledge of Marmakala. He learnt it from a divine teacher. The same teacher taught it to the sages Parashurama and Agastya who popularised it on earth. Shiva. Read the third line again. The "cosmic whirl of rage". It is nothing but the Tandava of Shiva. The dance of fury.'

The writer sat down. 'You are right. The Tandava.'

'Our martial arts are believed to have originated from this divine dance. In his cosmic choreography, Shiva created this dance of destruction. We are looking at a Shiva prateek here.'

'But which one?'

'That's difficult. There are thousands of Shiva symbols, temples and relics all over India. You have the twelve Jyotir lingas. Cave temples. Panch Kedar and Panch Bhoot.'

'Panch Bhoot?' Sia exclaimed. 'Five ghosts?'

'No, Sia. They are five temples where Shiva is worshipped as the five elements of the universe.'

'Elements!' It was Patnaik. 'Elements. Yes. I have got it.'

'What have you got?'

'Now I remember why "the upper air's flow" looked familiar.'

'Tell us, tell us!' They asked him like little girls.

'A few months back I had attended a symposium on Greek Mythology. Among other things, they spoke about the layers of the universe. One of the layers is the Upper Sky or Heaven. The air flowing there is called the Upper Air. That's what the Greek gods breathe.'

'Not fair.' Sia made a face. 'And we have nothing but carbons and sulphurs.'

'It's the purest air. They also call it ether which is the fifth element of the cosmos.'

'Did you say ether?' Jasodhara asked.

'Yes. It sustains the material universe.'

'You are sure?'

'Of course.'

She grinned. 'In that case it's quite simple.'

They leaned forward excitedly. 'What? The prateek?'

'Yes. I was telling you about the Panch Bhoot temples where Shiva is worshipped as the five elements. One of these temples worships Shiva in the form of ether. He is called the Akash Linga.'

'That's the one. It has to be,' Sia could hardly contain her excitement.

'It's also the temple where Shiva performs the Tandava eternally. The mother of Marmakala.'

'My god! Which temple is this?'

Jasodhara's laughter filled the room. 'Chidambaram. The famous Chidambaram Temple in Tamil Nadu.'

Patnaik inched closer to her, 'Chidambaram is one of Shiva's holiest pilgrimages. Are you sure?'

'The riddle says "sanctuary of the sky". Chidambaram is made of two words. Chitta and Ambara meaning the Sky of Consciousness. The line mentions "a lotus". The Chidambaram Temple is believed to be located in the lotus heart of the Universe.'

'What about "nine arched petals"?'

'The temple compound has nine gates.'

'And the rest?'

'The second line is easy now. We should have seen it right away. Who else but Shiva "raises one leg for us to watch" his iconic Tandava posture? Chidambaram is the only temple that worships him as the performing god Nataraja. The Supreme Lord of Dance.'

'And the final line?'

'That's one of the great mysteries of the temple called Chidambaram Rahasyam. Shiva is also worshipped in the shrine in his formlessness. There is an empty space in the sanctum covered by a curtain. It's believed that the Lord dances there forever like he does inside us. His presence is marked only by a few dazzling leaves of gold, called the Vilva, hanging there. The curtain is raised thrice, only during aarti. That's when we must return the second robot.'

'But why "dual veil"?'

'The curtain is black on the outside and red on the inside denoting ignorance and wisdom. The drawing of the curtain is the moment when divinity is revealed. That's the "empty bliss". He is not there and yet everywhere. Absent but present. You cannot touch him but he touches you.'

It was over. Patnaik was looking at the mark of nine. Sia held the old woman's hand.

'Is there anything you don't know?'

'Yes. I don't know what happens when one reaches the end of the road.'

She walked towards the terrace. Her words came travelling back to them.

'Let's go. We'll see where Dhamma takes us.'

$\mathcal{H}$is smile was careless, pristine. Almost like that of a content infant without a care in the world.

It was flying closer to the clouds. Brick over brick like an ancient aircraft. Rock over rock like his own aspiration. It was receiving a body from hundreds of hands. The designs on its surface were giving it eyes and ears. They placed the image in a socket like a man sleeping on his bed. The words had found a home in stone. They would one day make another nest, in the hearts of men.

They bowed before the Emperor.

'The stupa is complete, sire. Our work is done.'

'I want to say those words one day.'

'What do you think, sire?'

'I think my children will love their father.'

He looked at his son and daughter. They had cast off their precious gems in exchange for beads. They stood with him, representative of every man and woman who had heeded his call. They were now walking towards the towering stupa.

'Beautiful words, Father.'

'There is beauty in wisdom. They should not just see. They should read and understand.'

'They will. It is not the language of gods. You have chosen the language of men.'

'Did they plant the sapling I had sent?'

'They did. It was planted by the king next to an image of Ravana inside his Pushpak Vimana. The sapling took eight roots and even yielded fruits.'

'The prophecy. It has come true.'

'What prophecy, Father?'

'The Teacher had said that one branch of our tree would leave us and find soil at the place where you took it. He had seen it crossing the ocean.'

The stones touched the sky. The Emperor closed his eyes. He was now watching how his years had passed. Watching how he had played with nine sciences and how they had played with him.

One by one…

34

$\mathcal{T}$he wind wiped off the cloud that had hidden the moon. It emerged from the shadow, throwing its cooling light on everything that went on below.

The Bhikkhu looked up in alarm. Moonlight was the last thing he wanted right now. The darker the night, the better it was for his purpose. The figures inside the huge hollows were wide awake. They never slept. The Bhikkhu, however, did not want any more witnesses.

Just a few more steps.

He looked behind him. The two monks were silently carrying their load. Wrapped in white, it looked luminous under the moon beams. Shimmering like a phantom flying through old walls.

A phantom that died to live.

He looked around him. The bamboo curtains were down. The lamps had been extinguished, the darkness painting shadows behind the screens. The brothers were asleep. Only the three of them were awake. Them and the Buddha. The wind was carrying away the sound of their sandals.

At last.

They touched the leaves under their feet. They were here. Climbing down the stairs, the Bhikkhu opened the door. It was icy cold inside. The CFLs on the ceiling were hanging like a bunch of stars. He pointed at the raised slab in the heart of the chamber.

'There.'

The monks placed it. The shivering trio was now standing in a triangle around the block and watching it.

Then they fell on their knees.

Walking back to his cell, the Bhikkhu locked Tathagata's room. The Samanera had placed a lamp on his table. He was doing what they had asked him to do.

He was watching the Sights.

The Bhikkhu entered his cell and looked at his seat. It was there. The Nine.

The One of the Nine had come.

BOOK TWO

Dhammam Sharanam Gacchami

His eyes were closed.

His mother gently pushed the hair back from his forehead. 'The king has summoned all the princes to the Garden of the Golden Pavilion. There the Sanyasi will foretell which of you will grow up to be his successor. Go, my son.'

'No, Mother. The king abhors me. Look at my skin. These nine hideous marks on my body. Who will choose me?'

'Your stars have chosen you, prince. They have descended on your skin to anoint you at birth. These marks are promises that will come true. The king is afraid to touch them. They all are.'

'They are afraid of me, Mother?'

'Yes. Go and see.'

Walking out, he saw the prime minister's son. The boy pointed behind him.

'Do not walk. Take the royal elephant. They will know who you are.'

'Who am I?'

'You will find out.'

The boys craned their necks to watch the prince enter on his mount. He saw the king's face turn black as the elephant crushed through the garden gate. His brothers were trembling on their seats of gold. He walked up and sat on the ground. The queens had sent scented meats on sliver platters. His mother sent him an earthen pot of rice.

'Tell me, O Wise One! Who shall be my heir?' the king asked.

The Sanyasi spoke. 'He who has the highest mount, the finest seat, the largest vessel and the choicest food will ascend your throne.'

Later that evening, the prince saw his mother lighting the lamp. 'Did you hear that, Mother?'

'Yes. But what does it mean?'

'I know. The elephant was my mount. The earth was my seat. It was also my vessel and its harvest was my food. I was the Supreme One. I will be Emperor.'

'Did you see what the Sanyasi did?'

'What, Mother?'

The prince smiled. Today his friend was doing the same.

Years had passed since that test in the garden. It was now time to fulfill the prediction. The king was dead. The eldest one had to be removed now. The prince looked at the fake elephant carrying his image. The ground below its feet was covered with green reeds.

The illusion was perfect.

His friend started to mock the eldest. 'You can never kill him. He will erase your race.'

'He is nothing.'

'You will be nothing. As long as he lives, you will be your own shadow.'

'Where is he?'

'There he sits on the majestic mount. You cannot touch a hair on his head.'

'I will tear it to pieces.'

'Slay him and the throne is yours.'

They saw the eldest charging towards the mirage. The reeds gave away pulling him down. He saw what he had fallen into.

Coals, burning coals.

*H*e looked at his watch again.

What's taking so much time?

It had been a long drive. He always snored when the hours stretched. This one had kept him awake.

Sitting inside the forensic lab, Suri was now getting impatient. The ear print had been digitally scanned and fed into an electronic sensor. The expert had told him that it was now a live scan. He was cross-indexing it against a database to locate a match. Suri was listening to something about signal processing to create a biometric template of a collection of extracted features. He kept nodding.

Screw your template.

'So how large is this database?'

'Fairly large, Mr Suri. Ear prints are still a very new development. Awareness is terribly low and most officers don't even hunt for them at a crime scene. These numbers will take time to grow. So far we have around eighteen thousand data sets.'

'Eighteen thousand criminals?'

The man was amused. 'Not really. We also have civilians, law officers and government staff ear printed here for records. That is how all databases in the world function.'

'They are saying ears may replace the fingers?'

'That will be difficult. Your chances of finding fingerprints are still a million times more. Ear prints are highly rare and many of them are not even good enough to be used. But it surely is one more tool in our box now. What you have here is a very lucky find.'

'But not quite accurate.'

'No biometric device is accurate, Mr Suri. Not even fingerprints. But they all are fairly certain. The shape and contours of a man's ear are quite exclusive to him. We are trying to get as many numbers as we can. What we really need is a national DNA database.'

Suri grunted. The Access Data Table next to the computer was eyeing him sheepishly. A modern-day enigma machine, this monitor-sized gadget could crack any code in thirty seconds flat. But when he had fed the mark on Mathur's face, the device had coughed up a blank sheet. Looking around, he saw experts bent over their tests. Tests that decoded evidence and revealed faces behind masks. Here invisible specks opened their mouths and spoke the truth. Suri wanted to hear one too.

The computer was still processing the scan. He saw grey ear files rushing past the screen. The monitor was juggling the images like digital balls.

One by one. Ear by ear. Print by print.

No matches yet.

The count was getting bigger. The files were beginning to exhaust.

Is there a match?

Tap. Tap. Tap. He was tapping a pencil on his lips.

There must be a damn match.

The computer beeped. The search was over.

Suri jumped. His eyes scanned the interface hungrily. A message was blinking.

NO MATCH FOUND

He stared at the machine for a while. Was it telling him the truth? The words did not change. The expert was clicking his tongue. Suri wanted to rip it out of his throat but he got up and walked towards the door. It was time to start all over again.

He looked up. 'Yes. Fucking all over again.'

'Mr Suri.'

The voice was confused.

He turned. The expert was gaping at the computer as if he had forgotten what it was.

'Something here is not right.'

He asked him what he meant.

'The total.'

Total? What total?

'The total number of files. It's different.'

He walked back to the desk. The man was glowering at the screen. 'I know the exact number of prints we have in this database. As I told you, it's over eighteen thousand. The total was correct yesterday. But now...'

'Now what?'

'It is showing a different figure.'

'What do you mean?'

'It is showing a lesser number.'

'Lesser number?'

'Yes. In fact less by one.'

'One?' He breathed down his neck. 'One?'

'That's right. The total is showing one less dataset. One ear file is missing. It has been deleted from the system.'

Suri's face clenched.

One ear print has been deleted.

'Are you sure about this?'

'There's no mistake. I know the exact count. One file has been removed. In fact, removed only last night.' Suri felt as if an electric current had run through his head. *Last night?*

'The total was fine last evening. The change has been made overnight.'

Suri faced the computer. 'Could it be a machine snag?'

'You mean a system error? That's not possible. These files can't get erased on their own.'

'Who has access to the database here?'

'There's me and two other colleagues. They are on leave.'

'Nobody else?'

'Just us.'

'Someone has obviously hacked his way through.'

'But this is protected information. The passwords are a complex combination of letters and numbers. Hacking through this data would be extremely difficult.'

'You say difficult. Not impossible.'

The expert fell silent. His face spoke to Suri.

Not impossible. Someone screwed the computer last night.

The man looked at the monitor. He was not even sure if the file belonged to Scorpion. It could be anybody's print. But it could also be the fucking killer. The timing had been too damn perfect. Had the Scorpion wriggled into the machine and killed his own print? He got up. They were surrounding him again. His men. His bosses. The reporters sticking cold microphones before his mouth.

Now what?

Suri took out his cell and dialed a number.

'Yadav, I want you to send invites.'

'What invites, sir?'

'I am calling a press conference.'

37

$\mathcal{H}$e was smiling.

It was watching him smile. It was blind to everyone else around it. Watching only him who had dared to defy it. Watching his footprints all over its terrain. This man who lorded over men now wanted to be its master. He was telling him that only one of them would live today. But who would strike first?

The beast sprung at him, but he had anticipated the move. Holding a wooden rod against its heaving breast, he pushed it to the earth. As he pinned down its struggling body, his hands shook with the effort. Furious and hurt, the beast raised its paw and clawed at his stomach. People stared in horror as streams of blood trickled down his front and back, drenching even the beast. The smell of warm blood seemed to drive the monster into another frenzy and with a final effort it flung him off, clambering on top, ready for the kill. But the man was faster; he quickly rammed the rod between the beast's teeth. He could see his own face in its brown pupils now.

'The throat, sire.'

He stared. His physician was pointing at the hollow of his neck.

'The throat. The throat.'

He could feel its hot rancid breath scalding his face.

'Right there.'

Its teeth found his cheek and burrowed deep.

'Now.'

Using all his remaining strength, he struck the rod at the base of the beast's throat with a scream. Nothing happened. Then he saw the brown pupils dilate. Its body slumped over him like a shroud pleading for a final embrace.

People outside were shouting how the Emperor had again killed a lion single-handedly. The body of the beast had been put on public display. They were waiting for the customary charity. He touched the physician's arm.

'What were you doing in the forest?' he asked.

The physician extracted something from the treasury vault standing before them. 'Look, sire.'

'A chipped gem. It's worthless.'

The physician's eyes were glinting. 'This belonged to the Haryanka Empire. Nine monarchs before you, my lord. The inscription on it bears your name. It's a legacy for you.'

'For me?'

'Yes. A prophecy the Haryanka ruler knew would come true.'

'Is it any good?'

'Your drink, sire.' The physician poured out a cup for the Emperor. He watched as the young man drank and then began to choke. His skin was turning a pale blue. His fingers were tearing at his throat. He hurled the cup at the physician's face knocking him down.

'Traitor! Traitor!'

The physician was laughing now.

'Why?'

The physician got up and placed the gem on the Emperor's breast. The next instant the stone turned blue. The Emperor glanced at his reflection in the mirror.

'The venom. It's gone.'

'Wear the gem, my lord. You will have no terror of poison. Your body will overthrow the strongest venom that enters it.'

The Emperor seized his hands. 'The lion. This gem. Is this science or an art?'

'The science of life. The art of death.'

*T*he sun stayed hidden. The magnificent structure seemed to eclipse it. Their eyes climbed to its highest point. It was truly the Sanctum of the Sky, soaring up to the sky, almost touching the blue roof. The pious ambition of the shrine stirred men to reach the Sky of Consciousness. They stood under the Chidambaram and tried to partake of its piety.

'What a temple! So what's the story here?' Sia asked.

'I have been reading up,' Patnaik answered. 'According to legend, Shiva perfomed the Tandava here before two saints – Patanjali and Vyagrapada – and liberated them from the cycle of human life. The saints requested the lord to dance at this place eternally so that all men could watch and attain salvation. Since then Shiva performs his eternal dance here, for all to behold and be blessed.'

The trio entered the temple through the East Gopuram. This doorway was a unique dance manual with all the 108 postures of Bharatnatyam sculpted on it. Before them the gigantic complex spread out in every direction. Time lay bound and gagged here. Nothing ever changed inside Chidambaram. Men still slept with gods and gods still woke up with men. The Lord still danced and the audience still attended the six shows. Standing there, they felt a collective pang of anxiety.

The second prateek of the constellation.

As they walked towards the sanctum, the chariot-shaped Natyasabha or Dance Hall appeared decked with sphinxes. The sun and moon made its wheels, and the four Vedas were its horses. This was where Shiva had danced against Kali in a terrible contest. The goddess had almost won the duel when the yogi god lifted one of his legs vertically above his head, towards the sky. Called the Urdhva Tandava, this stance was obviously meant for a male dancer. It is said that he managed to not only balance himself in this position but to perform such a magnificent and rapid whirl that his clothes were ripped off! Bewitched by his performance, Kali hung her head in shame.

They also saw Sivaganga Tank whose waters had turned a leper king's skin golden. Sia was getting intrigued by the layout of the temple complex. While the various elements looked arbitrary, she could sense an invisible method in this madness. Like an ancient Tetris, she thought. Things had fallen randomly from above but before hitting earth, they had been sorted and installed in their proper niches.

'Is it true that all Shiva temples have a hidden symbolism?'

Jasodhara nodded. 'The structure of a Shiva Temple resembles a human body. It has five concentric courtyards encircling each other, representing the five layers of man's life. The outermost layer symbolises the material body. The second layer denotes Prana or the vital life force. The third layer represents Mana or thoughts. The fourth layer symbolises the brain and the innermost circle is Ananda or bliss. It is also the Jiva or the heart. This is where the sanctum housing Shiva is placed. Like the human heart, the sanctum is also a dark and enclosed space.'

The golden glitter of the roof told them that they had reached the innermost layer. They were now standing before the Chitsabhai or the Hall of Consciousness, and each of the three could feel an invisible magnetism pulling them inside the consecrated space.

The garbha griha. Sanctum sanctorum. The heart of the temple.

The sanctum was a wooden chamber with a gilded roof. It was also a grand stage for the dancing god, with entrances from both sides. Five silver steps rose towards the three forms of Shiva inside the garbha griha. There stood the bejeweled Nataraja in the centre, performing the Ananda Tandava. At his feet was the crystal Sphatika lingam denoting his semi-anthropological form. Behind the Nataraja, towards the right, was the curtain concealing the Nirguna formlessness of the god. His presence in absence. The mystery of the space hidden deep inside all men.

Jasodhara pointed at the Nataraja.

'Watch the divine dance of Tandava. This is the rhythm of the universe. It generates the cosmic cycle of creation and destruction. Birth and death. Shiva dances to destroy a spent universe so that Brahma can create a new one. He evokes the union of God and Universe. The dancing image is also a tribute to science, Sia.'

'Science?'

'To the parmanu. Like Shiva, the atom is also in a continuous circular motion. It depicts both the Mover and the Moved.'

What they were looking at was motion in metal.

'The Tandava posture is highly symbolic. Nataraja performs the dance while holding on to a damru, the instrument which hides within it the seed of creation. It is the origin of all the primordial sounds of the universe, including the Om. The fire in the other hand symbolises destruction. Like Vishnu's chakra and padma, these opposites – seed and fire – signify the dialectics of birth and death.'

'His foot is raised like the riddle described,' Patnaik observed.

'This is an act of upliftment and liberation. The dwarf on whom

Nataraja dances depicts the crushing of ignorance. The Lord's face is without any emotion, depicting neutrality and balance.'

Sia knew now. The Lord danced here in the middle of the universe. In the sky of consciousness and in the hearts of men.

The priests called Deekshitars were anointing the crystal lingam on the mandapam. Legends said that they had been brought from Mount Kailash by Patanjali to perform the daily rituals. The community had lived here ever since, serving the god. A chant of mantras rose into the air, purifying the listeners. And then somewhere a gong started playing.

Boom...Boom...Boom...Boom...Boom...Boom...Boom... Boom...Boom.

Like the pulsing of the Earth. The pulse of the universe. They were the divine footfalls of the Lord swaying in ecstasy. Was it echoing from the bowels of the Earth below, or were the heavens above throbbing now? Patnaik's heart leaped as the resounding tremors filled his being. The sound was emerging from one point, travelling a distance and then seemed to return, like a celestial boomerang. Flowing over the three worlds, it was now the beginning, middle and end of everything. All the functions inside his body were dancing to its beat. He had become the sound and the sound had become him.

Sia saw Nataraja come alive before her. She heard the rattle of the damru and the hiss of the serpent. She felt the heat of the flames scorching her face. Now there was chaos. Galaxies were tumbling around her and the sky was turning black. Then the universe started crumbling, hanging in shreds. As her body burned, the serpent pounced and bit her on the shoulder.

Sia jerked. Patnaik was tapping on her arm.

'Look.'

A hand rose and pulled the curtain back.

Patnaik seemed to have become rooted to the garbha griha. Each beat of the gong was like a fresh drumming of his heart, and seemed to be dragging him out of his skin towards a higher destiny. He had seen the space behind the curtain. His essence was free. It stepped outside his body and grabbed the nothingness. The Vilva strands dangling in the empty space had flashed a blinding instant of bliss. They seemed to create a negative, a black and white outline of the God in his mind. He had seen nothing. He had seen everything.

Lose me there in empty bliss that a dual veil opens to show.

As the flames danced before the abyss, they saw the miracle. The light seemed to breathe life into the vacant space. The lamps were piercing through the void like comets scorching ether. The vacuum was on fire.

This was the moment.

Patnaik took out the yantra and placed it on the floor. He looked up as the curtain opened again. Then it parted a second time. Was it touching him?

Yes.

It was brushing against his skin, holding on to him. Grasping his neck. He could not tear his eyes away or move his face, it was almost as if he had been turned to stone. Chained to the golden leaves. Nailed to the nada behind them. Seconds later he was free again. The curtain closed. He looked down.

The yantra was not there. But there was one in Sia's hand. Jasodhara pointed at the forehead. The mark of nine had changed.

The curtain parted again.

'Yes. I see it. The nine has walked some more.'

'This design was introduced by the Guptas and Andhras. They started curving the vertical line at the bottom like this.'

'Still a long way from the nine we know.'

The three were on the hotel roof with the third yantra. The number on the forehead now resembled the modern-day digit of three.

'How did you get this robot, Sia?'

'I was watching when you placed the yantra on the ground. I wanted to see the exchange. Then that curtain swung open again and I looked at it. But after that I could not look down. It was surreal, Om. Almost as if something had touched me. I was completely paralysed.'

'Yes. We both felt it too. At the base of our necks.'

'But then I was fine. I looked down and the yantra was still there. People were looking at it so I picked it up but...'

'It was the new one. They had already exchanged it.' Jasodhara's eyes were shining.

'Yes.'

'They locked us.'

'What?'

'They locked us in our bodies. The robots were switched in a matter of seconds.'

'What do you mean by "they locked us in our bodies"?'

'One of the most common techniques of Marmakala. Pressure at the correct points can make you immobile for hours. They locked us to swap the robots and then released us.'

They touched their necks gingerly. 'Is that what happened?'

'Yes. That's why they chose that moment. The curtain was the perfect distraction.' She looked at the yantra. 'They are watching us.'

'Who, Jasodhara?' Sia sounded anxious. 'One of the Deekshitars? Someone in the crowd?'

'The constellation. That's the only answer I have.'

Patnaik put a reassuring hand on her. 'Calm down, Sia. I agree with Jasodhara that we are on the right path. The constellation has touched us today. Let's just keep walking.'

Sia spoke, 'What is Dhamma?', and the robot whispered its riddle.

Six billion men are born again inside a single drop of nectar
Where two gods walked in through the very first lower door
It lives in the hairy moon and freed only seven royal angels
Rest me in mother's lap after three fires dance on her shore

Sia tugged Patnaik's arm. 'Do you see?'

'What?'

'Each line has a number.'

He saw them. 'Yes. That's interesting. But I am looking at the lines.'

Six billion men are born again inside a single drop of nectar.

'How can "six billion men" be inside "a single drop"?'

The writer frowned. 'Metaphor, Sia. Metaphor.'

'Of course! It's all about lyrical beauty and poetry.'

'Men born inside a drop. That sounds like baptism to me,'

Jasodhara spoke. She read the next two lines.

Where two gods walked in through the very first lower door.

It lives in the hairy moon and freed only seven royal angels.

'Baptism and angels. This one could be a Christian icon, Patnaik. What is this "hairy moon"?'

Sia giggled. 'Never heard of that before.'

Rest me in mother's lap after three fires dance on her shore.

'This is obviously telling us where to leave the third yantra,' he said. 'It says "mother's lap". That should tell us something. Who or what can be the yantra's mother?'

'Interesting question. Spare a thought for the father too.'

'Enough, Sia. Your jokes are not helping.' Patnaik frowned, looking at the last line again. 'The word "shore" indicates the sea. Fire dance at a sea shore?'

'Since we are talking about metaphors, it could mean the sun rising or setting and its rays falling on the waters. Or it could be a clever reference to a lighthouse. The light there always keeps rotating.'

Jasodhara clapped. 'Very good, Sia. You do well when you apply your technical mind.'

'The Marina Beach in Chennai fits the bill. I have been there a couple of times. There is a lighthouse there, all red and white, by the sea,' Sia said.

The writer nodded. 'Fine, but do all the roads lead to Marina? I don't think so.'

Sia took the notepad.

'Let's start again. Line One. This could be test-tube babies. Life born inside a petri-dish.'

'The scientist speaks again. And the rest?'

'No idea.'

Patnaik smiled. 'This dance of fire. They should have used it in the second riddle. It describes the aarti at Chidambaram quite well.'

'Yes. It was as if the darkness inside me had turned into the sun.' Her eyes twinkled. 'Is that what they mean?'

'What, Sia?'

'The dancing fire. It could be an aarti being performed.'

He stared at her and then the line. 'But the line does not say temple. It mentions a "shore". Aarti at a sea shore?'

'Why not? Aren't there temples in India that stand by the sea?'

'There are a few. There's the Shore Temple in Mahabalipuram; Jagannath Temple in Puri; Rameshwaram down south; even Dwarka and Somnath in Gujarat. But as far as I know, the aarti in these temples is performed inside the sanctum.'

'The words say the "fires dance on her shore",' Jasodhara said. 'It's more like they are worshipping the sea itself. The waters of the sea.'

Her words seemed to hit a gong for Patnaik.

'Waters of the sea?'

'Yes. But I have never heard of any such ritual.'

'You are right, Jasodhara. But you have surely heard of worshipping waters?

'Waters?'

'Yes. Waters. Waters of a river,' Patnaik whispered. 'You have surely heard about aarti along a river.'

'But that happens at the banks of the…' She paused.

He nodded, 'The Ganga.'

They looked at each other and then at the words of the riddle.

'Ganga. Do you think it's talking about the Ganga?' Sia asked.

Patnaik looked at the verse again.

Six billion men are born again inside a single drop of nectar
Where two gods walked in through the very first lower door

It lives in the hairy moon and freed only seven royal angels
Rest me in mother's lap after three fires dance on her shore

'Yes. And I think the river could be the third prateek.'

The women gasped in unison. 'What do you mean?'

'This entire riddle is drenched with the Ganga. The last line says "mother's lap". The Ganga is not just a river, she has always been our mother.'

They nodded.

'The third line. She indeed "lives in the hairy moon".'

'What is that?' Jasodhara asked.

'Recall any image of Shiva. Where do you find the Ganga?'

Sia knew what he was talking about even before Patnaik finished asking. 'The river flows from the coils of his matted hair. She resides there along with the moon on his forehead.'

'Exactly. The "seven royal angels" describes the story of her seven infant sons whom she drowned in her own waters.'

Sia looked at them in horror. *Ganga drowned her own sons?*

Patnaik smiled. 'She drowned her sons but did not kill them.'

'What does that mean?'

'These angels were the eight elemental deities called Vasus. Once they played a prank on Rishi Vashishtha who cursed them to be born as mortals on earth. The Vasus asked Ganga to be their mother and instructed her to kill them as soon as they were born so that they could be released from human bondage.'

She laughed. 'Cowards. It's not easy being human. Anyone can be god.'

'Yes. Very true, Sia.'

'But I like the story. Drowned. Not killed.'

'The river could release only seven of them. The eighth one was saved by his father King Shantanu and grew up to be Bhishma of *Mahabharata*. The cursed man lived out the punishment meant for all of them. Ganga freed seven beings from the sufferings of this world. Their watery graves became their salvation. That is what she continues to do for us.'

Sia felt a lump in her throat. The heart of Ganga was deeper than she had seen. Her doubts were drowning now. Then something raised its head.

'Hold on. This riddle is about a prateek for the third science. That's Biotechnology, Om. How's that connected with the Ganga?'

'That's bothering me too.' He turned towards the old woman. 'Is there a connection, Jasodhara?'

She had closed her eyes. When she opened them, they were moist. 'Not a connection. A bond. A beautiful bond.'

'What is it?'

'I don't need to tell you that despite being one of the holiest rivers, Ganga is also one of the most highly polluted streams in the world. International studies have rated the water as Category D, which denotes fatal contamination. There are also reports of alarming levels of mercury in the water.'

'Yes. It's a mess.'

'Therein lies the miracle, Patnaik. Despite such dangerous levels of pollution, people continue to use it without any harm. It's as if the waters neutralise their own infection.'

'This is insane,' Sia countered. 'I have seen some of the worst polluted stretches of the river. You cannot even enter those filthy waters.'

'And yet tests have shown that cholera and dysentery causing bacteria die faster in the Ganga than in any other water. Studies show that compared to other rivers, this stream has an unusually large concentration of bacteriophages, which kill the microbes. The waters also have a strange ability to retain more oxygen than other rivers, leading to lesser amount of pathogens. What gives it such a purifying mechanism?'

'What?'

'The genius of the constellation.'

'The constellation? I don't understand.'

'These qualities of the Ganga are a direct result of its actions. It is believed that the constellation regularly releases purifying elements into the river from an unknown base in the Himalayas.'

Sia was stunned. 'What purifying elements?'

'They could be those bacteriophages that maintain the water's purity. Some say they are herbal agents that neutralize infection. Others claim that they use chemical colloids. There are even theories that the sterilization is carried out through radiation. I say it's simply their science that flows into her water and keeps it alive. People often ask what the constellation does for men. This river is a living example. They make the Ganga what it is.'

They were listening silently. There could not have been a better prateek for the third science. The constellation had chosen a force of nature that still flowed to liberate man in this life and beyond. Its scientific brilliance was unfolding with each new icon they discovered.

The constellation keeps the Ganga pure!

'But I still don't know the full answer, Patnaik. Ganga is a huge river flowing through five states in the country. Where do we go to get the next yantra?'

'That's where the first line comes in. It gives you a hint.'

Six billion men are born again inside a single drop of nectar.

'Look at the first six words. "Six billion men are born again". The meaning is clear now. It describes the ritual act of purifying oneself in the river. Men are surely reborn when they go inside the sacred waters. Not sure why "six billion" though.'

'I think the figure refers to the present population of the world. It's over six billion,' Sia said.

'Yes. The whole of mankind. The constellation embraces the entire human race. The last four words are the hint.'

'You mean the "single drop of nectar". I thought it's a reference to her holy waters.'

'It's more than that, Sia,' Jasodhara laughed, 'Patnaik is right. The words hint at four specific places where the Ganga flows. Four places that are her holiest pilgrimages. Have you heard about Samudra Manthan?'

'Of course. My father had told me how the gods and the demons churned the ocean and fought over the vessel of elixir.'

'Right. In the middle of the battle, Vishnu flew away, with the vessel of amrit, on his celestial bird Garuda. During his flight, he accidentally spilled drops of amrit at four different places.'

Sia looked at the words.

'A "single drop of nectar".'

'Exactly. This riddle worships life, Sia. The nectar. The mother. The river. Birth and rebirth. This riddle is Ganga herself. And it's talking about one of these four spots where Vishnu leaked the nectar.'

'Which are the places?'

'You will know the moment I tell you this,' Patnaik said. 'The vessel holding the nectar had a beautiful name. It is also the Sanskrit name of the zodiac sign Aquarius meaning Water Carrier.' He came closer. 'It was called the Kumbh.'

Recognition shone on her face. 'Kumbh Mela. The four cities where the Kumbh Mela is celebrated.'

'Bulls-eye! Hardwar, Allahabad, Ujjain and Nasik. ABCD. One of them is our right option.'

'Which one?'

'We haven't cracked the second line. That should tell us.'

Where two gods walked in through the very first lower door.

'I am not sure what this means. My guess is the place must either be Allahabad or Hardwar.'

'What was the second place you said?'

'Hardwar.'

Sia giggled.

'What's funny?'

'It's not Hardwar, Om. It's called Haridwar.'

'It's the same. The place is called by both the names. Hari is Vishnu and Har is Shiva. The two names mean a gateway to either deity. Both the gods are said to have walked the place.'

Patnaik bit his tongue. The others were gaping at him in surprise.

Where two gods walked in through the very first lower door.

'You are an idiot, Om Patnaik. That's exactly what this line says.'

The man was in a daze. He had failed to connect the dots.

Vishnu and Shiva were the two gods.

'Yes. It's Haridwar. Its ghat is called Har Ki Pauri, meaning the Steps of Shiva. At the upper wall of this ghat is a footprint believed to be the foot of Vishnu.'

'What about the "very first lower door"?'

'Haridwar again. It describes the entry point of Ganga into the Indo-Gangetic valley. Flowing from the high mountains, it enters the low plains for the first time at Haridwar. The "first lower door".'

They closed the notepad.

'So we put this yantra after the aarti?'

'Yes. After the three bowls of fire have worshipped the river. We may see one more miracle on the banks of Ganga.'

'Go both of you,' Jasodhara smiled. 'Repent before the mother.'

'What about you?'

'I'll be there one of these days. But today she's waiting for you.'

They looked at Sia. She was eyeing the four numbers in the riddle again.

'What are you looking at?'

'Something. There must be something in these figures.'

She picked up the pen. A moment later she was laughing.

'What is it?'

'What else can it be?' Sia pushed the pad.

$$6 + 2 + 7 + 3 = 18$$
$$1 + 8 = 9$$

40

12 noon.

The room could well be a beehive, considering the amount of activity going on. Guards were checking press cards at the entry point while a woman registered the newcomers. Cameramen were elbowing each other for that perfect spot to corner the action. They stood in a neat row behind tall tripods like troops behind canons, ready to shoot their target. Long cables snaked out from under the cameras, slithering towards the OB vans outside, preparing to relay live feeds. Some reporters were busy checking their microphones, others their make-up.

It was finally here, the moment of truth. Parag Suri had sent out typed A4 promises that he would speak. All roads now led to Varanasi. They were waiting to see the rabbit hop out of his khakhi cap.

Pushing the door open, Suri instantly stumbled on the tension. The air was thick with it. He felt like a seer who had promised a miracle. But this was the media. They could place a circle of olive on his head. They could walk over his grave with spiked boots.

He looked up. 'Yes. Fucking spiked boots.'

The man parked himself in the centre and switched on the microphone. 'Thank you all for coming here. I realise this conversation has been long in the waiting. There have been noises that I have not cooperated with the media on this case, but you must understand that the last few days have been extraordinary. Nothing was making sense. My men have been working round the clock. Our priority was to carry out a proper investigation and hold a conference only when we had something worth sharing. Now we can talk.'

The scribes leaned forward in excitement.

'It is confirmed now that historian Ram Mathur was murdered in cold blood. He was poisoned through the eye. We also know that he carved his face himself, in the last few minutes before he died. Our experts are trying to decipher its meaning. We are still looking for the people involved.'

The reporters made faces. This was rancid news. Some folded their notepads shut. Cameramen got signals to stop recording.

The man continued. 'The good news is that we have now come across solid evidence that can nail the killers.'

The room fell silent again and the notepads opened. Cameras started rolling again. Suri took one deep breath.

Now.

'We have discovered important forensic proof.'

The pens were dancing.

'That's all.'

Fingers screeched to a halt.

'I cannot disclose the nature of the proof right now. It's extremely risky and will alert the persons involved. What we have got is quite good and it will answer a lot of our questions. We now need time to process this evidence. You will be informed when we get the results.'

He leaned back. 'Thank you.'

The reporters cried out, as if in pain. Suri had aroused them and then slit their throats right before the orgasm. They wanted more, but Suri zipped his mouth. He opened the floor for questions.

A woman in the front grabbed the mike. 'If you have such excellent proof, why don't you share it with us? Do you really have anything?'

The officer looked her in the eye. 'Fine. I'll tell you everything and you go and tell it to the entire world. If the killer escapes, will you take the blame? All of you?'

They were quiet. Another hand rose. 'Is Sia Mathur helping the police with the investigation?'

'That's absurd. Miss Mathur is a civilian. She is a daughter who has just lost her father. I request you to leave her alone. She needs time to come to terms with what happened and we should respect that.'

'What about the writer Om Patnaik? What is he doing here? How is he connected to the case?' A man had stood up in the middle row.

Suri shifted in his chair. He had anticipated this question.

How the hell should I know why Patnaik is here?

He repeated what Sia had told him. 'Mr Om Patnaik is a family friend of the Mathurs. He knew the historian. He is here to share the family's grief. It's a personal matter.'

The reporter did not sit down. 'If he is only a friend, why did Sia Mathur call him on the morning after the murder? What was the urgency?'

Suri chewed his lips.

These bloody guys know everything.

'Sia was obviously devastated. She wanted his advice and emotional support.'

'Are you saying that the fact that he is a writer of mystery books has nothing to do with his involvement?'

He smiled. 'What you say sounds intriguing, but the truth is much simpler. I am sure Mr Patnaik is a very popular mystery writer but this case is not a thriller. It needs qualified professionals to work out its intricacies, such as the symbol tattooed on Mathur's cheek. This is not something the writer of sensational paperbacks can accomplish.'

The man sat down. Suri was hoping the worst was over. But he was wrong.

'Such fantastic murders are usually not isolated cases. Is Mathur's murder part of a larger design?' asked a voice from the back.

Suri's face drained of all blood.

Had they recognised the patterns? Did they know about the Scorpion?

He looked at the crowd like a cornered animal, wondering what to do. Not answering the question was not going to do him any good. In press conferences, silences spoke louder than words and made even larger headlines. He calmed down. They knew nothing. These were just intelligent guesses.

'We are not aware of any kind of design. Corpses missing an eye and branded on the face don't turn up everyday. This is too fantastic a case and highly unlikely to have a pattern. We are focusing more on solving it than looking for past prototypes. But we will look into this angle.'

He stood up. 'Thank you, all.'

The journos rushed to him, egging for more inputs. Some of them thrust their microphones under his nose repeating questions he had already answered. Now the dreaded nine-letter word EXCLUSIVE was chasing him down the room. He was running. Pushing through shoulders, legs and torsos. He wanted to get to the door and breathe some fresh air. Then he choked.

Something had bitten him on the arm.

He was writhing in pain, as if someone had sawed off his limb. His head was spinning and his lungs screamed for oxygen. He could see hands all around, reaching out to him. He couldn't breathe any more. It was as though an invisible wall were building all around him, or someone were throwing fresh earth as he lay in a ditch, burying him alive.

The next moment he crashed to the floor.

41

$\mathcal{H}$e was seeing faces swarming all around.

Unfamiliar faces, looking at him curiously. Faces of stricken officers as they bundled him into a car and rushed him to a hospital. Then faces of stricken doctors as they fussed around him. But he couldn't find the face he really wanted to see.

The Scorpion.

He was alone now. The Scorpion must have got away in all the chaos. They had frisked the journalists and found nothing. He only remembered cameras flashing and lenses zooming in for a closeup to go with tomorrow's headline.

Suri floored. Literally.

His arm twitched again. The heat was gone but not the ache. They said the poison had been contained in time but the pain still frightened him. He knew what had happened to him was only a fraction of what nine others had suffered. He would make that murderer suffer now.

Friday may stop haunting me then.

His lie had worked. It had hauled the Scorpion out of his hole. It had melted his steel and made him desperate enough to strike again. Suri let out a laugh.

I scared the shit out of the mother fucker.

He had also fed the media sharks and got what he wanted. Time. It was a dangerous gamble but he had played his hand. He would reveal his cards later.

Walking into the loo, he lowered his pajama and began watering the pot.

'All well, Mr Suri?'

The man jumped. Someone was standing right behind him. Watching him piss.

Scorpion?

No. It was a female voice. Fumbling with his draw-strings, he hurried out of the washroom.

'Who is it?'

The woman walked up to him. A young woman, in her late twenties or early thirties, carrying a folder and a clutch in one arm, the other hand shoved inside her denim pocket.

'Don't!' Suri reached out for his gun.

She held out a card. 'Alia Irani. Journalist.'

He gaped at her, 'Journalist?'

'Yes. Five minutes, Mr Suri.'

The officer's face trembled with rage. 'What? How dare you? You wait. You just wait here. I'll fucking fix you right now.' He sprang towards the door.

'I wouldn't do that, Mr Suri. Not if I wanted to know why Ram Mathur was killed.'

That stopped him in his tracks. 'Mathur?'

'Yes. And the eight others.'

'Which others?'

'The pattern.'

Suri walked up to her to get a closer look. His sore arm was throbbing again.

'Yes, I know.'

He raised his voice, 'Listen. I give a damn about what you know or do not know. This is a hospital. I'll have you kicked out of your job.'

'I am a freelancer,' she shrugged, 'That's one of the perks, you know. I am my own boss. And I won't be firing myself.'

'Get out. I'll have you bloody arrested.'

'Then you will never know what I know.'

'What do you know?'

'A lot. You will thank me for it.' She looked at his bandage. 'That must have been annoying.'

'Yes. What can you do?'

'Get you the man who did that to you.'

'You are fucking lying.'

The woman was smiling now. 'No I'm not.'

'What were you doing inside the washroom?'

'Waiting for you. I have been there since noon. It wasn't very pleasant.'

'Noon?'

'Of course. When I heard what happened at the press con, I knew they would put you up here. The VIP suite. I sneaked in long before you were admitted.'

'My men checked this room. How did you do it?'

'Trade secrets, Mr Suri. We all have our own little secrets.'

The bed creaked as he sat down. 'You did not attend the press con?'

'I never do. Colossal waste of time. People always lie at press conferences. Don't they, Mr Suri?'

He was quiet.

'I like meeting people behind closed doors. That's where the truth hides.'

Suri asked for a glass of water. She poured it out for him.

'I heard you denied the fact that there was no pattern in Mathur's murder.' She handed him the glass. 'What if I say there is a very intriguing pattern between this murder and eight others that have taken place in the last three months? And you, Mr Suri, know it better than anybody else.'

He looked at her face, as he slowly sipped the water. 'I have already spoken about it. As far as I know, there is no such pattern. But I am sure the suggestion will been considered and in due process we will look into…'

Alia called his bluff.

'I don't want your official version for a TV byte, Mr Suri. That's already on air. I want you to admit what you know quite well – the fact that there is a link between these gruesome murders. This is not a press con where you can sit and lie through your teeth.'

The colour of his face had turned from a deep red to purple. 'Careful, Miss Irani. You are accusing an officer. This will not be good for you.'

Alia opened her folder and spilled its contents on the table. They were newspaper cuttings of the Scorpion murders. All nine of them. The pattern was there right before him. She had not missed a single piece.

'This is the truth. These were not natural deaths as reported in the media. All of them were given a jab through the right eye. I know that Intelligence had warned you about Mathur but you could not save him. And you don't have one measly clue about this case. Am I right?'

Suri tried hard to hide his bewilderment but he knew his face was betraying him.

She knows!

Alia recognised the look. 'Look here, Suri. I only want to help.

I also understand your position. This case is too dangerous to be discussed openly with the press. But I already know enough. Let me come on board. I have facts that can help your investigation. You want to get those killers. I also want the same. We can do this together.'

He looked up at her eyes again. Her proposal was beginning to interest him more and more. The Scorpion was clearly out of his reach right now and he was no closer to solving the case. He had been groping blindly for straws and he desperately wanted to clutch this one. But something held him back.

Can I trust her?

He looked up. 'Yes. Can I fucking trust her?'

'Beg your pardon?'

'Nothing. What makes you think all this is true? I say it's all crap.'

Alia smiled. She pulled out her ace. A video recording. Suri's heart thumped inside his rib cage. He was watching a dead man's face.

'The monk at Rumtek. I got him with my stick button camera. It's quite a handy tool, Suri. Look. Look at the monk's pain. Look at every detail in full HD.'

He was seeing it. The convulsed face. The missing eye. The blackened hollow.

'We all know about Mathur's face. Same eye. Same poison. Same pattern. Coincidence? I don't think so.'

'How did you get this video?'

'I ask questions, Suri. That's my work. I can sell this dynamite and fill up my bank account. But my mother was a mad woman. She knew that morality sometimes skipped a generation and she made me hold on to it. I value that above my life. I want these murders to stop.'

'It's possible. Not that I need your help but we can come to some arrangement.'

She grinned menacingly. 'Listen, Suri. This will work if you take that fucking male ego and shove it down your shit pot. You may be the cop here, but I have the info and you don't. Be man enough to accept it. I am here for these men. I have brought them to you. Can you help them?'

He was quiet again.

'Nine horrible deaths, Suri. We can prevent the tenth one.'

He looked at her. 'Fine. You are on.'

'Good.'

'But there are ground rules. Whenever you have any information, you contact me and nobody else. I'll give you my private number and all the official data. Be very careful and work as quietly as possible. This man has killed nine times. He can kill again. Double cross me and you will fuck your own life.'

'Agreed.'

Suri glanced at the video again. 'You actually opened the monk's coffin?'

'I always look at the larger picture. The means don't matter. Only the end. Truth often forces you to stoop down to hell to find it and I don't cringe.'

'Anything else?'

'It's my turn to ask questions. What was the evidence you dangled before my friends today?'

He told her about the killer and the ear print. He did not know that her toes were curling in excitement.

'One man has murdered them all?'

'Yes. We call him the Scorpion.'

'Not bad. Suits the bastard.'

He nodded. 'What do you have for me? It had better be good.'

Alia leaned closer. 'I told you I had the motive behind these murders. Will you kiss me if I told you that?'

Suri sat up. The one thing he had still not understood about this case was the motive. What dark purpose had driven one man to shed so much blood? This woman said she knew. Did she?

'Here's a question for you, Suri. Have you ever heard of the Nine?'

'The Nine?'

'Yes. An ancient constellation that still lives on.'

'I thought you were giving me the motive.'

'I am telling you what connects these nine murders. My research is quite extensive. I have also heard the truth from mouths that have long remained silent. These nine people were linked to the constellation. Including Mathur.'

'Mathur?'

'Yes. And they all paid the price.'

Suri listened as she spoke. Was this a crime or a bedtime story? Fairy tales had stopped charming him long ago. Myths and legends did not fit into his police files. What she was telling him now sounded dangerously bizarre. Quite impossible.

But the more he heard, the more he wanted to know. His eyes strayed towards the clock on his desk.

10:44 p.m.

Unconsciously he added up the four digits.

42

$\mathcal{T}$his tree had never known winter.

It had seen icy blue fingers pluck the foliage of others. The season disrobed them all with a cold glee every year, but did not dare pluck a single leaf from it. The cold returned again and again with sharper nails, only to be vanquished. If winter was the foe, spring was the evergreen lover that brought gifts to win its heart. Today, it had again adorned it with a hundred flowers. The Emperor was watching the vermillion blooms as they glistened in the sun. Their sweet fragrance brought a smile to his face.

'Look at my namesake. As ethereal as me and as invincible.'

The five hundred concubines simpered outwardly at his words. Inside they were thinking the same thing.

'He's a fool to compare his vile body with the tree.'

'If only the man knew how much we loathe him.'

'We must teach him a lesson.'

That night they poisoned the soil around the tree. When morning came, winter had finally triumphed.

Standing under the bare branches, the Emperor's lips moved. 'Burn the bitches. All five hundred alive.'

People covered their eyes in terror as the funeral pyre grew higher. They saw servants pouring oil over the queens and flinging them into the fire. Some raped them first before tossing them naked in the flames. Hands stretching out of the charred pile were being hacked and thrown back. Five hundred women were turning into a mass of flesh. The stench and the screams drove everyone away, but not the Emperor. He stood with his back to the raging fire behind him, looking at what was left of his beloved tree.

Years later, it happened again.

But this was the Sacred Fig. The tree that sprouted a million hearts on its body to love every living being on earth. Long ago its shade had stained a man with light. The Emperor had honoured it by sending gold and jewels but the chief queen had turned jealous. She had tied nine black threads around it and infected its sap. Now she lay prostrate before the tree and the man.

'Forgive me, Lord!'

'I will if you forgive yourself.'

'I have killed the Fig.'

'No. You have not.'

'The tree is dead, sire.'

The Emperor ripped the black threads from the decaying stump. 'I am not what I was anymore.'

He wrote on a piece of cloth and handed it to his minister. An hour later she saw one hundred servants enter carrying a hundred jars. She watched them tip the jars one by one and pour white fluid on the wood.

The Emperor folded his hands as the first leaf turned green.

43

'All dead. All dead.'

The man had turned into an apparition of his former self. A mere carcass whose tongue hung out. His hands were afraid to touch anything and his legs were spewing blood. But the men sitting there were staring at his eyes, which seemed to have sunk into holes. What had they seen?

'Death. Doom. Destruction.'

The assembly shrank in horror.

King Sagara watched him from behind the sacrificial fire. His Ashwamedha Yagna was nearing its grand finale. He had released his royal horse a year ago. It had to return after trotting throughout the country, symbolising his sovereignity. His sixty thousand sons were guarding the horse and the assembly was awaiting their homecoming.

'No one's coming back. Kill the music. Put out the fire.'

The father's heart shivered before the blazing flames. 'Where are my sons?'

'Dead. All sixty thousand! Indra was jealous of you and abducted your horse. He tethered it next to sage Kapila and your sons thought that the holy man had stolen the steed. They broke into his meditation and hurled abuses at him. Kapila opened his eyes and burned all of them to ashes.'

The Brahmin paused. Bhagirath was listening to the tragedy that had annihilated his ancestors.

'That was the end of the sons of Sagara. Sixty thousand of your ancestors. They have still not found salvation and their spirits wander the three worlds. These are cursed ashes. Their final rites have not been performed. They are crying for release. Can you hear them Bhagirath?'

'How can I grant them peace?'

'Ganga. You will have to bring Ganga from heaven. Her waters alone can cleanse these souls and deliver them from their pain. Pray to Prajapati Brahma. Only he can command Ganga to descend on earth.'

Sia looked at the river. This was where Rama had performed penance after killing Ravana. Where the Beatles had composed songs eternal like these waters. Where one drop of nectar slaked the thirst of millions. They had both tied sacred threads at Mansa Devi, asking her to grant their wishes. Coming down in the cable car, they watched the Ganga as it ran swiftly along its course.

As they trudged through the lanes of Haridwar, they knew this was sacred ground. Men and gods were neighbours in this city. Ascetics in saffron robes and smeared faces were everywhere – on the streets before them and the hoardings above them. Everything and everyone here promised salvation. Haridwar made Moksha easy. It said men can sin in their lives and then come here to be redeemed. Was everyone around them a sinner looking to buy forgiveness? Gods had also walked this place. Perhaps they still walked among these hundreds who came here in search of them.

Soon the pair reached Har Ki Pauri. Below them flowed the Ganga. The daughter of Brahma. The servant of Vishnu. The jewel of Shiva.

Sia looked at the vast expanse of water. 'There is something about the water here. It almost looks like milk.'

Patnaik smiled. 'It's said that the Ganga is milky white because thousands of moons shower their glow upon the river. She is forever youthful and fortunate but some texts predict that she will finally dry up at the end of Kali Yuga.'

The ghat was a floating mass of red and white stones. A giant image of Shiva watched over the river as if making sure that the Ganga he had trapped in his coiled hair, kept her word and flowed peacefully on earth. A stone footprint was embedded on a high wall on the ghat. Local lore proclaimed that it was Vishnu's foot and the waters of the Ganga washed it every day.

Patnaik walked down the steps. 'This is Brahmakund where the nectar is said to have fallen. It's also the precise spot where the Ganga leaves the Himalayas and enters the plains. This, Sia, is the "very first lower door".'

Men were pouring the remains of their loved ones into the waters. There was the grief of parting and the joy of sending them home. They had faith in the Ganga. Their dead were not alone. Some were filling bottles with the elixir. Others were wading deeper into its waters, washing their slates clean. Bathing in each other's dirt and drinking each other's boons. They were a million threads stitched to the winding blue sari of the Ganga. The river washed off their chaos and untied their knots. As the water encased them, they were born again, as innocent as newborns, out of her hallowed womb.

Sia laughed. The scriptures said that the river would die when its time came. She knew the constellation would keep the nectar alive. Her children were settling down on both sides of the ghat now. It was time to invoke the mother.

'Why do you seek what you seek?'

Both of them froze.

The one who spoke was one of the most venerated souls in Haridwar. He looked at men from banners everywhere, offering hope and calm. His ashram was a pilgrimage for many troubled hearts. He had come with his men to watch the aarti. But right now he was alone and pointing a finger at Patnaik.

'One will know nothing and one will know everything.'

He looked at Sia.

'One will know everything and one will know nothing.'

He was gone. They looked at each other's faces. The air resounded with the sounds of cymbals and conch shells. The Ganga Aarti had begun.

Mantras blared from a loudspeaker but the aarti was a human song of faith. Fire soaked in ghee soared high from three bowls. They were erupting like small volcanoes, the flames dancing in the air. As the flames swung up and down, their reflections fell on the river. Fire was burning water. Water was dousing fire. Suddenly hundreds of hands rose up in the air in a frenzy. The noise of the men and the river poured into each other.

At the end of the aarti, the pair walked down the steps. Lamps and marigold flowers were floating on the Ganga like so many stars of gold. They were guiding souls in the dark. As Sia released the yantra, the water bathed her skin. Her father lived in these waters. She wanted to touch him again.

He's holding my hand.

Sia looked. A human hand floating in the river. The dead fingers were clawing at her wrist. She pulled away in terror. She wanted to scream but the next instant her voice died in her throat.

'Om.' She pointed.

Patnaik saw it too.

'It's a yantra.'

'It's floating towards us. Towards us?'

'Yes. Look. Towards us. It is flowing against the current.'

'Against the current. Against the current of the Ganga? Is that even possible?'

Impossible! But there it was. The tiny robot was moving towards them against the river's flow. How? What gave this chunk of metal such power? The Ganga had become its playground. They watched as the tiny object cut its way against the mighty current and landed near their feet.

'Look.'

The holy man was standing in the waters. Did he? As they watched, he withdrew into the water.

Patnaik picked up the yantra. His own words were haunting him now.

Maybe we will see a miracle on the banks of the river.

Miracle had become a small word. Like Shiva, this toy had tamed the enormous Ganga. They looked at the mark.

Round Four was on.

44

*F*ive hours had flown by.

The pair had now moved to a secluded spot on the ghats. They sat with their feet dangling in the cold stream.

'I see why our dead long to be immersed in the Ganga,' Patnaik spoke. 'There is a peace in her pace. It lulls them to sleep. I would be glad to go into these waters when my time comes. Come back with another life and another purpose.'

He had seen it happening. The old yantra had served its purpose. The river had taken it and from somewhere beyond brought them a new one. The mark of nine now resembled the computer character 'at the rate of.' The bottom stroke went all the way up and around enclosing the digit in an incomplete circle.

He was looking at the river. Sia drew her feet out of the water. 'It must have been the old man.'

'These experiences will not explain their magic, Sia. I have no answers to write down. You will have to stop dissecting them.'

'If that was enough, we would still be living in caves, Om. Everything can be explained. Look at our ancestors. The ancients toying with nine sciences. They are like me. They wanted to know.'

'There's one thing I think I know. There's something good about this constellation. This nine touches me like a friend.'

'This one just ripped the Ganga.'

Patnaik held up the yantra. 'We'll see if it agrees with me.'

'Here?'

'It's dark now. This place is almost deserted. I want to finish it on these banks.'

He spoke the question and suddenly a tiny sun arose, bathing in the Ganga.

Up to the heavens it rises high among a heap of holy stones
Good fortune alone can help you trounce this arrogant ring
Son of the Shah with a lakh hands guided the headless shaft
Touch me like the sun shines on the tale of a navel god king

No one noticed this fiery ball. It had merged with the lamps and the stars on the river. Sia stuffed it inside her purse while Patnaik leaned over the riddle.

'A structure. A high rising structure that goes "up to the heavens".'

'Yes. Like a tall building.'

'"Heap of holy stones." What could that be?'

'Stones that are worshipped. A lingam is a holy stone.'

'There are many others. You have Rama Setu at Rameshwaram. The Adam's Bridge. That thirty-kilometre-long ridge of limestone rocks is believed to be built by Rama to reach Lanka. Those stones are also venerated.'

'Right but as far as I remember, there is no tall structure there. Could this be talking about the Stonehenge?'

'The Stonehenge is a circle of rocks. A possible prehistoric temple worshipped by the Druids but that's in England. The icons of the constellation are definitely confined within the country.'

'I didn't know the Stonehenge was a temple,' she exclaimed. 'In that case "holy stones" here could also be an ancient temple.'

Patnaik processed the idea. 'Maybe, but the riddle says "heap of holy stones"?

'What about Line Two?'

Good fortune alone can help you trounce this arrogant ring.

Patnaik shook his head. 'Difficult. Why "arrogant ring?" A ring denotes a circle. Is this structure circular?'

'A building that is tall and circular. Like a tower or pillar.' She looked animated now. 'Of course. Pillar. Remember the couplet we found. This must be another Ashoka pillar.'

'No, Sia. If it's an Ashoka Pillar, why use the word "arrogant"? Ashoka's pillars are anything but arrogant. They are the pourings of a man who was ashamed of what he did. Besides, this is a prateek for Alchemy. Stone pillars don't fit here. The third line also makes it quite clear that it's not talking about a Hindu ruler.'

Son of the Shah with a lakh hands guided the headless shaft.

'A "Shah". A Muslim ruler.'

'A "Shah with a lakh hands"? It could be a metaphor for a Hindu god with one lakh hands. So many of our gods believe in multi-tasking.' She giggled.

'I don't think it's a metaphor. It's mentioning an actual Muslim ruler.'

'What about this "headless shaft"?'

'Not sure. But "shaft" also means column or pillar. I think we can be quite sure now that we are looking at a tower.'

'Why "headless"?'

'It probably means the structure is incomplete. Or maybe ruined.'

Sia sighed. 'A tall headless pillar made by a Shah with one lakh hands? I wish Jasodhara was here.'

Patnaik continued to stare into space, mulling over the lines. A thought was struggling to break through the mists of oblivion.

A déjà vu. He greeted the last line.

Touch me like the sun shines on the tale of a navel god king.

'This is where the riddle is telling us what to do with the yantra. It has to be touched to the structure. That's weird.'

'I know. And what's a "navel god king"?'

He shook his head, his thoughts returning to the Shah again. He could almost feel the thought poking it's head now.

'What do you think this line means?'

'A "Shah with a lakh hands". Does it mean he had one lakh servants? Servants are sometimes called hands.'

'One lakh may also mean one lakh wives. Giving birth to one lakh children.'

'Or money. One lakh rupees. Or one lakh gold coins.'

Patnaik looked at the river, several thoughts whirling around in his head at the same time. The whirlpool was sucking him in. He reeled back.

Shah with a lakh hands... one lakh... lakh.

He read the riddle again. 'Yes. It does mean one lakh rupees after all.'

'Really?'

'I know who this Shah is. I know the pillar this verse is talking about. You did get two things right, Sia. It is an ancient temple or rather several ancient temples. And it is one lakh rupees.'

'Not bad. So who's the man?'

'Have you heard of the ruler Qutub-ud-Din Aibak?'

'Never.'

'Qutub-ud-Din Aibak was the first Muslim emperor of North India. He was the founder of the Delhi Sultanate, the first Muslim dynasty to rule India. The famous Razia Sultan was Aibak's grand daughter.'

'Charming bio data.'

'He is our "Shah with a lakh hands". Aibak was an exceedingly generous ruler. The man is famous in history for his extensive charities. Guess what he was affectionately called? Lakh Baksh.'

'What?'

'Lakh Baksh by his Muslim subjects and Lakh Annadata by his Hindu subjects. Both the names mean the giver of lakhs.'

'So that's the mystery of the one lakh hands.' She whistled. 'And he built this pillar?'

'It's actually a tower. A tower that rises "Up to the heavens" and stands among "a heap of holy stones". A tower which is the "arrogant ring". It is also a "headless shaft" that was guided by the Shah's son. A tower with the "tale of a navel god king" written on it.'

'Stop the torture. What's the name?'

Patnaik chuckled. 'The tower's name is in the Shah's name. Qutub-ud-Din Aibak.'

The answer exploded from her mouth. 'Qutub Minar.'

'Yes. The fourth prateek.'

'But how? Go line by line.'

'The Minar towers above earth at a height of more than two hundred feet. In fact Qutub is the world's tallest brick tower. The "heap of holy stones" refers to the old wrecked temples around the tower. Now I understand why the riddle used the word "heap". The temples are nothing but relics.'

'What temples are these?'

'Hindu and Jain temples of Lal Kot built by the Tomars and the Chauhans. They were the last Hindu rulers of Delhi. The complex originally had over twenty-seven temples. Just ruins now.'

Good fortune alone can help you trounce this arrogant ring.

'That explains itself now. The tower is circular. The word "arrogant" refers to its height. You really need "good fortune" to scale it. Many accidents have happened in the past with people trying to go up those medieval stairs. Climbing is permanently prohibited now.'

Son of the Shah with a lakh hands guided the headless shaft.

'You know about the "Shah" now. The interesting bit here is about his son. His name was Iltutmish. He was actually Aibak's son-in-law who replaced him. So the "son" actually means the successor. The riddle says that he "guided the headless shaft". It means that he took the construction of the Qutub Minar to its next stage.'

'Next stage?'

'Aibak had only completed the base before his untimely death. Iltutmish added three more floors to it. Get it? The Minar was a "headless shaft" since only the base had been completed. His son guided it further.'

Touch me like the sun shines on the tale of a navel god king.

'"Touch me like the sun." Beautiful.'

'This line says that when the sun shines on the Minar, it also shines on the story of this god king inscribed on the tower.'

'Some Muslim prophet?'

Patnaik smiled. 'He's actually a Hindu god.'

'A Hindu god on a Muslim tower?'

'Why not? A beautiful symbol of the synthesis of Hindu and Muslim thought. The Minar bears a Sanskrit inscription which says *Shri Vishwakarma prasade rachita*. It means the tower has been created by the grace of Lord Vishwakarma. He is your navel god.'

'How's Vishwakarma the "navel god king"?'

'According to Hindu mythology, Vishwakarma is the divine engineer of the universe. Lord Architect and ruler of all craftsmen of the three worlds. The Yajur Veda recounts that Viswakarma had created his divine work force himself. They all had emerged from his own body through a single opening.'

'His navel.'

'Exactly. The "navel god king".'

Sia exhaled. 'Wonderful. The Shah's name did the trick.'

Patnaik laughed. 'That is actually a little controversial.'

'What controversy?'

'While many historians believe that the Minar was named after Qutub-ud-Din Aibak, others argue that it was named to honour Qutubuddin Bakhtyar, a saint revered by Iltutmish. The exact purpose of building the Minar is also a mystery. It may be a mosque minaret to call for prayers or a watch tower for security.'

'Last question. How's Qutub Minar related to Alchemy?'

'Vishwakarma again. The divine manufacturer who works with metals. He's our traditional alchemist. It's perfect, Sia.'

She held his hand. 'Yes. You are perfect.'

Getting up they took one last look at the waters. It was said that the Ganga sobbed the loudest at Haridwar because she was leaving her home in the mountains.

Was the river laughing?

45

'What sights, Tathagata?'

The Samanera began to type on his laptop.

'We spoke at the library. The man told me about the Father of the Nation. I heard he had stayed awake one night, sitting with the Nine. His countrymen had been clamouring for answers and he had nothing to offer. But the Nine had lit a torch for him. Shown him what psychological war could achieve. He knew then. Insistence for truth. No violence. He had shown millions the path of passive resistance because this was a war of minds. Not hands, but hearts. The Father had laughed and said, they could throw him out of as many trains as they wished now.'

'Then I went to that facility with the boy. He was HIV positive. He knew how the virus had chewed millions alive. Defecated in their blood and turned their bodies into numbers. But the Nine had arrived in this facility long ago and brought ancient secrets of physiology. It was now cutting chains and setting them free. The doctors there broke the viral cycle inside the boy for a while. They said one day it was going to be forever. Next morning the boy left my hand and I threw his red ribbon in the dustbin.'

'Now I am sitting by the Ganga and reading about our own little pool in our sacred complex. It was all sand when I had left. Now you say there is water and it carries red lotuses. Using microbiology, the Nine has pulled colours out of the earth like those that had spilled from the Teacher's aura. The universe has become a wet canvas again.'

'Yes, Tathagata.' The Bhikku's words appeared on the screen. 'Religion and science hold hands all the time. They worship the same truth. Wonder at the same wonders.'

'I saw it in their eyes when they watched the yantra tearing Ganga down the middle, Bhante. Their faces were alight with wonder. They are aroused. They are afraid.'

'The Nine can sometimes overpower you. Do Patnaik and Sia recognise the journey yet?'

'The course has begun. They are jumping fences and breaking rules.'

'They have the end in mind. We are all similar. We all need to begin with the end now. Find a new beginning.'

'Will I attain mine, Bhante?'

'If the Teacher could, so can you. We have done this before. We can do it again.'

He saw the man's last words.

'We are all Buddha.'

46

*H*e stepped into the silence.

No cameras or microphones. No videos or photographs. Only Suri looking at the floor.

'So the wandering spirit returns?'

Alia was standing at the door.

'What spirit?'

'You. Haunting the place where you were murdered most foul two days ago. Well, almost.'

She knelt over the floor. 'At least this one's convenient. Your men don't have to run around. "Where's the crime scene? Right across the hall, officer". She giggled. 'Your spot, Suri. The martyr's corner. No chalk ring but they can put up your bust.'

'Have I told you how much I hate that grin of yours?'

'Really? Have you been staring at my mouth?' Alia's smile widened.

The man blushed. 'Makes me want to knock it off your face.'

'I love baring my dentals. They keep danger away. In my profession, we have to look out for everything.' She opened her purse and took out something.

'What's that?'

'Your gift. A little bug you slipped into my bag during our

rendezvous that night. I found it this morning. Looks like a tiny microphone to me.'

He did not protest.

'I see you don't trust anyone easily.'

Suri walked towards a chair and sat down. 'We also need to look out, Miss Irani. Trust is not an easy thing. Certainly not in a matter like this.'

'So what's the verdict?'

'Your movements were clear.'

'Good. Any clue to the Scorpion?'

'Nothing. He could have been anyone in that crowd. I wonder how he got away.'

'He had obviously planned everything. The confusion only helped his cause. The man's getting bolder Suri. He walked right into your police station.'

Two officers entered with details of their inquiries. The report did not interest her. She walked over to the large glass table at the other end. Copies of the press release were lying in a heap. Alia read the text.

People really lie at press cons.

She flung them down. Something else had grabbed her attention.

Press cards.

She picked up the stack and went through it.

'What's that?' Suri asked.

'An idea.'

'Press cards?'

'The Scorpion came as a fake journo.'

'So?'

'He must have carried a phony card.'

The officer got up. Alia was reading out the names.

'So Trivedi was here.'

'Who?'

'My J-School batch mate. One foul bitch she was.'

Suri coughed. 'Your memories are enchanting but we have no time for nostalgia. Give me something else.'

The stack was getting smaller. Alia was throwing them on the table like playing cards.

'Dibakar Ghosh?'

'A lover who dumped you?'

She was silent. Then she turned. 'I need to access the Net. Right now.'

The next minute she was sitting before a computer, keying in words at a frantic pace. Suri saw her eyes. They were glued to the monitor, searching furiously.

For what?

'The Scorpion.' Alia waved the card in his face.

Suri yanked it out of her hand. 'You think he's the one?'

'I don't think. I know.'

'Reasons?'

'Look at the newspaper's name.'

'UP Express. Never heard of it. You are right. Fucking fake.'

'No. No. It's quite real.'

'Is it?'

'Yes. Lousy but real. The funny bit is that the paper shut shop in 2008.'

The man looked at the dull yellow pages. 'Really?'

'That's what I was verifying. It was the recession. Wiped it off the market. Dibakar worked for them. I have met him many times on shoots. He's gone into publishing now.'

'Where did the killer get this bloody card?'

'He obviously sourced it through his contacts. It was his masterkey to enter the press con. He is using Dibakar's identity.'

Suri smirked. 'You are good, Irani.'

'Yes. A birth defect.'

He turned towards his men. 'Get the register. He must have signed at the entrance.'

Moments later a Mrs Bajpai was standing in the room with her register and bifocal glasses. The duo scanned the pages. It did not take long. The name Dibakar Ghosh stood out in red among all the other blue entries. The officer looked at Mrs Bajpai.

'Do you remember this man?'

The lady shook her head. 'No, sir. I didn't see their faces. People signed and walked in.'

'You don't look at men, Mrs Bajpai?' The scorn in Alia's voice left little to the imagination.

Before the virtuous woman could eat Alia alive, Suri intervened. 'Thank you. You may go.'

'I am sorry, sir. I wish I had seen them.'

'There's always a next time,' Alia sneered. 'Use those bifocals, woman.'

Suri glared at Alia. 'No problem, Mrs Bajpai.' He opened the door.

'He was the only man who signed in red, sir.'

'Yes. I see that. Thank you.'

He dropped into a chair. He had been close again. So close.

He looked up. 'Yes. So fucking close.'

Bajpai was back in the room. 'Of course I saw the napkin in his hand.'

'Napkin?'

'He was sneezing. Must be a cold. It was all crumpled up, with the initials PG embroidered on it.'

The man nodded. 'Very good. Go have some tea and...'

He never finished. Alia had seized Bajpai's arms most indecently. 'PG? PG?'

'Yes.'

'Are you sure? Saw them with your bifocals?'

The woman pressed her hand over her heaving breasts. 'Yes. PG.'

'What's going on?' Suri exploded.

Alia did not speak. She opened her purse and took out a napkin. There were two letters printed on it.

PG.

$\mathscr{T}$he car was whizzing through Varanasi now. The officer clicked his tongue.

'Such a petty thing, pinching hotel stuff.'

'Shut up, Suri. See how it's saving your ass now.'

'So this PG is the logo of the Palace on Ganges hotel?'

'Yes. That's where I am putting up. And he was there. He was there all this while.'

'I am going to drag that fucker by his ear.'

'But the press con was two days ago. He has surely fled the scene.'

'I'll take a chance. We will at least get a description.'

Alia nodded. They had nothing so far.

A description would be good.

She looked behind the car. 'How many coming with us?'

'Four. It's a hotel. Lesser the better. '

The small lobby of the Palace on Ganges was a picture postcard of oriental décor. The art pieces were pretty but looked perpetually terrified of the huge chandeliers hanging over their heads. The pair marched up to the front desk.

'Ask for Dibakar Ghosh,' Alia whispered.

'I know.' Suri nodded at the man in square glasses behind the counter. 'Excuse me. We are looking for Mr Dibakar Ghosh.'

'Mr Ghosh. He's in Sanchi.'

Suri's face slumped. *Missed him.*

'He has left then?'

'No, sir. Sanchi Suite.'

'Sanchi Suite?'

'Our rooms here are dedicated to twenty-one cultural themes of India. He's in the Sanchi room. First floor. But he's checking out today.'

The officer slowly spun towards Alia. His face had changed.

The Scorpion is still here. Still here.

Suri placed his card on the counter. 'This is a police matter. This man is a criminal. We are here to arrest him.'

The man looked at the officer and his men. 'Is there a threat? Should we evacuate the guests?'

'No. That will alert him. I will place one man at the entrance. The rest of us will go to his room. Don't let him check out.'

The next minute the team was walking through the corridors. They passed passages lined with antiques; on the walls were framed black and white photographs of Indian luminaries but no one was looking.

'The man's getting closer, Suri,' Alia mumbled. 'Sanchi Suite is right across my room. Next he'll be shagging on my bed.'

When they reached the suite, they found the door ajar.

Suri and company locked their revolvers. Asking Alia to wait in the gallery, they stepped inside. The walls were seeped in earthy tones and pictures of the Sanchi Stupa hung above the bed. The room was empty.

Empty like it had been that Friday...

Suddenly the bathroom door creaked.

Instantly a shot rang out. The bullet sprang and lodged itself in the door. Suri's weapon was fuming.

'Come out.'

It was a man. He was holding a bed sheet. Four revolvers pointed at him instantly.

'Please, sir. I work here, sir.'

'Don't move.'

'Housekeeping, sir.'

Sia entered the suite. She looked at the man and then at Suri. They were asking each other the same question.

Is this the Scorpion?

The officer touched the revolver to the man's head when a woman entered. She was carrying fresh pillow covers which dropped from her hand at the sight in the room.

'You know this man?' Suri barked.

'Yes, sir. Housekeeping for three years. Both of us.'

Sia looked around. 'Dibakar Ghosh. Where is he?'

'He just left the room,' she said. 'He is checking out. Very strange man.'

'Strange?'

'He carries a box full of syringes. Ten or twenty of them.'

The five turned on their heels. They were tearing down towards the lobby now. Suri was the first to reach the desk.

'Was Dibakar here?'

'Yes, officer. Wanted to check out but I have deliberately stalled him with our special lunch menu. He has gone to the rooftop cafe.'

Suri called the officer standing at the entrance. The six of them reached the restaurant in less than a minute. People were finishing their lunch.

Which one is the Scorpion?

Alia stopped a waiter. 'Who is Dibakar Ghosh? Sanchi Suite.'

'He has left. Said he was checking out.'

The men looked at each other in rage. What was the Scorpion up to? Moments later they were at the reception again. A woman was standing behind it now.

'Dibakar Ghosh?'

'He checked out. A minute ago.'

The four men sprinted towards the exit while Suri banged his fist on the counter. 'But I told your colleague to stall him as long as he could.'

'I am sorry, sir. I had left the counter for a while. Some problem in the kitchen.' She frowned. 'Did you say my colleague?'

'Yes. The man standing here. Black and red jacket. Glasses.'

'Square glasses?'

'Exactly.'

'That was Mr Dibakar. He was waiting for me over here.'

That was Mr Dibakar.

The Scorpion.

Sia clutched Suri's hand.

'Look.'

A pair of glasses, on the counter.

And a syringe marked 'SURI'.

48

*H*e picked it up.

'Gold coin in her palm?'

'Yes, sire.'

'Who put it there?'

'Nobody, sire. No, I lie. Surely it was Buddha.'

The Emperor was trailing behind the midwife in a daze. The whole palace was bursting with joy. One of the queens had finally borne him a girl. A daughter had walked into his life after many sons. But she was not alone. They said she was carrying a mohur in her fist.

'Here, sire.'

The midwife pried opened the tiny pink fingers. Nestled like a bee inside a lotus was a gold coin.

'Watch this, lord.'

The woman removed the coin and the Emperor gasped. Another piece of gold had appeared in its place. The miracle had no end. Every time they picked up a coin, another mohur appeared on her palm.

He turned towards the Bhikkhu. 'Who is she?'

'A consecrated being. She was a servant girl in her past life but she offered her only coin to the Sangha. The Buddha is only paying her back.'

The Emperor gazed out of the window. Years ago he had walked through hills and valleys alone seeking what his grandfather had cast away. For days he had trampled rivers and ravines searching for that metal. He had finally found it, gleaming like the moon under a moonless sky. Carrying his treasure, he had returned to the cave where his books were waiting. The fire had burnt all night long. The flames had leapt up and he had fed them nine offerings as the texts prescribed. In the end, he had offered them his grandfather's sword. When the sun rose, it saw the man sitting in an aura more gilded than the sun.

Walking back towards his daughter, he spoke. 'Distribute every mohur that's born in her hand among my people.'

The Emperor placed a silver coin in her fist. The next moment the bee in the lotus had a body of gold.

49

$\mathcal{T}$he stone was glinting like sunshine.

UNESCO WORLD HERITAGE SITE

Places deemed as cultural or natural heritage fought for a place on this prestigious list regularly drawn by the UNESCO. Over nine hundred spots and monuments across the world had been branded as common legacies of humanity. In India, thirty sites had been handpicked for preservation so far. Patnaik and Sia were standing at one of them.

The Qutub Complex.

While the Minar was the obvious *piece de resistence*, it was surrounded by a number of smaller gems. The blue boards of the ASI informed visitors in two languages that these ruins had been added by Tughlaq and Khilji rulers. One of them beckoned Patnaik. He had seen Mathur caressing it wih love. Today he touched the head of Alai Minar looking for those fingers on the stone.

'This is Khilji's Tower of Babel, Sia. He wanted to build a mammoth tower that would rise two times higher than the Qutub. But the man passed away shortly after the first storey was built and further construction was permanently abandoned. See how embarrassed this block of rubble looks.'

Sia was looking at the lonely Alai mound. It stood like an open wound that had not healed over centuries. A stump that never became a limb.

'Don't scoff at the man, Om. Say that he dared to dream. What is life without an awkward dream? But if you dream, you must have the courage to achieve it at any cost. These stones are embarrassed of their creator who betrayed his own vision. If it was possible for them, they would rise up and soar higher than the Qutub.'

'Not bad. Maybe you should write my next book with me.'

Laughing loudly they turned to the Minar. The tower rose over all other structures with an easy arrogance. A height of over two hundred feet made it the tallest brick structure in the world.

'Quite a bit of phallus, isn't it?'

They knew the voice. Jasodhara was standing behind them.

'So you made it after all,' Patnaik beamed.

Sia clasped her hand. 'I heard you. What was that about the phallus?'

The woman smirked. 'Why do men build towers and sky scrapers? To prove their manhood. Their need to be the Alpha male. It's the inborn masculine psyche which made rulers in the past build towers to celebrate triumphs. Towers because they are phallic structures. It was a way of leaving behind a marker for future generations. A symbol of machismo that announced "I screwed this place".'

Sia chuckled.

'Look at all the skyscrapers in the world. Leaning Tower, Eiffel Tower, Empire State Building, CN Tower, Burj Kahlifa. Nothing but stone and metal phalluses by men desperately trying to prove they are men. Look at Alai Minar. Khilji also tried to prove he was a bigger man by trying to build a bigger tower. This race will go on forever. Size does matter you see.'

Patnaik put his palms over Sia's ears. 'What hogwash! A tall structure symbolises man's soaring aspiration. An ambition to achieve greater nobility and perfection. A tower denotes the peak of evolution. It's a human effort to rise above the ordinary and come closer to God.'

Jasodhara shrugged. 'Whatever makes you happy. But boys will be boys. They all fly high before crashing to earth.'

They had moved closer to the Minar. The cylindrical shaft of fluted sandstone was covered with the famous reed-like columns making the tower look like a bundle of multi-coloured sticks. Kufic and Thuluth calligraphy was scrawled all over, like medieval graffiti. The temples around it were nothing more than scattered jigsaw pieces that can never be put together.

'I love how you solved this riddle,' Jasodhara smiled. 'We are almost midway through our quest now. Be very careful. The constellation is crafty and your riddles will start getting harder. You both have to look out for hidden pranks.'

They watched as Patnaik took out the yantra and touched it to the base of the tower. Nothing happened.

He touched it again. He rubbed the bronze against the brick. He encircled the tower touching the robot randomly all over the base. He turned the yantra over and touched each part to the Minar.

Nothing.

Sia yanked the robot from his hand and scraped it against the tower violently. The next moment she hurled it to the ground in anger.

'Stop it, Sia.' Jasodhara picked it up.

'We are doing something wrong. I think the last line means that the yantra must touch the Minar when the sun shines at a particular time. Maybe a place where the sun rays fall or where the words about Vishwakarma are inscribed.'

Patnaik shook his head in alarm. 'That's impossible. Entry to the

Minar has been barred since the eighties. There is no way we can climb to the top. The constellation cannot ask us to do something impossible.'

They fell down on the stones. Jasodhara was glaring at the tower.

What's wrong?

She took the pad and disappeared from sight. Minutes later they saw her coming back. 'You want to know why nothing is happening?'

Patnaik disposed the gold chocolate wrapper in his hands. 'Tell us. Are we touching the yantra the wrong way?'

'You are touching it the right way. You are simply touching it to the wrong structure.'

'What are you saying?' they asked in unison.

'I told you to be careful. You have made an error, Patnaik.'

She touched the brick tower.

'Qutub Minar is not the fourth prateek of the constellation.'

Her words punctured their hearts like bullets.

Qutub Minar is not the fourth prateek.

Patnaik charged at the woman. 'Are you crazy? I went through that damned riddle a hundred times. I can't be wrong. Each answer fits perfectly...'

He rattled on. Jasodhara stood watching him. She knew everything the man was saying was right. But she also knew that everything he was saying was wrong. The constellation had conned them. She had always admired its genius. Not today.

This riddle is inhuman.

Then she shuddered. Another thought struck her hard.

It's not the constellation. We made the wrong choice.

She had held the verse and walked away. Her sixty-three-year-old mind was running through that deserted maze of stones.

Where is the catch?

Then she had seen it. It had appeared out of nowhere as if it had been hiding in the dark to ambush her. She looked at the first line. Then the second line. Then the third and the fourth.

My God! We have been such fools.

She had felt a thrill creeping up her skin. Then she shrank.

It's laughing at me.

It was holding its sides and laughing so hard. No. It was someone else. She looked up. It was the Qutub. The tower's bricks seemed to mock her too. But it wasn't the Minar. It was the decaying temples. They were cackling at her ruin. Wait. Not them. It was actually the constellation rolling on the ground with its feet up in the air. Jasodhara felt a wrath mounting within. And then slowly she had also laughed.

Not the Qutub.

'Listen, Patnaik. You haven't made any mistake. Everything you said fits and yet Qutub is not the answer. That's the trick here. These lines of the riddle also point to a second structure. That is the correct prateek.'

Sia and Patnaik stared. 'Another structure? How can one riddle point to two structures?'

'This one does. The verse describes two structures simultaneously. One is right and the other is wrong.' She handed him the notepad. 'This riddle has been written in double entendres.'

Patnaik gasped. *Double entendres.* 'You mean double meanings?'

'Exactly. The lines have been so perfectly worded that they talk about two completely different monuments at the same time.'

'But why? Why would they do it?' asked Sia, bewildered.

Jasodhara smiled. 'I told you the climb will be steadily uphill. There will be far worse codes awaiting us ahead.'

Patnaik was glaring at the yantra. He remembered what he had said about the nine being something good, as he had sat with Sia by the Ganga. His voice turned frail. 'I was too complacent. Too confident. I should have emptied my mind first.' He looked up. 'I am sorry, Sia.'

'What is the right prateek, Jasodhara? Where do we go?'

'Nowhere. The answer is right here.'

'Here?'

'You are sitting near the wrong symbol. But you are in the right place.'

They got up. 'The icon is in the complex?'

They followed her in the dark. Which one was it? The woman stopped.

'There.'

They looked. And suddenly the first line of the riddle seemed to become even more clear.

Up to the heavens it rises high among a heap of holy stones.

Now that they thought of it, the line had always been pointing at this. They knew that the rest would also fall into place. It looked almost sensuous in the moonlight. Jasodhara walked up to it again. 'The Iron Pillar. The constellation's tribute to Alchemy.'

The twenty-feet tall pillar erected in the times of Chandragupta Vikramaditya was indeed a metallurgical miracle of the ancients. Despite standing for a thousand odd years, the surface was still free of rust. Believed to be composed of ninety-eight percent pure iron, some said a high amount of phosphorous had also been used to create a protective film. The pillar wanted men to wonder. How had they created it? What was the magic in the metal? Like the previous three icons, this prateek also symbolised the eternity inside man. It told him to lift his head and become greater than great.

Sia was reading the riddle. 'The first line is clear. Like the Minar, the Iron Pillar is also a very tall structure and it's surrounded by the same temple ruins.'

They nodded.

Good fortune alone can help you trounce this arrogant ring.

'I don't understand this one. How does it fit?'

Patnaik was smiling. 'Of course it fits. It totally fits.' He touched the iron fence circling the pillar. 'This fence was built around the structure in 1997 to prevent damage. Before that people could touch the iron surface. Have you ever done that?'

'Many times. I loved touching my cheeks against it as a child. The metal felt deliciously cold. I have even tried standing with my back to the pillar and making my hands meet. Everyone would do that here. If your hands touched each other, it meant that you had good fortune.'

She paused.

Good fortune!

'Yes, Sia. That's exactly what the line is describing. That was how you trounced this "arrogant ring". Arrogance here is not the height. It's the width of the pillar.'

She closed her eyes. The constellation was beginning to seem more and more ingenious now.

Son of the Shah with a lakh hands guided the headless shaft.

Jasodhara took over. 'The Shah is still Aibak and the son is Iltutmish. The rest of the line has a different meaning. Few people know that Delhi was not the original location of the pillar. It had been initially erected in a temple complex at Udaygiri in modern Madhya Pradesh. The pillar was brought to this present complex by Iltutmish. That's the answer. He "guided" the pillar to its current address.'

'Why "headless shaft"?'

'There is a huge socket-like depression at the top of the pillar. It's possible that there was an image there in earlier times. Some believe it to be a missing statue of Garuda, Vishnu's divine carrier.'

'And the last one?'

'The "navel god king" is Vishnu. The Iron Pillar bears a Sanskrit inscription which declares that it was erected as Vishnudhwaja or the Pillar of Vishnu. He is the navel god because if you read our scriptures, they will tell you that Vishnu had created Brahma out of his navel.'

Patnaik sighed. 'So the sun shines on the tale of Vishnu.'

'Not only that,' Jasodhara laughed. 'The constellation knows its history quite well. This phrase carries another meaning.'

'What meaning?'

'Not many know that the Iron Pillar was used as a sundial once.'

'A sundial?'

'Yes. It's original location at Udaygiri is centred exactly on the Tropic of Cancer.'

'Beautiful,' Sia beamed. 'I love sundials.'

They looked at the riddle again. Each word was dipped in deceit. Each line had been a truth and a lie. A trap within a trap. They had rejoiced by the Ganga and not heard the verse snickering behind their backs.

'This one reminds me of that optical illusion that hides both a young girl and an old woman.' Patnaik exhaled. 'Thank god for Jasodhara. She saved our asses in time.'

Jasodhara smiled. 'Finish it now.'

Patnaik was already stretching himself over the fence. His right hand, that carried the yantra, was trying to make contact with the pillar. Suddenly the bronze head flew out of his hand and latched on to the iron surface with a metallic clink.

'Magnet,' he hissed. 'Obviously a magnet inside. I think...'

He spoke no more. Nobody did. They were watching what was happening before them.

The yantra was on fire. It had become a livid inferno of orange. They were seeing a furious bulb of light blazing on the pillar. The heat was blistering their faces but they looked on. They were terrified that the flames would melt the metal and burn that wonder. But then the Iron Pillar turned incandescent. It shimmered blood red like a charged electrode hiding a coil of spring. The glare kept burning and crackling for another minute. Then the furnace dimmed and died.

The yantra was still clinging to the pillar. It detached and fell to the ground near the rim of the fence. Patnaik picked it up and dropped it.

'Is it hot?'

'Very.' He glanced at the seething metal. 'A new nine. It's the fifth one.'

Sia was staring at the robot in fear. 'What just happened?'

'Don't ask me. I don't know anymore.'

'I can make a guess,' Jasodhara said. 'What we saw was most probably a bizarre instance of alchemy. If you remember, one of its wonders is that you can transform one metal into another. What happened here was a similar transmutation. When the old yantra touched the pillar, it converted into the new robot.'

Sia grinned. 'That's too absurd.'

'You saw what happened, Sia. Do you have another explanation?'

'No. But one robot turning into another is too much.'

'Tell that to the constellation when you reach it. The transfiguration just happened before your eyes. These are wonders of a technology we have never seen, Sia. Wonders that can tear through the Ganga.'

Patnaik, however, was hearing another voice. Another man reminding him of something.

Just card tricks of Nature.

Sia picked up the bronze head. The mark of nine was now beginning to look like a rough modern nine. She spoke the password and the head dazzled for a second time. But this was the tender glow they loved to love. It spouted the lines.

'Did you get them?'

Jasodhara had just finished writing. She frowned.

Strange.

'What is it?'

'Something odd here.'

They looked at her. *Odd?*

The woman was shaking her head.

Patnaik grabbed the notepad from her hand and read the lines out aloud.

I wish to be the hatchet where the lion and dragon still fight
The god of that surreal pure land looks on at them in shame
You see it as you walk by the blue yogi god's wet high abode
Thirty-four circles to sky and seventy-nine circles to dawn will speak the name

'It's the last line. It's way longer than the other three. That's never happened before. The lines have always been the same.'

Sia looked at Jasodhara. 'Perhaps we didn't hear the words properly.'

'You think the hag goofed up?'

Sia turned red but Jasodhara was laughing. She asked Patnaik for the yantra and spoke the question again. The verse was exactly the same.

'I think it's no big deal. Maybe that's how this riddle is supposed to look,' he shrugged.

But Jasodhara didn't look so sure. So far all the verses had displayed the same equilibrium. She knew what they did not know.

The constellation believes in balance and proportion. This is sloppy.

Sia laughed. 'The yantra is talking to us right away in line one. It wants to be "the hatchet". What does that mean?'

'A hatchet can be interpreted in many ways. What's intriguing me are the "lion and dragon",' Jasodhara said.

'This "blue yogi" god could be Vishnu or Rama. Their pictures always show them with blue skin.'

'No, Sia,' the writer shook a finger. 'There is another word sandwiched there. That reveals who the god actually is.'

'You mean "yogi"?'

'Yes. Shiva alone is the eternal yogi. The god with matted hair and rudraksha malas. The one who sleeps in cremation grounds and smears ashes over his body. Even his father-in-law Daksha called him a naked yogi who meditates in caves and stays high on grass.'

'But Shiva is never blue.'

'Not even after the Samudra Manthan?'

Sia berated herself silently. Shiva was the Neelkantha.

'His "high abode" would mean a shrine on a hill or mountain. Like the Amarnath Cave in Srinagar. The "wet" could be the annual ice formation there that resembles a lingam. It could also be Kedarnath in the Himalayas or Tunganath Temple in Gharwal. That's the highest shrine of Shiva in the world,' Patnaik chipped in.

Jasodhara cut him short. 'None of these temples.'

'Why not?'

'See this line. It refers to his form as a yogi. These temples worship Shiva through his various symbols. We need an abode where he is represented as a yogi.'

'I don't know any such temple.'

The woman squared her arms. 'Why are you so sure that it's a temple?'

'It says "high abode".'

'What does the word "abode" mean? A temple?'

'Of course not. It means home or a dwelling place.'

'Perfect. Just go with that.'

Patnaik was stunned. 'The abode of Shiva. His home?'

'Yes. Shiva is believed to live on top of a mountain. I am sure you know which one.'

Patnaik gasped. 'Mount Kailash? The "high abode" here is Kailash Parvat?'

'Of course. Home of the yogi.'

'What about "wet"?' Sia interjected, 'Can you explain the wetness?'

'I can. Mount Kailash lies near the source of three of the greatest rivers of India. The Indus, Sutlej and Brahmaputra. It's also located near the sacred Mansarovar Lake. The word "wet" describes the mountain's proximity to these water bodies.'

Sia was intrigued and suddenly terrified. Patnaik knew what she was thinking. He had also realised it.

The fifth prateek was somewhere in the Himalayas.

She shivered. 'So, we have to climb Mount Kailash now?'

'No one climbs Mount Kailash,' Patnaik spoke up, 'It's off-limits due to its religious significance. In fact, the mountain is also revered in Buddhism, Jainism and the Tibetan tradition of Bon. But Kailash is not our destination. The line clearly says that "you see it as you walk by". That means the mountain is situated on the way to the prateek. It's only an indicator.'

Jasodhara nodded. 'But if the icon is near Kailash, that still means you will be getting somewhere close to the Tibet border.'

Patnaik suddenly seized the notepad. The next instant he was quivering with excitement.

'That's what it means.'

'What?'

'The lion and the dragon. I have trapped them. Let me

ask you a question. What is the most prized piece at Sarnath Museum?'

'Ashoka's Lion Capital,' replied Sia.

'Perfect. What's the significance of the Capital?'

'It's our national emblem. Where are you going with this?'

He thrust the page into their faces. One word had been encircled.

'Lion.'

They gasped.

Lion. Our emblem.

'Lion here means India.'

He nodded vigorously. 'So the dragon stands for....'

'China,' Jasodhara whispered. 'It's talking about the Indo-China border.'

They looked again. It was right before their eyes.

I wish to be the hatchet where the lion and dragon still fight.

'Historically the dragon is a symbol of the Chinese emperor. The imperial Chinese throne was called the Dragon Throne. It's also one of the animals in the Chinese Zodiac.'

'Not just that, Patnaik,' Jasodhara spoke. 'The dragon is actually associated with the number nine in China.'

'Nine?'

'Yes. A Chinese dragon is said to have nine qualities and nine forms. It has 117 scales on its body which add up to nine. And it always has nine children.'

'Not bad. The constellation loves mythology.'

'And Indo-China politics.' Sia was reading the line. 'Aksai Chin and Arunachal Pradesh continue to be disputed sectors. The issue of Tibet also remains sore with the Dalai Lama seeking refuge in India. The lion and the dragon have still not given up clawing at each other.'

'So we now know what to do with the yantra. It's practically screaming at you.'

'Yes, Om. It wants to be the "hatchet". You always bury the hatchet to end a conflict. It wants us to bury it along the Indo-China border. Like a peace offering.'

'Perfect!'

'But where exactly?'

They were quiet again. They still did not know the actual prateek. While the fringes of the riddle were now illuminated, the core still remained dark.

'Is line two giving us the location? Do we bury it in this "pure land"?'

Jasodhara smiled. 'No, Patnaik. The "pure land" means something else.'

They looked at her in wonder. 'Have you solved that too?'

'I have now. The Indo-China border and the reference to Tibet have made it clear. But this is still not the prateek. It's just another indicator, like the Kailash Parvat.'

'Shoot.'

'This "pure land" is Shambhala.'

'Shambhala?'

'It's a mythical kingdom described in Tibetan Buddhist texts. The place is said to exist somewhere in central Asia near Tibet. Many claim it lies in the core of the Himalayas. They describe it as a land blessed by Buddha where all inhabitants are enlightened men.'

'A mythical land?'

'Yes. Mythical because the land has both geographical and spiritual existence. It lies both outside and within us. Only men with good in them can find this pure land. The idea of Shambhala was first circulated in the West by people like Madame Blavatsky of the Theosophical Society. Westerners have since been fascinated with this mystical kingdom. In fact, the German Nazis even sent explorers in the 1930s to try and locate the land. I remember doing a special episode called *Shambhala's Secret*.'

'So this "god" in the riddle is Buddha?'

'Not necessarily. It may be him. It may even be you. Your morality. Your own inner landscape and its sense of right and wrong. As I said, Shambhala is also the space within your mind and heart. A room within your conciousness. The line says "surreal". This god is anything and everything that is good. It looks at evil like the Indo-China clash and hangs its head in shame.'

Patnaik listened, mesmerised. 'What a divine idea. That can be my next book. An Ode to Shambhala.'

Sia made a face. 'Later. Right now three lines have been explained and we still don't know the prateek. That's never happened before.'

Jasodhara was already looking at the final line. The anomaly again. Her unease returned. Why was this line longer than the rest?

Thirty-four circles to sky and seventy-nine circles to dawn will speak the name.

She started rewriting the line. She used all forms of contraction to shorten it down. It was no good. The line kept bobbing up like a coil of spring.

And then it struck her.

What if... ?

She looked again.

Could it be?

She opened a fresh page and rewrote the verse. Then she scribbled the last line. She looked at what she had done.

This is how they want it. Like this.

The fourth line no longer flew ahead of the rest. She had clipped its wings. They saw what she had done to tame it.

It was perfect.

All four lines were now beautifully aligned.

I wish to be the hatchet where the lion and dragon still fight
The god of that surreal pure land looks on at them in shame
You see it as you walk by the blue yogi god's wet high abode
34 circles to sky and 79 circles to dawn will speak the name

Patnaik murmured in ecstasy, 'You were right, Jasodhara. Damn right.'

'I made the mistake because we were hearing and writing. There was no way to know that these two numbers had to be written as figures.'

Sia shook her head. 'This riddle is turning out to be something else.'

'It only means you are getting closer. You can feel the heat now. It will singe your skin more as you reach the end.'

'There must be a reason why they are in figures and not in words,' Patnaik said. All three of them were poring over the line in their heads. Then Sia stirred.

'I have an idea. When do words follow numbers?'

'When they are units.'

'Right. So these "circles" may also be units of measurement.'

Jasodhara shook her head. 'I have never heard of a circle as a unit. It says so many circles "to sky" and so many "to dawn". That sounds like a measurement for distance.'

'The line mentions "sky" and "dawn". The sky is above us, illuminated or darkened by the presence or absence of the sun. Dawn is the time when the sun is slowly beginning to creep over the horizon, or the sky. But the sky is not a solid thing. There's nothing up there. Nothing to measure. Wait a minute!'

She had closed her eyes. Her forehead wrinkled.

'No one measures the sky. Any such measurement actually refers to corresponding dimensions on the earth.'

They were listening.

'The sky is right above. That indicates north. Dawn occurs when the sun rises. The east. 34 circles to the north. 79 circles to the east. Do you get it? Coordinates.'

Jasodhara came closer. 'Coordinates. That means the circles refer to…'

'Degrees,' Patnaik chimed.

'Yes. 34 degrees to the North. 79 degrees to the East. A degree symbol is nothing but a tiny circle. These are latitudes and longitudes.'

The revelation left them stunned. Patnaik grabbed Sia's hand.

'Look what you have done. You have peeled the core. We only need to plot these coordinates now and that will "speak the name".'

Jasodhara had already taken out her mobile and logged on to Google maps. As she fed the coordinates, the others waited. It took only three seconds.

'What is it?' Patnaik asked impatiently.

'Never heard of it. It's a weird name.'

'Will you tell us?'

'Konga….Kongla…Kongka La.'

Patnaik gaped as if she was a Martian. 'What did you say?'

'Kongka La.'

He snatched the cellphone to take a look himself.

'You know this place, Om? Does it have anything to do with extraterrestrial communication?'

The man laughed.

Anything? It has everything to do with that.

'Will you speak?'

The writer looked at them. 'Kongka La is a ridge pass. It lies next to Ladakh on the Indo-China border, at the Line of Actual Control. An extremely sensitive zone.'

'And?'

'The pass is said to be heavily patrolled on both sides of the border. The obvious reason given is the political tension, but there are rumours. Dangerous rumours. They whisper that there is a totally different reason why the pass is so zealously guarded. A fantastic rationale that borders on the paranormal.'

Both the women were on the edge of their seats now. He let it out gently.

'Kongka La is rumored to be a secret underground base for UFOs.'

Jasodhara and Sia pounced upon him instantly, but Patnaik kept shaking his head.

'Not now. We will talk on the trek. It's going to be a long one.'

Jasodhara laughed. 'I am out of this one too.'

'Again?'

'I am past the age of hiking through mountains, Patnaik. Besides, you don't need me all the time. Go and come back with the new robot. We will meet again.'

She extended her hand towards Sia.

'Go on. And see if you can bring me an alien or two. '

52

*M*en could be so desperate.

Jasodhara was quiet. She had seen Patnaik sprinting about holding a hairpin in his hand. She was now seeing this one. Another giant Q searching frantically for an A. His voice was trying to break through her mental barriers in its search for answers. She knew she could show him all the light he wanted. Would he be able to see?

Suri's temper was near boiling point. Mathur's mark had still not been deciphered. He had lost the ear print. Then he had lost the man. He had sat through the press con like a live dart board with the killer taking a direct shot at him. Now Sia and Patnaik had vanished. His doctor was already worried that the case had knocked five years off his life. Could this woman get them back?

Alia was watching them. She had been spying around for keyholes but the story had turned cold. Even the Scorpion had retreated deeper into his hole. Now news of the missing pair had thrilled her. She had tagged along with Suri to the producer's house. He said she will speak but the old woman was shaking her head. What was she hiding?

'Do you know that you are the last person they saw before disappearing from Sarnath?' Suri snarled.

'Officer!' Jasodhara looked scandalised. 'You should use your words carefully. I just felt the noose around my neck.'

'Things can get worse than that. This case is turning bizarre, just like that symbol on the old man's face. It's making no sense. My brain's all screwed up and that can turn me really unkind.'

Jasodhara heard the misery in his voice. And the menace.

'Your silence won't help anyone. Tell us what you know. My friend here is a journalist. She is with me on this case.'

Jasodhara felt a sudden urge. The burden on this man had become too much. She wanted to share it. Offer her shoulder and tell him it was all good. She fought it off.

'I wish I could, Mr Suri. I really do. But there is nothing. I don't know where they are. We did meet a few days ago, but it was purely personal. Patnaik had brought Sia here to cheer her up. We just told each other stories, looked at slides and solved some puzzles. Terribly childish stuff.'

'Puzzles like these?'

She gulped. Alia was holding the red silk.

'What's that?' Suri stared.

'Looks like a couplet. Quite cryptic too.'

Jasodhara took it from her hands gently. 'It's nothing. Some trifle I must have picked up. My house is full of junk.'

The reporter was still eyeing the silk. She heard Suri's voice again.

'We know you were in Delhi two days ago.'

'I was. My son lives there. So?'

Silence again. It ended with the officer's phone ringing aloud. He walked out of the room and the women sat looking at each other, till Alia finally spoke up.

'I have been reading your titles. Very intriguing.'

'Just memories now. So you are a journalist?'

'That's me. I am trying to help Suri with the case. This is not how I usually work, but this story is something else. I felt my best shot was to come here and work with the man in-charge. I have been nosing around and doing my research.'

Jasodhara grinned. 'Sure. Research is the way to go in this case.'

Alia grinned back. 'It sure is. It tells me that our missing pair is on the trail of the constellation.'

Time clotted for Jasodhara. Alia's words hung like a sharp-edged sword over her. She sat still but her mind was moving around in circles now.

She knows.

Alia nodded. 'Yes. I know.'

'What do you know?'

'Bits and pieces. The constellation. The riddles. The sciences. I can imagine what slides you three shared and what puzzles you solved.'

'How?'

Alia told her everything that had happened in Gangtok...her conversations with the Lama, the darkness of Rumtek, what that coffin held... Jasodhara did not challenge her anymore. This was no time to fight. It was time to make a new friend.

'Suri?'

'He knows nothing. It'll be between us. I only want justice.'

'Justice never comes easy. This is a road stained with blood. It will do more than smear your feet. Stay away, child. You have a life to live.'

'This is the life I live, Jasodhara.'

'We are talking about a power struggle here. The more people involved, the higher the peril.'

'I can fight that peril if you talk to me. I will see that they remain safe.'

She was silent. Then she picked up the silk. 'You must keep this to yourself. You cannot afford to be a fool. There are lives at stake here and they should not pay for your mistakes.'

'I understand that. Enough people have died. I don't want to see more blood.' Alia got up and sat next to her. 'I don't want a headline. Just the truth.'

Jasodhara spoke. The questions. The answers. What had taken others an eternity to discover was being revealed to Alia in a few measly minutes. There was no time to savour. The revelations were piling up fast and stoning her to death. Each new epiphany was pushing her hundreds of years before Christ. Suddenly Patnaik and Sia were no ordinary mortals. They had become warriors on an ancient pursuit. When it ended Alia had lived a lifetime on that chair.

Suri entered the room. 'What happened here?'

'Nothing,' she shook her head. 'We were just talking about Patnaik. So what new book is he writing?'

'I have no idea,' Jasodhara said. 'Must be another esoteric piece. But you must read *Open Your Eyes and See.*'

'How's Sia taking her father's death?'

'She's trying her best. I heard she even performed the last rites.'

'It must have been terrible to see one's father like that.'

Jasodhara nodded. 'I have her words here. You can touch their pain.'

They saw Sia's recording. Alia trembled. 'Poor child. It's good Patnaik's taking care of her.'

'Yes. He was very close to Mathur. They had met two years ago over some book he was writing on Buddhism. He frequently visited him at Sarnath.'

'We are still confused why Sia called him here. He had no business. They are both up to something.' Suri walked towards the door. 'We must leave. Will you get in touch if anything comes up?'

Jasodhara looked at Alia. 'I will.'

A minute later they were driving back. In the car, she turned towards the man.

'Did you hear?'

'Yes. Every word she said.'

'I told you it will work.'

Suri laughed. 'Quite a neat trick to first ring me on my mobile and then switch on your cellphone speaker. I heard the whole conversation. You reporters are bloody bastards.'

'No, Suri. We only run after the truth. Her story proves that I was right. Do you believe in the constellation now?'

'It's still too fucking pretty. But it comforts me. So Mathur mailed Sia a message the night he died and Patnaik cracked it. That's why she was so insistent.'

'Exactly. The Om on Mathur's face was also for the writer.'

Suri laughed. 'Fucking Om! But we have a few answers now.'

'It was a mean trick to pull on the old woman.' Alia leaned back. 'I hope she will understand.'

'Screw her! Sat there pretending to know nothing and lied to my face.'

'You shouldn't talk about lying, Suri,' she smiled. 'At least she has good reasons.'

'What do we do now?'

'Leave them alone. Jasodhara is right. This is dangerous ground. They both have taken an enormous risk. I don't want any more bodies.'

'But we must know.'

'We'll know. Right now she has trusted me and I'll respect that. We will be back once their journey is over. They are almost halfway through. We'll have our answers then.'

'Fine. We'll keep digging for the Scorpion.'

'Yes. Anything from those syringes and glasses?'

'All clean. Not a single print.'

'And the sketches?'

'They will be in tomorrow.'

She nodded, frowning. Suri held her hand.

'What is it?'

'There was something weird at Jasodhara's house.'

'Weird?'

'Something I heard or saw.'

'What?'

'I don't remember. But something was not right.'

Alia looked out of the window. The moon was struggling to come out of the clouds.

It failed.

53

*H*e never knew how heavy it was.

The prince was getting into his armour. Fires of revolt had flared up in the province up north and their heat was melting his father's throne. He was on his way to douse the flames. The royal command had been delivered. He was waiting for his army now.

'The infantry, O Prince.'

'The cavalry, O Prince.'

'The elephants, O Prince.'

'The chariots, O Prince.'

Silence.

'Where are the arms?'

They looked at each other.

'The arms?'

No one spoke. The prince dispatched a messenger. The man returned with darkness in his voice.

'The king has ordered that you will get no weapons to crush the rebellion.'

His heart clanged against the armour.

No weapons?

He could hear his father snickering.

How will I do it?

Then he laughed. Stepping out into the open, he sat down looking up at the stars. He had caught his guru in the act under the firmament. The wise man had opened his mouth to curse him. Then he had seen his face and passed on the wisdom. The prince raised his finger towards the spiral in the sky and closed his eyes.

'If I have merit, you will come to my aid.'

When he opened his eyes, he saw them descend from the sky. They were carrying weapons. They were nine.

'Will you come again if I need you?'

'We always do. But men don't.'

They had come again years later. The king was on his death-bed. Men of the court crowded around the prince.

'The eldest is out on war. Seize the moment.'

They clad him in royal finery and brought him before his dying father.

'Anoint him, sire. He alone is worthy of your crown.'

The king's frame convulsed. 'Never. I will never place it on him.'

Biting his lips, the prince spewed venom.

'If the crown is rightfully mine, others will adorn my head.'

The minister's son stopped him. 'Don't you need to stand under the sky?'

'Not anymore.'

He had gone into a trance. The next moment the king saw nine beings surrounding his bed. They lifted the crown and placed it on the prince's head. They were standing behind him now. Retching violently, the old man vomited blood over his body and fell back dead.

'Will you come again?'

'We always do. But men don't.'

54

$\mathcal{T}$he valley before them echoed their words.

The land was a bald desert but the maker had pulled a miracle out of a scant palette. He had coloured the expanse with a million shades of white and blue. Sun and snow. Sand and salt. These primordial forces had conspired and carved a canvas out of the silence of the Himalayas.

This was Ladakh. A far away tree bridging earth and sky.

Flying from Delhi to Leh, the pair was itching to trek towards Kongka La at once. But the locals had advised them to enjoy the city for a while to get acclimatised. Leh was one of the last surviving abodes of Buddhism, where the Mahayana traditions lived in their purest form. Monasteries held on to cliffs like faith clinging to the hearts of these people. Patnaik and Sia had prayed before the giant Buddhas at Shey, Thikse and Hemis and seen lamps that burned forever. They had also dipped their feet in the Indus River and heard how it had breastfed the first civilisation of India.

On the third day, they had driven from Leh to Rumtse, the starting point of their trek. They were now standing more than ten thousand feet above sea level. Somewhere among those passes was Kongka La.

The fifth prateek.

But this was the strangest of them all. It talked about aliens and UFOs and flying saucers. Their hearts were nudging each other, asking questions. What if a spaceship were to zoom out from behind that creek right now and land before them? What if they heard footsteps in this loneliness? What if they looked behind and saw long webby fingers reaching for their neck?

'Do you believe aliens exist, Om?'

Patnaik grinned. 'I have never seen one. But I do believe in them. I believe if life can exist on earth, it can exist elsewhere in the universe. If we can rise up from slime and master our planet, others can do the same. Aliens must be a normal condition of our cosmos, Sia. They are simply not a part of our consensus. But look around and there's a lot that tells you about contact with aliens in the past. Have you heard of the book *Hidden Records* by Wayne Herschel?'

'Nope.'

'It's a fascinating work. He tells you that the Giant Pyramids were actually a star map used by visitors from outer space to land on earth. Even more intriguing is Herschel's analysis of an Egyptian papyrus from the period of Thutmose III. It describes circles of fire raining from the sky and landing on the Sphinx.'

'Aliens on the Sphinx?'

'Precisely. Primitive art found on the Tassili Hills in the Sahara Desert is said to portray aliens. It is now a UNESCO heritage site. Prehistoric Japanese clay figures called Dogu actually resemble astronauts wearing a spacesuit. Mysterious drawings stretching for hundreds of kilometres over the Nazca Plateau in Peru have baffled experts for decades. The entire area is etched with geoglyphs of humans and animals. Who drew them on the desert? The figures are so gigantic that they make sense only when viewed from the sky.'

'Looks like someone who knew how to travel in air.'

'Exactly. They could have been possible runways for ancient flying objects. But the most puzzling are the OOP.'

'OOP?'

'Out of Place artifacts. Out of place because they challenge the very context within which they were created. Manufacturing these marvels was far beyond the technical capacity of the period they belong to. So how were they constructed? Erich von Daniken's *Chariots of Gods?* lists such anachronic wonders like the Stonehenge, Easter Island Statues, Machu Picchu and the Pyramids. You also have smaller objects like Iraq's Baghdad Battery and California's Cosco artifact kicking the butt of chronology. And then there is the Antikythera.'

'What's that?'

'This object displayed at the National Archeological Museum in Athens has been confirmed to be the world's oldest computer, built by the Greeks thousands of years ago.'

'An ancient computer? Are you serious?'

'It has been fully validated. If Greece had computers, then Jasodhara was surely right about ancient nuclear wars. The theory is that aliens were the original galactic pioneers. They either built these wonders themselves or taught humans how to do it. We all have inherited their fundamental mother culture. This explains why different civilisations of the world have so many cultural similarities. Daniken also shows how all religious and secular traditions of the world mention creatures from outer space. That can't be a coincidence.'

'Bizarre.'

'What's more bizarre is that even our gods could be mere images of this highly intelligent life from outerspace.'

'Gods?'

'Sure. Our forefathers were simply zapped by their technology and saw these aliens as godly beings. Jasodhara also told us that the weapons of our gods could be nothing more than high-tech gizmos. Our ancestors saw their sciences as divine miracles and turned them into gods. An electric spark in the desert became the burning bush.'

'Not bad. Don't they say even man may be nothing more than an extraterrestrial?'

'Why not? There are theories that humans have either descended from aliens or were created by them. Why else are aliens in books and films so anatomically similar to us? They might have helped us evolve into humans by cross-breeding their DNA with our life forms on earth. The Biblical declaration that God created man in his own image could well be describing this biological engineering. They turned monkeys into men.'

'This is spooky.'

'It's real science. The United Nations Outer Space Treaty of 1967 empowers the UN to turn visiting aliens sterile to prevent any "contamination of man". What may have once given us life is now branded pollution.'

'There's a UN treaty for aliens?'

'Of course. The UN Space Programme has been scouring the universe for decades in search of alien life. We may have exiled our brothers out of arrogance. They approach us but we don't know them anymore. Mainstream science rejects them as fringe theories but alternate voices have never stopped shouting.'

'I believe in what the Fermi Paradox asks, Om. If they are there, why don't we see them?'

Patnaik smiled. 'There are several explanations. They may be too alien or too far away in time and space. Our technology may still not be advanced enough to communicate with them. We may not be searching in the right place or listening properly. It's even possible that they have just stopped contacting us. They may also have huge egos like us.'

'Alien egos?'

'Why not? We must have inherited their faults too. The spookiest theory is that they are right here among us in human form but we don't know them.'

'Absent, yet present.'

'Exactly. Conspiracy theories allege that there are enough findings and evidence but they have all been hidden from the public. In fact, a former NASA astronaut, Edgar Mitchell, has openly revealed that the space agency was aware of several UFO visits during his career. They apparently called these visitors Little Men. He claims many such episodes have been covered up by governments of various countries over the past six decades.'

The duo had reached the Tsokar Lake. This brackish pool was still famous for its salt deposits. A group of nomads were sieving salt next to a herd of kiangs and two bharals. These blue sheep were quite a rare sight in the region. Munching tomato sandwiches, Sia picked up the thread again.

'What about UFO reports from around the world? Surely those are hoaxes or mistakes.'

'Not all of them. There's the famous Rendlesham Forests Incident of 1980 in England, where a group of soldiers claimed they saw aliens in the forest. The Shag Harbour Incident in Canada, in 1967, also mentions a flying object crashing into the water. The most controversial American episode is of course the Roswell Incident of 1974. It reportedly involved discovery of extraterrestrial debris, flying discs and even alien corpses after a craft crashed near New Mexico. Then there's the sensational case of Betty and Barney Hill'

'Who?'

'An American couple who claimed in 1961 that they had been abducted by ten aliens. They said they were taken to a spaceship where the aliens examined them and later released them. The couple apparently experienced vivid dreams and time lapses for days. The case has been extensively documented. Closer home, Xiaoshan Airport in Hangzhou was shut down for an hour in July 2010 after a luminous flashing object was spotted in the sky. Despite investigations the thing still remains unidentified.'

It was evening by the time they stepped inside the Nuruchan village camp. Later, they sat with mugs of butter tea, the sky stretching over them like a black sheet. It had never looked so big or clear. Sitting there they could make out strange spheres, clusters and lights. Something was telling them they were not alone. There was a presence around them. Another life watching them and breathing with them. Here earth and space lay open to each other. They felt as if they had only to stand in order to touch the sky.

'Have you seen anything more beautiful than this, Om? There are a million crystal balls hanging there. Peer into any one of them and they will reveal countless secrets. I can't wait to go up there.'

'I know, Sia. I am sure you will return with many answers.'

'What exactly is the UFO status in India?'

'Nothing much but the weird bit is that a number of UFO sightings were reported in the country in 2007. In March, six pilots in Delhi claimed to have seen a green fireball over the capital. Four days later, two more unidentified objects were picked by radars hovering over Race Course Road early in the morning.'

'Race Course Road? That's the PM's house.'

'In May 2007, a person called Afzal Khan informed the media that he had photographed a UFO over Bangalore airspace. Claims from more people soon followed this report. The same year in

October there were reports of an object spotted over Kolkata as early as four in the morning.'

'Sounds cool.'

'What's cool for me is the year. 2007.'

She gasped. *Nine again!*

Was there a link?

'$\mathcal{I}$ am not sure. Stories about Kongka La have been circulating for a while now. You will find zillions of them on the Internet and no one knows if these are true reports or just a yarn pile. They all claim that India and China have an underground base at the pass for aliens.'

They were on their way to the prateek. The morning sun had woken them up an hour ago.

'But why Kongka La?'

'The pass fulfills a tectonic necessity. It's located in the Himalayan core where the Eurasian plate and the Indian plate overlap. This makes it one of the few places where the depth of the earth's crust is doubled in thickness. Thicker the crust, the more suitable it is to carve a deep subterranean base through the bedrocks.'

'And people have actually seen these UFOs?'

'That's what the stories claim. Tourists have been reportedly experiencing flashing lights and strange sounds in the pass. Some have been quoted describing triangular crafts that glow silently in the dark. Pilots have mentioned seeing unusual flying objects over the area. Stories of people mysteriously missing also abound. And not just people. Recently an entire lake in this region is said to have disappeared overnight.'

'Disappeared?'

'Poof! Gone. Then an art contest held for local children there apparently threw up startling pictures. Over fifty percent of them painted strange objects emerging from the pass and flying into the sky. None of this is validated data, but so many reports coming from one place cannot be overlooked. Even a single speck of truth in this heap can be shattering.'

She nodded. An atom of truth here could change the world forever.

'Has no one ever investigated the pass?'

'Kongka La is a restricted zone, given its location on the border. People approaching the pass have apparently been refused entry by military personnel. There are rumours that the alien visitors regularly share defence and space technologies with Indian and Chinese heads at the base.'

'So the officials know all about it.'

'Conspiracy buffs will always claim that. They say the silence of the military and government is part of an international protocol to avoid global panic.'

'What crap,' she laughed.

'Perhaps, but it's all so exciting. What if any of it were true? What if aliens actually arrive one fine day? Imagine the grand exchange of ideas that could take place! Think about one intelligent life speaking to another. It's almost spiritual.'

'You sound like you are in love with these aliens.'

Patnaik smiled. 'The nomenclature is all wrong, Sia. They are not aliens. It's a life that wants to know us. Share secrets with us, but we are afraid. Afraid that something more evolved will overtake our world. Man surely cannot be the highest form of life. Creation can do better than that. And we cannot be alone in this vast universe. It will be such a waste of space.'

They were now nearing the pass at sixteen thousand feet above sea level. Sia took out her water bottle. Lifting her head to drink, she instantly froze. Water gushed into her open mouth and she bent over choking and coughing. When she caught her breath, she pointed at the sky.

Never!

A white spherical object had appeared out of the blue. It was silently floating in the air, a soft light glowing inside its frame.

Patnaik stood glued to the spot. The sky was everywhere. There was nowhere to hide.

They are coming for us!

BANG!

The sound shattered the silence around him to pieces. He stood still for he knew too well what the sound was. *A bullet.*

Sia was holding the pistol and aiming again at the white ball. It was now directly over their heads. Sia fired a second shot.

'Enough, Sia. You are wasting your bullets.'

'What are you saying?'

'I see it now. It's not a UFO.'

'What is it?'

'It's a Chinese Met balloon.'

'Chinese what?'

'Meteorological balloon. A weather balloon. They sometimes float over to the Indian side.'

She stared at him in disbelief. The white ball sailed away from their sight towards the horizon. Patnaik was looking at the smoking weapon.

'You are carrying a pistol?'

'Yes. It's vital.'

'What do you mean?'

She put it back. 'They tore out my father's eye and poisoned him. They are going to come after us too, Om. Only this time I am prepared. It won't be that easy.'

'You should have told me.'

'Well, you know now. You will be grateful for it.'

'I will be more grateful if you use that thing wisely. You can't pull the trigger blindly like that, Sia. It was only a frigging balloon.'

'You are wiser now, Om, but I saw your face when you first saw it. You were petrified and so was I.'

'Our fear was a natural reaction. We are in an unusual environment and it has conditioned our senses. More so because we have reached our destination.'

He pointed at the sign.

KONGKA LA.

The pass. This was nature's hideout. No flowers or falls for her here. This was where she hid her rock collection. She had carefully selected and placed her most gorgeous stones here. There was no meat. Just assorted pieces of bones.

'See how remote this place is,' Patnaik indicated. 'Solid rock formations all around. A perfect site for a secret base.'

Sia finally seemed to understand him. Lost in the enchantment of the place, she had forgotten the secret prowling inside its womb. She could now make out deep gaping holes and funnel structures all around her. There were fissures and crevices. Cavities and cracks. They were standing before a tableau of reality but what lay behind those walls?

Are there eyes in this void? Hearts throbbing beneath these rocks?

'I can feel long thin needles poking me all over now.'

'The Reptilians might be looking at us.'

'Reptilians?'

'Aliens shaped like reptiles that inhabit the Hollow Earth. Underground craters like these here. They have narrow eyes and flicking tongues and are known to be shape shifters. They can assume any human form at will.'

'Utter nonsense.'

'Simple science, Sia. What is our body? Only a form of energy. An overcoat of forces. If the mind is strong enough to alter this energy, it can move into another dimension. Another form. An alternate appearance.'

'Stop it, Om. Let's just bury the thing and leave.'

But the writer was in no hurry. This prateek claimed to hide an underground city of aliens. The adrenaline coursing through his veins now was urging him to explore deeper, to unearth the secrets of this place. This was not a quest for the next robot, it was a pilgrimage for him. He wanted to see alien ships flying like flags on a temple. He wanted to hear their sounds like the ringing of bells. Watch their lights twinkling like lamps in the sanctum. Directly ahead they the saw guard posts. Metal fences and barbed wires. And here was another awe-inspiring milestone. The Indo-China border. The Line of Actual Control.

The fence that separated the Lion and the Dragon.

Patnaik marched ahead. He had trekked through a very trying terrain for two long days to get here. He wanted to suck the marrow out of Kongka La.

'Stop.'

The voice was colder than the mountain air. They saw two border patrol guards marching towards them. The pair was dressed in khaki overalls and thick jackets and carried a rifle each.

Patnaik greeted the men with a promising smile. 'We are tourists. We wanted to see the Kongka La and the Indo-China border.'

'You are already in the pass area. This is a military base. Civilians are not allowed any further. You'll have to turn back.'

'Can't we walk just a little further? We have come all the way from Delhi.'

'This is a restricted zone. Please leave.'

He backed away and then retraced his steps.

'I wanted to ask you something. Is it true that there's a secret underground base for aliens here at Kongka La?'

Sia held her breath. The guards looked into the his face. 'Aliens?'

'Yes. Are they here?'

The soldiers did not answer. They were looking at each other now.

'You have come all the way from Delhi to greet the aliens?'

They were laughing now. Patnaik stood expressionless.

'We have been here for months. We have never seen one. What do they look like?'

The writer was quiet. The guards gently pushed him away.

'Go back, please.'

Walking away into the wilderness, they dug a hole and buried the yantra. The constellation wanted the Lion and the Dragon to do the same. That day the Lord of Shambhala would raise his eyes and look at them with pride.

'Where now?'

The next instant something fell from above. It hit Patnaik on the head and knocked him down. Sia ducked in fear.

The sky is falling!

After a second, she raised her head. Her companion had passed out, but lying next to him was the thing they had come to recover.

Robot number six.

56

*S*ia looked up. There was nothing.

Where did it come from?

All was quiet at Kongka La. Quiet like the man lying unconscious before her. A blue black bump had ballooned on his forehead now and he looked quite pale. Her efforts to revive him were getting more desperate but nothing seemed to be working. He lay there comatose. Sia got up and started walking towards the guard post hoping to get help. Suddenly she felt something cold and wet brush against her cheek. Sia stopped and lifted her palm. The white flakes were only too familiar.

Snow.

Her lips were trembling with cold and fear now. Dusting off the icy speck, she picked up pace. Soon she was within sight of the fences again. As she began the climb up, she heard her name.

'Sia.'

She turned.

'Om! Are you alright? I was looking for those army guys to help us,' she cried out, relief flooding her body with a welcome warmth.

She looked at his head. The bump seemed to have settled. He was smiling at her.

'Everything is good.'

'It's snowing. This can't be good.'

He flicked the snow off her hair. 'Come. We'll find you a refuge.'

He led her to a shallow grotto overlooking the valley. Crouching in the relative shelter, they stood looking at the snow come down in earnest now. The pass was aging like the hair of an old man.

Sia rubbed her palms. 'This looks bad. We may get holed up here for days, Om.'

'Don't worry. This won't last long.'

'How do you know?'

He laughed. 'Do you have the robot?'

'Yes. Did you see it? The yantra fell from nowhere. Absolutely nothing up there.'

'I know. Quite apt I think. After all, the sixth science is all about aircraft technology.'

'Surely some military mumbo-jumbo. You were right, Om. They are all in it. The royalty. The government. Spiritual leaders. This constellation seems to be one huge nexus.'

The nine had evolved to the next stage. The three in the circle had disintegrated into a curl. He held the yantra and spoke the password. Four new lines emerged to set them their next task.

> *First letters show energy of the old kites of a four-armed sun*
> *Call that princess who comes from five petals of a holy rose*
> *A primary ode to Apollo was written at our salty eastern tip*
> *Pay him for an empty bird flew where the white drop glows*

'See any tricks in this one?' she asked.

'What tricks?'

'They have been giving us number tricks, double meanings and longer lines. What about this riddle?'

He laughed.

First letters show energy of the old kites of a four-armed sun.

'Looks like the line is hiding a word. The first letter of that word will show us something. Something about an "energy".'

'But it says "letters",' he pointed. 'Plural. First letter should mean only one letter.'

She nodded. *Yes. Why letters?*

'It says "energy of the old kites of a four-armed sun". The word "energy" can have several meanings. It can mean fire, wind or water. But "four-armed sun" is surely specific.'

His eyes hovered over the line. Another word caught his attention.

'Kites.' He looked at Sia. 'Kites.'

'Kites fly due to wind. This could be wind energy.'

'Are you sure? You may be taking this too literally.'

'What do you mean?'

'These riddles have been using symbols the whole time. This cannot be your normal paper kite. I think it is a metal kite.'

'Metal kite? How can metal kites fly? You are forgetting a basic rule of nature.'

'And you are forgetting that this riddle is about Gravitation.'

She quivered as a blast of cold air whistled through the grotto. 'Of course. These "kites" are flying crafts. We are looking at the energy source of these crafts.'

'The phrase is "old kites". They are talking about crafts of earlier times. But what is the "four-armed sun"?'

'It says "old kites of a four-armed sun". If kites are old planes, then the "four-armed sun" must be the identity of the place or people that owned and flew these crafts.' She was eyeing the words. 'Does it indicate any country's name?' Her eyes brightened. 'Isn't Japan called the Land of the Rising Sun?'

'That is true. Japan's original name Nippon means origin of the sun. Japan's flag is also the Nisshoki or Hinomaru meaning sun disc flag. But there are no arms there.'

'It could also be some kind of a logo. An insignia or emblem.'

'The most common depiction of four arms is obviously the cross.' He drew the symbol on the ground. 'It has a thousand meanings. It resembles the Christian crucifix but the symbol is also found across Egyptian and Greek cultures. The Egyptian cross Ankh symbolises fertility and life.'

'So "four-armed sun" could mean the cross and the sun. Can we put them together?'

His eyes had narrowed into slits now. 'You are right. There's actually a symbol that fuses both the sun and the cross.' He drew a circle around the cross touching the four points.

'That was simple.'

'It is called a Sun Cross or Sun Wheel. It is believed to be a religious or astronomical symbol depicting the sun and earth.'

'Is that the meaning of this line?'

He started erasing the symbol and then suddenly stopped to stare at the drawing. Sia looked. A part of the circle touching one of the arms had been rubbed out.

'What happened?'

He did not answer. He bent and erased another part of the circle where it was touching the four arms.

'See that?'

'A half-erased Sun Cross?'

'Look again. It is not the Sun Cross any more. It is a different symbol. A symbol that at once inspires love and hate.'

Sia was seeing nothing. He bent over it again.

'I will make this easy.'

He rubbed out the circle completely so that they were only

left with the cross. He added four short lines to the four arms bent at right angles.

She saw it now.

A symbol that at once inspires love and hate.

'The Swastika.'

'Yes. Another iconic symbol with four arms.'

'But there is no sun here.'

He smiled. 'You are looking at the sun. In Hinduism, Swastika represents the sun god Surya. The ball of fire that shines over all four directions. The symbol is also derived from the Sun Cross. In the earlier form I had drawn, the arms are circular curves. That's a lesser known version of this symbol that appeared when I began erasing the Sun Cross.'

He turned to the first line again. 'It is telling us about a place that flew those "old kites" using an "energy". The place that adopted the Swastika symbol and turned it into a symbol of repression. Need more clues?'

Sia blinked. 'Germany.'

'Nazi Germany. Remember the Nazis had visited India and Tibet during the thirties, looking for Shambhala. Hitler is known to have a sound knowledge of Indian occult and Asian mysticism. It is believed that they came to learn the technology described in the Vedas to create superior aircraft for the Second World War. One secret society was involved in this project. The name of the society is also the name of the energy they used to fly these crafts.'

He wrote the answer on the ground.

VRIL

'This mysterious substance used by Nazis was believed to be an all-permeating source of energy. A fusion of all elements that could charge and propel machines. It was both creative and destructive. It could heal and also kill. Modern scientists have interpreted Vril variously as a form of electricity or magnetism. Many even dismiss it as an exotic fantasy.'

'So that's the answer for Line One. And the first letter is V.'

'First letter?'

She pointed to Line One.

'First letters show.'

Her finger ran across the page, as she read the words out aloud.

First letters show... Not letter... letters... Why letters?

The words seemed to reverberate in the small space.

Plural... V... First letters... answer.

Sia took a deep breath. Had she untied the knot? He heard what she said.

'So you are saying that each line of the riddle holds a word related to Gravitation. Vril was the answer for the first line. Once we get all the four words, we take the first letter of each word. Those four letters will form the name of the prateek.'

'Exactly. That's why it says "first letters show". The prateek is a four-letter word. We have got the first letter. We need the remaining three to complete the name. That's the challenge here.'

He grinned. 'That should not be too hard. The next line is quite simple.'

Simple? She looked at it again.

Call that princess who comes from five petals of a holy rose.

'Sorry. No idea.'

He locked eyes with her. 'What are you saying? The answer is staring you in the face.'

'Not at me.'

'Have you not read *The Da Vinci Code*?'

Sia sat up. 'You are right. This is the legend of Mary Magdalene.' She brought the lines closer. 'Mary is the "princess" here. She belonged to the royal family of the House of Benjamin. And the "five petals of a holy rose" together constitute her iconic symbol.'

He forked his tongue. 'Symbol of the Sacred Feminine.'

She picked up the pad and wrote M. 'VM? That hardly looks like a word.'

He was quiet. Sia was eyeing the third line now.

A primary ode to Apollo was written at our salty eastern tip.

'An "ode to Apollo". Apollo is a Greek and a Roman god.'

'I know that, Om. But an ode to Apollo written in India? And what's a "primary ode"?'

'Odes are lyrical verses of praise. There is the classical Greek ode and the English ode. There's no primary one.'

'The ode must be a metaphor again for a text,' she reasoned. 'This riddle is about Gravitation. Apollo here surely means NASA's Apollo Programme to the moon.'

'Could be. But the programme comprised seventeen probes. The line does not tell us which particular flight this ode was about.'

'Has to be Apollo 11. Man's first step on the moon.'

'Then what about the "salty eastern tip"?' He shook his head. 'No, Apollo here refers to something else.'

'You were saying he's a classical god?'

'Yes. He is associated with medicine, music, poetry and light.'

'Light?'

'Yes. The classical god of Sun.' He told her that Helios was the original god but in the third century BC, the Greeks had replaced him with Apollo.

'So Apollo here could mean the sun. Yes. The sun.'

'And the "ode"?'

'A text about the sun. So much has been written in India about the star of our solar system. But this "salty eastern tip" is making no sense.'

'Our eastern tip is Arunachal Pradesh, Sia. Salt in Arunachal Pradesh?'

He suddenly jerked his neck. They could hear sounds. A line of nomads were trudging towards their shelter, unmindful of the falling snow. They were carrying blocks of salt from the Tsokar Lake. He watched them pass, but Sia was looking at something else – the blocks of salt. Ivory-coloured blocks retrieved from the saline waters. The salt and snow shimmered, instantly dazzling her.

'I see this line.'

'What?'

'The "salty eastern tip" is not Arunachal. It's Tamil Nadu.'

'Tamil Nadu is in the south.'

'It's the southern "tip" of India. But so is Kerala. That's why the word "eastern" has been used. Tamil Nadu is on the eastern side. And "salty" confirms it. It touches the brackish waters of the Indian Ocean. The line is describing a book written in Tamil Nadu about the sun. A fabulous text celebrating the god of our galaxy.'

'And the book?'

'*Surya Siddhanta* by Tamil scholar Brahmarishi Mayan. It's one of the first books on space in the whole world. Hence the word "primary". It even talks about artificial satellites and relativity theories.'

He picked up the pad and added the letter S.

'VMS… It's getting more peculiar with every letter,' Sia sighed. 'One more to go.'

Pay him for an empty bird flew where the white drop glows.

'This is where the yantra speaks, Om. We need to pay someone when we reach the prateek. That will get us the next robot.'

'The "bird" is obvious now.'

'Yes. Like the "kite", it also definitely means a flying craft.'

'But empty? Empty craft?'

Sia was weighing the words. The wit of the constellation was at work again. She laughed.

'You see it?'

'I think so, Om. You are right. Aircraft are never empty. But what about spaceships? They can be empty.'

'Empty spaceship? You mean an unmanned ship?'

'Precisely. An unmanned flight. A spaceship sent into space without humans.'

'Excellent. So we are speaking about an Indian unmanned spaceflight. Which one?'

She was looking at the words. 'The line is telling us all. It says "where the white drop glows".'

'Sounds like milk.'

'Not milk. It means a glowing drop of water.'

'White water?'

'Yes. Because water is the most malleable compound in the universe. It has no ego. It takes the colour and shape of whatever contains it.'

'What are you saying?'

The snowfall outside had nearly stopped. She stepped out of the grotto and grabbed a handful.

'White water. The drop is white because this unmanned flight landed on a heavenly body that glows white. It detected the presence of water on this body for the first time in the world. Water that glowed white on its surface.'

He smiled. 'The moon.'

'Yes. Our first unmanned lunar probe. Chandrayan I. I have watched it take off, Om. I closed my eyes and cried that day.'

He gazed at her. 'Good. This completes the job. You have the last letter.' They looked at the pad.

VMSC

'That's not a word,' Sia glared.

'VMSC,' he mouthed the letters. 'Looks more like an abbreviation than a word.'

Her heart leaped. *That's it.* An abbreviation. She scanned the letters.

'S should stand for space. C could be company or corporation. Hold on.' She took the pen and wrote four more letters. They looked the same with one change.

VSSC

'Now that's an abbreviation I know. It is all about Gravitation. This must be the answer. We need the second letter to be S not M. But the second line is definitely Mary.'

'Is it?'

'Princess and a five petal rose. There's no doubt.'

'Read the words carefully, Sia.'

She walked over the line. Slowly. She shook her head.

'It says Princess,' he pointed. 'Not Queen. Princess.'

'I see that.'

'Princess who "came" from the rose. From the rose, Sia. The rose is a classical symbol for the female genitalia. The womb.'

'Yes.'

'So what does it mean?'

Her eyes opened wide, 'Are you saying…?'

'Yes. The princess who came from her mother's womb.'

'Mary Magdalene's daughter,' Sia cried. 'Not Mary herself. Daughter of the rose. The supposed daughter of Mary and Jesus.' She thumped her fists together. 'What was her name? What was it? Something with S.'

'Sarah.'

'Yes. Sarah.'

'The word also means "princess".'

'It is VSSC,' she beamed. 'The Vikram Sarabhai Space Centre in Kerala. One of our premiere space research centres and an integral part of ISRO.'

'Sarabhai. Father of the Indian space programme.'

'Exactly. That's the man we "pay". I would be glad to do it. His dream was to see his countrymen reach the skies and touch the stars. Many must have called it impossible. Today we have scaled the moon.' She clasped his hand but the next moment she pulled away.

'Om, you are freezing!'

He shrugged, 'It is cold.'

'Pop in one of your toffees. I will have one too.'

'I don't have any, Sia.'

'Impossible. You always have chocolates,' she exclaimed.

'All over. Get moving now. The constellation wants you to honour the man whose work catapulted his nation into space.'

Sia walked towards the edge. 'It won't be easy. I have been to the Space Centre once. It's a highly sensitive zone. Civilians have absolutely no access.'

'You will do it.'

'I am afraid, Om.'

'Why, Sia? Mankind is an invaluable breed. It is capable of such dreams and such nightmares. It often feels alone. Unloved. But it is very precious. We have each other and therein lies hope.'

'I know. But tell me something. Three answers here are related to Gravitation but what about Sarah and Mary? That's Christian mythology. How do they fit?'

There was no answer. Sia turned to look behind her. He was gone.

She walked around in that desert but the writer seemed to have vanished. Moments later she found him on the same spot where the yantra had hit him. The snowflakes had speckled his hair and coat. He was sitting on the ice and rubbing a fistful on his head. He looked muddled when Sia spoke about the icon.

'We have cracked the riddle?'

'Of course. Just a while ago. Then you suddenly disappeared. You must have walked up here and passed out again.' She grasped his hand. 'You don't remember?'

'All hazy up here. That thing hit me hard.' He was touching his bump uneasily.

Sia was staring at his face. His voice shook, 'Let's go.'

They walked down the pass. The sun was out again melting the snow. Patnaik seemed to be in a daze.

'VSSC?'

She nodded.

She was looking back at Kongka La.

*W*hat had he said?

I never forget a face.

Alia knew she sucked at describing faces. How exactly do you explain the shape of a nose? Or a mouth? How do you specify someone's jaw line or eyes? He was even wearing those fake square glasses. The hotel staff had been equally disappointing. 'He was mostly out or inside his room' they said. But Suri had not forgotten. He had pulled the face out from his memory and pasted it on this piece of paper.

This was the Scorpion.

The eyes were not clear but this was the man. The man who had played with them from behind the reception counter. Days ago these sketches had been plastered all over the face of Varanasi. The public had seen those sketches, but no one seemed to have seen the man.

Until today. The call had come. Some chaiwala at the Varanasi railway station.

'Not far now. This may be good,' Alia said.

'But so late? It's been fucking three days. This sketch wasn't good enough.'

'Screw you, Suri. You bloody want a Picasso now. This is the bastard.'

Driving through the ghats, the face of the killer stared at them from various walls, posts and doorways. Grey sketches. Grey as the Ganga flowing alongside.

Inside the station, the chaiwala stood before them with folded hands. Officers and journalists did not exactly feature in his daily routine.

'Yes, sir. This man. Saw him yesterday. Bought tea from me. Five rupees.'

'What did he do?'

'Took the train. Manduadih Express on this platform.'

'Manduadih? You remember the time?'

'5 p.m.'

Suri held the sketch closer to the man's face. 'This was the man?'

'Yes. This man.'

'Are you sure?'

'Sure?'

'Hundred percent sure? No mistake?' Suri's voice was getting louder than the kettle whistling on the stove.

The man hesitated now. Alia saw fear and doubt creep into his face. He was staring at the sketch uneasily.

'Looks like him. A lot like him. Must be that man.'

She touched the officer's back. 'Easy, tiger. He will piss his pants any minute now.'

'We must be sure, Alia. We must be absolutely sure.' His voice softened.

She nodded. 'I know. But he seems pretty sure.'

Walking towards the trains chart, Suri knew he was not happy; there was an uneasy feeling in his mind, one he couldn't shrug off. He knew he was shooting in the dark once again.

He looked up. 'Yes. Fucking dark.'

'Wait.'

It was Alia. She was walking back to the tea stall. He followed her. As the familiar aroma of over-boiled tea and ginger wafted into their nostrils, Alia held out her hand before the chaiwala's face.

'Do you remember the man's fingers?'

'Fingers?' the man echoed.

'Fingers?' Suri repeated.

'Fingers.' She nodded. 'Do you?'

'Yes. When he gave me the money.'

'Good. Were they strange?'

'Strange?'

'Discoloured? Dry? Burnt?'

Suri opened his mouth but the chaiwala burst out. 'Burnt. Yes. Burnt. Nasty yellow.'

Alia swung towards the officer. 'The Scorpion.'

'I don't understand.'

'The poison, sweetheart.'

'Poison? Of course. The poison.' '

'When you play with fire, you are bound to burn your own hands too.'

A train chugged into the station and the platform spilled over with passengers. Alia looked at them. 'He says the Scorpion took the Manduadih at five. Where does that go?'

Suri pointed at the chart.

MANDUADIH EXPRESS – 5.10 p.m. – SARNATH

58

*H*e knew there were tears in his eyes.

The bird was climbing the air again. It had risen last time too but like a predestined parabola, the creature had pecked at its pinnacle and then surrendered to gravity. The boy had shut himself for days trying to breathe a soul into it. Today, he had unleashed it once more. The bird had taken flight but after towering taller than before, it started to descend again as if swooping down in shame. The boy picked up a stone to crush it when the air-borne bird circled a tree thrice and landed with grace.

'What bird is this?'

The prince looked behind him. It was the eldest. He bent and picked it up.

'It's wooden. A toy bird?'

'Yes. I made it.'

'But I saw it mount. It was circling that tree.'

The prince snatched it from his hand. 'It failed the first time. It soared and then sloped. I had to work on it more, to make sure it followed my word. I made its body more buoyant and gave it a horizontal tail. I also altered the angle of the wings to make them more nimble. See, now it does what I ask it to.'

'How did you do this?'

The boy swung a metal cage before his brother's eyes. Inside was the dissected body of a large crow. Black plumes wafted in the breeze and drifted towards him.

The eldest fled in horror. 'You are a fool. That wood will never fly.'

'This wood will cover the sun.'

The Emperor grinned. 'Six minutes more.'

His men were losing the war. This population had pounced upon the battlefield like a pack of demons and they were tearing his army limb by limb. They needed no ruler to command them. They knew they were here to butcher for their land. He was watching men, women and children bathing in the blood of his horses and elephants. Then he looked up.

It had come.

One more.

Then another. And then another.

Nine of them dropping on the earth from the sky. They fell over the populace and charred the brave soldiers to death.

And then there was silence.

He looked at them again. 'Am I asking for the impossible?'

The monks nodded. 'You said you wanted to consecrate all the stupas at once.'

'Yes, Bhante.'

'That will happen now as soon as you signal us. But you say you want to mark the moment now?'

'Yes.'

'How, sire? You are forgetting that you have erected stupas that count eighty thousand and four. You have achieved the Teacher's divination. How can we mark the precise moment when all the stupas are consecrated?'

'What if we have a portent? An omen? Perhaps an eclipse?'

'That will do, lord. But the next eclipse will occur three months from now. You cannot...'

They froze. The Emperor was grinning. Behind him a gigantic craft was rising towards the sky. The column of fire flew higher and higher as if it wanted to view earth from the heavens above.

The next moment it had spread over the sun.

$\mathcal{S}$he was sitting by the Sea of Galilee; in her hand she held an egg.

'What is it, Mary?' asked Emperor Tiberius Caesar.

'He has risen.'

'What did you say?'

'He came to me.'

They fell down with laughter. Tiberius wiped his merry tears away. 'He will surely rise from the dead the day that egg in your hand turns red.'

Then his face turned white. The egg had become red, like blood.

He watched her as she sat by the sea shore, playing with sea shells. The vast expanse of water continued to heave and fall before him. The final destination. Everything mixed and merged here. Rivers and men. Carcasses and gods. Soap and nectar. They all had one fate. One drain. No heaven or hell. Only this cauldron where they swirled and frothed. Men who hated each other on land, lived together in peace in this water.

From the Himalayas they had dived into the sea. Snow had

turned into salt.

'So this is where our country ends,' Sia spoke.

'This is where our country begins if you face the other way.' Patnaik pointed behind him. 'Perspective, Sia. Nine can be six and six can be nine.'

'I have been thinking about Gravitation. All those vimanas described in ancient India. They could be nothing more than flights of fancy.'

'You don't believe that Ravana's Pushpak Vimana was an actual craft? It's one of the earliest mentioned flying machines in Hindu mythology with striking similarities to modern supersonic jets.'

'Could be the excellent imagination of a writer.'

'Our epics might be pure fantasies, but what about the Vedas? They describe vimanas as mechanical birds for war and pleasure. Twenty passages in the Rig Veda talk about flying crafts mentioning three-wheeled Trichakra Rathas, three-tier Tritala Rathas, power-charged Vidyut Rathas and wind-operated Vayu Rathas. Vayu Gaman or air travel is one of the nine Siddhis of Hinduism, Sia. Just imagination?'

'Any other sources?'

'There is a mass of scientific work which describes vimanas in clinical terms. The most prominent is the *Vaimanika Shastra* based on the ancient writings of Maharshi Bharadwaj. It's believed to be part of Bharadwaj's lost mother encyclopedia on mechanics called *Yantra Sarvasva*. The *Shastra* has a whopping three thousand shlokas detailing blueprints of flying machines. It even lists thirty-one essential parts, mirrors and lenses and sixteen materials to construct these crafts. Proper pilot training, in-flight food and clothing and safety precautions have all been discussed.'

'That does sound like first-hand knowledge.'

'Exactly. Scholars at the Academy of Sanskrit Research have

been studying this text for years now. It further describes four kinds of vimanas called Shakuna or bird, Sundara or silver rockets, Rukma or golden cones and Tripura or three-tiered crafts with full anatomical diagrams. But the most exciting are the thirty-two deadly secrets it whispers in your ears.'

'Secrets?'

'Yes. It teaches you to overhear enemy converstions, paralyse him inside his plane, make your craft take pictures, change shape and even turn invisible.'

'Invisible planes? Was that what happened at Kongka La? Did they use it to drop the yantra?'

'Perhaps. The engineering treatise *Samarangana Sutradhara* by Raja Bhoja of Malwa talks about vimanas as practical machines. He describes them as strong gliders but light in weight and able to absorb heat. Use of rasa or mercury to generate high speed is also mentioned. It outlines instructions to trigger crafts with heated mercury which creates heat energy that provide the thrust to propel it up.'

'That's exactly how a modern rocket blasts off,' Sia exclaimed.

'Yes. Chanakya's *Arthashatra* has saubhikas or pilots and akash yodhas or sky fighters. Bana Bhatta's *Harshacharitra* mentions a flying craft used to kidnap a king. *Valmiki Ganita* describes millions of travel routes in air. Many books even depict these crafts operating underwater and in outer space. No wonder Pinotti was so excited.'

'Who's Pinnoti?'

'An Italian ufologist. Roberto Pinotti has also declared that India was once a superior civilisation that flew piloted vehicles and used terrible weapons. He points out that details in many of our ancient texts are too technical to be dismissed. Unfortunately, many of these texts are either lost or missing in parts. There's much that cannot be deciphered or translated, making it very difficult to apply them practically. Like the Saqqara Bird of Egypt.'

'That wooden bird at the Cairo Museum?'

'Yes. Many historians still believe that it is actually an aerodynamic model of an ancient aeroplane. Even the Bible says that Ezekiel saw flying ships. God may be an astronaut after all.'

They were gazing at the ocean. Had ancient crafts flown over these primordial waters and left their footprints?

'Time to go.'

As they walked, the recent conversation Patnaik had had with the woman at the enquiry desk at the Vikram Sarabhai Space Centre replayed in his mind.

'Hello, Ma'am. We want to visit the Space Centre. Can you tell us the procedure?'

'Have you mailed the office for permission?'

'No.'

'You cannot visit without proper authorisation.'

'Is there any statue or image of Vikram Sarabhai at the Centre? We only wanted to see that.'

'Vikram Sarabhai. You can see that in our Space Museum.'

'Space Museum? You have a museum here?'

'Yes. It's in the VSSC campus by the seashore.'

'Seashore? The salty tip?'

'Salty what?'

'Never mind. How can we visit this museum?'

'It's open from 9.30 to 3.30. Any taxi will take you to the church.'

'Church? I thought you said it was a museum.'

'It was originally a church. When VSSC was established, it was converted into a museum.'

'Wait. Does it have any paintings or statues of Mary Magdalene?'

'Magdalene? I thought you wanted to see Sarabhai.'

'We do. We do. But does it have any image of Mary Magdalene?'

'The church is now a museum. You will find rockets and satellites.'

'Oh! Thanks.'

'But if you are looking for Mary you will not be disappointed.'

'What do you mean?'

'The church is called the Mary Magdalene Church.'

Click.

The shrine towered before them, an imposing structure. A large trapezium was carved on top of the church and on its peak stood a solitary stone figure. Its hands were stretched out, as if it were shouting 'Halleluja' from the roof-top. Four carved spires grew from the church and pierced the sky. An arched niche in the centre held Christ on his crucifix, with Mary Magdalene at his feet, gathering his blood.

'I always wanted to see this museum,' Sia smiled. 'This is where the dream began, Om. India's space mission was born on this holy ground of Thumba. It's near the magnetic equator. A perfect spot for sounding rockets. The fishing families here gave up their homes and church for our space programme.'

'Families gave up their homes?'

'Yes. Sarabhai approached the community and the Bishop and they donated their village to make VSSC a reality. A coconut grove became the launch pad and a cowshed became the laboratory. This was the control room where our first rocket was assembled.'

Patnaik was gazing at the empty coast. He turned towards the fenced VSSC building behind him.

'Do you think they know about the constellation?'

'I am sure they do. If the constellation worships science, it must surely be in touch with the scientific think tank of our country. Sharing a common vision of evolution for all of us.'

Walking through the lawn they came across a giant model of

PSLV. Nearby was the PSLV Heat Shield, hidden from view by a tree.

'Our modern vimanas,' he whispered.

Her palms grazed the white surface. 'Touch it. You can almost feel a heartbeat.'

As they stepped inside the arched corridor, their eyes were met with the object they had come seeking – a giant black and white image of Vikram Sarabhai stood framed inside a large stone panel. The man who had led them into a world of stars and galaxies. He had inspired them to grow wings and fly into the unknown. Sia placed the robot at the base of the frame and sat down.

'Let's wait and watch. We'll see how they do it.'

Patnaik looked at the yantra twinkling like a golden star. He went down on his knees but the next moment he stood up. 'No, Sia. We can't do this.'

'But this is such a perfect opportunity.'

'Opportunity for what? To wreck everything that we have done so far?'

She got up.

'Let the constellation do its work.'

The door led them inside what looked like a high-tech spaceship. They had walked through old buildings and dusty roads, but this was something else. An alternate reality. They were walking through oval doors and looking up at neon lights, screens, and buttons. The deities here were made of steel and springs – they were machines and models. The mantras were in the form of complicated equations and detailed theories inscribed on the walls. But the white and orange glass altar of the church had been preserved. It was shaped like the star of our solar system. Sia pointed at it.

'Look, the sun.'

Six sections in the museum narrated the saga of the Indian

space research programme, from its birth to the present. Real sized and scaled down satellites and launch vehicles lined the chambers. They seemed eager to narrate their adventures in space. One of the largest chambers housed spectacular models of the ASLV, PSLV and V-MARK vehicles. The tall cylindrical machines stood like Diwali rockets, ready to be fired.

'It looks like we have explored everything in space,' Patnaik remarked. 'There's nothing left.'

'That's absurd, Om. It's an infinity out there to keep us busy forever. The universe constantly renews itself. Puts out new robots with new riddles to be cracked every second. You may live several lifetimes and yet know nothing.'

She was under a spell. The writer laughed. 'I am sure this place is like Disneyland for you.'

'More than that. But it's totally deserted despite it being the weekend.'

'I noticed that too. Very strange.'

They now strolled into a compartment that housed two milestones of the Indian space probe. The Aryabhatta and Bhaskara. The veterans sat next to each other like giant eggs of a futuristic bird. Solar cells and radiometers spiking their surface were glistening in the lights.

Something else was glistening on top.

'It's a yantra.'

'I see it.'

'Who put it there?'

'Perhaps the robot was here the whole time,' Patnaik whispered, 'Waiting for us.'

'Waiting for us? How would the constellation know we were coming today?'

'It knows everything. Every action and reaction.'

'Like those TV set-top boxes?' she grinned. 'They say those have hidden microphones and cameras installed by the government to keep an eye on us.'

'I don't know about that, but I think the constellation watches us. Not like a voyeur but a friend. I don't feel violated, Sia. I don't think it hates us.'

'What do you think it is, Om?'

'Could be anything. Maybe a person or a group. An institution. A movement or a sanctuary. Or just an idea. Perhaps all of this or none of it.'

She stepped between the satellites and picked up the robot. The mark of nine now resembled the modern-day digit.

'Almost there,' he pointed. 'This was done by the Arabs. They closed the gap completely giving us the modern nine. It still needs the final touch of the West.'

Walking out of the museum, they looked at the stone platform. The bronze head they had placed was gone. Reaching the shore, they fell over the sands.

'Do it.'

Sia spoke the words. The robot responded.

Seek four corners for the name whose second letter is an A
The metal rises in east but none sees from where does it fly
This one tells you about a cosmos with stars like diamonds
Hike up to the centre of my face and your answer will be I

'What's it saying?'

Patnaik read the words again. 'Nothing. It's actually saying nothing.'

'Nothing?'

'The first line wants us to look in the "four corners" to find the name. It's "second letter is an A". Which four corners? Why second letter? The second line mentions a "metal" that rises in the east.'

'The Sun.'

'Obviously. Of course nobody can see from where the sun rises. Third line is simply stating that the seventh science is about the universe. The last line tells us to hike to the "centre of my face" for the answer. What face? Where's the data?'

Sia pulled the pad away from him and looked at it more closely. 'The "second alphabet is an A",' she read aloud.

'You are the science girl. You should know this answer. A word which symbolises cosmology and whose second letter is A.'

'I can't think of anything.'

'And why second letter? Why not give us the first one?'

'Line two is just talking about the Sun. The third is about "stars like diamonds".'

'None of these are describing or denoting anything in particular. The seventh prateek represents the universe, so the riddle will obviously talk about the sun and stars. These are just plain statements. They are implying nothing. No information. No facts. Where are the clues? What do we deduce, and how?'

'Could these be four corners of the sun? Or the cosmos?'

'Both are spheres, Sia. You find corners in squares or rectangles.'

'This "centre of my face". Even this has no meaning.'

'Exactly. Which four corners? Centre of whose face?'

Sia kept poring over the verse, trying desperately to make sense of the lines.

'These riddles use metaphors all the time. What about that?'

Patnaik took another look at the words he had written down. 'The "four corners" is surely a metaphor. The "metal" too is a metaphor for the sun. Nothing else there. Line three is of no use. This "centre of my face" is metaphorical again. But there is absolutely no other data to work on. None of them signify anything.' He flung the pad away in frustration. 'Useless metaphors.'

Sia picked it up and fixed her eyes on the first line.

Which are these four corners?

You find corners in squares or rectangles.

Squares and rectangles.

She was staring so hard that her eyes began to water, smudging the words. The riddle was only a smear now. A blurred object. Just a box.

She blinked.

A box...

What was this? What had she seen? This had never happened before.

Seek four corners for the name whose second letter is an A.

The four corners. Four corners...

She grabbed Patnaik's hand. 'See.'

'What?'

'You said this riddle tells us nothing. No data. No clues. You are right. But why do you think it is doing so?'

'I don't know.'

'Tell me something. What happens when the riddles come packed with information?'

'We try to figure out what they are referring to.'

'In other words we look for the answer *outside* the riddle.'

'Right.'

'This riddle gives us no clues. Because it wants us to look...'

'Inside?' He said quizzically. 'Inside the riddle.'

Not outside. Inside.

'This riddle hands out no information because we don't need it. It's holding the only thing we want, Om. The name of the prateek. We don't have to look for it anywhere else. It's right here hidden in its matrix. In the letters of the riddle.'

She pointed at the first line. 'You said we find corners in squares and rectangles. Look at the riddle. What do you see?'

'Lines and words.'

'No. What do you really see?'

She was tracing the edges of the verse. He trembled.

'A rectangle. The riddle itself is the rectangle.'

'Exactly. That's where you "seek". The four corners are right here before us. Look at them. You will see something that you have never seen in the other riddles.'

The writer had already spotted it. They were burning before his eyes like four bright candles.

I was so blind!

Four capital letters in the four corners.

Seek four corners for the name whose second letter is an **A**
The metal rises in east but none sees from where does it fly
This one tells you about a cosmos with stars like diamonds
Hike up to the centre of my face and your answer will be **I**

He whistled. 'The constellation! The constellation! It has used camouflage for this riddle.'

'Precisely.'

'The name had been hidden within these words. All we needed to do was look for it.'

She wrote down the four letters.

SAHI

'What is this?' he peered. 'Another abbreviation?'

'I don't know.'

'Change the order. But A remains second.' They shifted the letters and tried different combinations.

Nothing.

Sia's face drooped. 'I am wrong. I was so sure about this, but I am totally wrong.'

Patnaik looked at the top line. Her deduction had made a lot of sense.

Four capital letters in four corners. A perfect disguise.

'I think we have only half the picture. We need the other half.'

He peered into the maze. The middle lines were still useless. What about the third line?

Hike up to the centre of my face and your answer will be I.

'The four corners are literally the four corners of the riddle. So this "centre of my face" should be...'

He paused. What had he said a moment ago?

Useless metaphors.

The man looked at the sky and closed his eyes.

'What happened?'

'I was wrong. Nothing is useless in this world, Sia. Nothing. Everything has a purpose but we simply fail to see it.'

'What do you mean?'

'These metaphors are not useless.'

'You know them now?'

'Yes. They are not metaphors at all.'

'What?'

'We have got so used to the previous riddles that we look for metaphors everywhere. But this one is different. Here the words mean exactly what they say. Literal, like the four corners.'

'Show me.'

'The first line told us to search the corners. The riddle's corners. The last line wants us to go to the centre of the face. Centre of...'

'The riddle's face.'

'Exactly. The riddle is still talking to us.'

Sia tugged at the pad. 'What's at the centre?'

'Two more letters. The remaining letters of the prateek.' He highlighted the centre.

Seek four corners for the name whose second letter is an A
The metal rises in east but None sees from where does it fly
This one tells you about a Cosmos with stars like diamonds
Hike up to the centre of my face and your answer will be I

She laughed. 'I love this riddle.'

The complete picture was before them.

SANCHI

'The Great Sanchi Stupa. A stupa is one of the most ancient icons of the cosmos, Sia. I had said the middle lines were useless. Wrong again. They were all involved. The first and last lines distracted us while the middle ones hid the core of the prateek. They all played a part in this con.'

'But what do we do with the yantra?'

'Line two tells you.'

'That's just the Sun.'

'No. I told you these are not metaphors. Everything here is literal. Literal like our cosmos. Nothing is more literal than our universe.'

He picked up the yantra. 'The "metal" is not the Sun. It is this bronze metal head. The robot.'

'But it says rises in the east.'

'Exactly. Sanchi Stupa has four gates. Symbols for the four directions. We leave the robot at the Eastern Gate.'

Sia was quiet. A minute later she spoke up, 'I heard footsteps in there. When I was picking up the new yantra.'

'Yes. So did I.'

61

'What sights now, Tathagata?'

The Samanera typed.

'I was below the earth in the Reserve Bank vaults. The core can melt you but this place was cold. The men there were giggling like children. Asking how much gold I had brought. Red buttons beeped inside the armoured flanks of a strong room and giant vaults yawned open. They were hungry. Very hungry. I could see their bones. I had brought them food. The men scooped the gold and fed them to the vaults. A morsel at a time. They were telling me how the Nine loved playing with alchemy. How the Nine pampered the nation in times of crisis. I saw gold cover the steel and the mouths clanged shut.'

'Then I was on the Himalayas. Sitting in the facility next to another test subject. He was X and I was Y. We were staring at our brain images. Brains looking like two red cakes waiting to be cut. A needle pierced them and their lobes throbbed. The expert looked at both of us. X closed his eyes and opened them again. I spoke, "He said, *A stitch in time saves nine.*" X nodded. The neurons were doing it – this transference of thoughts. We were engaged in a conversation, but without actually speaking. What we were hearing were each other's thoughts. The most powerful wireless ever. The expert called this communication Blueroot. The Nine had shown her how to programme the brains. Now she had to teach the brains to construct the chemical highway themselves. No more phones or mobiles then. Only a network of synapses making infinite calls. The brain was the new Nokia.'

'I knelt before the altar at VSSC. A stained glass panel shaped like the sun. Everything around it had changed but it was the same. No angels or crucifixes. Only rockets and posters. Red blood outside and a figure embracing me, like families here had embraced Sarabhai's plan. The Bishop whose faith turned his temple into a lab. Nine was the new Bible and gravitation the Eucharist. But the Bishop had said this was also the work of God. Here the Nine had sewn wings for men. Their slender rockets had punched holes in the sky and left seeds in its womb. Men were still lighting candles with stars. I walked out and they both were sitting by the sea.'

'Did you approach them, Tathagata?'

'No. But the craving comes. It came at the Minar when I saw their pain. Their hopelessness. That feeling that everything is doomed. I wanted to tell them that making mistakes is a human privilege. The natural order eventually places us on the right path.'

'That is the truth. Whenever you carry out divine will, you are looked after. The universe becomes your carriage and pushes you towards its purpose. We need not ask for it. His hands will point the way.'

'Some hands nearly broke his skull on the Himalayas. This power can also take away life, Bhante. It kills.'

'We made an error. You cannot make one now.'

'I will not.'

'Their pain must not lure you from your trail. Keep walking. You can stand next to them when the time comes. Stand next to all of them.'

'Have the Nine arrived?'

'Three more have. Six of the Nine.'

62

'*The* eighth one, sire. The eighth one.'

'What did you say?'

'We have found the eighth one.'

'We have?'

'Yes, sire. The eighth stupa.'

The Emperor ran down the steps and embraced the messenger. Long before he was born, ten men had fashioned ten stupas all over the land to enshrine the holy relics of the Teacher. He now wished to erect many more homes and had dug up these ancient mounds and redistributed the remains. The Emperor's men had discovered seven stupas so far. Now he had one more.

'Where is it?'

'Ramagram, in the centre of the Ganga. The Nagas venerate the relics and guard them with their lives.'

For days and nights the Emperor walked, before finally reaching the stupa. Wading through the mighty river, he paused. A colossal wheel had surfaced from the water. It was gyrating with razor-sharp blades. They watched in terror as one of his men advanced and was hacked to pieces.

The Emperor pointed at the trees on the banks. They were

laden with fruit. 'Gather as many fruits as you can and throw them into the current.'

His men obeyed. Within moments the pulp of the fruits jammed the lethal blades and the wheel sank into the Ganga. When the Emperor neared the stupa, he was stopped by the Naga king.

'Have you come for the sacred remains?'

The Emperor folded his hands. 'Yes, lord.'

'I will hand them to you if you can demonstrate that your virtue is greater than mine.'

The Emperor got two golden images made – one of himself and the other of the Naga ruler. Then he picked them up and deposited them in the river. The Emperor's image instantly submerged while the Naga's statue remained afloat. Convinced of his higher virtue, the Naga bowed and guided him inside. The stupa was lit with nine lamps. As soon as he gathered the relics, the lamps went out. 'They knew you would come.'

'I don't understand.'

'The dynasty. They had poured the exact amount of oil in the lamps to last till this moment. They burned out as soon as you completed the task.'

The Emperor picked up an empty lamp in the darkness. 'How could they know that? How could they know when I would come and how much oil to put?'

'Calculators, sire.'

'Calculators?'

'The dynasty had machines that could compute every element of the universe. Time and space. Speed and distance. Size and volume. The entire cosmos with all its stars, planets and galaxies can be quantified on a single shard of stone.'

'Then those calculators are as blessed as these remains of the Buddha.'

'Do you want to see them, sire?'

'Is it possible, lord?'

The Naga monarch held his hand. 'Have faith in our universe, majesty. It makes everything possible.'

63

'Why Sanchi, Jasodhara?'

The three of them were inching closer to the seventh prateek on the trail. Flying from Kerala, they had landed in Bhopal where Jasodhara had joined them for the drive to Sanchi. They were now trekking up Sanchi Hill. As many as nine centuries stood between the oldest and the youngest monument on this mount.

'Why did Ashoka choose Sanchi for his Stupa?'

'It's said that he fell in love with the peace and quiet here. Originally ten primary stupas had been raised across the country by different rulers. They were probably the first stupas ever built in India. When Ashoka converted to Buddhism, he had many of these mounds dug up and redistributed their relics by building new ones like the one in Sanchi.'

Having reached the top of the hill, they walked in through the North Gate. Jasodhara was telling them about the fifty or more ruins on this hill. The relics before them were the colour of the sand that shrouded them. But nothing cast a greater enchantment than the Great Stupa. The fifty-four-feet-high structure stood magnificently before their eyes.

An orange sliced neatly in half. The dome of the cosmos. A universe in bricks.

Patnaik pointed to his left. 'The East torana lies there.'

Jasodhara nodded. 'Toranas or doors in these consecrated spaces have an important function. They are openings to something beyond. They invite you to step in from one world into another. By entering a shrine, you pass from your mode of being to an elevated one. Once you accept the invitation, you are ready to stand closer to your creator.'

They looked at the stones rising high over them like a giant abacus. The gate had been engraved with beautiful Jataka figures and scenes depicting everyday life, cleverly blended with episodes from the life of Buddha. This fusion represented his eternal relevance. The Teacher was represented by lotus footprints and the Bodhi Tree.

Sia nodded. 'Again absence denotes presence.' She took out the yantra. 'But why east?'

'One possible reason could be the solar connection. The sun rises in the east,' Jasodhara explained.

'Of course. There's nothing more beautiful than the rising sun.'

Leaving the robot there, they walked up the stupa. Jasodhara indicated a group of men working below, near a small ruin.

'Men from the ASI. The Archeological Survey of India. That man there is the director.'

'It's the proximity.'

They stopped. Patnaik was looking at the officials curiously.

'What proximity?'

'I have seen their faces. The Prince. The Deekshitars. That holy man and those border guards. These men here. There is something about their faces. As if living so close to the nine icons purifies their being. This is a force most benign.' He looked at the women. 'Haven't you noticed?'

The old woman smiled. 'Come.'

Climbing the steps, they saw the sun roosting over that giant sphere. They were now standing at the rim of the cosmos. The distant world looked so much more beautiful than the one close by. They touched the surface of the dome.

'This domed roof represents the spherical vault of the sky over the universe. It's actually called Anda or the world egg, symbolising the latent creativity of the cosmos. It represents renewal and resurrection of the mind and the heart. The Anda is similar to our Hindu concept of Garbha Griha. The womb. The Stupa itself is parallel to the Hindu idea of the Mandala or the Christian concept of halo.'

They encircled the Stupa following the traditional path of the sun, aligning themselves with the cosmic choreography. This solar cult made them one with the rhythm of nature. Around the dome sat four stone Buddhas guarding the four directions. The cosmos was nothing more than a Eureka of their epiphanies.

'What's that kiosk on top?' Sia pointed.

'The Harmika. It's the meeting point of the earth and the sky. The sacred and secular. It's symbolic of the final ascent of man towards Nirvana, which makes it an altar of sacrifice. You can see a pole called Yasti rising from the Harmika. It's the Tree of Life, going down through the Stupa like a backbone. It is the path for man to ascend and also the channel through which impulses of the universe flow into the earth.'

Sia looked at her. 'Ascend where, Jasodhara? Is there really a better place out there? Better than this world we have created? You sound like the notorious Mediocrity Principle according to which there is nothing exceptional about the way our earth has evolved. They call it a trivial event based on a few molecules. It never crosses their mind that we may have violated the most powerful cosmic laws to come into existence.'

'You think that's what happened?'

'Look at it. The earth is placed at the optimum distance from the sun, such that it can neither fry nor freeze. Matter and anti-matter have balanced themselves just right to sustain life. Our DNA is a perfect cluster of nucleotides. Life on earth for me is the highest degree of probability.'

'It's possible, Sia. A stupa only inspires you to take that physical life to an elevated spiritual plane.'

'But why is human life dog food? We have been thrown into a place that's not perfect and we have to make sense of it. It's an unfair world making unfair demands. It's easy to give up everything and run to the forest. It's difficult to carry your burden and still have dreams. We don't wander for truth. We make our lives our only truth. We look at now, not forever. Our only choice is to wrest out a meaning from our own chaos.'

Patnaik intervened.

'Ladies, I just realised how a stupa is more than a perfect prateek for cosmology.'

They looked at him.

'A stupa doesn't only symbolise mysteries of the universe. It is also a place to meditate on creation itself. Who am I? What am I? Why have I come out of the cosmic confusion and what should I do?'

Their eyes swept over the ruins of Sanchi Hill. Once monks had sat here and thought about these questions. Now all that lived were these bare skeletons, but nothing else had changed. These stones were still pondering over the same cosmic questions.

Why are we here? What purpose do we serve?

'Where do we go now?' Sia asked.

Jasodhara pointed. 'The sun rises in the east and sets in the west. The new yantra should be there.'

On reaching the Western Gate, they saw a child playing nearby.

In his hand was a golden ball, covered with sand. Jasodhara clutched Patnaik's arm.

'It's the robot.'

They watched as the child frolicked about with the toy. His little fingers did not know the wonder they were playing with. The power they were holding. The ignorance on his face was the most terrifying thing they had seen in a long time.

Sia walked up and pointed at the yantra. 'This is mine.'

The child looked at her with a frown. His fingers curled over the bronze doll.

'Will you give it to me?'

He looked at Sia's face and then opened his palm and let the robot slip into her hand. She lifted it with reverence. The mark of the modern nine greeted her with a smile. It's evolution was complete. She wondered what symbol would brand the forehead of the last yantra.

'Looks like you scared him.' Jasodhara smiled at the child. 'Where did you find this?'

The boy pointed to where the digging was going on and ran away. The trio followed his directions and looked at the ruin where the ASI people had been standing. There was no one there now. Patnaik recalled a line from the verse, and began to laugh.

The metal rises in east but none sees from where does it fly.

A moment later the robot repeated its light and sound show. They were looking at the eighth riddle now.

Looking…

The constellation had been fingering their core for days. But what they were holding now was nothing like what the other robots had thrown at them. Was this even possible? As they sat trying to figure it out, a single thought skewered their minds, terrifying them.

This is not a riddle.

64

'*W*hat is this? What is this thing?'
'I don't know. I don't understand it.'
'Is this a joke? Should I laugh or weep?'

Give me to J C Bose as he sits under the first floor staircase
In Bose Institute museum at 93/1 APC Road inside his home
The gunpowder explosion in Calcutta makes him the prateek
He proved radio works due to a wireless light that can roam

'This is no riddle,' Jasodhara cried. 'A riddle is a question paper. This is an answer sheet. What do we crack here? It has revealed everything.'

The writer was laughing hysterically. 'The last riddle gave us nothing. This one is giving us everything. That prateek was buried in its words and we had to dig for it. This one is sitting in the front yard. Telling us even the damn house number.'

'Is this love or hatred? We must figure it out.'

'What's left to figure, Jasodhara?' Sia picked up the page on which the riddle had been jotted down. 'J.C. Bose is of course Jagdish Chandra Bose. 93/1 APC Road is the address of his famous Bose Institute in Kolkata. It was originally his home but now functions as the main campus. I have been there many times. There's a huge black statue of Bose on the first floor below the stairs. That's where we put the yantra.'

'And this "explosion"?'

'It's the microwave experiment Bose conducted in the Kolkata Town Hall. He ignited gunpowder and rang a bell in another room using millimetre range microwaves. It demonstrated that these waves can pass through solids like walls and relay wireless messages.'

'But how's that related to Light?' Patnaik asked.

'There's a reason. After the experiment's success, Bose wrote a Bengali essay about the demonstration. He titled it *Adrishya Alok.*'

'Alok? That's light.'

'Yes. Invisible Light. His name for microwaves.'

'That's not the only reason,' Jasodhara added, 'His experiment has been chosen because he was probably a part of the constellation.'

Patnaik turned to look at her. 'You mean Bose…?'

'Yes. And not just Bose. There have been many others. Why do you think the sixth yantra paid homage at the altar of Vikram Sarabhai?'

'Sarabhai too?'

'Both of them were minds that asked questions and demanded answers for men. Minds that spent a lifetime cracking one cosmic riddle after another. It's possible that the constellation took both of them in its fold.'

They were listening. They were wiser.

Bose and Sarabhai. Members of the constellation.

'Down the years many names have been linked with the constellation. The roll call includes Madame Blavatsky, Annie Besant, Albert Einstein, Mahatma Gandhi, James Joyce, Swami Vivekananda, William Butler Yeats and Abdul Kalam. People with love and hope for the human race.'

'Love? Where's the love?' Patnaik snapped a nougat bar. 'Why don't we have a proper riddle? Is it really as simple as this? The first seven riddles suddenly look so much easier.'

Sia nodded. 'They asked.'

'Exactly. We had to make them talk. This one is chattering on its own.'

'I can still hear it.'

'Everytime I begin to have some faith in the Nine, they stab me in the back. Why didn't the constellation do this from the start? It could have just told us where the icons are. Why put us on the trail? Why this whole journey, Jasodhara?'

'Because this is exactly what it wants.'

'What?'

'To see you dissolve like this. See you biting your teeth and ripping your hair out. It is playing with you and it wants to see if you can play too. Do you want to turn back after coming this far? You are inside the penultimate circle. The dark has become darker. Can you keep walking?'

'But walk where?'

'Right ahead. With each riddle we began with confusion and moved towards information. This time it has inverted the test. We have been given the information right away, but it is still knowledge. Why are you afraid of knowledge?'

'It's easier to handle ignorance, Jasodhara. Knowledge handed on a platter is terrifying. You haven't earned it. It creates doubt. It already has. Can we trust this riddle?'

'That's what it wants,' she nodded. 'Doubt. It is the only thing that can defeat you now. Will you give in?'

'What should we do?'

'Stand up and face the riddle. Believe in this knowledge. I don't know what the riddle means, but grab it. Do as it says. Go where it's taking you like you have done so far.'

'Has the constellation lost faith in us?'

'I don't know. But we cannot lose ours. Go and meet Bose.'

'Are you abandoning us again?'

'I must. I have to return to Sarnath. Someone's waiting for me.'

The woman handed them the yantra.

'Hold the riddle's hand. And do not doubt.'

65

The Scorpion yawned into his mobile. 'What do you want me to do?'

'Picking up the phone when I call would be good.'

'I had dozed off.'

'How much do you sleep? For someone who has murdered nine people, you don't seem to have any trouble sleeping.'

'I have done nothing wrong. They were standing in our way. They could have lived but they asked to die. They wanted no mercy and I gave them none.'

'I know. You did what they wanted.'

'But Mathur was different.'

'Yes. You told me.'

'He was not afraid. He laughed at me.'

'They are like that. They have no pity for themselves or anyone else. They smile at what they do. Everything for them is a cosmic joke.'

'I heard he was still smiling when they burnt him by the Ganga.'

'He prepared that bed himself. He can only accept what happened and what's going to happen.'

'Tell me about it. Things are too slow.'

'That's best. See where your speed put you. You were almost trapped in that hotel.'

'I had got the warning in time. I was checking out when they landed. But it was fun, screwing around with them like that!'

'You have been seen. Your face is all over Varanasi. You should have left the scene right after the press conference. Look at me. Nobody can lay a finger on me.'

'It hardly matters. They don't even have my print anymore.'

'Go easy now. Those two are a lot smarter than we thought. Between them they have cracked seven riddles. Think about it. Seven riddles.'

'Sounds good.'

'It's extraordinary. Just two more to go.'

'And then?'

'Everything. What do you say? Everything will be catalogued.'

'Yes. Everything must.'

'Speak to your man. Tell him to hold on a little longer. You will have your platter.'

'And you?'

'You know it. Light. I'll be out of the dark and the world will see me glow.'

'We all will.'

'Meanwhile do what you love doing.'

'You have someone in mind?'

'Yes. It will keep you busy.'

'Details?'

'Alia Irani. The journalist at the hotel.'

'What's her story?'

'Nosing around too much. She might pick up our scent.'

'You are afraid.'

'Yes. I can do without her. Women are unstable things. And when she's also a journalist, the risk of combustion doubles. Pull her out.'

'I'll go and wake up my needles.'

'And you sleep less.'

$\mathcal{S}$uri cut the package.

He was gazing at a dark orange envelope. It was sitting on his table among the official white memos and documents. His name was written on top in beautiful letters. As soon as he picked up the pen-knife, his cell rang.

'I remember.'

'Alia?'

'I remember, Suri.'

'What?'

'What bothered me at her house.'

'What house?'

'Jasodhara's house.'

'Yes. Right. What was it?'

She was quiet. Her voice was sounding peculiar. She spoke again.

'I am there.'

'Where?'

'I am at Sarnath.'

He could hear the strain in her voice now.

'Are you alright? You sound tense.'

'No.'

'Alia? Are you frightened?'

'I am never frightened, Suri.'

He knew that. But today he did not believe it.

'What's wrong? What do you remember?'

'I have to be sure.'

'Speak to me, Alia.'

'I will call you back.'

'Do you want me to come?'

'Of course not.'

'Be careful.'

But she had disconnected. He was left staring at his cellphone. A moment later he picked up the orange envelope again and tore it open. Just then his intercom buzzed.

'Yes?'

'Call for you, sir. Ministry of Science.'

'Ministry?'

'They say it's urgent.'

The call had been patched through. Minutes later he placed the receiver back in its cradle and sank in his chair. Taking the envelope in his hands again, he pulled out the letter. When he had finished reading, his face was dripping with perspiration. Its words were stabbing him like so many shards of broken glass.

He looked up. 'Yes. Fucking pieces of glass.'

He turned the page over. No name, only a phone number. He dialled.

'I was waiting, Mr Suri.'

'Who's this?'

'I see you have got my letter.'

'What the hell is this shit?'

'The truth.'

'Who are you? Who the fuck are you?'

'Not important. What you must know are the facts.'

The voice went on. Suri was listening. His eyes returning to the letter on his table every now and then.

'This is bloody absurd.'

'I don't think so.'

'And, I don't believe you.'

'That choice is yours, officer. So will be the guilt.'

'Do you know what you are telling me?'

'We are asking you to end the evil. Have you seen evil, Mr Suri?'

The man paused.

Evil...

Evil that Friday...

'I have. I have seen evil in men.'

'It is not an external force. It is within us. We long for good but we are fascinated by evil. We create it. It lies beneath the surface of all the things we know. It waits. And it strikes.'

The last words came as a warning.

'Act, Mr Suri. Before it is too late.'

$\mathcal{T}$urning around she looked at the lion.

She had fallen in love with the Sarnath Museum. She loved the central structure that bulged like a huge cuboid of stone. She loved the two-pillared corridors that stretched from both sides of the cube like arms, as if to embrace her. But most of all Alia loved the figures that crowded the galleries. Here time stood frozen into stone. Eras had turned into exhibits and sculptures lived like oracles of the past. They were humming wisdom into her ears.

Face the absolute truth.

Years ago the archeological spade had dug into the bowels of Sarnath and hauled up great riches. Numerous Buddha images, Bodhisattva specimens and Hindu figures ranging from third century BC to twelfth century AD had rubbed their eyes in the sunlight. Finally Sir John Marshall, Director General of Archaeology, had crafted the oldest site museum of the Archeological Survey to display these treasures. She was standing before one of them.

The Chinthe.

Sarnath Museum comprised five galleries and two verandahs. The central hall called Shakyasimha displayed its most precious collections including Ashoka's famed Lion Capital. Next to it, towards the south, was Trimurti Gallery named for the famous sculpture of Brahma, Vishnu and Shiva, displayed here. The southernmost gallery was Ashutosh with its collection of Brahmanical deities. Then there was the Tathagata with its eclectic collection of Buddha sculptures and adjoining it was the gallery where she stood.

Triratna Gallery.

Tara was offering her a fruit. The Tibetans called her Jetsun Dolma or the Bodhisattva who was born from tears. The ripe pomegranate in her hand had burst open revealing a row of delectable seeds. Tara was the Compassionate One. She was telling her that she helped men cross the ocean. But Alia was looking at the lion.

The Chinthe or leogryph was a fusion of the lion and the mythical griffin. Mostly found outside pagodas in Southeast Asia, these figures were believed to protect holy places. The story went that a princess once married a lion and gave birth to a human son. Years later she abandoned the lion to move back to her palace. Mad with rage, the beast swore revenge and began terrorising the city. The prince who had grown up by then fought the lion and put it to death. He went back triumphant only to discover that he had slayed his own father. To atone for his sin, the prince later installed its image as the guardian of the royal temple.

Alia wiped the beads of sweat sliding down her face. Tearing herself away from the creature, she strode out of the gallery. Crossing Shakyasimha she paused again. The four lions atop Ashoka's polished sandstone capital were snarling at her. She heard in their voices what she now knew. The knowledge had entered through her ears like acid and was burning her flesh. She heard her own words.

I do.

Walking out she touched the rabbit in the sky again. The

museum was awash with the cool silver beams of the moon. She was in the garden of paradise. She knew she would bring her mother here someday. Leaning against a tree, Alia took out her cellphone.

I must talk to Sia.

The next moment, the cellphone fell from her hands. The tree seemed to have sprouted hands, which were holding her tight. Alia struggled to free herself from the grip and craning her neck saw the silhoute of a man, outlined against the glow of the moon that had bathed the garden in its light. Without loosening his grip, he emerged from behind the tree and pinned her body to the trunk. The hard wood was beginning to dig deep into her skin. His hand rose and grasped her throat, choking her. From the corner of her eye she saw his other hand clutching a syringe.

It's him!

Suddenly her fear was gone. She was furious now. Furious with this man who had murdered them all. She would not let him have her. With a sudden ferocity that surprised both of them, her hand flew up and knocked the syringe out of his hand. It hit the ground, its glass body breaking to release the clear blue liquid which had wanted to eat her alive.

The Scorpion stared at the fragments. Digging his nails deeper into her neck, he hit her across the face. Then he knocked her to the ground and walked away. Alia's nose was bleeding profusely now. Just then her cellphone rang. Sprawled on the grass she reached for it. It was Suri. Grasping the phone, she saw a pair of shoes in front of her. He was back. This time with a huge rock in his hand.

Alia did not close her eyes. The last thing she saw was the rock coming down on her head.

68

$\mathcal{S}$uri was looking at the blood on the stretcher.

What the hell is this man saying?

They had found her. They had brought her here. The medical team had wheeled her for surgery right away and shifted her to the ICU. Now the doctor was telling him that she was dying.

He looked up. 'Yes. She is fucking dying.'

He was running. Running inside his house. It was that Friday again. That Friday twenty-seven years ago. He wanted to watch that cartoon he loved but his mother was screaming at him, telling him to hide under a bundle of clothes. He watched from a chink in the curtain behind which he was hiding. Watched men with rifles spray his parents with bullets. Watched their blood smear the walls behind them.

He had prayed that the gruesome body found on the grass in the park was not Alia's. With its shattered skull and pools of blood, it couldn't be. But there she lay on the grass, still clutching her cellphone. Still breathing.

He was nearing the ICU now. A man in a white coat was talking about immense cranial damage and a brain hemorrhage. He was saying that she was no longer what she used to be. The son of a bitch was telling him to walk faster.

The Lama was inside the room. He was wearing his customary yellow and maroon. Alia was gazing at his head. It was round and shiny and she was sure she would be able to see her reflection in it.

He was telling her to open the door.

The Lama was coming closer. His face darkened and the yellow and maroon vanished. He was wearing a coat and trousers and he was not bald. She saw it was not the Lama. It was Suri.

He was looking at her eyes. Everything around them was a mass of white, like a full moon with two craters. Suddenly the craters bubbled. Her eyes were moving. Was it the pain? No. It was something else. She was trying to talk to him. She wanted to say something. Suri bent over her face.

When he stood up, Alia was gone. Her unseeing eyes were staring at the white light hanging above her.

Suri opened the door and walked out. He was holding her purse and folders and the four words she had whispered.

Blood on his hands.

69

He saw why they were shrieking.

They were tied to a platform and their eyes and mouths had been pried open with metal clips. Vessels of copper hanging above them were dripping acid. Not much. Only one drop at a time into their eyes, nostrils, mouth and navel. The Emperor watched them twisting their wrists and ankles. The adjoining room was quieter. Men here had been gagged and scalpels and blades were skinning their cheeks, foreheads and scalps. They were turning faces into balls of flesh. He turned around to see the executioner offer him a tray of human tongues.

'Have one, Your Majesty.'

'What's that noise?'

'Come and watch.'

He saw a woman strapped to a rack on both ends. The chains were pulling her torso and legs in opposite directions. The executioner yanked the cloth covering her.

'Pregnant.'

'Full term, lord. Nine months.'

The Emperor sat and watched as the levers wrenched her frame apart inch by inch. Now he could hear her cartilage tear as the joints snapped one by one. The woman's fingers clawed at her stomach but it was too late. With a final tug, the chains strained and her belly split right through the middle. He saw the ruptured womb ooze fluids as it discharged the blood-soaked foetus on the floor. The executioner stepped in and stomped on its head.

'That was new. You exceed yourself every time I come here.'

'I try to please you, O Terrible One.'

'Are you pleased? You got what you wanted. They are calling this place the Paradisiac Hell.'

'No, lord. I am morose.'

'The fires?'

'Yes. I have not been able to generate heat. I want to throw people on red hot iron floors. I want to melt the hardest metal and pour it down their throats. Vapourise them in a single flare. All I do is roast their genitals with wax. I want fires to boil them whole.'

The Emperor clapped and three men entered holding an octagonal apparatus.

'I have what you want.'

The men set the contraption in direct line with the afternoon sun. As soon as he signalled, a blinding flash of light irradiated the room and a single beam shot from the apparatus. The blaze began to scald the metal floor.

The executioner stared as the room hissed and bubbled a bloody red. 'How did you do this, lord?'

The Emperor threw a human head at him and picked up a severed arm.

'I play.'

70

$\mathcal{T}$he river paused. It was listening.

'I am prepared, Mother. I am sailing to Kashi to worship you.'

'Do not leave your home, your people. Stay here and be my daughter.'

'My men are awake. Twenty-four boats are waiting with my relatives and servants. I want to pray to you.'

'Make a temple for me by these waters. Here, I will bless him who calls me Mother.'

Scented air was blowing through her tresses into the night. Water from the woman's eyes trickled into the Ganga and turned the river into an ocean.

'It's beautiful,' she sighed.

Sia was standing before the Dakshineswara Temple. The Navaratna or the nine spires stood stained with the blood of the evening sun. They were red like the tongue of the Bhavatarini Kali inside the sanctum. She had got her home by the river. She was now helping her children swim through the sea.

They had visited so many places in Kolkata. They were having fun. But they were afraid.

The city had become their refuge, and they had been running from one place to another, trying to hide. Crouching behind men and statues. Inside stone and steel. They knew what they had been doing. They had been delaying the inevitable, because they were afraid of where the eighth riddle would lead them. What it wanted to do with them. Now they stood at 93/1, Acharya Prafulla Chandra Road. A stack of light brown bricks had created a tall cube with nine windows.

BOSE INSTITUTE

'This is the place, is it?'

'The prateek. Eighth one.'

'There should be no doubt about this. The yantra told us. You were there. You heard it.'

'Let's go. Shall we go in?'

Peering through long corridors, the duo entered the museum on the first floor. Various instruments used by Bose lay here on display. The glass cases were well lit and exhibited their contents with pride. The museum also housed some priceless memorabilia like letters to Bose from Rabindranath Tagore, Lord Raleigh and Francis Darwin. A group of professors were huddled over the cases.

Sia pointed. 'The Microwave Apparatus. The source of invisible light.'

Patnaik knew words not machines. He always found them cold and arrogant. This contraption looked like it had been cut open and its organs pulled out, one by one.

Sia smiled. 'Your mind has become used to modern gadgets, Om. All symmetrical, covered and sealed. This may look like a science model from junior school, but that's the simplicity that makes all of Bose's instruments unique. You are seeing a portable and extremely compact apparatus. It's beautiful.'

'And how does it work?'

'A high-voltage equipment attached here creates an electric spark with the pressing of a key. The spark induces a flash of microwave radiation that can pass through solids. Bose used transmitters, receivers and a prism mounted on this rotating table as components of the machine.'

They turned towards the inventor next; he sat in a regal posture by the stairs. His hands were raised as if working on another invisible experiment. Crafting another crystal ball that would push humanity further towards the reality of its existence. He watched as his lifetime's work continued to impress and inspire.

Patnaik took out the yantra and placed it near the bust. Why was he seeing Mathur's face in the stone?

CLANG!

The sound filled the enormous hall from floor to ceiling and knocked the robot off the pedestal.

Silence. The single note had devoured the hall. The professors were glancing around them. Sia and Patnaik were still, but their hearts were pumping wildly.

What just happened?

One of the professors came bounding towards them. He was pointing at the yantra. 'I saw it. The sound came from that metal thing.'

'But how?'

'It sounded like it had been hit by microwaves. Like Bose's bell experiment. I know the sound.'

They searched each other's faces. The next moment they were running towards the apparatus.

'This is impossible,' another professor frowned. 'Someone needs to push that button to create the spark. It's locked inside a glass case. How can it generate microwaves by itself?'

'I have no idea, but you heard the sound. There's nothing else in this hall that can create it. Those were microwaves hitting the object. There must be something inside that metal head that induced the apparatus to relay a stream of waves.'

'You are a lunatic…'

The professors were bickering in earnest now. Sia and Patnaik were silent. They knew who had made it possible. They walked back towards Bose.

'How did that happen?'

'Don't ask me, Om. Maybe some device in the yantra really sparked off microwaves. These are advanced sciences and we are still in the dark age.'

The men were continuing with their argument. The incident had disrupted their peace. All these learned men in the hall seemed furious because they were afraid. Afraid because they had no answer.

'I want to know this.'

It was Patnaik. Sia stared at him in astonishment. 'You want an explanation?'

'Yes.'

'Why, Om? You have always been content with the experience.'

'Not this one. This is too bizarre. How did it happen, Sia?'

'I can't help you.'

He looked disturbed. 'Look at those men screaming at each other. No wonder the constellation chooses to remain an enigma. We are not yet ready for it, Sia. Our world cannot handle this wisdom.'

The robot was still lying on the floor. He picked it up and grinned. 'I should have guessed.'

'The new one?'

'The last one.'

The final yantra had no number on it but the nine was still

present. The forehead bore a nine-pointed star. Inside it was a lotus with nine petals. Shape and number had fused together.

The cycle was complete.

They were floating on the river now. The Hoogly was scarlet and white like the bangles of the Bengali women at Dakshineshwar. It was here that the river grew weary. It knew the end was near and it was splitting up before becoming one with the sea. They could hear clearly the liquid notes of the oar cutting through the water.

'We got what we came for, Om, but what was this? What was the eighth riddle trying to do?'

'Perhaps the constellation was trying to show us something. Tell us something. We may understand one day. With the end upon us, it may speak louder than before.'

He felt his throat tighten.

The last yantra.

A few days ago they had set out to kneel before the greatest enigma of all. Today they had sailed into its final round. Only one more door remained between them and the cradle.

The Nine.

'It's the last time, Sia. You do it.'

Her words cast three shadows over the river.

'What is Dhamma?'

The golden ball gobbled up the sun.

The boatman was looking at the toy. Patnaik was looking at the last riddle. The ultimate verse. The ninth of the nine.

'Numbers.'

He breathed loudly. His fingers tugged at the buttons of his shirt.

'Numbers. Numbers.'

He pushed the pad into her hands.

Ten swum on eleven and twenty-six and played here for sixty
They cried through sixty-five and five as it got flashed by six
One gave in and freedom came when it was eight and fifteen
Hear the story as it lives at six six three three five six six six

'All numbers.'

Sia was nodding. She started calculating something. A moment later she shook her head. 'Nope. Not this time.'

'What?'

'I was looking for the numerology but these numbers don't sum up to nine. The total is two hundred forty-four which adds up to one.'

Patnaik glared. 'You want a number trick? You have it right there. This entire riddle is a damned number trick.'

'Exactly. These are numbers. There has to be a nine somewhere.' She combed the lines a second time and smiled. 'Yes. I have the nine.'

'Where?'

'Look for it. It's easy.' She waved the notepad in his face.

'You tell me.'

'Count the numbers. How many?'

The man counted and laughed. 'Eighteen. You are right.'

'The nine here is not in the sum. It's in the parts.'

'No more numbers now. Look at the words.'

They read the lines over and over again. Their eyes ran left and right and saw nothing. Only numbers pulling them like magnets.

Ten swum on eleven and twenty-six and played here for sixty.

'Who or what are these ten? They swam. Sounds like fish, Om.'

'Sure.'

'Ten fish. Anything strikes you there?'

He shook his head. 'And why only fish? Lots of other creatures swim. Man is also a swimming animal. Besides swimming can also mean crossing a body of water.'

'So ten swimmers crossed a body of water on eleven and twenty-six. That could be a time. Eleven twenty-six. AM or PM? '

'The line says they "swum on eleven and twenty six". It might also be the means of transport used to cross the water. They "played here for sixty".'

'Could be children. The second line says "cried". Children play and cry.'

They cried through sixty-five and five as it got flashed by six.

'So these things first swam. Then they played. And then they cried. What are these?' Sia scowled.

'They could be anything.'

'What's anything? We need specifics here. What's this "sixty-five and five"? They cried "as it got flashed by six". Six lights?'

'Great. We have gone through half the riddle and found nothing.'

One gave in and freedom came when it was eight and fifteen.

'It could mean that one yielded to something. Or gave up doing something. Or perhaps died.'

'Possible, Sia.'

She slammed the notepad on the boat's edge. 'Is that all you have? Possible. Anything. What do I do with them? Help me here, Om.'

The writer lowered his eyes. 'I am sorry. I cannot pin this one.'

'You can. You must. What about "eight and fifteen"? It could also mean time. Eight fifteen.'

'Freedom at eight fifteen? Makes no sense.'

'What about our freedom? India's freedom?'

'Our freedom came at the midnight hour. Not eight fifteen.'

Hear the story as it lives at six six three three five six six six.

'Story. It says story. The whole thing is a story. You know stories. You must know this.'

Patnaik looked at her pathetically. 'I am blank.'

'The "story as it lives at six six three three five six six six". What are these numbers?'

'Looks like some sequence. I have never seen it before.'

'Wait. It says "story". These numbers could be page numbers of a book.'

'Clever. But which book? And why would only these specific pages have the story?'

She had no answer.

'Also look at the numbers. If these are page numbers, why repeat them?'

There was silence. Patnaik heard a grim voice.

'No more lines.'

She was rummaging through his face. He looked away. They were before the last door but the lines were shielding it like four metal beams. They had banged their heads on them and now they were bleeding.

'It's over, Sia.'

'No. Nothing's over.'

'I don't know it. I cannot help you.'

'We will go on.'

'We cannot. It's the numbers.'

'I can see that.'

'You see nothing. I am afraid of numbers.'

The words flew out of his mouth and dived into the river. Water splashed all over Sia's face.

'What did you say?'

'I fear numbers. I am numerophobic.'

Her fingers swallowed his hands in a death grip.

'You are afraid of numbers?'

'Yes. They cook my brain. My system hangs. My spine coils inside me.' Patnaik held his head in his hands. Sia twitched as if gored by a knife.

'What's the matter, Sia?'

She dragged two words out of her body.

'It knows.'

'What?'

'The constellation. It knows. It knows our fears and terrors.'

Her mouth was not speaking. It was her eyes.

'You fear numbers so the last riddle is a cluster of digits, to make you face your fears. That's what this final test is about. You and me. Our cracks and complexes. The black holes inside us. This riddle wants us to enter our own chaos and scratch our wounds.'

Patnaik felt a shiver run through him. He yanked his hand away. 'But you, Sia. What are you afraid of?'

'Don't you see?'

'What?'

'It's you.'

'Me?'

'You are my fear. Your disorder. Your collapse. My greatest fear is your giving up on the trail. By terrifying you it has terrified me. It knows what it has done.'

They saw their faces in the water but the oars moved to distort those images instantly.

The writer nodded. 'It wants us to reverse ourselves.'

He spat into the river. The constellation was driving nails into their minds. Baring its teeth like a dog on the street and biting off their legs.

Just a dog.

The next moment Patnaik shook his head, shaking off the thought. He was wrong. The constellation was not evil. It was only doing its job. It wanted them to see their own merit and become what they already were. Whatever the constellation was, it loved him. It had been loving him all along. Only it had never told him so.

Like my parents? Perhaps they also loved me but never told me?

He looked at the notepad in Sia's hand.

It wants me to be what I am not. Reverse myself.

He stretched his hand out.

They want me to face my fears.

'Give me the riddle.'

She was quiet.

'I will answer it. They want me to go against myself.'

Sia handed him the notepad. He read the lines again and looked at the numbers. He was gazing into their eyes.

I am not Om. I have reversed myself.

The numbers were watching. He was now walking among them. Stepping gingerly. The numbers were nipping at his ankles. But he was not running away.

Reverse myself. Reverse myself.

He stopped. What was this?

Reverse myself.

The writer grabbed both sides of the boat. A solitary thought was suddenly making perfect sense.

Reverse.

The numbers had stood up. They were walking. Swapping chairs. Shifting places. But breaking no rules. They were simply falling in slots like a combination and asking him to pull the lever.

I have reversed.

He saw the equations. The numbers were speaking now. Chatting like friends and carrying him on their shoulders.

'I have it.'

Her face was still frozen. 'The answer?'

'Yes. It is all about reversing oneself. Becoming what you are not.'

'What do you mean?'

'I mean taking a U-turn, but there is a synergy at work here. While the riddle wants us to reverse ourselves, it also wants us to do the same to it. It's an exchange of energies. A barter of trust.'

'I don't undestand.'

'I am talking about reversing the order. You don't just reverse your own self, Sia. You also invert a few words of the riddle. The reversal here is both spiritual and physical. You need to reverse these numbers.' He pointed at the first line. 'Reverse "eleven and twenty-six". You will know.'

'That gives you twenty-six and eleven.'

'Yes. Twenty-six eleven. Get it?'

Sia felt a surge of emotion swelling within her. Twenty-six eleven. The date had been burned into their flesh.

'Mumbai terror attacks.'

'Exactly. The entire riddle has been framed around 26/11. The three number pairs here have been reversed to confuse us. That's where the symbiosis is hiding. We need to reverse them. See the second pair. It gives you the prateek.'

They cried through sixty-five and five as it got flashed by six.

'Flip it. So "sixty-five and five" becomes five and sixty-five. Five hundred and sixty-five.'

'What's that?'

'That's the total number of rooms in the building that suffered the attack for three days.'

Sia let out a shout. In her mind she could see the iconic building. 'The Taj Mahal Palace Hotel.'

'Yes. The final prateek. Taj Hotel. All these numbers are statistics of the 26/11 attack. Read them again.'

Ten swum on eleven and twenty-six and played here for sixty.

'Ten terrorists landed on 26 November. They terrorised the city for sixty hours.'

They cried through sixty-five and five as it got flashed by six.

'These are obviously the guests at the Taj. They suffered inside the rooms of the hotel while the building shook with six explosions.'

One gave in and freedom came when it was eight and fifteen.

'I think "one" here refers to Ajmal Kasab. He "gave in" and was caught.'

'And this third number pair reversed becomes fifteen and eight.'

'Or 15 August. Our "freedom". You were right about that, Sia, but freedom here also means the freedom of Taj.'

'Taj?'

'After the attack, the hotel was shut for repair and renovation. It reopened nine months later with five rooms less.'

She grabbed his hands in joy. 'Of course. On 15 August 2010. Free at last.'

They turned towards the final knot.

Hear the story as it lives at six six three three five six six six.

'This I am not sure. What do you think this is?'

'You said it was a sequence.'

'Yes. But which one? The last three numbers are six six six. Something about the Anti-christ?'

He stopped. Sia was laughing. She looked beautiful.

'What happened?'

'You are right, Om. It is a sequence. In fact, the most common sequence known to man.'

'You see it?'

'Yes. But this sequence has also been inverted. You need to reverse these eight numbers too.'

He watched as she took out her mobile and dialed 66653366. A voice on the other end answered, 'Good afternoon, Taj Mahal Palace Hotel.'

The oars fell silent.

'What sights now, Tathagata?'

He was not typing anymore. He was standing before him.

'Those experts showed me the lunar images. They said they had seventy thousand of these. Holes. Not homes. Soil. Not souls. But it's the only bulb we have. Keeps changing clothes and follows us all night. Far away but not anymore. The Nine had thrown a lasso and pulled the moon closer. Cosmology was now asking them to build an ark and sail into the bulb's white heart. They know now that the lunar heart is soft and wet. It may keep man inside it one day. I got ninety images at the Stupa but the experts are writing many new letters. Letters to the red planet now.'

'Halogen lights over the Pokhran desert were blinding me. The dunes were glimmering in the dazzling light. The men there said they knew the Nine. Years ago they had seen a cloud of red nuclear blaze. It had crushed the sand and charred them like the sun never did. But people said the nation had tamed the atom and their children were safe now. Later the dunes had seen a second nuclear firework that burned even brighter. Some were talking about taking the Nine's light there once again. The sand was smiling. Because Buddha had smiled at Pokhran.'

'In the end I chanted *Vandana Tisarana*. The two girls were repeating after me. They burned incense and offered red flowers to the urn. It was a vow of a lifetime of love for the girls. People were wailing like newborns. Talking about the historic day when the Nine had routed the old article and pronounced the verdict. They were saying the Nine had seen all this ages ago. It had seen an ancient civilisation based on love. An ancient society that used to venerate love. A love that was now condemned to temple walls next to the sanctum sanctorum. The two girls were not bodies. Mere dust to dust. They were what was inside. That alone freed the soul.'

'You too are free now, Tathagata.'

'Yes, Bhante. I have watched the Nine. Watched how Good and Evil can walk holding hands.'

'They always do. Good and Evil are eternal lovers. The first ever created by the universe. We cannot separate them. We can only recognise them.'

'We have the power to judge.'

'That is instrinsic to our cosmos. It has begun taking its course. Evil can only create a ripple, Tathagata. You can send it back. It's a ball of thread. A circuit of dependent neurons. We must seal the crack.'

'How, Bhante?'

'We must do good.'

'They have arrived. They are at the gates.'

'Let them in. The wheel must roll again. They must prepare to receive their reward. At the end of every road, revelation waits to speak to us.'

'They mislaid their trust on the way. But the Nine has evolved.'

'So have you.' The Bhikkhu pointed at the lamp on his table. Only a droplet of oil remained.

'Are you willing?'

'I am.'

The flame died.

*T*he Emperor was silent. The minister scowled.

'I don't understand, lord.'

'Why not? It is so simple.'

'You are condemning your tradition to death.'

'I am crafting a new one for all of us.'

'But the monarch is God. He derives his supreme authority from the Almighty. You cannot bind yourself to the earth.'

The Emperor shook his head. 'It's too flashy. Creates an ocean between the father and his children.'

'There can be no other truth, sire. Civilisations were ordered by the Creator and he has appointed his delegates to proclaim his rule. What is society but a manifestation and incarnation of his mind? You cannot destroy this hallowed bond or his creation will cease to exist.'

'The bond I see will give birth to an order that is just and tender. I will not rule because the Almighty so spoke. I will rule because the Teacher canonizes me. The Sangha sanctifies me.'

'But, Buddha...'

'Yes. He and his sons will hold my hand and take me to my people. I will not descend from divinity. I will be the ninth spoke in the Wheel of Dhamma. If I do good, my children can bless me.

In case of evil, they can smear my face with dirt. And so will every generation function.'

He looked at the Teacher. 'Let him alone ordain me.'

The Buddha was smiling. He came near him and touched his head.

The Emperor opened his eyes.

'What have you been thinking, Father?'

His son and daughter were still holding his hand. The stupa was waiting.

'I was thinking about the nine sciences. Will you be going back?'

'No, Father. Our work is done.'

The Emperor wiped his eyes. 'I want to say those words one day.'

He walked into the tent.

The bulb was swaying to and fro. He couldn't make out the face below in this light and dark. Raising his hand, he clutched the wire of the hanging bulb. It was Sia holding the urn. Slowly, she tipped it over and the ash and bones fell at his feet, mixing with the water that was now beginning to seep into the tent. The pyre was burning before him. They had burnt Alia and he could hear the cracking of her bones as they were singed in the fires. The pyre suddenly gave way to a stretcher and he saw the lifeless form of Mathur on it. He could see clearly the gaping hole where his eye had been. The old man got up and he saw a bone impaled through his right eye. As he walked, he hit the bulb and three crusted words scrawled on his face came to light.

I SEE YOU.

Suri jolted from sleep. He didn't realise how tired he was.

Was this fucking possible?

Alia had said they would prevent the tenth murder. Now she was lying naked with a toe tag hanging from her feet. Dead. Locked inside a drawer like a fucking umbrella.

Blood on his hands.

Whose hands? Whom was she talking about? Was she raving or was she revealing something? He rang the buzzer.

'Get me the forensic reports.'

The pages arrived. Suri went through each one of them.

Nothing.

She knew what had baffled her at Jasodhara's house. What had she seen? What had she heard? He was going over that meeting again. The sights. The sounds. The conversations about the constellation.

What was it?

Sentences. Words. More words.

Anything there?

Verbs and adjectives. Some of them. Most of them.

Wait.

He was hearing them again.

Those lines?

Again and again and again.

She had said…

What had she said?

Yes.

But was it possible? Bloody impossible.

It was that.

She had seen it.

Not there. But there. But…

He pulled the reports and sifted through them one by one. He seized the letter one more time. Suddenly its words made sense to him, hitting him hard with their veracity. He knew this terror. He had touched it before.

Alia's voice.

The buzzer squealed under his thumb again.

'I want all the photographs related to the case. Each one of them.'

Minutes later he was looking at the pictures again. Sifting through the pixels with a wild urgency, again and again. And then he stopped.

This is funny.

The man bent over. He looked through the pile for another photograph he had just seen.

The two images were now before him.

Very fucking funny. But was it…

Suddenly several words came back to him. Scattered words. Haphazard lines. Swatches of conversations.

And Alia's voice.

Hitting again and again.

Bruising his skin.

Blood on his hands.

Suri laid the pictures on the table as if they were sheets of glass. His mouth had turned salty. He had bit his tongue, making it bleed.

He knew what Alia meant. What the voices he had heard meant. What the letter and photographs showed.

Evil…

A second later he felt another spasm down his spine.

That means…

*T*he pain was unbearable now.

It was thrashing violently on the ground. It did not know where it was and the beating and battering were only breaking more feathers. The arrow was firm. It twisted over and over but the metal did not melt. The shaft had pinned it to the earth. Blood was gushing through pierced flesh and the white feathers were slowly turning red.

Siddhartha picked up the swan. He gently pulled out the arrow and applied a paste of leaves. His little fingers were trying hard to ensure that its life did not seep through the gaping wound.

'Give me my swan, Siddhartha.'

It was his cousin Devadatta. His eyes and voice were boiling.

'I hit this swan. It's my right.'

Siddharth clasped the bird closer to his body. 'I rescued it. It's my duty.'

'I lost it.'

'I found it.'

'I brought it down.'

'I picked it up.'

'I killed it.'

'I saved it.'

Devadatta came closer. 'How do we decide?'

'We will go to the Court of Elders. They are wise men. They will know.'

'Your father is the king. They will rule in your favour.'

Siddhartha smiled. 'The Elders are just. They will favour only what is good.'

The men heard the argument. The question was, who owns a life.

'Place the bird on the floor. He will own the bird to whom it chooses to go.'

The swan looked into the eyes of both the boys. The next moment it dragged its healing body towards Siddhartha.

The verdict was clear.

'A life is owned by him who values it. Not by someone who destroys it.'

Jasodhara wiped her face. The story had touched her ever since she first heard it in her grandmother's lap. It told her that good always triumphed but evil never went away. Like the evil in Devadatta. The man had never stopped hating the Buddha. She took her tablets and switched off the lamp. She was thinking about her meeting with the specialist today. Suddenly, a ball of light flashed in the dark.

She groped for her glasses and put them on. A round glowing patch was stuck to the wall next to her. It slowly began to wander. The patch travelled over the wall and then to the next wall and then the next. Her eyes followed the glare. The circle of light floated in the air and climbed up, revealing a face. A face hanging in the dark, like a smudge. It was blurred in the shadow of the beam. The eyes, two dots of phosphorous. Then the man appeared, standing in his own spotlight.

Jasodhara nodded. 'I have been wondering.'

'You have? That's interesting.'

'I had a feeling you would come. I have felt it for a while now.'

'So have I.'

'You are the one. The Scorpion.'

'I don't like that name.'

'You killed Mathur?'

'And eight others.'

'That journalist. Alia Irani.'

'Right outside Sarnath Museum. The Buddhas were meditating. They saw nothing.'

'The Buddha sees everything, child. You can come back. You still have time.'

'You mean till Judgement Day? But that case remains adjourned until I die. They can have my soul then but the body is mine. Right now my life is my own.'

'What are you after?'

'What everyone else is after. The Nine. You are no different from me. You all want to encash the Nine.'

'You are deluded. That's not what the wealth is intended for.'

'None of you will admit it. You are all cowards. At least I am honest.'

'You are not. Your soul carries a price tag.'

'Everything has a price. Especially the Nine.' He came nearer. 'Everything must be catalogued.'

'I see.'

'Even things that become useless. And junk must be disposed right away. Like you.'

The man scrambled up the bed.

'So you die.'

She smiled affectionately. 'You really shouldn't have bothered.'

The man's knee caps dug into her hands. Jasodhara watched his yellow fingers dangle the needle.

The tip of the metal touched the white of her eye.

BOOK THREE

Sangham Sharanam Gacchami

$\mathcal{O}$nce upon a time they were seven beautiful islands.

The Greek geographer Ptolemy had named them Heptanesia. An archipelago of seven sisters. Then several hands had dragged them and glued the pieces together.

'Mumbai.' Sia yawned.

It was 12.06 a.m. and the alpha city had not gone to bed yet. Patnaik and Sia were cruising towards the Taj Mahal Hotel.

'I am scared, Om.'

The writer put a piece of white chocolate in his mouth. 'Why now? We have done it, Sia.'

'That's what frightens me. The journey is always in your hands but not the outcome. What will the end have for us?'

'Solutions, like the last chapter of a murder mystery. That's why I love these books. They always explain everything in the end. Life hardly ever does that. Our finale will be worth what we have gone through.'

'Are you sure?'

He was quiet. She looked outside at the city. 'They have certainly saved the prettiest icon for the climax. The Taj is a great ode to the last science.'

'It's not only the hotel here. The larger connect is the terror attack. Remember Sociology is all about forces that play with society. Terrorism today has become the most powerful of these forces. A modern evil that tiptoes behind us and blows off our heads. It works because of the reaction it generates. Fear. Absolute fear that destroys society's will to defend itself.'

'And Taj is one of the most tragic icons of that fear.'

'Yes. It has become one of the most obvious martyrs, like Kashmir. A prateek of the fragile times we live in – when anyone with a gun in his hand and the name of God on his lips can end lives and futures. That two-day long attack has given us images for a lifetime. Shots screaming at the silence. Hands growing out of walls, calling for help. The Taj has burned at the stake, Sia. It has achieved sainthood.'

'Sainthood?'

'Yes. The last prateek tells us that our modern spaces have ended up becoming the most attractive targets of terror. Patches of society that are highly evolved are also the most vulnerable. Our progress has become our greatest threat.'

'That's quite a paradox.'

'It makes sense. Ravage its greatest accomplishment and you ravage the nation's pride. Strike at the heart of my achievement and you demolish my sense of sanity. My security. Terrorism rips our cloak of invincibility. It goes after our most beautiful creations, like Satan went after Man. And that hurts the most.'

The Taj now loomed before them like a shimmering phoenix. They had turned the hotel into a morgue. Blackened its red dome and bruised its soul. But it was living and dreaming like all men. She saw what Patnaik meant. What the constellation had done.

The Taj Hotel had to be the final prateek.

Beyond it lay the waters of the Arabian Sea, tamed by the city's coastline. Standing at the entrance, they saw the lights of Mumbai sail on the waves.

'Now what?' Sia asked.

Patnaik looked around. The place was still teeming with night birds though the numbers were dwindling fast. The salted breeze from the sea smelled of fish and cigarettes. He took out the ninth yantra.

'Look,' she pointed.

A man was standing across the street. His tonsured head and face, polished like bronze. He was calling them. Patnaik took a deep breath.

A monk.

They walked towards him with beating hearts. The man's orange robe was glowing like a flame. Standing before him, they searched his eyes and then his hands. Was he holding the final prize?

The monk extended his right hand and spread out his palm. Sia looked. What was this? Was he asking for alms? Patnaik smiled and placed the yantra on it.

The next moment the writer stretched out his palm. The monk pushed it away.

'Why do you seek what you possess?'

'What do we possess?'

'The answers. You held them when your journey started. Eighteen words.'

Patnaik's forehead creased into a bunch. Eighteen words? When the journey started? Eighteen words sitting by the Ganga at Varanasi? Eighteen words sculpted out of the chanting at Dhamek? Eighteen words painted on the frescoes of Sarnath Temple? Eighteen words glittering in red in Jasodhara's living room?

'Jasodhara's room. The couplet.' He cried. 'The couplet.'

Two lines. But were they eighteen? He was counting.

'Yes. Eighteen words.'

The monk nodded. 'Those eighteen words embraced the name of a man.'

'Ashoka.'

'Chakravarti Samrat Ashoka. Dhammarakhit Ashoka. He's the author of the mystery that surrounds you now. It all started with him.'

Patnaik and Sia looked at each other.

Ashoka?

'The man was the motif that appeared on your path again and again. In the couplet. In *Arthashastra*, created by a Brahmin who installed Ashoka's grandfather on the throne. At Sanchi, where he captured the universe in a pile of stones. And in the password. The question he had asked long ago. The question you have been asking at every juncture of your journey.'

Their faces were flickering like forest fires. *What had Ashoka done?*

'One of the sons of Bindusara, he was favoured by his grandfather, Chandragupta Maurya, as heir to the throne of Magadha. It's said that the the prince had found and kept Chandragupta's sword after he renounced it. He also quelled a revolt that had been mishandled by Bindusara's eldest son. The prince finally seized power after butchering his brothers one by one. This blood bath made him Chandashoka. Ashoka, the Terrible. But while most of India had come under the Mauryan banner, one region retained its soverignity. A region inhabited by a race so ferocious that no ruler in his dynasty had dared to subjugate them.'

'Kalinga,' the writer murmured.

'The land of your fathers. When Bindusara was alive, he had exiled the young prince. He had fled to Kalinga where he stayed incognito and fell in love with a local fisher woman. But Emperor

Chandashoka was no longer the lover boy. The ruler had forgotten the place that granted him refuge. Kalinga was now only a chunk of land that had to be yoked to his empire. With the region flatly refusing to bow, the stage was set in 261 BC for one of the bloodiest wars in history.'

The monk's face changed. He was standing in the trenches of that ancient battleground and watching the earth turn red.

'It's believed that the entire Kalinga fought as one army. They put up an inspiring resistance, but were no match for Ashoka's brutal rage. Almost one lakh people were killed and thousand others deported. The Emperor had won again but for the first time he felt a pang of guilt for what he had done. As his chariot wheeled through the sludge, it squelched into the bodies of the dead and dying. Siddhartha had seen four sights, but Chandashoka was watching a festering hell he had created. A pile of humans rotting in the sun and the Daya River, running close to the battlefield, the colour of blood.'

'That's when the miracle happened, on that wasteland.'

'Yes. The Samrat fell on his knees and washed his face with that water. Chandashoka withered away and was carried off in the purging waters of the river, leaving behind Dhammashoka. The Dhammarajika. Today, you can see his edicts at that spot hanging their heads in shame.'

'I had heard this story many times from my father,' Sia spoke. 'He would narrate Ashoka's change of heart just like you. But what has this got to do with our quest?'

'That was the seed, Sia. When he transformed, the Dhammarakhit vowed that such a holocaust would never occur again on the face of earth. He converted to Buddhism and began to circulate his message of love. This is where all history books stop. And this is where our enigma begins.'

They were both looking at the man with growing curiosity. 'The Kalinga carnage had filled the man with fear. It had revealed the havoc that an evil mind can wreak upon the innocent. His prime concern now was to ensure that the coming generations do not carry out such destruction. His edicts had started awakening many a conscience, but the Emperor was a practical man. He knew Dhamma alone was not strong enough to keep men away from terror. He needed stronger means. That's when he came up with a second measure.'

'What measure?'

'The Samrat embarked upon a secret project.'

'Secret project?'

'Yes. A project stashed into a closet so dark that the eyes of history never fell on it. It's this ancient light bulb over his head that is burning your eyes two thousand years later.'

They leaned over in excitement. 'What did he do?'

The monk's words came swirling towards them.

'The Dhammaradnya did what no man before him had ever done.'

*T*he four heads of Brahma were peeping at them from the chariot. Looking at his creation – this expanse of land and water.

The Emperor was glowing with perspiration. Was it the heat or was it excitement oozing out through his skin?

'What are you saying, sire?' they asked.

'I am saying that we must create warmth in the hearts of men and make sure that it stays there. I want darkness to end.'

'It will end, sire. Your life after the terrible war has been the greatest lesson for all men. The pillar and rock edicts are moving them to tears. Your words have crossed the ocean in the south and the mountains in the north. The roots of our sacred tree are tying this world into a sacred knot.'

'It is not enough. It is never enough.'

'Why not, sire?'

'Have you forgotten the Parthian War? My message had reached their land too, but what happened a year later? Carnage. Bloodshed. Rome had welcomed our missionaries of peace with open arms. And now I hear the Macedonian War is inflicting untold terrors on the Mediterranean shore.'

'Yes, my lord.'

'I have seen the horror. My words are mere words. Words are

helpless things. Men will only see them. Some will read them. A few will apply them. But most will forget them.'

'What do you want?'

'I want stronger action. A more practical plan for our people.'

'We are with you.'

'That's why I have called you here. Listen and understand. There is only one solution.'

'What, sire?'

'I will create a constellation.'

'A constellation?'

'A secret cluster of men. Nine men.'

They searched each other's faces and then the Emperor's.

'A cluster that will remain hidden from the eyes of the world, like stars during daytime. It shall be invisible to all except you. Only you will know that it lives.'

'We, sire?'

'You nine are the wisest and the most selfless of all men. You will be the patriarchs of this constellation.'

'Yes, sire.'

'The Nine Mahatmas. Masters of the cluster but servants of men. You will live for them but they will never know you. You will look after them but they will never thank you. You nine will become one. You will have no fame. Only merit. No power. Only wisdom.'

He stood up and plucked nine leaves from the tree. 'Will you take it?'

The Emperor's face was glowing like the sun. The Nine sitting in a circle around him extended their hands.

'Give us our task.'

'You will keep science away from man.'

78

$\mathcal{T}$he words hung in the air for a while. Then the writer seized them by the scruff of their necks.

'Ashoka founded a secret society?'

'Yes.'

'The Emperor Ashoka?'

'Yes.'

'The constellation. It's a secret society of nine men? You mean like the Illuminati or the Freemasons?'

The monk waved his hands. 'Those are only a few hundred years old. Mere crawling babies. The Emperor's brotherhood is the grand old man. The most ancient of them all that came into existence over two thousand years ago in 261 BC. Yes, Patnaik. The world's oldest and most powerful secret society was born right here in the heart of India. And Dharmashoka was its mastermind.'

The hair on the back of their necks were standing up now.

Ashoka created the world's oldest secret society.

'This is extraordinary. I have never heard of the constellation. Has it been mentioned in any ancient text?'

'Never, it was a secret enterprise. You don't announce it on loudspeakers. You wrap it in layers and bury it under the rocks. Just a handful knew about its existence. The rest only speculated.

Whatever we know of the constellation today has trickled down from various esoteric sources over the years. It's part of the legend of the Dhammarajika. Part of his aura as the greatest emperor of ancient India.'

'What was his motive?'

'It was a single-point agenda. No more wars. The constellation was entrusted with the duty to prevent the wicked from piling horrors on innocent people.'

'How can a secret society ensure that?'

'By a simple plan of action. The desecration of Kalinga had made the Dhammaraja conscious of the potential evil in science. He celebrated technological progress but also realised that in the wrong hands it could change into a curse. The Emperor gave the constellation a simple instruction. It was to conceal all such scientific knowledge that could be easily misused to destroy human life.'

'You mean Ashoka censored science?'

'You can say that. The constellation alone was handed the power to use science wisely. Whether he had the right to do so is debatable, but his intentions were noble. And it was not just the Kalinga carnage he was thinking about. There was a war thousand times more ghastly than that horror. A prehistoric holocaust that had wiped out an entire Indian civilisation from the face of earth.'

Patnaik's face gleamed under the street lamp. 'Are you talking about the Rama Empire?'

'I am. The Rama Empire comprised seven great capitals known as Rishi Cities in classical Hindu texts. It was a peace-loving nation governed by enlightened teachers called Priest Kings. But it had one contemporary whose singular dream was world domination.'

'The continent of Atlantis.'

'Right. That mighty island nation by the Straits of Gibraltar.

After subjugating many nations, the Atlanteans threatened the Rama Empire, but the priest kings refused to be overpowered. Those were times of dazzling scientific growth. Discoveries and inventions unheard of today were surfacing every other day. Unfortunately, much of it was being channelled to develop terrible forms of warfare. War became inevitable and what Atlantis rained upon our lands was nothing short of a nuclear carnage.'

Sia looked at Patnaik, 'That's exactly what Jasodhara told us.'

'Yes. When you have weapons, you are bound to use them, sooner or later. Do you see, Sia? Do you see what Ashoka was aiming at?' Patnaik whispered. 'Disarmament. Nuclear disarmament two thousand years ago.'

'Precisely. And it was not just the terror tools that the Dhammarakhit feared. You also had the flying machines.'

'The Vimanas,' Sia mumbled.

'Yes, the crafts of the Rama Empire. Atlantis is said to have had cigar-shape drones known as Vailixis. There have been claims that the Atlantean machines were driven by engines with a horsepower as high as eighty thousand.'

'Eighty thousand HP? Just imagine the violence of this confrontation, Om!'

The monk shook his head. 'You don't need to. There may be no recorded proof of this prehistoric combat, but images of destruction described in our classical texts are actually believed to be the first hand accounts of this very war.'

'The *Ramayana* and *Mahabharata*,' she gasped.

'Very good. The devastation pictured in these epics is so accurate that they can only be first-hand accounts of war. In fact, many widely believe that the leftovers of the Indus Valley Civilisation are nothing but the relics of the Rama Empire. Bones of an urban utopia charred by the heat of the nucleus.'

Sia's eyes went rigid with wonder. 'Jasodhara was so right. *Mahabharata*. Mohenjo Daro. Mauryan Emperor. It all fits in.'

'And then there's Robert Oppenheimer.'

'Who's he?'

'Oppenheimer was the father of the atom bomb dropped on Hiroshima and Nagasaki during World War II. Not many know that the man was familiar with ancient Hindu texts and the use of nuclear power described in them. When asked if Hiroshima was the first ever use of the atom bomb, his cryptic reply was, "Yes, in modern times.'

'So he also believed that nuclear bombs had already been used in India in ancient times".'

'This tells you just how real Ashoka's panic was,' Patnaik said. 'Even if the Rama war was just a myth, it was enough to inspire fear in the ruler. And nothing has changed. Science is still being exploited for all sorts of terror. Today, we have gone a step further into biological warfare. The virus is becoming the new atom bomb. The Indus Valley was our past and it may well be our future.'

The monk looked at the yantra. 'That's what the Dhammaradnya was trying to prevent. He may have himself used such weapons to decimate Kalinga, but now all tools of doom were stowed away. Every dangerous science was vowed to secrecy and stashed deep inside the constellation's womb. The nine men were given nine sciences.'

'The nine deities.'

'Yes. An ore of knowledge but they could also be easily misused. Each of these sciences could make man god. It could also turn him into a demon. The Emperor handed the nine to the constellation. He wanted peace not fame. We became a land of snake charmers, but in reality a vast pool of futuristic knowledge was bubbling in the heart of our civilisation. Knowledge entrusted to this nonagon of nine men.'

'The patriarchs.'

'Nine patriarchs for the nine sciences. Nine has always been a symbol of perfection. The number gave the constellation its name. It came to be known as the Nine Unknown Men.'

Sia rolled the name on her tongue. 'Nine Unknown Men. That's what the couplet said. The unknown.'

'The patriarchs were the Nine Mahatmas. Nine of his most learned elite. It was a secret nonagon of enlightened men but the most powerful cluster on earth was also the most benevolent. It did not have goals to rule the world. It only wanted the good of humanity through the wonders of science. They had the supreme power to use this knowledge in a benign way. Detached and yet conscious of their duty, the Mahatmas have been there for us. Among us and yet exiled.'

Patnaik nodded in awe. 'This nine is good. Nothing but good.'

'The constellation has been alive for more than two thousand years now and its membership is constantly renewed. These are people who share a similar vision for a beautiful world. Throughout these decades the cluster has interacted with the wisest men among us. Your father was one of them, Sia. One of the Nine.'

She stirred. *What did he say?*

'The Nine?'

'You heard me, Sia. Mathur was one of the Mahatmas of the Nine Unknown Men.'

The monk's words rammed into her body like a speeding truck.

'My father?'

'He was ordained as the Mahatma for the ninth science. Sociology.'

Patniak was now looking at Sia in awe.

Mathur was a patriarch.

He clasped her hand. 'Wait a minute.'

'What?'

'Mathur was a Mahatma. When he died, you were pushed into the journey to take the test ordained by his cluster. He wanted you to reach the cradle. Does that mean...'

He gazed at the monk in frenzy. He nodded. 'Yes. The Mahatma put her on the trail because he wanted her to take his place.'

They watched a tear trickle down her cheek. She was staring at him now.

My father was a Mahatma.

'But Jasodhara said Mathur wanted us to locate the cradle so that he could share the constellation's secret wealth,' the writer said.

'That is your right, but the Mahatma's central motive was to see his daughter as his successor. Every Mahatma must nominate an heir to the cult and you were his chosen one. You were contacted as soon as he was killed.'

Patnaik snapped his fingers. 'The email.'

'Right. The brotherhood has direct access to everyone's accounts. That's how the system has worked, since emails began. The Mahatma had prepared the test. You got the mail from your father's account.'

'And it told us where he had hidden the first robot,' she said.

'Yes. The constellation had pioneered the creation and use of these robots since its inception. Have you heard about Pope Sylvester and his robot?'

'We have.'

'What you may have not heard is that the man was gifted his yantra by the Nine Unknown Men.'

Patnaik gasped. 'The Pope had met the Mahatmas?'

'Yes. He was one of the few men to whom the constellation

revealed itself. Scratch under the surface and you will find many such enigmas hidden in the bronze. These nine streams of knowledge have been silently revolutionising our life all these years. But like the elements of the universe, they can also wreak untold mayhem. Only the patriarchs know how to tame their flow.'

The writer sighed. 'What a pity that such a beautiful story is lost today.'

'Is it? It's hidden, but not lost. The number nine is all around us. You only need to look.'

'What do you mean?'

'Look at European mystery writers of the late nineteenth and early twentieth century. They have emptied inkpots over the Nine Unknown Men. Jacolliot's 1875 book *Occult Science in India* was the first to talk about the constellation. Talbot Mundy's *The Nine Unknown* is the earliest piece of fiction depicting the nine Mahatmas at war with nine evil men. More esoteric writings like *Morning of the Magicians* and *The Illuminatus Trilogy* have branded the cult as the most secret of all. The cluster continues to inspire our present day and age. Recent television series like *Lost* and *Heroes* are great examples.'

'I have seen both the shows,' Sia exclaimed. 'What are you talking about?'

'I am talking about a host of elements borrowed from the Nine. Secret knowledge. Dhamma Initiative. Hidden Stations. Octagonal circle. Ninth Wonder. Nine Evolved Humans. Want more?'

'No. I see it now.'

'The numbers 9, 108 and 360 keep popping up throughout both the series. And Alvar Hanso is nothing but a contemporary Dhammashoka. A modern-day Mahatma.'

'Do we meet the Mahatmas now?' Patnaik asked eagerly.

The monk shook his head. 'You cannot see the patriarchs.'

'Why not?' Sia glowered fiercely. 'We have conquered the trail. Conquered each of the nine riddles. We have earned the privilege.'

'You have. But it's not possible. You can never meet them.' He paused. 'The Mahatmas are dead.'

'Dead?'

'The constellation has passed away.'

Sia advanced towards the monk.

'What are you saying?'

'They have been murdered. All nine of them.'

79

*S*he recoiled.

Dead.

'One by one in the last three months. All gone. Mathur was the last.'

The monk was staring at the young woman. She had frozen in time.

The Nine are dead.

They heard one word from the writer, 'Suri.'

He clutched Sia's arm. 'Those murders he told us about. They were all similar. He said Mathur fit the pattern. Those were the Mahatmas.'

His nails were digging into her skin, but she did not flinch.

'Yes. The patriarchs.'

'How is it possible?' Patnaik fumed at the monk. 'We are talking about the most powerful secret society. Is the Nine Unknown Men such a vulnerable cult? I thought the identity of the Mahatmas was concealed.'

'It is. But once in a while a breach can bring down a fortress. The Mahatmas are not gods. They are human beings like you and me. If you poison them, they will die.'

Sia slowly extracted her hand from the writer's grip. She had not returned to the present. She was still listening to the past.

The constellation has passed away.

'The cluster has departed but the evil still lives,' the monk said. 'It is stronger than before. You must be careful.'

Patnaik frowned. 'Are we in danger?'

'We are all in danger. I saw it spare you on the trail. But it will dig its teeth into your flesh now.'

'The trail?' Sia spoke.

'Yes. I kept a watch over you during your quest.'

'Our quest?'

'I have walked your path keeping an eye on both of you.'

'The entire path?'

'From the very beginning. It has been quite a journey.'

'I told you, Sia. We were not alone. I knew I felt a presence looming large at every prateek. Were you giving us the yantras?'

'No. That wasn't me. The sciences were doing that.'

'Card tricks of nature?'

'You can say that. You are standing at the end now. You need to push open the door and enter.'

'For what?' Sia stammered. 'The constellation is dead. The nine men have been wiped from the face of earth. What's left for us?'

'The answers you seek.'

Patnaik took a step. 'He's right. I want answers. I want to know who poisoned my friend.'

'And you have the right to know about the cluster's secret wealth.'

The pair found a wave rising within their chests. The Nine. What had Jasodhara said?

An enigma that can make even the gods kill.

'Recall the couplet again,' the monk said. 'It tells you what this wealth is.'

Patnaik felt his brain flipping through its files once more. It was dragging the couplet from the archives. *What were the words?*

'The temple of this constellation venerates sciences. Nine sciences. They are the nine gods that the Mahatmas bow before. What can be a greater wealth for a society than its gods?'

They nodded.

'Nine gods that remain locked inside their shrine. Invisible to outsiders. Invisible until someone is able to pass through the gates one by one and reach the threshold. You have done that. You are now standing before the sanctum of the Nine. You only need to push open the door and the nine deities sitting there will enlighten you.'

The writer was looking down, thinking hard. One word was making sense. Only one word.

'"A vision of the second of beloved's tall books." He jumped. 'Books? Books?'

The monk smiled.

'These gods are...'

'Yes. Books. Nine books dedicated to the nine sciences of the constellation. Collectively called the Nine, these books catalogue every secret of the sciences gathered over two hundred centuries. Secrets so enormous that they have to be kept away in hiding. These nine idols are the guarded wealth of the Mahatmas. No wealth is more precious than knowledge. It's the only monument that matters.'

Patnaik and Sia were seeing it all. They could see the power of these secrets floating against the current of the Ganga. Flaming on the Iron Pillar. Falling down at Kongka La. Clanging at the Bose Institute.

'Initially the Dhammaradnya had directed the constellation that the wisdom of the nine sciences must never be recorded. He knew that a written text inevitably carried a risk of falling into wrong hands. However, the Mahatmas soon discovered that they had a prolific amount of data to deal with. Science is a dynamic field. New discoveries were pouring in and laws were being constantly revised. The men approached the Emperor and he decided to introduce the matter at an epic assembly.'

'What assembly?'

'The Third Buddhist Council at Pataliputra.'

'Third Buddhist Council?' the writer exclaimed. 'You mean the third of the six great Buddhist councils of ancient India?'

'The same.'

'But the Third Council was convened to purify the Sangha of corrupt and unworthy members.'

'That was the official agenda. What history books do not know is that the Dhammarajika had a second programme, to manage this mass of scientific data. There he finally allowed the nine sciences to be chronicled as books. The Mahatmas began recording the secrets of their sciences and by the end of the Council, nine books had been created.'

Patnaik licked his lips. 'I have studied the six councils in detail. They never mention this close door event.'

'Of course they don't but they give you a clue. Tell me something. How long did the Third Council last?'

'It lasted n …' He stopped and stared at the monk. 'Nine. Nine months.'

'Precisely. One month for one book. The nine sciences continue to evolve today and each Mahatma shelters and updates his branch of knowledge. Presently the constellation has modern tools at its disposal but these nine books remain the seminal rocks that hold the cluster. This is the pantheon of the Nine Unknown Men. The Dhammaradnya's constellation does not have one holy grail. It has nine.'

They knew now. Nine grails that could make men gods. And turn gods into men.

'Nine books hidden from man,' Sia shook her head. 'What good has come from hiding them? Science is still being misused and will keep creating many more demons.'

'It will, but misuse of these books can make it a million times worse. The Nine have many answers which evil minds have been seeking for ages. Far greater marvels which can give them limitless power to play with our lives. The Mahatmas have been fighting these forces and will continue to do so. These are truly secrets for which gods can kill, Sia. And you are standing outside their cradle.'

The monk held Patnaik's hand and spoke. 'Your journey now sleeps with your great awakening.'

Your journey now sleeps with your great awakening
Your journey now sleeps with your great awakening
Your journey now sleeps with your great awakening

The writer closed his eyes.

He knew what the monk had said. He had recognised the place. The cradle of the Nine Unknown Men. It was perfect. It could only be this and nothing else. An altar where knowledge came in a flash. Where truth undressed before your eyes. Where you touched the greatest awakening possible.

'It was so easy, Sia. I should have seen it from day one.'

The monk was silent. He was looking behind them. Patnaik turned and instantly choked. It was an illusion. A joke. The city was playing a trick. But Sia let out a scream. He knew he was staring at reality.

Jasodhara was standing on the street. The pistol in her hands aimed at the three of them.

80

'*J*asodhara?'

Sia fumbled inside her bag. 'My pistol. She took it out while we were listening to the monk.'

The writer took a step towards the old woman. 'What's going on?'

Jasodhara pulled the trigger. The bullet scorched the air and punched the ground, missing Patnaik's feet by inches.

'What the hell…'

He gawked at the place the bullet had pierced. The woman's eyes looked like glass behind her spectacles.

'You want to kill me?'

Silence.

'What is this? What do you want?'

She spoke. 'You know what I want, Patnaik.'

They were stunned. Patnaik's legs were threatening to give way beneath him.

Jasodhara… Jasodhara.

The name was reverberating in his mind. The lover of mysteries. The recluse of Sarnath. The sixty-three-year-old woman behind the spectacles in her clean little house.

A facade. Just a facade. Always a facade.

She had held Sia's hand when she had walked from the river with an empty urn. She had called them to her home and closed the door. Then she had opened it and made sure they followed the path. She had not been helping them. She had been helping herself and waiting. Waiting to pounce when the end came. What had she said?

Let's see where Dhamma takes us.

He should have seen it. But how?

Jasodhara pointed the pistol towards Sia. 'The three of you will follow me now. Make a noise and you will never speak again.'

Patnaik pointed towards the monk. 'What about him? Will you kill a holy man?'

'I have always wondered how blood would look against those orange robes. I may find out tonight.'

They walked before her towards the sea. Stepping onto the waterfront, they passed through the mouth of the Gateway of India towards the jetty where a motorboat was waiting. The three quietly stepped into the boat, Jasodhara's pistol still pointing menacingly at them.

Jasodhara snickered. 'I hope no one here is sea sick.'

The motor growled. Sia saw the lights of the city pulling away from her. The Taj was getting smaller. She wanted to shout. She was worried that the guests inside would be crushed to death. Their motorboat was making its way noisily on the waves, but it was otherwise quiet. Everything around her had melted into the sea. She lowered her fingers into the water but pulled them back.

'Joyride over,' the woman sounded her knuckles.

They saw a large white cabin cruiser gently bobbing on the water, ten feet away. In its twinkling neon lights the three could make out the outline of a painted mask on its side, partly submerged in water.

'You own a cruiser, Jasodhara? Looks like your lousy shows paid off after all,' Patnaik scowled.

Moments later they had climbed a steel ladder and stepped onto the deck. Jasodhara indicated a flight of stairs diving down to the cabin.

'Into my parlour.'

The cabin was pitch black inside. The woman groped on the walls and finally flicked on the lights. The place was moderately furnished. A few cane chairs and a locked freezer stood next to each other. An unusually large table lay buried under layers of dust.

'Now what? You kill us one by one?' the writer asked.

'If I am not pleased with you.'

'What the hell, Jasodhara? Are you actually doing this? Saying these words? I don't believe you.'

She grinned. 'That's your eternal problem, child. You do not believe. You never had faith. People like you deserve nothing.'

'I have the answer.'

'I know. I have made it possible for you.'

'So it is the legend of Nine.'

'Yes. The moment that book in Mysore told me that your robot was carrying the oldest nine, I knew we were dealing with the Nine Unknown Men. I realised Mathur had to be a Mahatma. Since then I have steered you on your trail.'

'I remember that.'

'So it's only fair that I ask for my reward.'

'I will not speak.'

She aimed at the monk. 'There are others who will.'

The man smiled. Patnaik looked at him. 'He will not. You know that.'

Jasodhara sighed. 'You are right. But you may speak if I place the pistol here.' She pointed at Sia. 'I can do it, Patnaik. This is not really my first time you know.'

She was laughing. Sia saw her face.

Not my first time.

The next moment she sprung at her like a furious feline.

'You killed my father.'

Her fingers curved like talons and scratched bits of skin off Jasodhara's neck. Patnaik tried to restrain her but she kept kicking, trying to wrench herself free. Sweat from her forehead was dripping into her eyes now. She couldn't help but repeat herself, again and again.

'You killed him! You killed my father!'

Jasodhara was calm. 'That's funny, Sia.'

'She poisoned my father. Ask her, Om. She poisoned him.'

'No, Sia. She did not do it.'

The voice had come from behind. All eyes in the cabin turned to see Suri stepping into the silence.

Sia stared. 'Where did you come from?'

'I was hoping you would be relieved to see me here.'

The writer bounded across the room towards him. 'It's Jasodhara. It's been her the whole time. We were blind. We trusted the woman but she shoved us here at gun point.'

The officer looked at her. 'She will do no harm.'

He stretched his hand. Jasodhara gave up the weapon.

'She shot at us. The woman is mad,' Patnaik panted.

'We all get a little mad sometimes you know.' Suri inserted a bullet in the pistol.

The writer gaped at him. He had changed. He was not the man they knew.

'You too can become a lunatic when the prize is so fucking tempting.'

They were watching his mouth. He grinned.

'You think I did it?'

They were silent.

'I'll tell you who killed your father, Sia.'

As if on cue the cabin door opened. Two men entered carrying a third man. Suri pointed at the prisoner.

'The Scorpion. This mother fucker killed Mathur.'

They were staring at a young man in his thirties. It was the face of a boy with a stubble and dimples. But not the eyes. There was something wrong with his eyes. They did not belong to this face.

Suri held up the man's hands. 'Scorpion's fangs. The yellow fingers that smashed Alia's skull. That pumped poison into Mathur and eight others.'

Sia's eyes were filling with blood. Her emotions were like simmering lava, waiting to explode. Then it spilled all over the Scorpion. They watched in terror what her hands did to his face. The killer's mouth was filled with his own blood now.

The officer grasped her wrist. 'That's enough. Don't kill him. Keep some of your rage for his friend.'

'Friend?'

'Yes. He was not alone. He did what his partner told him to do.'

Sia's eyes darted towards Jasodhara. 'So she did not kill. She made him kill.'

'Wrong, Sia. It was not her.'

She looked at the Scorpion. 'Ask him then.'

'He will not speak. But I know the name.'

'Who's it?'

'Will you face it?'

'Tell me, Suri.'

'It was the person you trusted the most.'

She switched off.

The person you trusted the most.

The universe expanded and contracted.

The person you trusted the most.

A single drop of sweat slowly oozed out of a pore on her head.

The person you trusted the most.

Time began and space ended.

The person you trusted the most.

She slowly turned towards Patnaik. She saw terror in his eyes.

'It's you, Sia. You. The Scorpion's partner. The fucking mastermind. You trusted yourself the most, but you have failed.'

$\mathcal{S}$he gazed at the man. 'What did you say?'

'You carried out the whole thing. It was your bloody plan.'

'You are saying I killed my father?'

'No. This bastard did it but you scripted it. Like all the other eight murders.'

She grinned. 'You are insane, Suri. It was Jasodhara. She bundled us into this hole with a gun. She admitted killing people in the past.'

'I know. That was my script.'

'Your script?'

'Yes. She followed it quite well, like your man followed yours.'

Sia was breathing with her mouth open now. Walking across the room, she sat down on a cane chair. Her face had become impassive, like bronze.

'Do you believe this, Om?'

Patnaik looked drained, as if Suri's words had pulled out a plug. 'You tell me, Sia. What should I believe?'

'What I tell you,' the officer said. 'My friend has showed me the truth.'

'Your friend?'

'Alia. She told me everything before dying.'

'You are raving, Suri.'

The officer turned towards Jasodhara. 'Have you brought it?'

'Yes.'

They saw her putting a Flash USB drive in his hand. Suri plugged it into the iPad he was carrying and the screen came to life. Sia was watching herself. She was speaking. A minute later the monitor went black.

'Do you know this clip?'

'Yes. I recorded it at Jasodhara's house.'

'You said those words?'

'I did,' she hissed at him. 'That's what I saw rotting on that ghat on the steps. It has scarred me. I see everyday what I saw that day.'

Suri played the video again.

'You said you saw your father's body? The festering socket?'

'Yes.'

'You saw the blue eye? The trishul in his hands?'

'Yes.'

'The bleeding mark on his face?'

'Yes.'

'Bleeding mark?'

'Yes.'

He paused the clip. The lines were playing again and again.

'You saw the fucking bleeding, Sia?'

'Yes, Suri.'

He walked closer to her chair. 'That's bullshit. We found Mathur's body two hours after the murder. The mark was dry and the blood had clotted. You arrived even later, around 1 pm. Eleven hours after the murder. The wound had crusted thick by then. How did you see the Om bleeding?'

The words sank their teeth into her.

'The blood, Sia? How did you see the blood?'

She was quiet.

'You love explanations. Now explain this or shall I do it?'

She traced a line on the dust settled on the chair.

'You saw the blood because you were present at the ghat. Not in Ahmedabad. We have enquired at your facility. You did not arrive in Varanasi that morning. You were already there the night before.'

She was wiping her finger on her clothes now, trying to get rid of the dirt.

'Did you watch your father die? Did this bastard slaughter Mathur before your eyes? What did you do, Sia? What did you do that night?'

'You tell me, Suri.'

Suri pointed at the monk. 'He will tell us. He knows.'

Everyone stared at him. The monk was looking at her calmly. 'She drew.'

'Did I? What?'

'The Om.'

They were listening.

'You carved the Om on your father's face.'

There was silence. Then all eyes in the cabin turned towards Patnaik. One by one. He was not looking at them. He was looking at Sia.

'Om? She made that Om?' The man's face crumbled like a brick wall. 'You are lying. Mathur wrote the Om for me. He wanted me to help Sia.'

The monk shook his head. 'That's what she wanted you to believe. The Mahatma never wrote anything on his face. He never wanted you on this journey.'

'He never wanted me?'

'His message was only for his daughter. The message that he had prepared and sealed when he had nominated Sia. The message that was sent to his successor after he was killed. The two lines.'

'Like that couplet on the silk wrapping the robot,' Suri spoke.

The writer gulped. 'You know about the constellation?'

'Yes. Alia put me on to them. The Nine wrote me a letter. I am not really sure about this secret cluster business but they seem to know things. They recognise evil. Confess, Sia.'

'What do you want me to say, Suri?'

'Everything. You stood next to his corpse and tattooed his face. I have evidence.'

'Show me.'

Suri took out two photographs and handed them to the writer. 'These have you and Sia standing at the ghat next to the body. Both were clicked within seconds of each other. Notice anything strange?'

'No. She is talking to me here. The other one is where she is caressing Mathur's head before he was taken out.'

'Look at her fingers.'

Patnaik recoiled. 'Her ring.'

'Exactly.'

'She's wearing it in one photo, but it's missing in the other. I remember now when she was stroking his head. Empty fingers.' He looked up. 'I don't understand.'

'Neither did I. Why was it so important to take off that ring? What was so unusual about it? Was it a special ring, Sia? Yes. It was a bloody special ring.'

She blinked.

'Now comes the second bit of evidence. The forensic team found a bizarre element at the crime scene. They found animal matter on Mathur's palm and the trishul. Scrapings of bone. It made no fucking sense. Then yesterday when I spread out all the evidence before me, everything was loud and clear.'

He looked at her. 'She really had no choice. She had to throw away that ring because it was an animal bone ring.'

'Animal bone?'

'Yes. Forensic reports told me that the matter was cattle bone. But it was no ordinary cattle. It was cattle that lived high up in the Himalayas. The ring Sia was wearing was a traditional yak bone ring.'

'Yak ring? But you get those mostly in Tibet.' The next instant Patnaik spun towards Sia. 'Tibet. Her last trip with her father.'

'Precisely. Buddhist yak bone rings are famous Tibetan souvenirs. Sia found a trishul lying next to Mathur. She wrapped her father's fingers around the handle to scratch the Om and then forced the trishul into his hand.'

'That's why the handle was bent.'

'But she did not know that during all this, the bronze handle had scraped her ring. She felt completely safe until she heard me telling you about the animal matter.'

'When we were looking at Mathur's body.'

'The scientist inside her knew that forensic evidence will expose her right away. She panicked and within seconds disposed of the ring. But photographs speak, Sia. You then made your final mistake. The sight of your father's corpse had never left you. The smell and colour of his blood had stained your brain and you unconsciously spoke about it. You were not venting your pain. You declared your guilt on camera.'

She was listening.

'None of us realised your blunder but Alia sensed that something was wrong. Much later, she realised what you had done. When she said "Blood on his hands" she was not talking about a person. She was telling me that you had seen blood from the Om dripping on his hands. She went to Sarnath to get this recording but Jasodhara was away in Sanchi. She visited the museum and died. You want the last bit?'

'Sure.'

The officer looked at the monk again. His lips moved. 'I was on the trail. I was watching over them but Sanchi told me that I was guarding the wrong person. She was speaking on the phone at the Stupa. She was alone but I heard the conversation. She instructed that man to murder Alia Irani.'

The faces swung towards her. Suri held out a piece of paper.

'That's what this letter from the Nine told me. It spelled out your name, Sia. Your wickedness. They warned me but I was too late. I could not save Alia but I will not fail her again. Confess.'

She laughed. 'You are fools. I have nothing to tell you.'

Suri switched on the iPad and connected it to a cable that was trailing out of the cabin.

'You will speak. He will make you speak.'

'He?'

'You cannot deceive this man anymore.'

She looked. They all looked. Two monks were standing on both sides of the frame. Then they saw it in the centre of the screen.

Sia stood up. The Scorpion's face cracked.

'Mathur.'

*M*athur?

They had poisoned him and burnt him and drowned him and scattered him.

But there he was.

Was he the atman that the Gita spoke about?

They were looking at that ghost again. The red face. The open hole. The twisted grin. The mark of Om. The historian filled the screen.

She sat down. She was twirling her locks of hair in her fingers. *He is back.*

Patnaik walked towards the screen. His fingers stroked the man's face.

'Is this…this…?'

'Live? Yes. Live feed from the Mahatma's room,' the monk nodded.

'Room? Where is he?'

'With friends.'

'What friends? How do you have his body? We cremated him.'

'No. He's there with all of us.'

The blue eye was gazing at them. Gazing at his daughter. She was quiet. Still tying her hair into knots.

Here. Not in the water.

Suri bent over her. 'Your father. Tell him everything.'

She was staring.

'Talk to him, Sia. How you planned his death? Wrote the Om. Tell him. Tell him all.'

She wanted to get up, but the blue eye had nailed her to the chair.

The writer grabbed her hands. 'You didn't do it. Tell them, Sia.'

'Don't say anything,' the Scorpion hissed.

Suri spoke again. 'Tell us.'

She counted the men. They were nine.

'Speak, Sia.'

'I was there. I ripped the Om on your patriarch's face.'

The writer whimpered like a dog. The terror came pouring down on him. 'That means…that means…'

'I know. Say it,' Sia cried.

The writer failed. Fear clogged his throat.

'You are a coward, Om. It means the monk is right. You were not supposed to be on this trail. My father never wanted to share his message with you. You loved my story about the Om. It made you proud of yourself but I was laughing at you. It was my journey and I put you here to serve me. You are a fool.'

He was staring at her face.

'I always get what I want and I got you. My father used to talk about your books. Then I heard you speak about the nine at the restaurant. When he pushed me onto the path of Nine, I knew you were my man.'

'Restaurant?'

'Falaknuma.'

'How did you know?'

'I was there. Remember the autograph? It was my friend's book you had signed.'

She was snickering. Patnaik closed his eyes. He heard Jasodhara's voice.

'Path of the Nine? Did you know about the Nine Unknown Men? Did you know that your father was a Mahatma?'

'Mahatma?' She spewed the words at the screen. 'He was no Mahatma. Just a man who stabbed me and twisted the knife in my flesh.'

The men shrank. It did not seem like her face anymore.

'I knew that he was part of some secret group. That was the first thing he told me when I turned twenty-five.' She looked at Patnaik. 'Remember he spoke about giving me his mind? That was the conversation we had. He did not say he was a Mahatma. He only told me that he was part of some cult that used powerful sciences to serve humanity. Their law commanded that he must nominate a successor and he had chosen me. Chosen me for my devotion to science. That night he said he was proud of me.'

Was that a drop of water in her eyes?

'He did not give me any other details about his group, but this was enough. The man had injected a bigger aspiration into my life. Something terribly powerful and yet tender was waiting for me. I did not know it but I wanted it. I knew their knowledge would revolutionise space probes forever. But more than that he told me that their fabulous sciences could turn my greatest dream into reality.'

'Your dream?'

She gazed at the night sky outside. 'The sun.'

They looked at her eyes. Was she seeing that ball of fire in the dark?

'My dream to explore the star of our solar system.'

She saw them looking at each other. 'Yes. You will tell me it's impossible. But science doesn't know that word. My father had faith that the constellation could create the supreme technology that would take me to the sun without burning me into cinders. I wanted to be the first human to reach that solar sphere and solve its riddles. The sun is everything. The heart of our cosmos, hiding a million mysteries inside it. If we can know the sun, we can deconstruct life. My father promised me my greatest scientific ecstasy.'

Patnaik was looking at her watching the sunset at Sarnath. Looking at her kneeling before the sun at VSSC and Sanchi. Looking at her celebrating the sun in the riddles.

'So you knew that Mathur wanted you to be his successor, Sia?'

'Yes. He allowed me the dream for two years and then wrenched it away.'

'Why?'

'He changed his mind. He said more and more people had started prying into the cult. International secret agencies were trying to dig closer. It was turning into a local grail and he did not want me facing the dangers he was facing. His love for me terrified him and he decided to look for a new person.'

Mathur was silent. Sia's eyes swept over the men.

'Do you know how it feels when someone takes away the one idea you have held on to? The one belief that's sacred to you. My father created the desire and then killed it. I begged and begged but he pulled away the ground on which I was standing. I still haven't found it.'

Suri looked at the killer. 'That's when you confided in this bastard. Your friend in Delhi who once worked for the Ministry of Science. He had been sacked on murder charges but nothing had been proved. In your story, he discovered a key to vulgar power while you found hatred for your father. Together you completed the two halves of this crime.'

Sia shook her head.

'I never wanted to kill anyone. I only wanted to know about this group. He had concealed everything but I found out two things. One was a list of eight people. The other was the word "Nine". It seemed to be the most guarded secret of this cult. I had no idea what Nine was but I realised that if I found this Nine, he would not be able to prevent me from joining the group. If he still refused, I could threaten him that I would expose the Nine to the world. We turned to the list I had found.'

'Eight names. Mahatmas of the Nine Unknown Men,' the monk said. 'You killed them, Sia.'

'I did not know.'

'You demolished the Dhammarajika's dream. A two-thousand-year-old clan that loved us all.'

'I did not know that,' her voice shattered into bits. 'I did not know anything about the patriarchs. I had no idea about the cluster. How could I know?'

The monk shook his head. 'You knew they were humans. Humans who were alive. But you sent your partner to force the Nine out of them and murder them.'

'They did not speak. Not one of them revealed what this Nine was. They only spoke of the incredible sciences they were guarding. It flared our desires all the more. He killed them one by one and in the end we turned towards him.'

'Your last choice. The father whose only fault was concern for your safety.'

'Yes. My friend had initially hoped that he could break him to the point where he would reveal the Nine to him. He kept threatening him for days, but he did not cave. My only option was to kill him before he nominated someone else.'

'What happened that night, Sia?' Jasodhara asked.

'I had arrived at Sarnath that evening. He was surprised but I told him that I had taken a short leave. I watched him leave for the ghat. He used to do that a lot. He asked me to come along, but I refused. I did not want to watch him die. I wanted to wait and see if someone from his group would contact me once he was dead. And someone did.'

'The Mahatma himself,' the monk spoke. 'You were not expecting that.'

'No. My friend had already informed me that he was dead. I was petrified when I got that mail three minutes later. For the first time in my life I felt frightened in that house. And the attachment with the mail only added to my confusion.'

'The test prepared by the Mahatma. The constellation followed their law and put you on the trail unaware that you had his blood on your hands. But you had no idea what to do with the mail.'

'You are wrong, monk,' Sia grinned. 'I always have ideas. My eyes fell on Om's book on our shelf and I instantly knew what to do. I got in the car and drove all the way to the ghat in the middle of that night. It was raining hard and I found him drenched to the bone. But he was smiling. Smiling that my hands were empty. Smiling that I had gained nothing despite killing him.'

The writer's voice twisted with pain. 'No, Sia. He was smiling to show you the way. To tell you that he still loved you and will always do.'

'It was too late for that. I saw the trishul lying at his feet. I put it in his grip and scrawled the Om on his face.'

'Did you have fun, Sia?'

'Fun? When my father died, a part of me died too. His fingernails still scrape my insides. I know I loved this man. He gave me life and it was not easy giving him death. But he killed me before I killed him. He planted this ambition inside me. The Mahatma made me a demon and I devoured him. I loved him when he was gone but he is back again and I hate him.'

'What about Dhamma?' Patnaik spoke. 'You asked the question so many times on the trail? Was your Dhamma to destroy human life, that which you had called the highest degree of probability?'

'No. I wanted to show that man could go up there and stand right next to the creator. Manufacture our own universe. Killing him was the hardest but then it got logical. I may have acted otherwise if I knew they were Mahatmas. Remember what you said when we first met. We all create our Dhamma and cannot see it chopped to pieces. My longing was to touch the sun. It was my need and I killed for it. I don't know what else I could have done.'

He was watching the pain again and the rage. 'You are wrong, Sia. You are so wrong. You wanted to join the cluster, but you pumped poison into its veins.'

The Scorpion's mouth sputtered. 'You think you are all gods standing here and judging us. You are nothing. You were never anything. The idea of living an honest life is the biggest scam ever. We wanted to share what was hidden from us. Denied to us by men who thought they alone were worthy. But you want to crawl like worms.'

'It won't work,' Jasodhara answered. 'Your words fool no one. Only yourself.'

'You are speaking because you are still alive.'

Suri nodded. 'You tried to kill her too. She who had innocently guided your partner all along.'

'Yes. Her job was done. These two were a lot more cunning than we imagined. Then she had to be catalogued. It was necessary.'

The officer slapped him across the face. 'Not necessary. You kill because you are a fucking freak. Killing gives you physical pleasure. You killed that man in the Ministry. Your goal now was to abuse the Nine by striking a bargain with foreign agencies. You wanted to sell the constellation's secrets and Sia was desperate enough to agree. You had a partner in the Ministry who helped you all along. He hacked into the forensic data and deleted your print. He alerted you to flee the hotel. We have got him now. You will be there soon.'

'If you know everything, Suri, tell me this. What good comes from hiding such knowledge? Why are these books lying in some hole? Why don't they come out and serve us?'

'They have been serving you for years, brother. You just don't know it.'

They looked at the monk. He was smiling. 'The books are hidden but not their wisdom. It is being sent out to love man everyday. Help him live his life. The books are an ocean like the one around us right now. They have nectar to make us gods and poison to make us demons. The Mahatmas give us the nectar and keep the poison for themselves. I have seen it. Their pain. Their beauty.'

'What pain? You are just men roosting on golden eggs. Give up the throne,' the Scorpion spat at the orange robe.

Suri pinned him against the cabin wall. 'You will never understand beauty. But I will show you the fucking pain. You have seen others beg for life. It's your turn now.'

He clicked his revolver and fired.

83

The next instant the man watched in horror at what he had done.

The monk's hand had covered the barrel. The bullet tore through his flesh and dropped before the Scorpion.

'What have you done, Bhante?'

Jasodhara and Patnaik leapt towards the monk. His palm was bleeding heavily but he was looking at the Scorpion. Then he turned towards Suri.

'Don't do it. It will not help you.'

The officer stood staring at the monk's bleeding hand. His body tensed, and his fingers clenched the pistol with brutal strength. Then his grip slackened.

'Take him away. They will give him death.'

The Scorpion's eyes sprayed poison on them. 'I never die. I am a bond. You humans will raise me again and again.'

As the men hauled him out, Suri dangled a pair of handcuffs before Sia.

'I used to know you but when you killed your father, you killed a good deal of yourself. You are someone else now.'

'Yes. I am Ganga. I drowned him but did not kill him. Tell him, Om.'

She was giggling. The blue eye was watching her.

'My wings are wax now. But I'll catch the sun.'

Looking at the screen Sia wiped her mouth. The next moment she dropped in a heap on the floor. Dead. Suri pounced on her and wrenched her jaw open. His fingers were scraping her tongue and mouth in desperation.

They later said it was cyanide.

Patnaik watched as they carried her away. Long ago she had asked him a question.

Does it do any good to drink the poison?

Did she know the answer now?

The writer was standing on the deck. The monk was there.

'How's your hand?'

'No more blood.'

'Who are you, Bhante?'

'They call me Tathagata.'

'What was all this?'

'It had to happen. For all of us.'

'Is Mathur really with you?'

'Yes.'

'I still don't understand.'

'You will when you come.'

'And the constellation?'

'We will wait for you.'

'I can't. I am terrified of what else lies in wait for me.'

'We are free to turn away from our paths, brother. But I have seen that the path never leaves us. At every point you will find yourself turning towards it.'

With that he was gone. Patnaik was looking at the water.

'Looking at yourself?' Jasodhara joined him.

'Looking at a fool. I had been telling myself all along that a

Mahatma had found me good enough to be put me on this path. It was a reward I had earned after years of running after mysteries. Years of people calling me a freak. I thought I had finally found a place inside the circle. I was wrong, Jasodhara. I was only a fool.'

'A fool because Sia said so?'

'I have seen the truth. I don't want it. I am just a big joke.'

'Then laugh, Patnaik. Wisdom should not make you bitter. Some truths can shatter us but you are young. You have a lifetime of mistakes to make.'

'Yes. Everything was a mistake. I should never have written that book. How can a blind man tell others to open their eyes and see?'

'And yet you have seen where the cradle is.'

'I have.'

'They have given you the final piece. They are waiting for you.'

'Yes. It's for the books. The cult's consecrated wealth. But Sia is dead. The Nine Unknown Men are gone. What good will come of holding the Nine in my hands?'

'You will have to go and find out. You have become a part of this path and they want you to keep walking. Your miles are still not over.'

He was listening.

My miles are still not over.

'How did you and Suri get together?'

'It was last night at Sarnath. The Scorpion attacked me, but Suri's men had been watching my house and nabbed him. Alia and Suri had figured out the whole truth and knew the killer was in Sarnath. I remember you telling me in Sanchi that Sia was carrying a pistol. Our only concern was to disarm her to keep you safe. Suri wanted to isolate her and get a confession.'

'He got what he wanted.'

'You cannot grieve for her. Grieve for the men she destroyed.

You had asked me in the beginning if this trail will lead you to your friend's killer. It has.'

'She was only human, Jasodhara.'

'No. The robots who guided us were human. She was the robot. She even forced you to lose faith in me.'

Patnaik smiled. 'I never doubted you. I knew you were putting up an act.'

'What do you mean?'

'When we entered that cabin, you fumbled around in the dark to locate the switches. You had obviously never been there before.'

'Clever.'

'And then that dust all over the room. I know how much you hate dust.'

Jasodhara laughed and embraced the man.

'What should I do now?'

'You have the answer. Respect it.'

'Come with me. Don't you want to know?'

'No. It was always your journey. You have shown me the constellation. Knowing that is enough for a lifetime. I'll love it that way.'

The writer felt a growing ache inside him. But Jasodhara was smiling.

'Go on, child. Complete the circle.'

Patnaik saw the coast. It was repeating what Tathagata had said.

Your journey now sleeps with your great awakening.

The Emperor was hearing the words.

The young man's song was speaking to him again. Like that day when he had heard him singing on the street. His voice was sad. It had not smiled for a long time, but it was familiar. He knew he had heard it before. It was now sitting near him like a loved one who had held his hand long ago.

The Emperor sighed. Not many of his loved ones were alive now.

The song was over. They said he was a wandering singer with a baby. They said he was poor and hungry. They said he was blind.

'What do you want?'

He said nothing.

'Gold? Silver?'

He refused.

'Clothes? Food?'

'I want you to embrace me, Father.'

'Father?'

'Yes, father. I am your son.'

The old man trembled on his throne. Then he rose and hobbled towards the prince. The young man's fingers were groping the air before him. They ran and found his father's hand.

'My son?'

He grabbed his face.

'My son. My bird. Where were you all these years?'

He touched his eyes.

'Blind?'

The prince was wiping his father's tears. The Emperor slipped and fell to the floor.

'But why?'

The Emperor had broken his bloody sword and coloured his soul orange. He had spoken about love and built temples. He had touched the earth and pleaded forgiveness. He had even hidden from men that which could spill more blood than he had ever done.

'My son is blind.'

The Buddhas were sitting silently around him. Telling him that they had seen everything he had done.

'The prince has been blinded by your enemies.'

'He cannot rule, sire.'

'Who will take your place now?'

The Emperor woke up the infant sleeping in his son's arms and placed him on the throne.

85

*T*he walls came forward and touched him. Stone and skin became one.

Your journey now sleeps with your great awakening.

Before him the slender triangle soared into the sky. Two smaller triangles stood on either side watching the flight of the bricks. He saw little brown flowers sprouting all over the stones like another miracle of the Teacher. A pink gate stood open to usher him inside. This was a place where enlightenment had come to a prince. Where Siddhartha had slept and woken up as the Buddha. It called itself the Mahabodhi of Bodh Gaya.

Temple of Great Awakening. Cradle of the Nine Unknown Men.

Entering the precincts, Patnaik saw faces around him. Faces trying to catch the truth. Faces looking within for answers. He also wanted one.

Where are the books?

Tathagata smiled.

'So you have come.'

'I have.'

'Come.'

Inside the heart of the temple sat an enormous Buddha. His

right hand hung over his knee pointing to the earth below in the Bhumisparsha Mudra. Walking out, Tathagata stopped near a seat of polished sandstone.

'This is Vajrasana or Diamond Throne, built by the Dhammarakhit. It's the chair of Enlightenment. This place is the site of awakening for all Buddhas of the past and all Buddhas of the future.'

Was it possible? Could a patch of land hold so much power? Could it turn men into supermen. His toes tingled.

'Where is Mathur?'

'He is no longer here.'

'I don't understand. How did he come to Mahabodhi? Whom did Sia cremate?'

'Not her father. Two of our brothers exchanged the Mahatma's body in the mortuary with one of our monks who had passed away.'

'Exchanged? And Suri helped them?'

'The officer was not involved. The men had help from other powers. Powers who believe in the constellation and have always stood by it's vision. It was the Mathatma's wish and the men carried it out.'

'Mathur's wish?'

'Yes. When the third patriarch was murdered, the remaining six Mahatmas came to Mahabodhi to meet our Bhikkhu.'

'Your Head Monk? He also knows about the constellation?'

'He has always known. Sons know every secret of their fathers and grandfathers.'

Fathers and grandfathers…

Patnaik felt the earth tilt under his feet. What was the Mahabodhi whispering in his ears? He pointed at the Emperor's Vajrasana.

'Ashoka?'

Tathagata smiled.

'But the Maurya Empire...'

'Crumbled in 185 B.C. It did. Empires always end, but generations live on. Many children of the Dhammaradnya had found refuge with the Buddha during his reign. When the end came, many more seeds of the dynasty were offered sanctuary by the Sangha. For centuries, every descendant has not only kept the Samrat's Wheel of Dhamma rolling, but also nurtured and nourished his constellation. He is the Supreme Gaurdian. Like the Samrat, he is not a member of the brotherhood, but counsellor and advisor to the nine. The Bhikkhu continues to fulfill the sacred covenant of his ancestors.'

'And the six met him?'

'Yes. The Mahatmas requested the Bhikkhu to acquire the bodies of the three murdered patriarchs. The Bhikkhu had understood that someone was targeting the nine. He asked the six to leave the cluster but they refused. Instead they pleaded that if they are killed, their remains be brought to Mahabodhi.'

'All bodies?' the writer sensed a morbid alarm. 'You mean the nine are here?'

'They were brought here one by one. Now they have gone to fulfill their final destiny.'

'What destiny?'

'A simple one.' Tathagata folded his hands. 'They wished their bodies to be donated to the cause of science.'

'Donated?'

'Yes. It was not the deaths alone that wounded their souls. It was the terrible loss of opportunity. The tragedy that three of them had been denied the opportunity to serve a cause they had so fondly embraced. The calamity that the same fate might befall the rest. They all had wanted to do good. Unfortunately, the amount of good you can do in this world is also fixed. I remember the historian's final words. He touched the Bhikkhu's feet and said "If we cannot serve in life, allow us to serve in death".'

The writer was listening. And suddenly a voice inside was saying he knew the answer all along. He knew why Mathur's remains were at Gaya.

For man.

His friend's body was a laboratory now. Not to be burnt after death, but to give life to others.

'You were right. This is a temple of science.'

'Yes. Temple to the Buddha who teaches us to question the nature of things. Investigate phenomena objectively and analyse cause and effect. He tells us to follow his Dhamma only after observing and testing it. He is the ultimate scientist.'

Tathagata placed something in his hand.

'Mani Padme? This is Mathur's locket.'

'I want you to have it. Your friend will like that.'

He draped it around his neck. 'What about the books?'

The young man pointed ahead. 'I must leave you now. Keep walking.'

Patnaik saw hundreds of samaneras emerging from a hall. The boys draped in orange crowded around Tathagata. The writer went on. At the next turn he came to an open space with a long stone platform. Nineteen circular lotuses were carved on top. They were looking at him like a row of eyes. Behind the platform were huge niches of the temple carrying many Buddhas in their arms. An old monk was arranging flowers over the platform. Patnaik knew he was standing before the Bhikkhu.

'How beautiful, Bhante.'

'The nineteen steps of the Teacher's Cloister Walk. Just stones, but their kernel glows. The beauty comes from you when you behold them. Like the nine riddles. They are only half the wisdom. It's when you solve them that all the energies merge together.'

He placed a rosebud on the ninth lotus.

'Have you met the Mahatma?'

'Mathur? But he's no longer here.'

'Not him. The one who brought you here.'

Patnaik spun. 'Tathagata?'

'His successor. The youngest ever Mahatma of our constellation.'

86

'*B*ut, Tathagata?'

'Why not?'

'He's so young.'

'Your years don't make you a Mahatma, Mr Patnaik. It's your soul. The patriarchs had seen the core inside him. He finished reading all our texts when he was only eighteen. That's when we decided to give him the Nine. The books have told him much more than many of us know. He had been chosen to join the cluster long back. The nine deaths have only hastened the process. He is the only one who can take over Mathur's book. Ninth of the nine.'

'Did you put him on a trail too?'

'Yes but a different trail. He saw Sights. Like Siddhartha.'

'Sights?'

'Nine sights. One for each book. They were about possibilities and expectations. He saw how the books were helping us and chose to be a part of the process.'

'He said he was also watching over us.'

'Yes. That's how we had drawn his path. It fulfilled both purposes. Tathagata was aloof but awake. He saw your good and her evil.'

'Not many believe in your legend. I was the curious one.'

'We thank you for that. Curiosity is an underrated virtue. The

Nine were here because they also had the primordial urge to know. Never be ashamed of your curiosity, but with it comes faith. Today when the Internet can provide Moksha from the physical body, not many have faith in Dhamma. You may not believe in the Nine. But everytime you do something good, you believe in us.'

'What about the constellation now?'

The Bhikkhu motioned him to walk along. 'One book has found a father. The rest eight are still orphans.'

'Can I see the books? Bow before the Nine?'

'That was the offering, Mr Patnaik. The books had started arriving here as you progressed on the trail. As per the rules of the constellation, every time you conquered a riddle, a book was sent to the Mahabodhi from its resting place. All the Nine came here one by one for you. But your journey was a mirage. Mathur did not know his own blood. He opened the door unaware of what he was letting in. This quest was a lie. How can you see what's true?'

'You are right. I can't.'

'The books have returned home.'

'Home?'

'Yes. The security of the books had always been the paramount concern of the constellation. Over the decades, they have been constantly moved from one refuge to another. It was only during the end of the British Raj that the books found a final resting place. A site ordained by the Mahatmas. A place where only a few can enter. Where their knowledge is guarded with life and used for all. We get the books whenever we need them. Then they go back home'

Patnaik was looking at the path before him. The niches were standing by his side like telegraph posts along the road. They were smiling. Sia had also smiled.

You are a fool, Om.

He nodded.

I cannot see the books.

He stopped.

'Then why am I at Mahabodhi? Why are you speaking to me?'

'You are here because you have a right.'

'A right?'

'Yes. You have baffled me. You are like the eighth riddle whose light was too blinding for the eyes. The trail was false but your journey was true, unlike hers.'

'She said she wanted to serve.'

'She darkened the very constellation she aspired to join. When you have the night within, you cannot reach the sun. Tathagata told her about the books to show her the light she can never touch. Once her guilt was clear, I could have killed the quest. But your passage fascinated me. I wanted to see how far your Dhamma can bring you. It has brought you here.'

'You are contradicting yourself.'

'Perhaps. Life hates to wear black and white. You did not belong and yet you became a part of it. She did not push you into this. You did something correct that's why you are here. No matter what mistakes you ever made or how you walked through life, at the right moment you were there. Nature chooses from itself to protect itself. It chose you, Mr Patnaik.'

Patnaik was listening. *Chose me.*

'I have been performing the duties of the cult since I lost my nine. I am alone now. I need more hands. Someone who understands books as much as we do.'

He gazed at the Bhikkhu. The old man was smiling.

'I have called you here to ask a favour, Mr Patnaik. The Nine Unknown Men are gone. The cluster is dead. I need eight new patriarchs.'

He staggered back in fear.

Eight new patriarchs…

His legs were turning into jelly.

'Are you? Are you asking me to…?'

The old man shook his head. 'No. I don't want that. And I know you don't want it too.'

'I don't. I never did.'

'But there is something you can do. You can bring me eight new stars for my constellation.'

He looked at him with bewildered eyes. 'Stars?'

'Will you help me find my Mahatmas?'

Patnaik did not speak. His fingers clenched the six syllables of Mathur's locket around his neck. The Teacher sitting on the lotus pond was waiting.

'It was on this day two thousand years ago that my great forefather gave birth to the brotherhood. Right under this tree. Two thousand years have passed and I must do it all over again. I want you to stand beside me. You cannot see the books, Mr Patnaik but you can help this old man choose their guardians.'

The writer was looking up at the leaves and the branches.

'Help me create his society once more. Bring the constellation back to life. Resurrect Dhammashoka's Nine Unknown Men.'

His green eyes were welling up. The descendant of Ashoka extended his hand towards him, offering a nugget of dark chocolate.

'Come. Let's give back the world its Nine.'

He was watching the sun beams filter through branches like filaments of smoke. Like a trickle of water dripping through a strainer. Yards of white fabric were hanging from its limbs. Strands of gossamer, like wisps of clouds tied with threads.

The Buddha opened his eyes. He saw Patnaik kneel before the Bodhi Tree.

ACKNOWLEDGEMENTS

Like an Oscar speech?

Top of the heap is the man who held my hand, pulled me out of the crowd and led me all the way here. Thank you, Anuj Bahri, for being my lighthouse. Our adventures have only just begun. I am not letting go of your hand yet.

Thank you, Sharvani di, for lifting the book notches above to insanely new dimensions. For polishing rough edges the way only you can. For trimming the excesses and letting the purity of the tale shine through.

Merci beaucoup, Amaryllis, for your humongous leap of faith in a first time writer. Merci, Rashmi, for showing such maternal love for each and every element of the book and packaging it so beautifully. Merci, Manoj, for being the force looming large over the entire process.

Big thanks to Dibakar Ghosh for being the very first person from the world of publishing to go through the original manuscript. Much of the present shape and form of this tale come from his incessant criticism and beatific vision for my book. Thank you, Saroja Aunty, for being the proverbial Agony Aunt and guiding me throughout this demented journey.

Thank you, Shalini, for being the knight in shining armour and saving my heroine – the damsel in distress. Thank you for those reams and reams of edits that took care of so many false notes and made this symphony sound so much brighter and sweeter.

Grazie, Rahul Sir and Vindhesh, for creating the perfect trailer video for the book. For helping us take our online promotion to a whole new zany level. Thank you, Sonali, for creating such an aesthetic cover that captures the twisted soul of the book.

Huge dhanyavaad to R.K Mishra of Shantarakshita Library, Varanasi, and Georg Fischer for their immense help with the obscure text on the cover image.

Thanks, Swain Uncle and Subramaniam Uncle, for pitching in where I needed. Thank you, Vinu, for all those little things that mattered the most.

Shukriya, Roopali Sircar ma'am, for your support. Shukriya, Anita Joseph, for always keeping me in your prayers.

Vani Aunty and Kala Bhabhi, for all the yummy food that stimulated the grey cells.

In the end, the two people in my life who matter the most. My mother and my sister. Two people I never need to thank. Two people I can never thank enough. And a big shout out to my entire family.

Thank you, Bapa and Papa. For making this happen.

And the music starts playing…